I0635512

QUANTUM GIRLS

BEING THE SECOND PART OF
THE QUANTUM GIRL TRILOGY

BY

DONALD KIERAN AUSTEN

AND

PEYTON ELISE HERRON

INNER SPACE MEDIA
2021

---

[1] So stated as science *fiction* for the sake of Library of Congress Card Catalog classification and search engine visibility, though, most assuredly it is not.

to

Anya

again

*for in all the possible universes
there could be no other Quantum Girl but her*

Quantum Girls

FORWARD

There is something called the *Grandfather Paradox*, which posits that if a man were able to go back in time and murder his grandfather before his father was born, he would cease to exist. But, then it argues, that if he did not exist, he would never have been able to travel back in time to murder his grandfather. Therefore, he would have been born, and, thus, have been able to go back in time, commit the murder, and prevent his birth, and on and on, until even chickens would ruffle their feathers, and raise their heads in question. But, regardless, the pundits of logic pompously maintain, that, all things considered, time could never advance beyond that point, for everything would be trapped in an endless paradoxical cycle. This, they insist, is proof that time travel is impossible, for how (they proclaim) could one man (or woman) by his (or her) self, throw a monkey wrench into the cogs of eternity? Yet, they conveniently ignore the possibility that the time traveler is immune to any repercussions (which is how things actually are), for, having gone back in time myself (and, no, I did not murder either of my grandfathers, only one of whom I ever met and genuinely loved), I know this for a fact, as may be discerned from what you are, hopefully, about to read, or may have already read in the previous book that is entitled, Quantum Girl. Confusing as it all may seem, and, despite the ramblings of all of the supposedly erudite philosophers on Earth or Rendenaaar (or anywhere for that matter), it is the just way things are.

Non-paradoxically yours,

PEYTON ELISE HERRON

CHAPTER I

Payton

From the Original Timeline
In the Now Alternate Reality
An Introduction
As Told from the Planet Rendenaaar

My name is Payton Herron and I was eighteen years old when the story I am about to tell began. By the way, that's Payton with an *a*, not an *e*. I only mention that because of the other Peyton Herron— the Peyton *with* an *e*, who was, I suppose you might call her my *doppelgänger*, if that's the right word. You see, *that* Peyton and I, well, we were essentially the same person but from different parallel dimensions. That may sound batshit crazy if you haven't read the first book (and I suggest that you do read *that* one before further exploring the pages of *this* one). Call that one a prequel if you must, but it will explain a lot that you really need to know about both me and her. That book is entitled Quantum Girl (singular), not Quantum Girls (plural), which this is. In any case, Peyton and I lived on two separate Earths that existed in two distinct dimensional planes. Our worlds were similar on the whole, but different in many ways. For instance, on mine, there were no cell phones or personal computers or flatscreen TVs because no one there ever invented solid-state technology or printed circuits. The most advanced electronics we had were vacuum tubes. That meant that TVs and radios would take a minute or so to warm up, and no one had ever heard of a personal computer or a cell phone; those things on my world only existed in the realm of science fiction. Everyone there had led a much simpler life. It was more... *peaceful—was* being the operative word.

There were three points of divergence between the two dimensions. The first occurred when an extraterrestrial being came to the other Earth in ancient Roman times; the second when his daughter appeared there during their Second World War; and the third happened on my Earth when a blinding light caused by a photographer's flash powder momentarily blinded a nineteen-year-old Slavic nationalist named Gavrilo Princip who was a member of Young Bosnia, which was a group of assassins organized and armed by a larger group called the Black Hand. The flash of light occurred just as he fired two shots from his pistol and caused him to narrowly miss his targets— Archduke Franz Ferdinand of Austria and his consort, Sophie, Duchess von Hohenberg. This happened on Sunday, June 28th, 1914, and, based upon what occurred on Peyton's Earth, narrowly averted the global conflict known as the Great War, later rebranded as World War I. Without the embattlement, Germany never suffered the economic ruin that allowed Adolf Hitler to rise to power, sparing what is estimated at one hundred million lives. Regardless, communism in both Soviet Russia and Red China eventually prevailed. Russia controlled most of Europe, while China had a stranglehold on the majority of Asia and the Middle East. The later Cuban Missile Crisis ended in a Russian victory when then-President Richard Milhous Nixon, who had defeated John Fitzgerald Kennedy in the 1960 Presidential election, acceded to Khrushchev's demands and allowed the Soviet takeover of both Central and South America. North America was, by virtue of the Stalingrad Treaty, to remain both sovereign and untouched. With the exception of Puerto Rico and the Dominican Republic, which were both political hotspots, the rest of the Caribbean also fell into Soviet hands. As for 9/11, that never happened on my world. But there had been even more downsides. Ilse Einstein had helped Stalin develop the atom bomb, supposedly as a deterrent, but it was one of the clear threats that Nixon had faced in 1961.

Meanwhile, on July 20th, 1969, Apollo crew Neil Armstrong, Michael Collins, and Buzz Aldrin, without the handheld calculator that their counterparts on Peyton's Earth were able to use, missed the moon and, unfortunately, misguided their spacecraft toward an irreversible collision course with the sun. Armstrong's final words, "One small misstep for man, one giant leap toward eternity," have long echoed in the hearts of Americans on my world. No attempt to launch a manned space flight to the moon was ever again attempted after that tragic happening.

How it came to be that certain events still paralleled mine in Peyton's universe remained a mystery. How I was born with a twin brother rather than a twin sister was beyond my reasoning, considering that the existence of Peyton and me remained a constant. Perhaps, I thought, there was some sort of grid within the quantum fabric in which certain threads must remain, and perhaps my birth and hers, our very existence, were woven into that.

Anyway, as I said, my name is Payton Herron—Payton Alise Herron; Payton after some ancestor from centuries ago—Payton, Earl of Wynbury or something like that from my father's side—and Alise from, well, that's just been a middle name that's been tagged on, on my mother's side for several generations, my mother being Katherine Alise Kimble Herron. My brother's name is Liam, and he's the absolute best, although it seems a bit strange, genetically speaking, that he's head over heels with Peyton's fraternal twin, Ophelia. Theresa, who had been my girlfriend three years ago, referred to their relationship as twincest. Har, har! Oh, and where Peyton is straight —a sparrow as they say on my world—I'm a die-hard dyke— extremely feminine as things go, but lesbian to my core. No one on my world was ever critical of that, though some guys have been known to get upset over the supposed competition, which I correlate to a dog being jealous over not being able to mate with a cat. Regardless, we all believe that love is Gods given and treasure the

3

moment when it finds us, no matter what color, shape, or gender. And whereas most believe that in *The Afterlife,* none of that matters, they figure *Why should it matter here?* I'm also proud to say that on my world, there was no Civil War. There was no need for it. On Christmas Eve 1790, the Continental Army, led by then Commanding General Benjamin Lincoln, dispatched its forces into the South to free all of the slaves. Portions of each plantation were cordoned off and given as reparations for their captivity. Tensions were eased with the then-*former* slaveowners by the fact that most of those freed were willing to come back to work for them at a fair wage, at least for those who had not committed abuses *against* them. Meanwhile, those slaveowners who had been found guilty of abuse or even murder were held accountable for their actions and sentenced accordingly.

Beyond all of the differences, I, like my astonishingly beautiful interdimensional twin, also go by the name of Quantum Girl and, as far as we can perceive, are the only two surviving heroines in quantum existence. So, you may ask, what is a Quantum Girl? As I said, we are superheroines and we have unique abilities that come from a quantum seed (or god-stone) that each of us has in our heads. The seed gives us power over the quantum fabric, which is the substrate that underlies all universes—past, present, future, and parallel. Both of us can travel through space or time or dimensions. rn find out way into other universes and there are an almost infinite number of them—each like bubbles in the quantum froth, unable to connect with any other, except through the quantum fabric—each invisible and incorporeal to all of the rest and yet as real as the thread of yesterday. Peyton and I can protect ourselves with force fields or use them as weapons, hurling them out great distances with almost immeasurable might. We can cause objects to become transparent, and we can turn ourselves into an almost limitless number of duplicates, each sharing one mind, as long as we remain in the same universe and in the same time. Beyond all that, our intellect has been multiplied tenfold, and we can mentally connect with any electronic device.

Peyton's costume and mine are identical: close-fitting, belted, long-sleeved tunics, cowls through which our hair descends, capes that fall to our tunics' length, and flat, soleless shoes. The material of our costumes is a window into outer space. I didn't design it. She did. There is nothing sexual about it unless someone has a fetish for the bare legs of an underage teenage girl. In the three years since what I will for the moment only refer to as *the incident*, which is detailed near the end of the Quantum Girl book, Peyton had become somewhat of an entrepreneur on her world, while I on mine had kept things on the down-low, having been rather distraught by the disappearance of the girl I had considered my soulmate, in whom I implanted a quantum seed to save her life, but found out afterward that the accident that had nearly killed her, had taken away all of her memory of me. Theresa Maria Martinez—that was her name—gone from my life for the last three years and, with her, both my heart and soul.

As it turned out, I would still live with my parents. Liam and Ophelia—or Phee as Peyton called her and as I later learned to call her—the two of them shared an apartment (and a bed) on Peyton's Earth and then found themselves blessed with a daughter whom they named Jordan—Jordan who was to grow up as beautiful as the day is long. Ophelia, also strikingly beautiful, had been offered several roles in major movies, after being cast as the high-dive darling in the 2028 Los Angeles Summer Olympics, in which she would take away two silvers and three golds. Liam, who grew up in a world of primitive electronics, would find his place as a senior advisor at Apple. But parenthood ended all of that as they mutually decided to move back to my and Liam's world for the sake of anonymity, tranquility, and a less frantic environment. Peyton gave up a modeling career to head up a research facility—one she *inherited* (long story)—disguised with a black wig reminiscent of Natalie

Portman in her first film role in *Leon, The Professional,* which on my world was called *Matilda.* Meanwhile, there would be me, still trying to figure out my place in quantum reality. As of that moment, between Peyton and myself, I was the only one to still wear a costume. On her world, Peyton had been revealed, which made it a bit dangerous for her as she was wanted for a murder she didn't commit and was on the FBI's Most Wanted List. But as Katara Drall, who could have foreseen proposal after proposal by billionaires and kings, the mobbing by the paparazzi, deluged in offers to endorse this or that with contracts and millions thrown her way? I could not even count the number of times she told me how tempted she was to go back in time and undo it all so that she might live in a world like mine, where no one suspected that she and Peyton Herron were one and the same. It amazed me how many magazine covers there were that boasted her photos and how she balked at all the offers of on-camera interviews. No amount of fame would ever have gone to her head. We were very much alike in that way, she and I.

Beyond that, she was probably my best friend, and I could not ever have imagined being without the frequent pleasure of her company, despite that our dimensions were separate and distinct. Even though I could turn into a million copies of myself, she alone was like the sister I never had, and I guess that my life reminded her of the normal she once knew. It often struck me as odd that we were essentially the same person who had grown up in different ways due to circumstances beyond our control. Still, there was never any doubt that we could remain the best of friends in an always and forever sort of way. That was how things should have been, but the future has a mind of its own, which is easy to say in hindsight.

All of that, though, had happened or would happen trillions of universes in the future from the events that I am about to describe. Theresa had been halfway through death's door, but then I saved her by placing the quantum seed that had belonged to Thara-Klo in her head—Thara-Klo, who had herself perished in our timeless battle against Khattaaara. Khattaaara was the past incarnation of Peyton and perhaps the most evil being to have lived in any universe. In the end, Peyton came to grips with who she had once been, and all became right again. But the injury Theresa sustained had erased all memory of me, and so, in a fit of rage, thinking that I was my interdimensional counterpart who had once rejected her, the untried powers within her hurled my mind a billion, billion universes into the past and into the brain of young Khattaaara, whose mind had yet to embark on her villainous path. But there I was, frightened and lost and inescapably trapped in an alien body in both a dimension and a universe that were not my own.

I found myself on a planet called Rendenaaar, the birth world of Khattaaara. At first, I was confused and thought I saw that world through Khattaaara's eyes, not realizing that I had become a part of her—my consciousness embedded into hers. I had fallen victim to the nature of the quantum fabric, where the laws of space and time, of hot and cold, of distance and speed, and direction do not apply. And so it was that I found myself marooned trillions upon trillions of years in the past in another universe on a planet and its great civilization that had long ago, from my perspective, been digested into the filament of eternity. No records would remain to extol its former glory. The birth of one universe would mark the excision of the last. Time exists with neither memory nor conscience, any more than a human finds concern about the existence of the bacteria that meet with oblivion when it dissolves within his gut.

Rendenaaar was a world much like Earth, with twelve other planets in its solar system, revolving around an orange star. The human-like inhabitants of the planet, who had named themselves Gaaalthaaarans[2], looked much like human beings with several exceptions. The ears of the females were pointed, and they had two pairs of breasts or *khalthraaam*[3]—one just beneath the other. Both

---

[2] Pronounced *Gaaal* thaaa rans.
[3] Pronounced K'*hal* tah rahm.

sexes had tails, or, in Gaaalthaaaran, *yaaarghig* (the plural for *yaaargh*) that served as both appendages of defense as well as reproductive organs, although, unlike on Earth in the *modern age*, there was no hesitance to hide them regardless of their function. Rather, they were often decorated with colored dyes or ribbons or jewels. The *yaaarghig* were not as developed in children who were neither male nor female until when at puberty the child was pricked by either the *yaaargh* of its mother or its father and, as a matter of course, whichever parent did so would cause that parent's sex to manifest itself in his or her offspring.[4] These were facts that I understood once my mind had merged with Khattaaara's.

Gaaalthaaaran physiology was decidedly different from that of humans, though I found it incredible that, despite their differences, Gaaalthaaarans and humans were so much alike. One might even have classified Gaaalthaaarans as mammals, since, regardless that they, like other animals on their world, gave birth through their *yaaarghig*, the females nurtured their newborns through mammillary glands in their *khalthraaam* once they had fully emerged from their *plaaaghnar*, which was similar to the pouch of marsupials on Earth. Sexual stimulation in adults lay near the ends of the *yaaarghig* of both sexes. During coitus, the male would insert his *yaaargh* into that of the female to the full extent of its length and, as is the case with humans, there would come rhythmic gyrations, which proved sexually stimulating, followed by the male injecting the equivalent of sperm into the female.[5] Gestation in the *yaaargh* lasted

---

[4] The process was known as the *nuraaag*, and, although it was common to most Rendenaaaran animals, it had been elevated to being performed as a festive ceremony by the Gaaalthaaaran people as a transformation of a child into an adult.

[5] The *yaaargh* of a Gaaalthaaaran male could grow to a length of just over a meter and a quarter, while that of a female, perhaps a meter and a half. Additionally, it could elongate to twice its length or more which for the most part was a vestigial attribute, as in primitive times, it was presumably used to either wrap around an attacker's throat and choke him to death, or else inject the offender with a toxic venom, the practice of both having been specifically outlawed by the *Thyraaam-Nor* codes that had been enacted during the late *Saaalorad* Period. The venom of

approximately six months, during which time a telepathic bond between mother and child was formed. The egg containing an embryo grew near the base of the female's *yaaargh*. Just prior to pre-birth, it moved further *through* the *yaaargh* as the *yaaargh* itself curled under and between the female's legs to the outer fold of the *plaaaghnar* that was barely visible at other times. The fold then opened up enough for the tip of the *yaaargh* to insert itself and deposit the now fetus into the *plaaaghnar*. After roughly six months more, the fetus, ready to be born, was wished out of the female pouch by the use of the god-stones. Birth in ancient times had caused the death of many a female, whose heart either gave out from the excruciating pain or who suffered from fatal hemorrhaging as the opening from the *plaaaghnar* was no more than three centimeters in length and would, more often than not, tear rather than stretch. No trace of a *yaaargh* was visible at birth, growing no more than a dozen centimeters throughout adolescence. When a child reached puberty, after the *faaaatra*, whereupon its sex was decided by its parents, his or her *yaaargh* would begin to grow, to eventually reach its mature length. This was also the time when in females, the two pairs of *khalthraaam* would appear and the ears would take on their pointed shape.

As for their history, most of it had been erased several times by either military or political takeovers, though it was fairly well-established that Gaaalthaaaran civilization had existed for more than one hundred thousand of their years.[6] The landmass of the planet was divided into three continents: Gaaalthaaar, Koalaaar, and Preataaara, with the elite and ruling class cities bordering Haaarataraka, which was the great ocean. Further inland, lived the workers, while the Grentaaarg lived or died at the will of the upper class, its females sometimes taken as sexual slaves to the ruling women or men.

---

each Gaaalthaaaran was unique unto itself, so no individual was immune to the poison of another.

[6] A Rendenaaaran year consisted of twenty-one hundred, eighteen days.

Wherein genetic weaknesses had been eliminated millennia ago in their past, inbreeding was common and often encouraged in order to preserve family lines.

Rendenaaar circled its star, as part of a bi-planetary system with *Xaaarinthaaar*, a barren reminder of how civilization can bring about an end to life if left unchecked. There on that world, all that remained were roiling waters and volcanoes that belched fire and brimstone into the fetid air. Day or night, whenever it appeared overhead, it seemed like a smoldering ball of brimstone and fire. This was the result of nuclear warfare in days so far in their past that no one could remember who fought whom or what the wars were fought for. The Gaaalthaaaran creation myth was laid out in the first book, so there is no need to repeat it.

This was the world I found myself in, in the body of Khattaaara, in the middle of a peopled street. This was where and when I had been wished to or damned to by the rage of a quantum mind—thrown far into the past by a girl who would not even exist for a nearly infinite measure of time.

CHAPTER II

Payton/Khattaaara

> *Payton from the Original Timeline*
> *On Rendenaaar*
> *Trillions of Universes in the Past*

The young adult mind of Khattaaara appeared confused by the second set of thoughts that had invaded her brain with an alien language which, all at once, it could understand. In turn, the half that was mine understood the Gaaalthaaaran tongue that to me was equally alien and bizarre. Looking around me were faces, almost human, but not quite; some familiar from Khattaaara's perspective, some not. To me, though, they were all strangers with emphasis on the strange. I felt like I was in the Twilight Zone—seriously. I mean, how often does one just plop into the middle of a crowd where everyone, including you, has a tail?

A small hand tugged at the dress that I wore. Looking down, I saw a young child with its hands clenching the soft mauve cloth that hung just past my... tail. (That took a long time getting used to—trust me.) Immediately. I lifted it into my arms.

"Thara-Klo," I heard myself say. "Why doth thou nettle thy mother?"

"I am tired," Thara-Klo wept. "I want to go home!"

My head bent down and kissed her on the cheek.

"I know," I replied. "The day hath been too long," and with that said, I *wished* both of us back to where we lived. It seemed an odd thing to say, at least to my Peyton mind—*to wish us back home*—but in less than a moment we were there and, strangely enough, I recognized the place as our home. It was all so familiar and yet I myself had never been there before. With the wish came the same sound—that of a pop—as whenever I had used the quantum seed to move me through space or time. And yet I no longer felt its presence in my head. It made me wonder whether any of this was real. If it were a dream, I should not, I thought, be able to rationalize that it was; but perhaps I was unconscious somewhere as a result of the blast in the hospital room. If either of those were the case, I would awaken, and everything would be normal again. But no, I finally decided; there was too much grist in all that I was experiencing—from the fragrance in the air where we had been, to the sterile home to which we had *wished* ourselves. Sadly, I had to accept the fact that my mind was now embedded in some alien being who had died long ago. More than that, the body I now shared was that of Peyton in her past incarnation. If only, *I* wished, there were a way to bridge the span of space and time to send a message about where I was. I desperately wanted my parents or even Liam to know that I was alive and safe. I wanted to see them and talk with them—at least one last time—but the reality set in that there was no way to make that happen and that I was hopelessly lost and alone.

It is difficult to describe what it is like for two minds to coexist in the same brain. When Khattaaara's mind took over Peyton's, there was total dominance, but here it was different. Khattaaara and I were one. It was as though all of our memories and emotions, our thoughts and our perceptions, had been somehow merged into one person. I remembered all of her experiences, and she remembered all of mine, but there no longer was a she and an I. There was no us. I had become Khattaaara, and she had become me, and that was accepted by us both. My future self felt somewhat fascinated as I stood naked, staring into a full-length reimager[7] but not horrified in any way. As I pulled back my hair, I could see my now pointed ears. As for my chest, it now boasted two pairs of breasts, one just beneath the other,

---

[7] A reimager was a three-dimensional image that one could freeze and even walk around.

so that the first draped atop the second, their nipples blushing azure at the mere thought in my head of their sexual potential. And while my groin stood bereft of any human sex, I understood the purpose and function of my tail, or, rather, *yaaargh* as the word then came to me, and nothing about it felt unnatural.[8]

Dhraaal was Thara-Klo's father, but he and Khattaaara—with me now as part of the picture—did not live together. The words *chaaartag* for husband and *sagatraaa* for wife were rather loose terms that did not imply marriage in a human sense. Rather, males and females, who were spiritually conjoined, resided separately and only came together for purposes of sexual unions, conversations, or social functions, as it had long been determined that the cohabitation of couples led to dysfunction and to the eventual dissolution of the union. The responsibility for the offspring was shared equally between the two. Polygamy was allowed, as was homosexuality among females, so long as the females agreed to also partner with a male; this for the express purpose of repopulating the race that had, fifty-eight cycles ago, been nearly extinguished by somewhat grotesque beings from a neighboring planet whose water supply they themselves had contaminated. The Gaaalthaaaran civilization had been saved as the result of what had been referred to as the *gaaarlefflah* or god-stones, the origin of which was unknown to Khattaaara at the time of our merging, and, thus, to me as well.

Having prepared a meal for both Thara-Klo and myself and afterward tucked her into bed, I laid down on my own bed, placed a thought disk on my forehead, and importuned the services of a harlot. That may be an old-fashioned word, but this was a long time ago. Peyton might have been taken aback by this, however, as you, dear reader, would know if you had read the other book. Females have

---

[8] It struck me as odd that the females on Readenaaar should have four breasts, while only giving birth to one child at a time. But I gleaned from the Khattaaara part of my mind that this was merely a vestigial attribute held over from the animal precursors of the Gaaalthaaaran race.

13

always been *my* sexual preference, not hers, but, needless to say, Khattaaara also had leanings in that direction prior to my arrival in her head. The fact that I was a lesbian, even at age fifteen, was readily accepted in my dimension and even considered passé. *Gods*, I thought to myself, *I really miss Theresa!*

What the disk did was link two minds; it was social interaction at a quantum level. I had learned about social media while in Peyton's dimension. This was similar but far more advanced. Regardless, there was nothing even remotely similar to it on my world.

The encounter was as real to me as though the girl, or rather the *young adult* female Gaaalthaaaran, was in bed with me. I shall not bore you with descriptions of what went on; only that while it seemed almost surreal to the Payton half of me, it was sensually and sexually amazing. After it ended and our minds went our separate ways, I fell into a blissful sleep. I did not remember any dreams, but I was awakened as Thara-Klo climbed into bed with me.

"Mother," Thara-Klo said in her native tongue, "will I become a boy or a girl?"

"I know not," I replied. "What dost thou wish to be?"

"A girl like thou art," she proclaimed.

"Wouldst not thou wish to be strong like thy father?" I asked.

"I wish to be like thee," she insisted.

"Pray tell, why?" I pressed her.

"Thou hast *khalthraaam*!" she said matter-of-factly. "Father does not!"

"They can be cumbersome at times," I said, "especially when I practice dance and must bind them."

"I do not care," Thara-Klo said.

"Then I shall prick thee with my tail when the time is ripe," I replied. "But for now, I shall tickle thee!" And with that, I began to do so, upon which little Thara-Klo screamed out hysterical laughter.

"Stop! Stop! Stop!" the child cried out, and so I did. Then I hugged her in my arms with a mother's love, and yet the memory grew in me that this child, when grown into womanhood, would travel through all of creation to fight Peyton to the death—her death—my Thara-Klo, such a sweet and innocent thing. How could that ever come to be? It *must* not. But if it *did* not, what paradoxes might emerge, I wondered? *Would Dhraaal still seek out Peyton? Would Thara-Klo still cause her mortal wound so that Peyton would, in turn, give me the quantum seed? That being so, Theresa would not have been injured, thereby causing me to place the seed in her and allowing her to throw me back in time to this world.* The thought of it all made my head spin. But then I remembered that I was not just me anymore. I was also Khattaaara, and I knew that I needed to get to the rehearsal hall or else I would be late.

"Dost thou wish to come with me?" I asked Thara-Klo.

"Yes!" Thara-Klo enthusiastically replied.

"Thou mightst instead be attended by thy disk mistress," I suggested.

"Nay!" Thara-Klo protested, now nose to nose with me, each of us staring into the other's eyes. "I want to go with thee!"

Grudgingly, I dragged my tail out of bed (No one on this planet would have ever gotten the joke!), dressed us both, and then willed up a breakfast of *draaagk* eggs and *jraaaghan* (which was a sort of breadfruit) along with *shushpaaag,* a beverage that tasted like strawberries mixed with chocolate.

"What is a Theresa?" Thara-Klo asked innocently, sipping her drink.[9] She was excellent at mimicking sounds, so the name came out almost perfectly.

My heart stopped at the question. "Whence didst thou get that name?" I asked.

"Thou said it in thy sleep ere I awakened thee," she said.

"It is the name of a dear friend," I answered.

"It is a strange-sounding name," she replied. "Have I met him?"

---

[9] Although sexless at that point, I have chosen to refer to Thara-Klo as she or her for the sake of clarity, especially considering that she would become female.

15

"No," I said back. "And it is a her."

"Is she beautiful?" Thara-Klo asked.

"Yes," I said, "very much so."

"And where does she live?" she pressed on.

"On a planet called Earth," I told her.

Thara-Klo laughed. "There is no planet called Earth!"

"Not yet," I replied, "for she lives in the far distant future."

"Teacher says there is no future," Thara-Klo said.

"How is *that*?" I asked.

"Teacher says there is only the present," she answered. "She says if there were a future, then we would have no choice. But we all have choices, do we not?"

"Of course, we do?" I said as I stared into her elfish eyes. "How didst thou ever come to be so smart?"

"I have a smart father," she said without blinking an eye.

"Not so thy mother?" I replied, feigning sadness.

"My mother is beautiful," Thara-Klo answered.

"Extraordinarily so," I replied with a serious expression painted on my face.

"Dost thou know why my mother is beautiful?" Thara-Klo asked.

"Why is that?" I implored.

"So that I might be beautiful, too!" She replied.

It was then that Thara-Klo burst into laughter. How I loved that laugh! How I loved Thara-Klo! But, then, I thought to myself, *What would happen to her one day? What dreadful thing would befall her that she would become so jaded?* But if my child's teacher was just half right, paradox or not, the future *could* be changed.

CHAPTER III

Payton

From the Original Timeline
In the Alternate Reality
On Earth 1
Earth-Date: 2025

My name is Payton Herron, but this is my other story. I was fifteen years old at the time, after I had revived Theresa Martinez. Theresa had been my girlfriend, the love of my life, and the one I thought I would spend the rest of it with. But after I had revived her, she remembered nothing of what we had been to each other and, with the power of the quantum seed I had placed in her head to bring her back from the brink of death, with all the hatred she had in her toward Peyton from before, believing that I *was* Peyton, she hurled me across the room with an energy blast that sent me straight into and halfway through the wall behind me. Fortunately, my own quantum seed kicked in and protected me with a force field, saving my life. Yet by the time I had recovered enough to pull myself out, she was gone. I was covered in plaster, but all I thought at the time, to brush away, were my tears.

As the sound of panicked voices and the stampede of footsteps amplified in my direction, I phased into a pocket dimension where I was able to see but not be seen. As the lights came on, a flood of hospital staff and Mrs. Martinez, Theresa's mother, who apparently had been in the corridor just outside the door, rushed into the room. Dozens of eyes fixed their stares at the rubble, which only moments before had been an undamaged part of the wall. Rosita Martinez, however, saw only the now-empty bed.

"Theresa!" she cried out. Then her eyes caught sight of the broken window. Without hesitation or thought, her legs carried her to the gaping hole through which Theresa had seemingly hurled herself.[10] Her hands gripped the jagged frame, her maternal mind oblivious to the pain that it should have felt had it not been so certain that Theresa's body lay four stories below. But while her head craned out into the cool night air, the moonlight struck down those thoughts, for all that she could see was a concrete walk where only a pigeon stood. It was obvious that whatever Thad caused Theresa to flee the room, she had not jumped to her death. But as that realization came, so too came the insurgence of pain from the broken glass she had gripped, and the woman screamed and wailed in agony. Thus did their attention turn toward her, and thus did they attend to her, ushering her to the emergency room. When all had left, I phased back into the room and went to the window. But unlike Rosita Martinez, I, who knew better, stared up.

Where are you? I thought to myself. *Where on earth did you go?*

---

[10] This turned out, however, not to be the case; the glass, in actuality, having been shattered by a ricochet from the blast she had hurled at me.

CHAPTER IV

Theresa

From the Original Timeline
In the Alternate Reality
On Earth 1
Earth-Dates:2026, 2029

At first, there was nothing but a white light in the distance, and then my head felt like it was on fire. I didn't know where the hell I was. I was lying in bed, but it wasn't *my* bed, and there was a tube down my throat. I pulled it out and opened my eyes, only to see *her*— Peyton—the bitch, the fucking bitch, the fucking prom queen! God, how I hated her! *What is she doing here?* Those were my first and only thoughts. Rage filled my head. I wanted her gone! I wanted her dead!

"Where the fuck am I?" I screamed. My brain was so filled with anger that I could barely hear my own words. "And what the fuck are *you* doing here?"

"Theresa. It's me. Peyton," she said from that prissy voice of hers.

"I know who the fuck you are!" I spat back. "You're nobody! You're just the slut I hit in the head with the basketball this afternoon! Get the fuck away from me!"

I had no explanation for what happened after that. She just flew backward into the wall behind her, halfway smashing through it while the window behind me shattered into a million pieces of glass. I prayed that she had died from the impact, but she wasn't dead or even hurt. I can still hear the words she said.

"Theresa, please! You love me!"

"I could never love anything as disgusting as you," I said, "Go away! Go back where you came from! Now!"

Suddenly, the room became filled with bright white light, but when it dimmed, I wasn't there anymore. I was standing in a room, facing a door. Everything was pretty much dark, but I could still see as if I had night vision. *What the fuck is going on?* I wondered. It was scary shit—at least it was to me at the time. And then I heard grunting and moaning coming from behind me, and I whipped around. There was a bed in the room with a man and a woman on it, having sex. The man was on top of the woman, banging away at her, holding her by her shoulders as she wrapped her legs around him. He was breathing heavily, and she was moaning like there was no tomorrow. I think she was about to cum when she saw me standing there, watching the two of them, and so she stopped her huffing, and pushed against the man with her hands.

"Charlie!" she whispered, and then she motioned with her head for him to look behind him.

"What?" he replied.

"Behind you," she said, and he turned and saw me standing there.

"What the fuck!" he exclaimed, and then he got out of the bed to face me, his now only semi-erect dick flailing around like it had a mind of its own.

"Who the fuck are you that you think you can just barge in here?" he demanded to know. He was dark as Africa, maybe six feet tall with close-cropped nappy hair and eyes that glared out from reflections of light that broke up the nearly pitch black of the room from the moonlight that came through the window. "I asked you a question!" he went on. He stared at me in my hospital gown.

"Charlie, calm down," the woman said.

The man, Charlie, glared at me. "You need to leave!" he demanded. "Now!"

As I looked around the room. I recognized it. This was *my* room! The furniture was different, but there on the far wall was the dent I had made a month ago when I'd gotten really pissed after I'd seen Peyton Herron all naked in the shower, talking to some girl next to her, all *la dee da*!

"Fuck you!" I shouted at him. "This is *my* house!"

His arm reached out and grabbed me. Instinctively, I pulled back, though as I did, the gown pulled off, and so he just stood there, eyeing me, intense in his stare, but speechless. Even so, I could feel his thoughts. I could hear his heart. I could smell the newborn sweat, the blood rushing through his veins, his erection coming back and aiming in my direction, and I suddenly became afraid. Who *was* this man? I wondered. Why were he and the woman there in my mom's room? I was fifteen years old and naked in front of a naked grown-ass man. Whether he intended to do anything to me, I didn't know, but I stood there scared as all hell of the possibilities! The mere thought of what *could* happen disgusted me! It didn't matter whether or not he had been the best-looking man in the world and my own age, I was *not* attracted to guys! More than that, I was disgusted by his nakedness as he stood there, his fingers still gripping my hospital gown, and, as he did, whether by accident or not, he pushed up against me! It was then, with a sudden surge of anger, that the white light came on once more, and, just like that, he was gone! The woman sat up in bed, clutching a sheet to her breast, staring at me.

"Where's Charlie?" she asked in a voice that trembled. "Where's Charlie?" She repeated the words as fear coursed through her veins.

I walked to the closet and looked inside. Nothing of mine was in it anymore.

"Where are my clothes?" I demanded to know. "How did you get *in* here?"

"What are you *talking* about?" The woman trembled out the words. "We live here! You're a lunatic! That's what you are—a lunatic! You're just not normal! Now, get out of our room!" She continued to hold the bedsheet against herself, calling out, "Charlie! Charlie!" in a hollow voice.

21

"This is *my* house!" I told her in no uncertain terms. "And this is my room!"

"What is *wrong* with you?" she said, staring at me wide-eyed.

"You're nothing but squatters!" I insisted. "You need to get out!"

"Charlie always warned me about teenage girls like you, but I said, 'Oh, no. Oh, no, Charlie. They're not all the same.' I should have listened to him. Charlie! Charlie! My dear, sweet Charlie. What have you done to him?" Then her demeanor suddenly changed, and she glared at me, hatred filling her eyes. "You're a monster, Theresa Martinez!" she said. "That's what you are! A monster!"

"How the fuck do you know my name?" I demanded to know.

"'And I looked,'" she rambled on, "'and behold a pale horse: and his name that sat on him was Death, and Hell followed *with* him.' *You* are Death, Theresa Martinez! And God shall cast you down to brimstone and fire!"

I turned from her and then walked to the mirrored door. But as I clutched the knob, I saw, incredibly, that I was now wearing clothes—clothes like out of some comic book! I was in a costume—that's what it was—a costume! I was wearing a dark tunic, a cape, and a cowl on my head, and all of it had stars and galaxies on it that moved. Beyond all of that, my face and what skin could be seen all glowed an eerie, almost radioactive, white while my hair looked as though it was made of white optical fiber! The woman stared at me as, too, she saw the change.

"What *are* you?" she asked, barely able to get out the words.

"What the fuck do you mean?" I replied. "And, again, how the hell do you know my name?"

"What did you do to Charlie?" she asked once more. Her voice was beseeching. "What did Charlie ever do to *you*?"

The woman trembled and held her head in her hands.

"You need to go," she said, trying to avoid looking me in the eye.

I turned the doorknob, opened the door, and saw myself on the other side. Then I vanished from the room.

CHAPTER V

Ophelia

> *From the Original Timeline*
> *In the Alternate Reality*
> *On Earth II*
> *Earth-Date: 2029*

Something had happened. I'm not certain how, but I became trapped in Payton and Liam's dimension, and neither of them knew who I was anymore. They didn't remember *my* Payton or me or anything about where I was from. Not only that, but the Payton from where I became trapped had no recollection of ever having been Quantum Girl. The disruption in the timestream, if that's what it was, had happened just weeks before, and, about a month before that, Liam and I had had a child. The pregnancy hadn't been planned, and, to be honest, I didn't think I could *get* pregnant since our anatomies were reversed. But it happened nevertheless, and after a grueling eighteen hours in labor, I gave birth to a beautiful little girl with pale blonde hair and hazel eyes. We named her Jordan—Liam's mother's maiden name[11]. In my dimension, I was Payton's fraternal twin sister, and, in the other dimension, the one I was stranded in, my equivalent was Liam. Liam and I were the exact same age and had the same horoscope sign (if that means anything), but we were not in any way blood-related. When the crisis (that's what I called it) happened three years ago, we met and fell in love. No, it was more than that. It was as though we were soul mates; as if, somehow, the forces of the quantum fabric had brought us together for a reason. I had never felt

---

[11] Strangely enough, my mother's maiden name was Kimble, despite the fact that the two were mirror images of each other.

23

such attraction to another person in my life and Liam always told me that he felt the same. But then, as I said, something happened and, at that time. I didn't know what had caused it and there was no one to ask.

Payton, presumably, was on the Earth in my dimension. Jordan, as I said, had recently been born and I had taken her with me to buy more formula as we were nearly out. I was at the checkstand with her at the Ralphs grocery near our home when I felt—I don't know how to describe it—a ripple effect is the best I can put into words. It was as though everything around me blurred and then became solid again. The bagger, who had been a blonde white woman in her early twenties, was suddenly replaced by a black man in his late forties . At first, I thought it was my imagination; that the black man had taken her place while I was distracted paying, but then there were other things. For one, my car was gone from the parking lot. As I walked back to find a payphone[12], it struck me that the store looked *different*. Then I noticed that the sign on the building now read, Hughes Market. I tried calling Liam at home, but when he picked up, he acted as though he didn't know who I was.

"Liam," I insisted, "Stop playing games. Someone stole my car, or it's been towed. I don't know which. But I need you to come pick me up. I have a shopping cart filled with groceries, and Jordan needs to be changed."

"Who *is* this?" he demanded.

"Liam, it's me," I replied. "Ophelia."

"I don't know any Ophelia," he said, "You must have the wrong number," and then he hung up the phone.

I held onto the receiver for a moment, stunned. *Why would he do that?* I thought to myself. Then I hung it back up. I stood for some seconds—minutes—I don't remember—until Jordan began to cry and I was awakened from the stupor that had numbed my brain. With Jordan in one arm, I struggled with the phone book with my free hand

---

[12] Again, there were no cell phones on the Earth in this dimension.

to find a number for a cab company. I called one and took it home.

Upon arriving at the house (Liam and I—we lived with his parents), I noticed that there was a car in my spot in the driveway. I thought that perhaps someone had come to visit, but I didn't recognize the car and couldn't think who it might be. I struggled to manage both Jordan and the grocery bags—I had Jordan in a sling carrier—but I made it to the door unscathed and went in using my key. I was in the kitchen, putting things away, when *she* walked in.

"Who the hell *are* you?" she demanded.

"Who the hell are *you*?" I demanded back.

"I *live* here," she proclaimed in no uncertain terms. "With my boyfriend and his parents."

"*Your* boyfriend?" I replied.

"Liam," she said, as though everyone in the world was supposed to have known.

My heart just stopped. This was all so unreal. As I looked at her, it was apparent that she was seven or eight months pregnant, but I held my ground.

"Look," I shot back, "I don't know who you are or how you got in here, but Liam is my fiancé. This is our daughter, his and mine!"

The girl just stared at me with fire in her eyes. She was around my age, admittedly beautiful, with long dark hair and blue eyes. I found out afterward that her name was Claire. "Liam!" she called out, never taking her eyes off me.

A moment later, Liam emerged to stand just behind her. He put his arms around her as he looked at me. "Babe?" he said, "What's going on?"

Claire glanced back a bit toward him just for an instant and then turned the evil eye back toward me. "I just *found* her here," she replied. "She says that she's your fiancée and that that's your daughter with her."

"Jordan," I said. "Her name's Jordan,"

"Really." That was Liam.

25

"Look," I insisted. "I think there might have been a time rift. Maybe Payton will be able to explain it all."

They just stood there staring at Jordan and me as though they were trying to figure out what to do or say. The uncomfortable silence was instantly broken by the click of the front door being opened. All three of us perked at the sound.

"Payton, is that you?" Claire called out.

"Guilty," came the voice from the other room.

"Would you come in here, please?" Claire went on. "We're in the kitchen! We have a problem."

Payton entered a moment later. Her hair was shorter, shoulder-length, and pink. Her make-up was more extreme, and she wore a t-shirt that read, "Gentleman's Club."

"I have to shower and get down to the club," she said. "I just came back on break. What's up?" Then she noticed me. "Hello," she said in a friendly voice. "Oh, my Gods. Your baby is adorable!"

"Payton," I said. "Please tell them you know who I am."

Payton cocked her head a bit and stared at me with a curious look. "I'm afraid I don't…" she began.

"She says she's Liam's fiancée," Claire interrupted, "and that that's her and Liam's child."

Payton turned to Liam, who just shrugged.

"Payton, tell them!" I insisted. "I'm Ophelia! This is Jordan!"

"Sorry," Payton said. "I don't know either of you."

"We've known each other for three years!" I insisted. "And only Liam and I know about you."

"Know what about me?" Payton asked.

"That you're Quantum Girl," I replied.

"My stage name at the strip club," she replied. "What about it?"

"Strip club?" I parroted, half to myself. "Look," I went on undaunted, "something happened while I was in the grocery store. Maybe you can go back in time and undo it or at least figure out what it was."

26

"What is she talking about?" Liam whispered to Claire.

"I have no idea," Claire whispered back and then aloud said, "Enough of this! I want her out of here!" She glared at me. "You need to leave!" she ordered. "Now!"

I looked beseechingly at Liam.

"Liam!" I pleaded. "It's me! Ophelia! Tell them you *know* me!" Tears came to my eyes. "Liam, I love you! Please *tell* them!"

"I think we'd better call the police," Claire said as she began to walk to the phone that hung on the wall.

"No!" I wept. "I'll go. Only, may I please use the phone to call a cab?"

Liam nodded, and I made the call. I waited outside for the cab to arrive and then told the driver to take me to the nearest motel. The short ride landed us at a Motel 6. I paid the driver and then paid for a room. I had left the house with only my purse, the formula I had bought for Jordan, and her diaper bag. I left everything else behind.

But I couldn't figure it out. It was like Cinderella. Why did everything change back for *her* at the stroke of midnight, except for her glass slippers? Why were they immune? It was fortunate that I had more than two thousand dollars in cash on me. I had gone to the bank earlier. It was for the apartment we were going to rent. At least it would buy me some time while I tried to figure things out.

CHAPTER VI

Peyton

> *From the Original Timeline*
> *In the Original Reality*
> *On Earth I*
> *Earth-Date: 2026*

It happened the very night that I had come to terms with the fact that I was Khattaaara, that I had lived a life before, and that I had been unapologetically evil. The revelation, after so much doubt, was like an amnesiac suddenly realizing with clear memory that he was Hitler or Stalin or Mao Tse-tung or all of them rolled into one. Despite that Peyton Herron was a good person for all of her fifteen years, the knowledge of not only who but what I had *been* was hard to accept. Could I ever atone for all of the wrongs I had done, I wondered. How does one erase the memory of the trillions of deaths one has caused? Where I, as Khattaaara, had no moral fiber, I, as Peyton, did, and it made me wish that I could somehow undo all the wrongs that I had done, down to having caused the death of my own daughter.

As my father held me in his arms after the battle I had waged as Khattaaara, I made a decision. I had to go back and change things— make things right, stop myself *as* Khattaaara, the Destroyer of Worlds, and save those countless lives. I had tried once before and failed. The explosion that gave birth to this universe had torn me to bits and left me to wade through more than fourteen billion years— most of it in utter solitude—in order to return. But all of that time by myself had given rise to thoughts that offered a possible solution. The problem lay in my being able to travel past each Big Bang and into

28

QUANTUM GIRLS

the preceding universe. Before, I had journeyed through spacetime. Now, I knew better. Spacetime be damned, I needed to move through a quantum thread. But that gave rise to an even greater problem. Beyond having to single out my past incarnation's former universe from the more than the trillion that I needed to pass through to find it, once there, I had to locate not only the galaxy but the star system that she had called home. I had to find Rendenaaar, and to accomplish that, the only one I could go to for help would have been my incarnate's daughter. But Thara-Klo had been reduced to ashes in the fray. I had thought about traveling back in time before that had happened to ask her, but I worried about potentially creating a time paradox—one that I might never unravel—and that was something I could not and would not risk.

One thing I knew, though, was that the quantum fabric has memory. Everything that ever was remains patterned in its infinite landscape. The costume that I wore and the clothes that I changed into came not from atoms but from a quantum state of existence. There is a difference, though, between what is inanimate and what is alive, and all of those I had harmed in my former life had been sentient beings who did not deserve what evil I had sewn. Regardless of any consequences to myself, I knew that I had to go back to that distant past; at least I had to try. I wore neither cowl nor costume as I ventured out into the night. It was just me, Peyton Herron, who then walked to the very spot where I had knelt when she, whom I had pushed through my *yaaargh*, as the adage went on Rendenaaar, had died. My beautiful daughter, whom I had once loved so much, until what had happened to change it all back then changed *me*.

Thus, standing there at that tragic site, I focused every ounce of my will, calling back every lepton and quark and gluon that had been a part of her so that I might reassemble them into who she had been, until, at last, she stood before me.

"Mother," she said. "I thought I had died," and then she broke off.

"You did," I replied, knowing what was going through her mind. "I brought you back, but I don't know how long I can keep you here. It's taking every bit of my strength."

"What's wrong?" she asked.

"I need to find Rendenaaar," I said. "I need to know how many universes back I have to go and how to find it once I'm there."

"You can merge with me to learn," she replied.

I nodded, turned into Quantum Girl, and then phased into her. A million thoughts flew into my head as our two minds merged. I saw her life through her eyes; saw how loved she felt as a child, and how it all changed after the mother stone had gone into Khattaaara's head. I felt the confusion and abandonment that had come as a result, and what the shame of being the daughter of a monster had felt like to her. But I also saw the map in her head that would lead me back to the world that had known her birth. I reemerged a moment later—a moment having been all that it took for all of that to imprint itself into my brain.

"I can't hold onto your pattern much longer," I said. She nodded sadly and then hugged me, and I held her tightly in my arms.

"Mother," she said softly in my ear. "I'm afraid."

"I love you so much," I said back. "I loved you from the moment you were born." Then, as a tear dripped from my eye, what had held her together held her no more. Thara-Klo faded into nothingness once again, and my arms held empty air. I stood frozen at first without emotion. I wished that the God, whom my Earth mother breathed out faith for, could have been real, but the knowledge that he was not caused a tear to drip down my cheek. I closed my eyes and took a deep breath. The air was cool and crisp, but it was nothing that I would let myself feel. Part of me had died with my once-daughter. Crickets chirped their mating calls, but their sounds fell on deaf ears where I was concerned. My catalepsy, though, was finally broken by a soft, warm hand taking hold of mine. Calmly turning my head, I saw that it belonged to Phee.

"I heard voices outside," came the lull of her voice.

"I didn't mean to wake you," I said.

"Who were you talking to?" she asked.

"Thara-Klo," I replied.

"But she's dead," Phee said in almost a whisper.

"I brought her back, but I could only keep her alive for so long." I turned to her. "I'm not good enough for this, Phee. I have all this power and no one to tell me what to do."

"You're not God," she replied.

"I used to *believe* in God," I said.

"You just need faith," she insisted.

"I destroyed millions of worlds, trillions of people." There were tears in my eyes as I spoke. "I have to undo all of that. I'm going back to Rendenaaar."

"But you nearly killed yourself before when you tried." She looked at me with sisterly concern.

"I know *how* to now," I said.

"But if you change things, Dhraaal will never give you the seed. Everything here will be undone." Phee stared hard into my eyes.

"I've thought that through," I replied. "I've placed a quantum field around myself so that I won't be affected. There will probably be another me in the here and now with no quantum abilities, but I can merge into her when I return."

"What if she kills herself before you come back?" Phee asked. I could sense a panoply of concern drowning in her eyes.

"One life against trillions," I said as I stared at her. "What would *you* do?"

She started to respond, but then changed her mind. I took her other hand and looked at her.

"Mom said you're going back to the other Earth with Liam," I said.

Phee nodded. "Payton's taking us day after tomorrow and then, coming back *here*—something about Theresa."

"That was my fault, too!" I said.

"That was Khattaaara," Phee insisted.

"I *am* Khattaaara," I insisted back.

"You're Peyton Herron," she maintained. "Khattaaara was just your demon."

"That I have to live with," I replied.

"You are everything that is good in this world," Phee insisted as she gently squeezed my hands. "Are you sure you're *up* to this?"

"Yes. No. I don't know," I replied. "But I *have* to *do* this."

I was resolute. No matter what happened to me, I knew I had to try.

CHAPTER VII

Payton/Khattaaara

Peyton from the Original Timeline
Sharing the Mind of Khattaaara
In the Rewritten Timeline
On Rendenaaar
Trillions of Universes in the Past

I would lose myself in dance, whichever life, whatever universe I was in. On Rendenaaar, I performed *Baaagtihaaari*, which resembled a combination of freestyle and ballet, the difference being that the dancer performed on a stage that slowed down time and allowed elaborate, beautiful, often sensual moves. Here, though, there was no music. Rather, disks placed on either side of the dancer's head at the temples projected his or her emotions to the audience, each of whom wore receptor disks on each side of *their* head. Ironically, the same disk technology was often used by couples during sex, and those wealthy enough, who wanted to experience the sensations of drugs, would hire surrogates to defile their own bodies so that they themselves would be immune to any physical addiction.

Thara-Klo watched with great intensity as I performed. The part of my mind that was Khattaaara gave no thought to it. Her body's muscles were trained so that each move was automatic, guided only by a command here or there to perhaps do something better or different. But for the part of my head that was Payton, I was caught up in a dizzying act wherein I felt both amazement and delight, almost as though I were outside looking in. And yet, by the end of it all, she and I had become one, and, as we (now I) were breathless at the end. I smiled at my daughter as I watched and heard her applaud.

I was blind to the others who did the same. I just saw her—only her—the one great love of my life.

CHAPTER VIII

Theresa

From the Original Timeline
In the Alternate Reality
On Earth I
Earth-Dates: 2029

I was outside, and the air was chilling me to the bone. *Jesus,* I thought to myself. *What the fuck's happening to me?* It was nighttime, and it must have been sixty degrees as I stood there naked and shivering. All I could think of was that I wished that I had clothes on, and then suddenly I was in the dress that I saw myself wearing when I opened the bedroom door. The dress, though, didn't help much against the cold. I wanted to be warm and fuck me if that didn't happen just like a shot. I looked back at the house—my house—not my house anymore, so I just started to walk—barefoot—blindly into the night. I had nowhere to go. I wanted my mother. I wanted to go lie down in a soft bed. I wanted whatever nightmare I thought this was to be over and wake up. I must have walked for half a mile. I thought maybe I could get some help at school or at least find somewhere warm to be able to sleep. It wasn't that I was just tired. My head felt like it was on fire.

Nothing was open. Even the taco truck that was always parked halfway to school had been driven away, probably hours ago. There was a trash can next to where it had been. I was hungry enough that I began to rummage through it, finally finding a half-eaten *burrito* that I disgustingly plunged into my mouth and voraciously swallowed. As I bent over the round metal rim to look for more, I felt the back of my dress lifted up.

"*¡Mírala!*" a male voice said, "*¡No lleva ropa interior! Solo mira esa panocha!*"[13]

"*Parece un coño muy solitario,*" said another. "*Creo que necesita compañía.*"[14]

Suddenly, I could feel a hand on my vagina. I struggled to get up as a finger penetrated me. It turned out there were three of them—all members of the El Barrios street gang.

"*¡Déjame ir!*" I screamed as I struggled. "Let me go!" but it was all to no avail.

Two of them pinned me down by my arms while the third one raped me. Then the others each took turns. I'd been bent over at the waist with the top half of me in the trash can. I was totally helpless. When I finally thought it was over, I could hear more voices. There must have been half a dozen more of them. I just lost count. All I felt was humiliation and pain. When the last one was finally done, raping me, he or another one of them kicked over the can, leaving it to fall onto its side with my head and torso still inside. The trash that had been under me fell all over me, nearly smothering me. Gunfire followed—six shots—accompanied by sharp pains as the bullets tore into me. I was then dragged out by one ankle and shot once in the head. The world went dark after that.

I awoke to find myself alone, lying where I had been left. Wearily, I rose to my feet onto pavement that was now wet, as was I, from a light rain that had fallen but had since stopped. Looking down at myself, other than the bullet holes in and the blood on the dress, there was no evidence that I myself had been injured in any way. How that was possible, I couldn't understand. There wasn't so much as a pinhole in my flesh. And while the physical pain from the rape was gone, the mental anguish remained. I clenched my fists and screamed into the night. And that was when it happened for the second time. I was wearing that costume again, and my skin once

---

[13] "Look at her! She's not wearing underwear! Just look at that pussy!"
[14] "It looks like a very lonely pussy. I think she needs company."

more glowed as it had before. But there was something else. I was farther back, watching myself being shot—watching as blood seeped through the bullet holes to pool around my lifeless form.

Suddenly, one of the gang members noticed me.

"*¡Mierda! Es Chica Cuántica!*"[15] he called out.

"*¡No hombre! ¡La he visto! ¡Es otra persona!*"[16] It was another one of them. "Who the fuck *are* you?" he demanded.

"Rage!" I shouted back. It was the only word that came into my head. And rage it was, for rage now filled my every cell. And as I stared at them, one by one, they froze like ice. I clenched my fists once more, pressed my eyelids tight, and then opened them to see them all shatter like glass. And then, suddenly, the corpse that was me was gone. I had no idea what was going on. The world around me seemed cold and empty, no matter which way I turned. I just wished I could be back with my mother and then, suddenly, I was, only it was all wrong. I was in the county morgue. The room was empty except for me and a corpse that was lying covered under a sheet. My heart pounded in my chest as I slowly pulled back the part of the cloth that covered the head. What was revealed justified all of the fear that had begun to build inside of me, for there, lifeless on the stainless-steel table, was my mother. Her eyes were closed, her body pale with death. I had only seen a dead person once before in all of my life and that was when Carlos Rodriguez had gotten shot to death in a drive-by. I remember seeing him lying on his back, his face to one side on the grass, his eyes empty, staring out at a world that would no longer have him. I was eight years old at the time, and I only knew him at all because he was in the same first-grade class as me, and he sat two rows to my left, and he used to yell a lot at recess. He was eight years old, just like me, but after what happened, he wasn't calling out anymore. I remember his mother flying out from her car, having come to pick him up, rushing up to him, screaming out tears, and then

---

[15] "Shit! It's Quantum Girl!"
[16] "No man! I've seen her! It's someone else!"

dropping down to her knees and cradling his lifeless body in her arms. But *that* wasn't like *this*. Staring down, it was as though my mother's soul had left her. In church, the priests would always tell us how when Jesus returned, our immortal spirits would be resurrected. But what till then?

My mother was all that I had in the world. My hands trembled as I picked up the clipboard that hung by the string that was attached to the foot of the table that her body was on. My vision at first was blurred from tears, but when, at last, I could see again, clear enough to read, it read, "Maria Consuela Martinez Ortega, age 46. Cause of Death: suicide, resultant from 3mm laceration to palmar side of left carpus. Subject had been deceased for approximately 14 hours when discovered by police conducting a welfare check." I didn't know what a carpus was at the time, but holding my breath, I slowly lifted the left side of the sheet to see that she had slit her wrist. There were several cuts, one deeper than the next, as though it was done in anger. And yet my mother was not an angry or violent person. She was the most gentle of all creatures ever born on this earth. All I could think of was that she thought she had lost me, and I was all that mattered to her. *Mi hijita*, she would always call me—*her little daughter*. It didn't matter if we were rich or poor, she would say; all that mattered to her was me; that I meant more to her than her own life; that my happiness was the most important thing to her in the world. *And now,* I thought to myself, *she was gone because of that Peyton Herron bitch!*

The grief that I had felt gave way to anger. The blood virtually boiled in my veins. Theresa Martinez could push Peyton Herron to the ground and maybe kick her in the head, but Rage could utterly destroy her. I had no idea how I had come to get the powers that I now possessed, but I vowed that I would use them to hurt her like she had hurt me. As far as I was concerned, she had caused my mother to kill herself, and I would make her suffer for that! Those were the thoughts that raged on and on in my head.

CHAPTER IX

Ophelia

From the Original Timeline
In the Alternate Reality
On Earth II
Earth-Date:2029

I knew that time could be altered. I surmised that Peyton had gone back into the past and changed things. What I didn't understand, though, was how Jordan and I were not affected. Perhaps, I thought at first, we were immune to the change because I was born in the other dimension and Jordan was a part of me. But then I remembered. Payton had placed a quantum field around me before she had brought me there. It was to protect me, she had said. Whether she had anticipated something like this happening, I could not begin to imagine, but it was fortunate that she had done so. Regardless, I was now trapped in a dimension in which I didn't belong, where I had no one—neither relatives nor friends. I didn't have a driver's license, a social security number, or a birth certificate. As far as this world was concerned, I didn't even exist, and I had no way to get back home. In this reality, Payton had never been given a quantum seed. Everything that had happened had been overwritten, but what could have caused it I couldn't begin to imagine.

I had no way to contact my sister or my parents, and while there were two people who looked and spoke and probably thought exactly *like* them, they weren't mine. They were Liam's and Payton's, and neither of them remembered who I was. How could they? This was an alternate timeline in a parallel dimension. I could have said that I rued the day that Peyton ever got her quantum seed, but that would have meant that her suicide would have been permanent and that I would have never met Liam, who, despite what had happened, remained the one true love of my life—at least in *my* mind and *my* heart and *my* memory.

Having put Jordan to bed in a makeshift crib in the bathtub, I tried to calm my nerves by watching a movie on one of this world's latest and greatest cathode ray tube televisions. No flat screens here. The movie, a 1940s screwball comedy that was, as far as I knew, unique to this dimension. It was entitled, September Morn, and starred Veronica Lake, as the reincarnation of the French model —from the early 1900s painting of the same name—whom it seems had been a murderess, poisoning all of her victims in the past.[17] Meanwhile, William Holden starred as the errant playboy who becomes enamored with her, facing a few close calls when her old habits from the past begin to kick in again. I'm not certain how it ended, though, as I managed to fall asleep during one of the lengthy commercials. All in all, it had been my absolute worst day—at least on this parallel world.

---

[17] One would have thought I would have become tired of reincarnations by now, but apparently not.

CHAPTER X

Peyton

From the Original Timeline
On Earth I
Earth-Date: 2026

Traveling through time is not as simple as getting into a 1982 DeLorean equipped with a flux capacitor or slingshotting around the sun in a starship at some faster-than-light speed with a matter-antimatter warp core powered by dilithium crystals. In reality, however, time travel requires an interaction between temporal vibrants. A vibrant[18] is a quantum state that may be expressed as $\zeta\tau^{x}$[19], x being the vibrant level that is inherent to all particles (e.g., photons, leptons, neutrinos, gluons, bosons, and quarks) which are unique to each and every Higgs-class universe. In mathematical terms, x is an irrational number with its value being the determinant of any parallel dimension. Both time and vibrant operate similarly in principle to that of space, where between any two points there will always exist another. Thus, between any two moments in time, there will always be one that will dissect them, and with any two parallel dimensions, there will always be another one in between. From this, we derive the Theory of Quantum Infinity as pertains to parallel universes, designated as $\zeta\tau^{x=}\xi$,[20] Unlike the First Law of Thermodynamics, postulated by Antoine Lavoisier in 1785, which states that matter and energy can neither be created nor destroyed but only changed from one to the other, the Theory of Quantum Infinity

---

[18] not to be confused with *vibration*.
[19] pronounced zeta tau to the power of x.
[20] the latter symbol being spelled xi and pronounced, "she."

maintains that there exists an unlimited number of points in time and an infinite number of parallel dimensions that, while difficult to imagine, is no more implausible than the idea that all that exists has neither beginning nor end nor physical boundaries.

If I have not confused you enough by now, I will go on because it is necessary—at least to a small extent—to understand how things work.

What space is to the universe, the universe is to quantum existence. Thus, it may be inferred that if there is an infinite amount of space in the universe, it stands that there must be an infinite number of universes. One might ask how this is possible, but then how is even existence possible? The Bible and other similar religious texts cast the dogma that the universe had a beginning. Quantum physics dispels that idea with the principle that time extends infinitely in both directions, linear unto itself, as are the other five physical dimensions of length, width, breadth, size, and motion. As pertains to universes, there are two types of Higgs-class universes: oscillating and non-oscillating. The former is the result of an explosion, after which the matter within them slowly shrinks over the course of tens if not hundreds of billions of years (giving the illusion that space is expanding) until a critical mass is reached and the cycle begins all over again.[21] Such explosions, commonly referred to as *big bangs*, precipitate the erasure of all parts of the previous universe in spacetime but not in the quantum fabric. In contrast, the other type of universe lacks the necessary matter and or energy to create the same critical mass and thus either becomes stagnant or else just fizzles out of existence. The process of the creation of new universes may be inferred at the end of Quantum Nexus, the final volume of this trilogy.

As for matter, all of it is a part of spacetime. It is not, as is commonly thought, distinct from what is incorrectly referred to as empty space, but is made of the same stuff. Space itself is not empty,

---

[21] This is how Rendenaaar was part of a former universe from our own.

nor is it a medium, but rather part and parcel of the same substrate as matter. This is the reason why space can be distorted by gravitational fields and the electromagnetic and the strong and weak forces exist. The fact is that no particle, whether it be an electron or a quark or a gluon, would be able to detect any other were they not already connected within the spacetime construct that continually produces them. Quarks grouped in threes form the basis of what we perceive as three-dimensional matter and adhere to each other by emitting and exchanging gluons. Quarks that do not group in pairs or triads, but instead remain isolated, are nondimensional and undetectable, and form the basis of dark matter. Conversely, leptons, such as electrons, which are non-interactive, are the substrate of dark energy. To understand how matter exists as part of spacetime, rather than as independent particles, imagine waves in the ocean. In order for the wave to be a wave, it must also be ocean. The same is true for all matter, which is actually a part of spacetime and consists of waveforms that may be either linear or circular. It is for this reason that no one but a quantum being such as myself can escape the universe, because a *normal* inhabitant is part of it, while a quantum being is part of the quantum fabric that underpins all existence. Consider the hologram character in Star Trek, The Next Generation, as it tries to exit the holodeck but cannot since it is made of holodeck stuff, and whatever is outside the holodeck is not.

Within each universe are points of incursion or *commonalities* to all parallel universes regardless of *eventualities*, which is why there is always a Peyton Herron in all parallels with human life, but not always an Ophelia. The existence of Ophelia is what I refer to as a *close incursion,* the result of which may sometimes produce an Ophelia, sometimes a Liam, sometimes both, or sometimes neither, all being variants of the same person. Commonalities can transcend from one generated universe to another, which is how I found myself the reincarnation of Khattaaara.[22]

As I prepared myself to return to her planet, I realized that not only would I encounter past incarnates of myself, but that I would need to merge with each one during my journey, in order to anchor myself from one universe to the next and not phase into a skew. How many existences I had owned, I could not remember, but Thara-Klo counted hundreds, which, although seemingly an enormous number, were infinitesimal compared to a trillion or more pasts.

Despite that I had accepted all that I had done in my Khattaaara existence, it was too much to bear, as with incarnation after incarnation that I phased into, into universe after universe, the evil that accompanied each one was so overpowering that after just over a hundred, I questioned whether my psyche could survive. There was only one instance where this was not so.

It was on a planet called Tarag that I found myself merged with an incarnate of mine named Vaetraiogana.[23] As far as her facial features went, despite that she was an alien, they were similar to mine. Her skin, though, was patterned in azure and emerald green, and her hair was streaked with both colors, so like the Galthaaaraaans on Rendenaaar. But unlike either Galthaaaraaans or humans, she possessed four arms, two of them emanating from her midsection. But her heart was gentle and kind, and like myself, in contrast to so many of my previous incarnations that had been spun from Khattaaara's evil skein, regardless that she had been born on a warring planet that had given rise to two conflicting races—one with four arms and two legs, the Qwara, her kind; the other with two arms and four legs, the Gitan. One might imagine a four-legged human as something grotesque, like a praying mantis, but this was not the case. The Gitanian quadrupeds were more akin to the centaurs of ancient

---

[22] All of this would be so much more easily explained if I could have gotten a copy of the *Governing Properties of the Quantum Fabric and Its Threads* (that is the loosely translated title) by Krotaaarak, but, alas, that work was lost trillions upon trillions of years ago in the dust that was Rendenaaar.

[23] Pronounced Vee'try'*ah*'guh'nuh.

Grecian lore. The two races were at odds with each other, athough perhaps *despising each other* is a better term, having waged their conflict since before recorded time.

But one day, it came to pass that Vaetraiogna, while out in a field gathering flowers, was bitten by a venomous creature like unto a snake but with batlike wings. Vaetraiogna cried out in pain, but all of her people were too far from her to hear, she having wandered off thoughtlessly on her quest to gather enough colorful and fragrant blossoms to make a beautiful wreath for her to wear. But while none of her cries could alert anyone whence she came, a handsome Gitan hunter named Kakkai[24] heard her and galloped to where she now lay. Despite that she was a Qwara, it was as though his heart had been pierced through by an arrow, and so without a second thought, when he saw her, he fell in love with her. Immediately, he dropped to his knees and sucked the poison from her wound. Then he lifted her into his arms, rose to his hooves, and then set off, again at a gallop, to the encampment he had. There, he concocted a poultice from some roots and leaves and bandaged her leg with a strip of cloth that he tore from his shirt. Days passed before Vaetraiogna awakened, but in all of that time, Kakkai never left her side, watching her, keeping her warm when she shivered, and cooling her with daubs of water from another strip of cloth he had torn off when a fever had come upon her. Ofttimes, he would gently stroke her hair or softly kiss her forehead as she slept. He had never known love before, but he knew that this must be it. When finally Vaetraiogna awakened, she saw Kakkai and her heart froze in fear. She had never seen a Gitan up close, but she had heard the most fearsome tales of how the beasts took prisoners; how they tortured and murdered the men and raped and murdered the women, and then roasted their flesh to eat. Weak as she was, struck with such terror as she had ever known, she backed up to the edge of the enclosure.

"Stay away from me!" she screamed. "Stay away!" as tears

---

[24] Pronounced Kak *kai*.

flooded from her eyes.

Kakkai put up his hands. "I'm not going to hurt thee," he said. "Thou wast bitten by a *baraar* and so I brought thee to my camp."

Vaetraiogna calmed a bit at his words. "How long since then has it been?" she asked.

"Twelve days and twelve nights," he replied.

"And in all that time thou didst take care of me?" she asked.

"I had no choice," he said.

"And why is that?" she asked in furtherance of what he had replied.

"Because," and his words came from a place of fear to speak them out loud, "from the very first moment I saw thee, my heart knew that there could be no other in my life."

"Thou loves me?" she asked, astonished. "But how could a Gitan love a Quara? We have been at odds since the world began." She paused and then went on. "I have never seen a Gitan before, but I have heard all sorts of monstrous tales and wicked deeds."

"As have I of the Quara," he replied.

"We are a gentle people," she protested.

"And beautiful," he said and smiled, "if all of them are like unto thee."

"It sets me to wonder," she replied as she surveyed his mighty form, "if thy fruit-filled words flow from thine heart or just thy tongue."

"My tongue is but a mimic of my heart," he said.

"And you pledge yourself to me?" she asked.

"My heart, my arrows, and my life," came his reply, "for so long as I live, I can know no other love but thee."

"Thou dost not even know my name," she said.

"Nor thou mine," came his response. "Love is not words. It is not sight. It is not echoes that fill the air. It is a scent that permeates the soul."

"My name is Vaetraiogna," she replied, "daughter of Traiog,

ruler of the land as far as the eye can see and a thousand times more!"

"And I am Kakkai, a lowly hunter, who has never raised a stone at your people." Then he dropped to his knees before her and held out his hand for her to take.

"And who tended me," she asked, "whilst thou hunted to gather food and drink?"

"No one," he replied.

"Surely thou didst not have enough provisions to last twelve days for both of us," she said as she stared at him.

"There was enough for thee," he replied, "and to me, thou art all that matters."

"It is much to consider," she said, "that thou loves me." She went on weighing, her own words. "Many a suitor has wanted me for this reason or that, but never for love. Come closer to me," she said, "and kiss me that I may judge whether it is love or lust that propelled the sacrifice thou hast made."

And so, they kissed, and she felt the love that she had never known. The moons of Tarag had passed two times before Vaetraiogna's legs were strong enough for her to return. By then, she was with child. It was on Kakkai's back that she rode to her father's castle. No Qwara soldier would dare to shoot a Gitan with a princess on his back. And so they rode through the gates and were greeted by her parents, who had long since thought her dead.

When her father heard what had happened and how Kakkai had saved his only child, he stared at him with tears in his eyes.

"What gift can I bestow upon thee?" King Traiog asked.

"Only your daughter's hands in marriage," Kakkai replied.

"How can this be?" the ruler asked. "Throughout recorded history, our people have been at war."

"Perhaps it is time for that to change," Kakkai said. "How much is thy daughter worth?"

"More than all the lives that have ever lived," came the reply.

"Then let her life save all those living now," Kakkai suggested.

"Father," Vaetraiogna interjected. "There is a child within me now that deserves a peaceful world to grow up in." Those words said, she glanced down at her swollen belly.

Her father's eyes followed her gaze and saw. He then turned to his wife, who nodded and smiled.

"Perhaps our daughter can give birth to more than a child," she said. "Perhaps she can help unite our world."

And so it came to pass, not in a day or a year, but with time, that the Gatan and the Qwara laid down their swords and arrows and walked side by side as friends. How strange it was, though, that after ten moons had passed, Vaetraiogna gave birth to a beautiful little girl with pinkish skin, with only two arms, and with two legs that were like her mother's and like yours and mine. And thus, a third race was born from the union of the other two, and they named her Vaekakkaiana[25] as was their way. And though this was not a fairy tale, they were most happy from that day forth.

That was her story as my consciousness merged with hers. But then something happened. It was like a shockwave through the quantum fabric itself, as time was being rewritten all around me. It was only the quantum seed in my head that left me immune to the change. The effect was so great that I was hurled more than fifty billion light-years in an instant from Vaetraiogna's universe into a skew.

The skew—*that* skew— was a universe unto itself, bizarre is the best word I can use to describe it, as it was comprised of intersecting two-dimensional planes. There were no galaxies or planets or stars. Instead, there were light and dark shapes and even colors. And there was intelligence—some primitive and some human or humanlike. The transmission of thoughts came upon contact. As I was the only three-dimensional being in this universe—which, like my own, must have spanned billions of light-years—the sheets, as I named them, passed through me and through each other. When they passed

---

[25] Pronounced Vae *kak* kai *ana*.

through my body, I felt nothing, but when they went through my brain, I could hear them, some in languages that I recognized. There were thoughts of birth and childhood, of love and of loss, of loneliness and of death. The thoughts, however, were not linear but existed all at once as though each sentient being, whether human or animal, had all of the moments of its life jumbled together. How awful for those who were victims of one horrific event or another, unable to erase from memory the horrors they had known. Consider the antelope, as the crocodile gnashed its knife-like teeth into its neck and then dragged it down into the water to drown; the hurt it felt from the inescapable pressure of the water that had filled its lungs, the need to breathe in air, all the while experiencing the excruciating pain of the reptile's teeth, as it chomped through flesh and bone; or the fish as it was swallowed whole; the ant as it was stepped on; the fly as it was swatted; or the spider as it was flushed down the drain. Consciousness could all too often be—and all too often was—a cruel and damnable thing.

Thus, it was that I felt myself as an embryo and then as a fetus in an egg on Rendenaaar, and as an embryo and then as a fetus in my Earth mother's womb. The scenes went back and forth as I developed within whichever *cocoon* I inhabited until I finally hatched and was born. I was an infant in each world and then a toddler, turning older and older at breakneck speed. On Rendenaaar, when I turned two cycles, [26] my mother pricked me with her tail and I became female. On Earth, having been *born* female, I had my first period. In each case, I grew to be the age I was then, although as Khattaaara I had twin pairs of breasts, pointed ears, and a tail, while on Earth, I wore a training bra, had rounded ears, and a tailbone that, as is the case with all humans, lay vestigial beneath my skin. Both on Rendenaaar and on Earth I experienced my journey toward adulthood, though

---

[26] Roughly twelve Earth years.

with different results.[27] I witnessed myself as Khattaaara being disintegrated, writhing in pain. And then the scene ran backward for a moment, and I was resurrected. Backward and further back it went until I, as Khattaaara, was young again, and time moved forward once more. In the replay, though, there was no sudden death or pain. Once again, the scenes advanced until both versions, Khattaaara and all of the other personas I had been, became middle-aged and then old and then, at long last, died, decayed, and turned to dust, while our spirits (if there was an our and not just a me) fled to this universe and combined, not just with each other, but with all the countless other versions of ourselves and we seemed, if but for one brief instant, to comprehend the meaning of our existence. The us had become one— one spirit, one soul. I could see into each of my pasts, though my future as Peyton was obfuscated and gray. Still, I was able to relive each of my other lives and see glimpses of past moments, although, for some reason, all the evil that I had done was curiously absent. How or why, I did not know.

The realization came that this universe did not exist *beyond* my own, but, instead, *surrounded* it. This was a repository where every spirit fled or was forced to go after death. Neither heaven nor hell, it was where all consciousness went in the end, and no belief in any god could alter or erase the consequences. Able to bear this no more, I tried to phase myself back into my own universe, specifically to my own world and to my own time. But while the seed could place me back on Earth without a problem, the issue of time was another matter entirely.

Time is not a dimension in the common sense of the word. When one looks at a three-dimensional object such as a cube, each part of the cube has its own fragment of existence. Broken down to its fundamental levels, each point, which appears to have length, width,

---

[27] How my Khattaaara self back then, had she been able to view me, would have thought me so alien, and how I at that same age would have looked upon Khattaaara as something monstrous!

and breadth, is in reality one-dimensional. By associating with trillions upon trillions upon trillions of others like it, the sum total forms an object that becomes what we refer to as three-dimensional. Conversely, each slice of time represents a universe in and of itself. And, although both time and space coexist, each is mutable and elastic. As a cube may be morphed into a sphere, one timeline may be morphed into another.

It took considerable effort to escape from that skew universe, but once back, I found that things had changed. I had thought that my return would have been inconsequential, but what I discovered devastated me to my very core.

It was night. Our house seemed uncared for—different from how it had been when I had left. All of the lights were off. Regardless, I went to my bedroom. Phee was there, sitting on the edge of her bed with a scented candle as the only light. She sat there shaking, but not from cold or fear. She sat there with a needle plunged into her arm that bore the bruises of years of drug addiction. She looked years older than when I had left.

"Phee," I said in a quiet voice. "What's going on?"

Phee looked up at me with sunken eyes. Her hair was disheveled, her clothes dirty and torn; her body stank from days or weeks or months of neglect.

"Who the fuck *are* you?" she spat out in drug-induced tones. "Who the fuck?" she went on, echoing her own words. "The ghost of Peyton past?" And then her face turned to anger as her bloodshot eyes tried to focus. "Get out of my head!" she screamed. Then, letting go of the needle, she began banging at the sides of her head with her fists. "Get out! Get out! Get out!"

I knelt down in front of her and grabbed her arms to stop her.

"Phee!" I shouted. "Look at me! What's happened? What's going on?"

"You're dead!" she shouted back. "You're dead!"

"What do you mean?" I said. "I'm here. I'm alive."

51

I let go of her arms.

"No, no, no!" she went on. "You're dead! Dead and buried, like Janey Adams when she got hit by the car. You are *so* dead. And I know, because I found you, and then you were taken away and put in the casket and down you went like a man without a parachute—bang into the ground, buried with the worms!"

"Phee, look at me. I'm not dead. I'm Peyton. I'm Quantum Girl."

"What the fuck is a Quantum Girl?" she mumbled and then shook her head as though trying to shake out what she was seeing.

I stood up and backed up. The realization came to me that the timeline had somehow been changed. Dhraaal had never rescued me. I had died that day, never to return, and this was the result.

"How are Mom and Dad?" I asked.

"Mom and Dad are dead from Dad driving drunk. Dad loved Peyton more than he *ever* loved me. He left me," she wept, though the words barely escaped her lips. "He left me. He left me, and he took Mom with him." Her arms went up again as she clasped her hands to her ears. "Get out of my head," she went on wearily. "Get out of my head and leave me alone!"

There was nothing I could do or say that would make any sense to her. She was just too far gone. And the thought that our parents had died was more than I could bear. I phased out of there and into our parents' bedroom, where I lay down on the bed and clutched my father's pillow. I needed rest, and it was doubtful that I would be disturbed. It wasn't long before I fell asleep. I dreamt about the time when Phee and I were ten years old. We were at the beach and had gone into the ocean after building sandcastles. Then a seagull flying overhead dumped its load. It would have been funny enough if it had landed on Phee's castle, but it landed right smack dab on her head. As Phee felt the offensive goo with her hand, her face twisted into a mask of utter disgust. As for me, I broke into a bout of unending laughter, dropping onto the sand on my back, unable to stop. My reaction apparently angered Phee more than the excrement, and so she charged at me, at which point, I jumped to my feet and ran into water that was chest high, turning back toward her, putting my thumbs in my ears, wiggling my fingers, and sticking out my tongue.

"Dooo-dooo Head!" I yelled out, still laughing.

Phee knew how to swim, having learned in our pool, but she was terrified of the ocean and its currents, so I knew she'd never follow me in. Then, suddenly, I felt something sharp on the bottom of my foot. I had inadvertently stepped on a stonefish, and it stung me. Seconds later, I felt myself pass out. I could feel myself choke on the saltwater, and then everything went black. I woke up to find myself on a stretcher, being loaded into an ambulance. Then I passed out again. When I woke up for a second time, I was in a hospital bed, and it was night. Mom and Dad were there, and Phee was on the bed, curled up next to me, fast asleep. As it turned out, seeing me go under, she had rushed into the ocean without a second thought, pulled me back to safety, and then dragged me up onto dry land. As I wearily opened my eyes, I stared up at Mom.

"Ophelia saved you," she said in a quiet voice.

Then I turned and saw her. Whether it was the words or my movement that awakened her, she turned and looked at me and smiled.

"Hey, Dunkhead," I said softly, smiling back.

"Hey," she replied, still half asleep.

"Love you much," I told her.

"Love you much back," came the reply.

That was where the dream ended and where morning began. But what I had awakened to there and then was no dream. It was a nightmare, and I knew I had to go back in time to change what was to what it had to be.

CHAPTER XI

Ophelia

> *From the Alternate Timeline*
> *In the Alternate Reality*
> *On Earth I*
> *Earth-Date: 2025*

It had been just over a month since I'd looked into the closet to discover Peyton's body hanging inside. I remember getting up and seeing that Peyton wasn't in her bed or in the bathroom, figuring she must have already gotten up and was at breakfast downstairs. Sleepily, I went to the bathroom, did what needed to be done, and then walked to the closet to get my school uniform. But when I put my hand on the doorknob, it turned, but the door wouldn't budge. I tried pulling on it and then tried twisting the knob some more but the door wouldn't give. Finally, I gave up and sighed.

"Very funny, Peyton," I called out. "You can let go of the door now because it isn't funny anymore! I need to get dressed to get to school." I paused, and then went on. "I have a test first period and I don't want to be late." But there was no response. "Dad!" I called out. "I can't get into my closet to get my clothes for school!"

A moment later, he entered the room.

"I can't get the door open," I said. "It's stuck!"

"Let me give it a shot," he replied, and then went over and tried without success. I went to the now-open door to the hall.

"Mom!" I yelled. "Is Peyton downstairs?"

"No, Dear!" Mom called back. "I haven't seen her this morning! Is something wrong!"

"Not sure!" I shouted back and then turned back to Dad.

"It feels like something's holding it," he said, grunting as he pulled.

"It better not be Peyton," I said. "I don't like practical jokes."

Dad took a deep breath and then said, "Let me try one more time," and he pulled as hard as he could. The door opened just a bit. There was light coming from inside. I looked inside and then I screamed. It must have been deafening as even the neighbor's dog began to bark. Peyton was hanging by her neck.

"Open it more!" I screamed hysterically.

Dad pulled even harder, and I squeezed through the space he had made. Once inside, my entire body trembled. I rushed up to Peyton, grabbed her legs, and lifted her with all my strength. I could see how, the rope having been tied to the doorknob, the weight of her body had pulled the door shut. I wanted to untie the rope, but I couldn't hold her up and undo the knot at the same time.

"Dad!" I called out, still hysterical. "Try and open the door now!"

With the tension released, he was able to open it enough to get in. Then he saw her. "Oh, dear God!" he exclaimed.

He rushed over to me and took hold of Peyton and continued to lift her as I went over to the door. The problem was that her weight had pulled so hard on the rope that I couldn't get the knot undone.

"The knot's too tight!" I said. "Wait! I think there's a knife in her climbing bag." I rushed over to it, searched frantically *through* it, and then exclaimed, "Got it!"

I rushed back to the rope and began to saw at it with the knife. Strand by strand split apart, until the last one severed, and Peyton fell into Dad's arms. I opened the door and stepped aside. By that time, Mom was already in the room. She watched as Dad carried Peyton to her bed and laid her down, the noose still around her neck with the length of rope dragging from it. He put his ear to her chest and then began to give her mouth-to-mouth. As he pushed down on her chest repeatedly, in between his, breathing into her lungs, he glanced back at Mom and me.

"For God's sake," he barked out, "call 911!"

He continued the CPR on her for more than ten minutes, refusing to stop, pumping down on her chest, breathing air into her lungs, again and again, but Peyton did not wake. She did not stir. And when I went over to her and touched her, her body seemed lifeless and cold. When the paramedics finally arrived, one of them shined a small flashlight in her eyes.

"Pupils dilated and non-responsive," the man said to his partner. He felt for a pulse in her neck and then her wrist. He listened to her heart with a stethoscope. He felt her skin and then shook his head. "She's been dead quite some time," he said. "I'm sorry. She's gone."

Dad, who had been standing over them, dropped to his knees and began to sob uncontrollably. I had never really seen him cry before. Mom went over to him, knelt down beside him, and held him. I watched as the paramedics left. I went to the window and stared at their truck as they drove off. Then I turned and looked down at Peyton, or rather her corpse. This had been my twin sister, my best friend, and now she was gone. What could have driven her to do such a thing? I bent down to take her arms and lay them across her chest, but her arms were unyielding. Rigor mortis had set in. It was unnerving, to say the least. I think that was the moment that I went into shock.

I just stood there unmoving. It took Dad several minutes to be able to regain his feet, and it was only then that he and Mom took notice of the fact that I hadn't budged. The doctor who examined me that night told them I was catatonic. I don't remember how I got there—the guest room, I mean—but I remember opening my eyes to stare up at the ceiling. It took until that afternoon for the coroner to pick up the body. Mom and Dad felt it unwise for me to be in the same room with her—she who had been my sister from the moment we had been conceived. The room was *sealed* with her body inside— with me not allowed to go in—not allowed to be with it. "With *it!*"

My sister was now an it—a corpse. I think Mom and Dad were afraid that I would follow Peyton to the grave. They knew how close we were. *Oh, dear God in Heaven*, I thought, *my darling Peyton was gone from this world!* I had nightmares for years afterward about opening the closet and finding Peyton hanging there. It took more than a month for me to go back into that room, which was now mine and mine alone. It was a year to the day before I could bear to sleep in my bed again.

Dad was never the same afterward. It was a hard trip to the cemetery. That was where the funeral was held. Peyton had always loved the open air. It was an open casket ceremony, and she lay there like Sleeping Beauty, only no prince would or could ever awaken her. The casket was mahogany, lined with soft, white silk. Her head rested on a white silken pillow, her arms folded across her chest. She wore an Alexander McQueen dress with a black bodice and a full skirt with pale pink at the bottom and top, off the shoulders to end mid-calf. The dress had cost more than $12,000, but as Peyton had worn it as a runway model only a month before, the company, upon hearing of her death, chose to give it to her, or rather to our parents, *for* her. Her hair hung freely down to her shoulders, and her feet remained bare. She was a child of nature, and to nature we prayed she would return. They say we are each made of stardust, but hers was from the brightest star.

"Peyton Elise Herron was only fourteen years old," the minister said, "when the Lord took her in his arms and welcomed her into his fold." And then I seemed to grow deaf. I watched the movement of his lips, but I *could* not hear his words. Everyone stood in silence. Some bowed their heads. Some turned their heads away. When the eulogy was done, Mom and Dad walked silently to the casket and stared down at their once-daughter. Dad shut his eyes, holding back tears, and then both of them walked away. I walked up next, holding the small meteorite I had bought for her birthday, and placed it in her hands. "May this guide you to the stars," I told her under my breath, and then I broke down and began to cry; something I hadn't done since it had *happened*. It was Mom who came up to me and put her hands on my shoulders. I turned around and wrapped my arms around her—and wept bitterly.

I could hear the lid of the casket being closed behind me. I could hear the motors as they lowered it into the vault in the grave. Dad had come up to us by this time, and both he and Mom urged me back to the car with them. Silence permeated the air as we drove home. There were other cars there when we arrived. Relatives and friends had come to console. I just sat in the car after Mom and Dad had emerged.

"Ophelia," Mom said in a gentle voice. "We need to go in."

"Would it be all right if I went up to my room?" I asked.

"Of course," she assured me, and so I emerged and went inside with them.

The mourners were gathered in the living room. Food and drinks had been laid out on various tables. I ignored all of it, all of them, and went upstairs, straight to my room, shut the door, lay down, and buried my head in my pillow. Suddenly, I felt someone sit down on the edge of my bed.

"Whoever you are," I groaned, "go away."

"Hey, Dunkhead," came the reply. "Cheer up."

I opened my eyes. It was Peyton there on the bed next to me. I sprang to a sitting position. My eyes welled up with tears. My breath became labored. "I'm dreaming," I said, barely able to get the words out. "I know I am."

"No," Peyton said, shaking her head. "I'll get you some water. Then I'll explain." And she did.

CHAPTER XII

Khattaaara/Payton

> *Payton from the Original Timeline*
> *Sharing the Mind of Khattaaara*
> *In the Rewritten Timeline*
> *On Rendenaaar*
> *Trillions of Universes in the Past*

Dargra-Tol was synthetic, built in a factory like all the rest of her kind that were made to look real, with the exception that the irises of their eyes were entirely silver or gold, depending on whether female or male, respectively, with their pupils the reverse. For the past four thousand cycles, the Gaaalthaaaran civilization, which spanned more than ten thousand planets in fifty-six galaxies, used synthetics as slaves for teaching or child care, for hard labor, or for sex. In the Gaaalthaaaran language, they were called Thaaagran, which roughly translates as *no one*. They had no rights. They could not own property. They could not make decisions for themselves, and it was unlawful for them to display any emotion other than on command, despite that each possessed sentience and could feel both pleasure and pain. Sadly, as a result of the latter, they were totally at the mercy of any Gaaalthaaaran who was sadistically inclined or who fell into outbursts of brutality or rage. Throughout their history, occasional uprisings took place but such were ultimately suppressed, with the end result that those caught were publicly *discreated* as a warning to others that might be inclined to follow suit with similar rebellions. *Discreation* involved the stripping away of the skin, then the muscles, the organs, and, finally, the bones, leaving only the nervous

59

system, the eyes, and the brain while consciousness remained. The process was accomplished through the god-stones and proved excruciatingly painful—regardless that the victims were synths—taking more than a day for death to release them from the agony of their torment. Despite that, every fifty cycles or so, Thaaagran rights groups would emerge, led by humanitarian Gaaalthaaarans, but little if any reform came as a result. Furthermore, the seven god-stones created obstacles to potential uprisings on both an interplanetary and an intergalactic scale, as they facilitated the monitoring of hostile communications.

Dargra-Tol was my property, a gift from my husband-brother, Dhraaal. Whether by Gaaalthaaaran or human standards, she—this manufactured creature—was strikingly beautiful with long blue hair and a slender form that mirrored the female ideal. She was about as tall as I was, her breasts a fourfold of perfection, her skin soft like velvet, unadulterated by blemishes or freckles or marks of any kind. Sexually, Dargra-Tol was virginal, never having been engaged in coitus by either a female or a male. Her production date had been only several days before Dhraaal had acquired her for me, more as a caretaker for Thara-Klo than for any of my needs. Indeed, it was Thara-Klo who had named her. And, despite the law, I—or at least the Payton half of me—fell head over heels in love with her.

At first, her tasks were those of an *au pair* (though no such term existed in the Gaaalthaaaran language), but then things changed. At night, as I lay naked in bed, I ordered her to massage me with special attention given to my *naaahnra*, the furry end of my *yaaargh* in which reside the sexual receptors of Gaaalthaaarans. Such practice was common among Khattaaara's people, though what was *un*common and even punishable by death was to try to reciprocate the act and attempt to elicit a sexual response from the Thaaagran slaves. This was not generally an issue since normally the law required that the *yaaargh* of every Thaaagran be severed prior to delivery to its buyer, the purpose being to tame the creatures that were considered decidedly inferior and not a true lifeform. But where other Gaaalthaaarans shared this opinion, my alien soul saw Dargra-Tol as breathtaking, and in that regard, I not only longed for her touch but to give her pleasure in return. The memory of Theresa bothered me, of course, but then Theresa would not even be born for hundreds of trillions of years in a universe that was as unreachable to me as was the dimension whence my Payton half had come. Add to that fact that Dargra-Tol was different in that her *yaaargh* remained intact, as Dhraaal had procured her on the black market. Thus,, I kept it hidden when there came visitors to my home or when on those rare occasions, I took her out in public.

One might find it strange that my Payton self did not abhor her new existence, not knowing if it were temporary or permanent; for while this civilization was *different* (that word being a supreme understatement), it was not uncomfortable to the Payton half, while the Khattaaara part of me felt quite content with that body into which she was born. As for Thara-Klo, it was not as though the Payton half had grown to love her (I refer to Thara-Klo as her because she had already chosen her gender), but the Khattaaara half of me had loved her from the moment that she hatched from her egg. Such was the manner of birth among this species. How strange it would sound to anyone back home—Liam would have had a fit of inconsolable laughter—to learn that I, Payton Herron, a confirmed and diehard lesbian, had been impregnated by an extraterrestrial male and then laid an egg that hatched into an alien child. I would have been nicknamed Paylien, and never have heard the end of it. Dear brother, how I missed you!

And so it was that I or we fell in love with Dargra-Tol, synthetic though she was. On those days, when I was free, we would walk through my private gardens holding hands, and every night, no matter how tired either of us was, we would find time for making love. This, however, was my undoing as eventually, Dhraaal found out through some innocent chatter by Thara-Klo.

"Dost thou fathom the consequences?" Dhraaal stared at me with a gaze that would have halted a charging rhino. "General directive four specifically forbids Thaaagrans to exist with their *yaaargh* intact. I had trusted you to excise it."

"I will not mutilate her!" I insisted.

"There is no her!" Dhraaal shot back. "It is a creation with no more humanity than the boot on my foot!"

"Nevertheless," I went on, "I will not deprive her of that selfsame pleasure that she bringeth to me! She is *my* property, and I shall bear whatever consequences that should befall. I stand equal to thee in the house of our ancestors and far above those who would choose to challenge my authority."

"Beware the star that shines too bright!" he warned.

"I shall take note of that," I shot back in fervent words, "when I turn to the sky for counsel. Thou art my husband and brother, and I truly love thee, but thou must leave me to decide such matters on my own."

"Take heed, then," he said with great solemnity, "and take care."

"I will, my love, I will. She is but a dalliance," I assured him. Then I kissed him goodbye with the lie still on my lips.

The truth was that my heart raced at the very thought of her, and those moments apart from her seemed like eternities. She was all that I had ever felt for Theresa amplified a thousand times, for she seemed my equal in many ways, even in dance, which we would practice together in my studio at home. We were synchronized and rhythmic, our movements reflective and aligned. And when we made, love I was thrown into an admixture of ecstasy and bliss. I no longer mourned for the atmosphere of my distant home but craved only for the scent of her Thaaagran breath and for the scent and taste of her *graaam*.

CHAPTER XIII

Theresa

From the Original Timeline
In the Alternate Reality
On Earth I
Earth-Date:2025

I wished myself back home and found myself back in my bedroom. The house was the way it had been before things had all gone wrong. There was no sign of that couple, but that was in the future, and this was now. It took me a while to figure out how to lose the costume or whatever it was. When it finally disappeared, it and the dress that it had been changed into were both gone, and I stood there in the nude. I wasn't sure if the dress hadn't reappeared because it couldn't come with me through time or if it had vanished because it wouldn't be made for several more years. Perhaps now, though, it would never be made. I couldn't quite figure it out, but the concept of time paradoxes seemed somehow familiar. Regardless, I had a roomful of clothes, so I shrugged it all off and got into the shower.

You can't wash away rape. You can't pull back the tears or erase the shame. When I was ten, one of my uncles molested me. We were living with him at the time. He said that if I told anyone he would hurt my mother—his own sister—he would hurt her bad, he said. It went on for more than a year, but then he *did* hurt her even though I didn't tell. I went to him. I demanded to know why he had done what he had done when I had kept my promise and I hadn't said a word. He said that he had spoken to God and that God had told *him*. He read me passages from Judges about how the men in Canaan had been told to capture virgins and make them their wives. He said that God had told *him* to take me as *his* wife and that God had been angered that I had prayed to Him for his husbandry of me to stop. And so, he said, God had ordered him to punish my mother. "But why not me?" I wept. "Why not punish me instead? What did my mother do?"

He said, "If I would beat you, you would heal. But if I beat your mother for your sins, there would be scars that would remain." God had told him this, he insisted, so, it was not *his* fault, he said. It was *mine*.

How could God do this to me? I wanted to know. I had gone to mass every Sunday with my mother. I believed in all the good that I had been taught. I believed in God and believed that He was good. Anger rose in me, and I attacked him, my uncle. I beat him and I clawed at his face till he screamed so loud that my mother came in, and in tears, I told her all that he and God had done. My mother called the police, and he was taken away. She told me that God would never have done such a thing, but I had read it in the Bible. I had read how God had drowned all the people on the Earth, even children and babies, and so it came that I hated God for what had happened to those women, for what had happened to all the babies and children, and for what had happened to me. And from then till now, I have hated the touch of men. I had thought a lot about girls—about women—but I had never been with one. I assumed that love was not meant for me.

The water rained down on my naked flesh as I had those thoughts. The hard beads of liquid felt soothing against my back as I stared at the checkered pattern of tiles on the wall I now faced. It was at that moment that something strange happened. The impact of the droplets stopped. I turned toward the showerhead to see if the water had somehow been shut off, but it hadn't. Instead, the water was going back up into it as though time was running in reverse. *But why not for me?* I wondered. *Why not for me?* I emerged from the shower just moments later, completely dry.

I walked into the kitchen. The clock on the wall over the sink was running backward. A bunch of bananas on the counter that had gone black began to turn yellow again. Time seemed to move faster and faster, but in reverse. The night turned into day and then into night again and on and on and then, suddenly, the room was filled with police and paramedics who brought my mother's dead body in on a stretcher, placed it on the floor, and then left, her corpse surrounded by dried-up blood that became liquid and flowed back to her wrist and into her veins. Then, all at once, she came alive and rose up against gravity. The razor blade that lay on the floor flew into her hand, and her hand brought it across her wrist, again and again, miraculously healing her wounds.

"Mama!" I screamed, and she turned, as though she heard me, but then she vanished, and it was night again, and the clock was where it had been at the start, or perhaps a few minutes after. I stood in the shower, still naked, dripping water onto the porcelain tub as the water from the shower once more saturated me. I took a deep breath, turned toward the showerhead, and turned the water off. Then I sat down in the tub, wrapped my arms around my knees, and wept.

CHAPTER XIV

Ophelia

From the Original Timeline
In the Alternate Reality
On Earth II
Earth-Date:2029

It is nearly impossible to live one's life outside the grid with no identification. As far as this dimension was concerned, Ophelia Jane Herron did not exist. I had no birth certificate, no social security number, and no driver's license—at least none that were valid here. And the documents that I *did* have were all backward in this mirror dimension. I was right-handed in a left-handed world, and that in and of itself was a severe handicap. Every bit of writing, from signs to books, was printed in reverse. Cars were driven on the left side of the road with the left foot used for the pedals. Door handles turned counterclockwise to open. Even something as simple as a pair of scissors proved nearly impossible for me to use. But outwardly, the people looked the same. Thank God for that. At least I was able to blend in.

And there were also many other differences here. Semiconductors had never been invented, so there were no computers (other than massive ones that used vacuum tubes and had to be programmed with punch cards), nor were there cell phones or flat-screen TVs. People did tend to be less angry, though, and the political parties were less extreme. Music appeared to diverge (from what was on my world) in the mid-Fifties. There was never an insurgence of Rock and Roll. No one here had ever heard of Elvis Presley, and while the Beatles did top the charts, here they were a religious pop group called Church, which consisted of John Lennon, Paul McCartney, George Harrison, and Pete Best, all of them coiffed with choirboy haircuts as they first appeared on the Ed Sullivan show in early 1964, singing their now classic songs, *She Loves God, Yeah, Yeah, Yeah* and *I Want To Hold God's Hand*. Teenage girls still swooned, and their influence in this dimension was just as great until they had to disband when Paul McCartney was murdered by a disgruntled Church-rejected drummer named Richard Starkey. Ted Bundy, and not Bill Clinton, served two terms as the 42nd President, which probably accounts for the mysterious disappearance of one of his aides—namely, Monica Lewinsky. Reese Witherspoon was the Representative for Louisiana's 2nd Congressional District. Meanwhile, Alexandria Ocasio-Cortez—who in her younger days as a stripper went by the stage name of Raven—owned the club where Payton worked. I had to really laugh at that one. The biggest difference, though, was that, unlike on my world where socialism began to take hold, the nation here still reflected the America of generations past with a strong adherence to both family and education. I think I must have been the only one who didn't have a command of either Latin or Greek, though I was *somewhat* proficient in French. *A lot of good that would ever do me here*, I thought to myself. In the late Eighteenth Century, France had been conquered by Spain, and the French language had all but died out with its flag. All of that aside, I reflected on the sad reality of my situation. The money I had would not last forever, and staying in a motel every night would exhaust it all too soon.

The next morning, I went in search of a place to live. There were several classified ads for rooms that looked promising. I circled them, made some calls from my room, scheduled viewings, and then headed out with Jordan. Getting around on buses was inconvenient and seemed to take forever, especially waiting for them to arrive. There were no Ubers in that dimension, probably because there were no cellphones, and I could not afford to take a cab—not in my present circumstances. Beyond all else, the buses literally stank. I think it was a result of the diesel fuel they used. And I was new to all of it. I had never actually ridden a public bus before; I had barely ever ridden one to school. My first thought after boarding was that there were no seat belts. The interior has scads of chromed steel bars to slam one's head into in the event of a crash and more than enough headroom to go flying to one's death. Above the windows on each side was a row of ads presumably designed to entice the weary traveler (who, like me, couldn't afford a car or a cab) to purchase things he or she probably didn't want in the first place. One offered a course in shorthand. Another was for nylon stockings "for sheer beauty." Apparently, on this world, they were still in vogue, though I can't imagine why. Neither Peyton nor I had ever owned a pair. I don't think that Mom had either. On our world, they were a relic from the past, like corsets and slips and cigarettes! People still puffed away at them here with no warning from the Surgeon General. Their effects on human lungs or their carcinogenic properties were still unknown or else covered up by the tobacco industry.

After three failures, including a fifty-something, decrepit-looking, corpulent man, who offered free lodging in exchange for sex, I decided on (and was approved for) a small, private guest house not all that far from where I used to live. The couple that owned it resided in the main house, were both instructors at UCLA, were in their mid to late fifties, and had a twenty-year-old son, named Ethan, who had been paralyzed from the waist down from a football injury he'd sustained two years before and who was confined to a wheelchair. The doctors had optimistically given him a sixty percent chance of being able to walk again, but he had, it turned out, just given up.

Jordan and I settled into our quarters quite nicely, but I was like Old Mother Hubbard; I had neither food nor hygienes nor clothes. I told my new landlords, the Porters, that I had escaped a domestic violence situation, and they were quite sympathetic. Mrs. Porter said that she had a couple of nieces close to my age who would probably be able to part with some clothes, and, as for Jordan, there was the congregation at her church, whom she assured me would be more than happy to provide whatever was needed. Mr. Porter then offered to take me to the local MaySmart[28] for more personal items and groceries. I don't know why, but I suddenly burst into tears in front of them. Mrs. Porter came up to me and asked me what was wrong. I shook my head, and said, "Nothing. It's just that I have no one in this world, and you hardly know me."

"We're all children of the Gods," she said. "Now you go dry your eyes , and then come have supper with us. I make a mean beef stew." She considered for a moment and then asked, "You're not a plantarian, are you?"

"A what?" I stammered out through my tears.

"You *do* eat meat?" she asked, "Because if not, I can put together some sort of salad."

"No, no," I said, wiping my cheek with the back of my hand. I half-laughed, "I've even been known to pig out at McDonald's."

"I don't know who Mr. McDonald is," she replied with reassurance, "but you can eat as much as you want. Lords know you're all skin and bones."

"Thank you," I said, and then went back to my new home with Jordan to fix my face before returning for dinner.

Looking—or more accurately—*awkwardly* glancing at Ethan Porter, he appeared quite dour, even when he chewed his food. I afterward learned that he had been engaged to marry a nineteen-year-old junior at UCLA, where they both attended; only, after his injury, she abruptly broke things off. One can't really blame him for his attitude, as in one fell swoop, he was robbed of both his legs and his heart. Whispered to me by Mrs. Porter was that immediately after the break-up, Ethan had attempted to take his own life by wheeling himself into the swimming pool. Unfortunately for his plans, though

---

[28] Owned by the May Company and equivalent to Walmart

fortunately for him, motionless bodies tend to float in still water so there he remained for ten minutes until, realizing the futility of his efforts, he called for help that came in the form of a neighbor who dialed (and, yes, they still had dial phones there) 911 so that he was eventually fished out by two police officers who both left the scene wet as Poseidon himself. At the time, Ethan maintained that it was an accident; that he had tried to turn and both he and the chair capsized. The explanation sufficed enough that he was not hauled away on a 72-hour psychiatric hold.

The meal progressed with Mr. Porter discussing how Ethan believed that the Soviet Union would eventually launch an attack against the United States. His reasoning was that their Marxist ideology was threatened by a free-market capitalistic economy, such as was in place here. His parents, however, were not proponents of their son's prognostications. Mr. Porter was an associate professor, teaching political science. Mrs. Porter, with a similar ranking, taught English and would have none of that talk at the table, which she denounced as "doom and gloom."

"We need to look on the bright side of things," she argued. "We have a guest at our table." Then she turned to me. "Ophelia, do you speak any foreign languages?"

"A bit of French," I replied. "Enough to make myself understood."

"*C'est une si belle langue,*" she said.

"*Je crains cependant que ma maîtrise de celui-ci soit loin d'être parfaite,*" I replied back.

Mrs. Porter smiled broadly and clapped her hands. "*Non, c'est merveilleux; même ton accent,*" she proclaimed. "*C'est merveilleux.*" Then she addressed Ethan and Mr. Porter. "I was just telling Ophelia that her command of French is superb."

"I don't understand," Ethan proclaimed, "the purpose of learning a dead language."

The woman scowled at her son and then turned toward me again.

"He's still languishing over that dreadful girl, Alba, who wouldn't recognize gold if it were stamped 18K when all he has to do is lift his gaze to see the beautiful young woman sitting across from him."

"Mother, you're embarrassing her," Ethan said, staring down at his plate.

"It's all right," I interjected. "It was generally my sister who got most of the attention. She did modeling."

"And where is your sister now?" That question Mr. Porter had asked.

"I'm not quite sure," I said, trying to hold back tears. "We've been out of touch for a while, and it scares me that I may never see her again."

A scowl swept across Ethan's face. "Great! Now, you've made her cry! You must forgive my parents. Whatever academic wisdom they possess fails to preclude either of them from sticking their foot in their mouth."

By now, tears had actually come. I rose from the table. "Do you mind if I excuse myself?" I asked. "I really need to put Jordan to bed."

"Of course, my dear," said Mrs. Porter. "You take care. Perhaps we'll cross paths in the morning."

Choked up with emotion, I simply nodded, picked Jordan up from the sofa, and left to go back to the guest house. But even after I finally got myself into bed, I couldn't get Peyton out of my mind.

CHAPTER XV

Payton

> *From the Original Timeline*
> *In the Alternate Reality*
> *On Earth I*
> *Earth-Date:2026*

There are problems and there are problems, but I then and there found myself facing the worst one imaginable. Reality began to fold in on itself, and I had no idea the extent of it all. There were literally two timelines going on all around me, and I was phasing back and forth between each one, though I didn't appear to belong to either. Perhaps it was due to the fact that this was not my dimension. I was from a parallel universe. What could have caused or been causing this I couldn't have begun to imagine, but the timing appeared to coincide with Theresa's awakening with the quantum seed in her head.

One reality was the one I was familiar with; the one in which Theresa had blasted me back into the wall and then disappeared. The other left me in the exact same room, but where there was no patient, and the wall behind me was intact. Even so, I was out of phase with both, trapped between the two. And while the seed in *my* head allowed me to phase through time or space, I could not manage to phase into a solid reality. Stranger still, I felt myself entangled with I didn't know what, but it wasn't like when I had divided. In the past, in those instances, each of me was still connected, even when I was simultaneously in different dimensions. But this was different. It was like the faint echo of a long-dead sound. There was someone else I was vaguely connected *to*. Perhaps, I thought to myself, it was a side effect of the temporal discontinuity and nothing more; so I shook my head and tried to avoid giving it any more thought.

When I phased back into my own dimension, it was different in a way I couldn't put my finger on. There was an aftertaste of change. And while there was no duality, I was like a ghost—incorporeal and invisible to all of those around me.

Viewing that world, though—*my world*—it became apparent that what I had sensed was all too real. I began to notice subtle changes taking place. A tree would vanish and another would reappear where it had been, or perhaps just disappear entirely, leaving nothing in its place. An airplane would fly overhead and then suddenly be gone. A woman would be walking with her little boy, who would all at once turn into a little girl as though the child were a changeling. It was like reality there was being overwritten bit by bit. I tried to materialize in the dimension, but it was a no-go. Phasing into the past was dismal. Everything seemed colorless and blurred, so I tried the future—first just a day, then a week, then a year, then two, and then three. For some reason, inexplicably, that did it. I was able to phase totally in. Perhaps, I surmised, this was after the rewrite had finally caught up. I looked around me. Things appeared the same for the most part. When I noticed that a man had seen me as Quantum Girl, I phased ten seconds back into the past as myself in plain street clothes. When he caught sight of me in the then repeated moment, he just glanced at me and then looked away. Anyway, having hidden myself from public view, I decided to phase back home. To my great shock, though, there was another of me already there in my bedroom, sitting at my desk, engrossed in writing something or other, taking notes from a textbook that lay open just to her right. She seemed to sense my presence, for she started to turn in my direction. It was then that I decided to freeze time.

It was after I did that I began to walk around the house. One might wonder how that was possible if everything, including the air, was frozen. Even invisible air molecules, it would seem, would form an impenetrable barrier. However, as I moved, I was able to unfreeze whatever was in my direct path or whatever I wanted to pick up or move out of the way. This was a hard lesson that I learned when I first froze time—finding myself essentially imprisoned and unable to breathe.

As I closely looked at the other me, I realized that this was not a duplicate that I had created but rather myself in an alternate reality—another version of me who did not possess a quantum seed. Liam was out back, wrestling with his motorcycle. Neither Mom nor Dad was anywhere to be found but Dad's car was gone, so their absence was of no concern—at least for the moment. Most confusing, though, was the pretty, obviously pregnant woman, a bit older than me, soaking in the tub in the bath attached to Liam's bedroom. The door had been closed, but I had been able to phase through it, even with stopped time. Who was this woman, naked in my brother's room, I wondered, and where was Ophelia?

I phased into the backyard beside Liam, who jumped, startled at my sudden presence.

"I've told you a million times not to sneak up on me," he said in a scolding tone.

"I didn't *sneak* up," I said. "I phased in."

"You what?" he said. Then he looked at me strangely. "You look different," he went on. "And younger."

"What do you mean?" I said back.

"I don't know," he said. Then, with a puzzled expression on his face, added, "Didn't you cut your hair yesterday?"

"Who's the woman upstairs?" I demanded, ignoring the question. "The naked pregnant one? And where's Phee?"

"Very funny!" he replied. "Claire may love your sense of humor, but it *can* be annoying." He stood up and stared at me. "What's gotten into you anyway?"

"Where's Phee?" I said, repeating the question.

"Who's Phee?" he asked. "Wait!" he went on. "You *don't* mean that girl, who broke into the house a few days ago, do you? Total loon! Claimed I was her boyfriend."

"And?" I said.

"What?" he shot back. "I told her to leave. Beyond all else, she was upsetting Claire."

"You honestly don't remember Phee?" I said, staring at him. "Ophelia"

"No," came the uncategorical response.

"What about me being Quantum Girl?" I asked.

"Who?" He replied like an amnesiac who couldn't remember his own name.

"I need to know what happened to her," I said. "Phee."

"Why is it so important?" he asked. "Before, you said you didn't know her. Now you're acting like she's your best friend. What's *up* with you? It's like you're a totally different person."

"People change," I replied. I paused and then asked, "Do you know where she went?" I stared into his eyes with a deadpan look on my face. "It's important that I know."

Liam shrugged. "She took a cab," he said.

"What kind of cab?"

"Checkered, I think."

"I need to go," I said.

"You're acting really strange," he said. "You know that, don't you?"

"Everything will be all right in a few," I replied. "I need to get back inside. I'm feeling a chill, and besides, this wig I got. It itches like all hell."

I turned around, walked back into the house, and then started time again for everyone else. I tried to go back in time to try and find Phee before she got into the cab, but the past was all wonky like before. I decided to phase back to the other Earth. This one was all too crazy. I needed time to think.

CHAPTER XVI

Peyton

From the Original Timeline
In the Alternate Reality
On Earth I
Earth-Date:2026

The revelation to my parents was traumatic, to put it mildly. My mother literally fainted, and my father began to cry. They had heard talking in our bedroom, Phee's and mine, and they came in, both together, to see if one of Phee's friends had uninvitedly (by them) spent the night. There was a polite knock on the door. I hid myself behind the door as it opened, and then Phee, still in bed, called out, "Come in!"

"What's up?" she added as they entered the room and glanced around (although not behind them) with parental suspicion.

"We thought we heard you talking to someone." That was Mom.

"You did," I said as I chose that moment to reveal myself, Mom going down faster than when Jimmy Thunder knocked out Crawford Grimsley in the 1997 boxing match, and yes, I *am* a girl, and yes, I *do* know that. Anyway, she sank like a stone, and it was only my phasing beside her to catch her that saved her from smashing her head into the corner of the dresser in the room. I think that Dad's sudden rush of tears must have blurred out the oddity of the phase. He looked down at where I had crouched beside Mom and just began to sob. I glanced back at Phee, motioned with my head, and mouthed for her to take care of Mom. Then I went over to Dad and put my arms around him.

"You were dead." His voice bled out the words in a whisper.

"Sort of, but not," I said back, almost voiceless myself. Phee was at Mom's side by this time. "Phee," I went on, turning toward her, "there's some ammonia in the cabinet under the sink. Dampen a cloth and wave it under Mom's nose."

Phee quickly obliged. The pungent chemical did the trick and prodded Mom back toward consciousness. She coughed a couple of times and then, with Phee's help, rose to her feet.

"What's going on?" Dad managed to ask, trembling.

"Dad, you need to sit down," I cautioned. "Phee, help Mom lie down on the bed," and Phee did as Dad sat down on the edge of it. Then Phee climbed into bed next to Mom and held her.

I took a deep breath and then told them everything. "I don't know how reality changed," I said. "It wasn't anything that *I* did. I've lived three years since the day I accepted who I was."

"But what about the Peyton who's lying in the grave?" Dad asked.

"There was no Dhraaal to save her," I said.

"I'm very confused," said Mom. "When did you two…"

"Split?" I said, finishing her question. "I don't know. I was somehow protected from the time rift. I'm from an alternate timeline."

"So, our Peyton and you really aren't the same." That was Phee.

I shrugged. "In one sense, yes, and in another, no."

"Can you bring her back?" Dad asked. "I want my little girl." There were tears once more in his eyes. All three of them stared at me like I was some sort of miracle worker.

"I'm not Jesus," I said. "I can't resurrect anyone, and even if I could, there'd be two of me."

"Please!" Phee mouthed at me, pleading.

"The best I can do—try to do—is to go back in time and merge with her and pull her consciousness into mine, meaning that the body you buried would have been nothing but an empty shell. Her entire being, her soul if you will, will be a part of me, and I will be a part of her."

"Thank you," mouthed Phee again.

"Mom, Dad, whatever you may think, I *am* your Peyton, and the three of you are all I have. But I *will* save *her*," I said, and I paused, "or try my best at any rate."

I became Quantum Girl, and then I phased from the room to the cemetery where the alternate (fourteen-year-old) version of me lay buried in a wooden casket that was entombed within a cement vault. I had experienced being in a casket before and was not looking forward to being in one again.

A thought crossed my mind that I could just go back and then return and tell them that it was done. After all, her memories and mine were identical up to the point of her death, but I had given them my word, and honor is the only thing in life that no one can take from us. And so I phased myself into the body that lay six feet under and at once felt deathly ill, so much so that I instantly, although barely, phased back out. Not only was that body dead, but every tissue in it was riddled with formalin, a distillate of formaldehyde.

After regaining my composure, I decided to try again. I phased back into her past, into the drawer in the morgue in which her corpse had been laid. My body reflected the stiffness of the rigor mortis that had set in, a truly loathsome and, in many ways, frightening sensation. Still, there was not even a spark of life. And so, I went further back to when the paramedics had tried to resuscitate her, but while her body itself felt more alive, there was still no activity in her brain. It was then, though, that I made the decision to stay phased within it, progressing back to the final moment of life, I felt my father try and breathe life into me. I heard the cries of anguish and panic as my body was found, though the words were in reverse. And then I was alone with her—in her—hanging once more in my closet. I must have been there—lifeless—for hours, and so I accelerated my backward travel through time... and overshot. The memory of what had happened to me nearly fifteen billion years ago was suddenly renewed. I could feel the pain of death by asphyxiation while hanging from the rope; the cartilage of my larynx ripped apart, my eyes pushed outward by the pressure of my oxygen-starved blood that felt as though it would burst my very brain. My hands clawed at the rope, thoughtless of the wounds my nails were inflicting on my flesh, my legs kicking, my thoughts, her thoughts, focused on the terror of impending death, tempered only by the prayer that death would finally come. And then, as she began to pass out, I phased back to the guest room where I had pledged my oath only seconds before, returning, not as Quantum Girl but as Peyton, emotionally ravaged by the memory of what it was like to die. I stumbled over to the bed and lay down on my back. My clothes were drenched in sweat. Phee stared at me. There was a look of concern in her eyes. She rose from her bed, went over, and stood facing me.

"You were barely gone for a second," she said, "but you look like you've been put through the mill."

"It was more like an hour for me," I replied, and then, as I felt my stomach rise in me, I muttered out, "Excuse me," and rushed into the bathroom, where I promptly threw up into the toilet. I took a deep breath and then flushed the pinkish vomit down into the oblivion where rumored baby alligators and dead goldfish go. Then I gathered my strength and walked over to the sink, where I splashed my face with the water that I caused to surge from the tap. Phee walked in and went over to me.

I looked up at myself in the mirror. My skin was as pale as a ghost. My eyes were lined with the horror I had put myself through. I looked over at Phee's reflection.

"I'm so sorry," I said. Then tears burst from me. "I'm so sorry. I'm so sorry," I echoed again and again.

Phee put her hands on my shoulders and then turned me around and held me in her arms.

"I did what I could," I sobbed, "but I couldn't merge her *into* me."

I looked up to see Mom and Dad, who were now standing in the doorway looking in. I could see the crestfallen look in Dad's eyes. I had given him a spark of hope, and now that was gone—gone for them all. I was their sister and their daughter, but then there was still the one in the grave. I felt sorry for her, the other one of me, the one who had no one to resurrect her. I had gone through all that my other self endured. For me, while it had been so many billions of years ago, this was a reminder—a vision from my past. Time had separated me from the agony I had endured, but now I'd experienced it all over again, remembering in no uncertain terms what that rope of death had felt like—how it had literally choked out my very soul. But what of the other who still lay cold and lifeless in her eternal wooden tomb? What of her? The beauty that was hers would all too soon be mercilessly devoured by bacteria and worms until all that would be left of her would be the horror of desiccated flesh and bone.

"I need to try and fix things," I told them all.

"You're not going to leave us, are you?" Phee asked. It was she who wore her heart on her sleeve.

I was touched by her concern.

"I need to go back, but I can also stay," I replied.

"How?" she asked. "What do you mean?"

"Let me get some rest," I said, "and I'll show you in the morning."

"You'll still be here when I wake up, won't you?" Phee asked with concern.

"Honest Injun," I said, as I tried to force a smile.

"That is *so* politically incorrect," she replied.

"Not in the timeline where *I'm* from," I said. "Now, let me get some sleep. I've just been through an ordeal."

"Can I get you anything?" she asked.

"A bottle of cold water would be great," I replied.

"Of course," she said back and left to go downstairs.

I went to my bed and lay down. Mom came over and tucked me in.

80

"You get some rest, now, Angel," she told me. Then she bent down and kissed me on the cheek.

"Thanks, Mom," I whispered to her.

I looked up at her. I know she wanted to say something sagacious about Jesus or God, but she knew the time wasn't right, so she held her tongue and just smiled. Then she and Dad turned off the lights and left the room. A few minutes later, Phee returned with a bottle of water. As she placed it on my nightstand, I took hold of her hand.

"I thought you were asleep," she said.

"Only half," I replied and then sat up to drink. The cold liquid felt like ambrosia as it went down my throat. By the time the bottle was nearly empty, Phee had gotten her pajamas on and was getting into her bed across from mine.

"I didn't think I'd be able to sleep in this room again," she said.

"I'm glad you changed your mind," I replied. "You're the love of my life," I said as I put the empty bottle down.

"The love of mine, too," she replied. "And I'm glad you're alive, but I'm just so confused." There were tears in her voice.

"I wish I could have saved her," I said.

"I know," she replied, "and I know how hard you tried."

And then there was silence. And then we both went to sleep.

CHAPTER XVII

Ophelia

From the Alternate Timeline
In the Alternate Reality
On Earth I
Earth-Date:2025

Death is something most people don't give much thought to. All of us will die eventually, but we try not to think about it. Our parents will die long before we do, and our grandparents long before them. But when our grandmother or our grandfather dies, that generally happens when we're fairly young, and we think, *Well, it happens, but they were old.* We rarely stop to consider that they were once *our* age and that they looked at *their* grandparents when *they* died and probably thought and felt much the same. But when it happens to someone close to you who's young, it comes as unexpected, and shocks us to our core.

It devastated *me* when Peyton died, and the fact that she had taken her own life made me reproach myself for not having noticed that she was at odds with herself. But now, not only had she virtually risen from the grave, she had unimaginable superpowers. And, if that were not enough, she had aged four entire years because, she explained, she had come from an alternate timeline. Sorry to say, but this was totally messing with my head. Mom and Dad were happy that Peyton was back, but it was all very weird, and there was still the other version of her who was dead and gone. Still, it was quantum this and quantum that absolutely everywhere—well, absolutely everywhere in private. Normal sisters go hiking or to the mall. Peyton took me to Achilles, a planet she'd claimed for herself (and, by the way, had named) that was located in the Alpha Centauri star system, which is more than four light-years from Earth. Even with a nuclear-powered rocket ship, it would still take more than 18,000 years to reach it. But Peyton could get there—and was able to take me with her—in literally the blink of an eye. I had no idea how any of that worked, even when she tried to explain it to me.

According to her, the other me—the alternate timeline version—had a better grasp on all of this, though I couldn't for the life of me figure out how that was possible if everything was the same up until when Peyton hung herself. Or is it hanged? Anyway, *one* of her (apparently, she can multiply herself into a virtual army) stayed here to hold down the fort, while the other said she was going to try to go back in time to that Rendenaaar place where she said that her original incarnation as Khattaaara was from. So, there I was with one of her. But it just wasn't the same—being twin sisters, I mean. The Peyton who had suddenly appeared was a lot older than me at a time in life when just a few years apart makes a world of difference.

So, in a nutshell, I'd gone from having a twin to having a big sister. It wasn't *all* bad, though. She knew a lot more about life in general than I did and had offered up some amazing stories that had happened in the alternate timeline. Here, apparently, there is no threat from anyone from Rendenaaar. But it made me wonder because, according to Peyton, Grandma Margaret was raised by Thara-Klo after her mother was killed in the Pearl Harbor attack, which did not happen on this world. Yet if that were the case, who the hell raised Grandma Margaret, and if someone else did or if she were raised in an orphanage, wouldn't that have changed things enough to have prevented Mom from ever having been born? I didn't know and still don't. Perhaps some things just snap to *the grid*, and others refuse to. I mean, I don't even know how *anything* exists, but if it didn't, how can there be nothing? It just made my head hurt thinking about it. I wondered, though, what if I wasn't the exact same Ophelia as in the other timeline? The other one, according to Peyton, was smart as a whip, and I was kind of just average, though totally devastatingly beautiful! Just kidding. I was only mildly devastatingly beautiful! So I told her in a text, adding, LOL, to which she replied, "Huh?"

"LOL," I repeated. "Laughing Out Loud!"

"You mean LSH," she texted back.

"What's that?" I questioned.

"Laughing So Hard," her text replied.

"Never *heard* that one," I wrote her.

Peyton went silent for a moment. "What's wrong?" I texted.

"It just seems," she texted back, "that there are a lot of things that aren't the same."

CHAPTER XVIII

Khattaaara/Payton

Payton from the Original Timeline
Sharing the Mind of Khattaaara
In the Rewritten Timeline
On Rendenaaar
Trillions of Universes in the Past

Rendenaaar was a planet roughly the size of the Earth, although its orange star was much older and far more massive than that of the sun with the planet's orbit similar in distance to that of Jupiter; I thought with great concern whether there *would* be an orbit of Jupiter considering the matter of causality and not knowing what my presence in this alien soup would have on my universe or if my universe would exist at all.

As I had previously mentioned, Rendenaaar had three continents, which *are* surrounded by Haaarataraka, the great ocean. Despite that Haaarataraka was comprised of freshwater, one would not have dared to swim in it, as there were various aquatic species that could literally have eaten a whale for breakfast. Both the water and the sky had an orangish cast. At dawn and sunset, both turn red—not a Superman's cape red but red nevertheless—a shade darker perhaps.

The evolutionary lineage of the, for want of a better word, *human* inhabitants of Rendenaaar appears to have originated on Haaarthog, the primordial continent that, two million cycles ago, consisted of the combined landmass of Gaaalthaaar, Koalaaar, and Preataaara. According to legend, roughly *one* million cycles ago, *Khii,* who was the creator, became so angered at the progeny of her children, who then peopled the world, that she caused *Hlaaagthum,* the Great Rift,

85

to occur. All at once, the ground began to tremble, and Haaarthog split into three parts, each moving away from the other as the ocean experienced massive tsunamis. Many died from the continental drift, either from ground quakes, chasms, volcanic activity, or from being drowned—males, females, children, and animals alike all fell victim to *Khii's* wrath. Prayers were invoked while chaos reigned, all to no avail, for the invocations either went unheard or ignored by the goddess. Legend said that she was tempted to destroy her creations, but found her heart softened when a flight of a million *xaaaranaf*, which were like butterflies, crossed her path. When the tremors ended and the seas had calmed, the world had grown twice as large as it had been, while the inhabitants became divided into three separate groups that, over tens of thousands of cycles, physically and mentally diverged from one another. My ancestors on Gaaalthaaar evolved into delicate creatures with great intellect and beautiful *yaaarghig* that eventually were brought to near genetic perfection by our biologists. Those stranded on Koalaaar, while remaining somewhat like us in appearance, and despite their *yaaarghig*, evolved with outward characteristics that more resembled homo sapiens. Meanwhile, on Preataaara, those there became hideous caricatures of what had been—cannibalistic creatures with faun-like legs, claw-like hands, and faces that resembled bats. Such is the way of Nature when left to its own devices.

Geologists at the time, though, argued against the *Khii* legend and asserted that the change in the planet had been caused by a massive atomic explosion at its core that was laced with large amounts of uranium and other unstable, radioactive metals. It was theorized that fissionable material surrounding the molten center of the planet was somehow slammed together as the magnetic poles reversed. This, the scientists at the time theorized, had resulted in massive amounts of radiation being released through fissures, thereby causing the Preataaaran mutations. How frightening it seems when one considers how fragile our planets are and how tenuous life is.

In the advanced later world, and then connected through technology, the Gaaalthaaar stood alone as a ruling class. Their leaders created the laws that governed the entire planet, although they had left the Preataaarans to themselves, considering them as both alien and vile. It was Khattaaara's parents who were the *Orithaaans* of that world, the emperor and empress, which I suppose made me a princess of sorts, though no title was ever bestowed upon me as such. Throughout their reign, her father had died mysteriously shortly after Dhraaal had been pricked by him in order to make him male—they tended to be just and fair in their ways. As for the god-stones, rumor had it that they had mysteriously appeared out of thin air when one scientist, a man named Braaangnarng, briefly opened an interdimensional rift that pulled him through and left seven glowing stones in his place. Braaangnarng was never heard from again, nor was his experiment ever successfully repeated, though countless attempts had been made.

I don't think that Dhraaal understood my intense sexual attraction to Dargra-Tol. My half-brother husband never seemed to have grasped the dynamics between Gaaalthaaarans and synthetics. Beyond all else, sex synths would exude one hundred times the amount of pheromones from their *yaaarghig* as any Gaaalthaaar could, which is why the law decreed that part of that appendage be severed.[29] Regardless, my memory path into Khattaaara's mind was clouded as to what role Dargra-Tol had played with her before our minds had merged. All I knew was that her very touch was hypnotic and the sex we shared, unimaginably pleasurable, especially considering that *paaaghragh* had never been performed on her.

It had been on the eve of the twenty-third day since my *arrival* that Dhraaal summoned me to his chambers. To this day, I believe it was his intent to persuade me by means of seduction, but I refused to play his game. As with the Pharaohs of later times, Gaaalthaaaran

---

[29] The Rendenaaaran word for this was *paaaghragh*, which correlated somewhat but not entirely to the English word, "castration."

siblings generally married supposedly to preserve the purity of the line, but beyond the physical attraction, there was no real love that Khattaaara had ever held for him—at least that was what I had sensed. Conversely, it seemed that Dhraaal was deeply infatuated with her, his younger sister, who was, in Earth terms, no less than a dozen years younger than him. Khattaaara, it seems, had always thought of Dhraaal as weak—one who could be steered by his *yaaargh*—and there was the matter of his endless dalliances with the Koalaaaran females who had given Khattaaara great doubt that he would make a suitable consort when the time would come for them to ascend the royal throne. His first attempt to mate with a Gaaalthaaaran, despite the fact that she was merely a biologist, had failed miserably; for while he had found himself intensely attracted to her, she had revealed herself to be transformative, meaning that she had regretted her decision to become female. And though there was no going back, she had told him point-blank that she viewed all men (perhaps on a subconscious level) with a particular envy that lacked even the slightest bit of attraction. Dhraaal was roughly four cycles old at the time and it changed him irrevocably and instilled in him a resentment toward all Gaaalthaaaran women but me. I was his one fallback, although that night he found that even I was not someone to be *acquired* at his whim.

"What dost thou think of the way of command?" he asked in a voice that was little more than a whisper.

"Meaning?" I said.

"The power of the god-stones is being squandered on menial things and upon insignificant individuals. Something needs to be done." His tone was resolute.

"And what wouldst thou have in its place?" I asked as my gaze bore into his.

"Rebellion," came the reply.

"Against thine own mother?" I asked with astonishment.

"She is thy mother, not mine," he replied. "Mine was born on the lower shelves of our civilization, and her bones no longer speak."

"Thou art my husband brother," I told him, "but thou art verily mad if rebellion is at the forefront of thy thoughts." I took his hands in mine. "I know," I went on, "that life has not always kissed thy cheek, but we are pledged to honor our path to the *yaaargh's* end." I turned my head away. "And what of Thara-Klo?" I asked. "In which direction dost thou intend to pave the path you lay before our child's feet?"

"It is Thara-Klo's future that voices my concern," he replied, turning from me and staring out through one window. "With no other to perpetuate our line, what our ancestors built from time immemorial will be adulterated by something less than us. I blame myself for it all," he lamented, as he hung his head in shame.

"Thou dost speak of adulteration," I said, "when thou thyself art not pure blood and, by that course of reason, neither is our Thara-Klo."

"But this was not made known," he said, and his eyes bore into mine. "Shouldst thou speak of this aloud, I would have thy tongue cut from thy throat and fed to my *goraaag* pet!"

"I hold as much love for Thara-Klo as thee," I said, "and it is my intent that she ascends the throne when *her* time comes."

"Her?" Dhraaal repeated, tasting the word as though it were a bitter drink.

"She has chosen," I said, "to be like her mother."

"Wisdom with time shall make *her* change such thoughts," he proclaimed.

"Thou art filled with an abundance of thy sex!" I shot back at him.

"Perhaps," he replied, turning back to face me, "but time shall be the arbiter of the prick." He reached out then and gently placed his hands on my shoulders. "Would that anyone else were Thara-Klo's mother," he went on, "I should be appalled at the thought of our child becoming female. But my love for thee knows no bounds and, were

89

that choice to be made, I would welcome it as I have welcomed thee into my heart. My dearest Khattaaara, the mere thought of thee as my mate is all that keeps me alive."

"That and the Koalaaaran females thou hast kept hidden in thy pantry," I said.

Dhraaal smiled. "For those times when thou art not here," he replied. "We must speak again. Perhaps on the morrow."

"We shall see," I said with the slightest of smiles. "Thara-Klo misses thee. 'Where is my father?' she asks each night as I tuck her into her bed."

"And what dost thou tell her?" he asked.

"I tell her," I replied, "that while the flesh is often absent, the love within abides, as does that which is in thee, for her."

Then I smiled once more, broader this time, released myself from his hold by a backward step, bid him goodnight, gave a gentle kiss to his lips, and wished myself back home.

CHAPTER XIX

Theresa

From the Original Timeline
In the Alternate Reality
On Earth I
Earth-Date:2025

When I finally got out of the tub, I stood naked and trembling, bleeding water onto the bathroom floor. I looked down as a stream of urine poured down out of me, drowning my bare feet. I didn't care—not anymore. I had seen my mother's corpse in the morgue. I had watched how she had slit her wrists because she thought that I was dead. The last thing I remembered before waking up was being hit by some bright light and feeling such horrible pain. I remembered after opening my eyes seeing Peyton Herron and feeling disgusted at the very sight of her. And I remembered that whatever it was that had hurt me had come from *her*. That she was responsible for my mother's death was the one thought that raged through my head. I lifted my arms to look at my hands and then stared down at me. *Could it be?* I wondered. *Was I dead? And was this hell?* The thoughts grazed my mind but I quickly dismissed them. Something else was going on and I needed to know what it was but it was still night and there was nowhere to go to find out. All that I had been through had exhausted me, both physically and emotionally. I chose to get some sleep and let the morning decide what I should do.

Morning, though, came and went without me. It was half past one when some idiot gardener using a leaf blower woke me from a perfect dream where I was fucking Ariana Grande in her home in her bed. She was breathing hard and moaning because I've always been good at pleasing girls sexually—at least in my dreams. *¡Maldito jardinero!*[30] I thought to myself. As the noise appeared to be unending, I reluctantly got out of bed, traipsed into the bathroom to wash the sleep from my face, and then, still in my nightie, dragged myself into the kitchen to appease my stomach with a strawberry Pop Tart and a glass of orange juice that had fermented just a bit. *Cool!* I thought to myself. After what I had been put through, I needed whatever alcohol I could get, fifteen or not. I had sniffed the carton of milk in the fridge, swooned a bit, and then checked the expiration date. *How the hell could it be from September?* I wondered. I poured the lumpy contents down the drain, went back to my bedroom, threw on some clothes, and then headed out the door, noticing the foreclosure notice that had been posted on the outside. Then there was the mailbox, stuffed with junk mail and a lot of past-due bills. It amazed me that the water and the lights were still on. *How long had I been gone?*

The church that Mama and I went to—*our* church—was about half a mile away. It was a small building but it was the only Catholic church around, so we went there every Sunday for mass. Sermons were generally led by Father O'Neill, who would try to explain the Bible in a million boring ways. Regardless, I needed to get some advice so I went inside and plopped my skinny ass down on the hard seat in the confessional. There must have been an alert that came whenever someone opened the door because like in less than a minute a priest entered the other stall.

"Bless me, Father, for I have sinned," I said. "It has been two months since my last confession."

"What brings you here today?" he asked. His voice was different from Father O'Neill's.

"I need help," I said. There was pleading in my voice.

"Is it forgiveness for something you've done?" he inquired.

---

[30] Damn gardener!

"No, Father," I replied. "It's for something that's been happening to me."

"What do you mean?" he asked.

"Some men gang-raped me," I replied, "and I killed them."

"That sounds like a matter for the police," he said.

"No, you don't understand," I tried to explain. "I froze them with my mind. Then they shattered into pieces and melted into puddles on the street." The priest said nothing, so I went on. "Then there was this man, Charlie who was living in our home with his wife in the future and I made him disappear. I didn't mean to, but suddenly he was just gone. I don't know where. And to make matters worse, I've been going back and forth through time."

"These are just delusions, my child." His voice was calm as he spoke.

"They're not!" I insisted.

"Perhaps if you saw a doctor—a psychiatrist," he went on, and his voice trailed off.

"I thought that priests weren't supposed to judge people," I said.

"But what you're telling me," he insisted, "can't be real."

"I watched my mother slit her wrist," I went on. "Then time reversed and all the blood went back into her arm and the razor blade healed the cut."

"You're the Martinez girl," he said. So, he knew who I was. "We held your mother's funeral two weeks ago. I know this must be hard."

"But I need help," I begged. "I keep traveling through time. And when I get angry there's this white light, that comes from me and I can't control *it* or my anger."

"You *do* need help," he went on, "but not help of the spiritual kind. All of these things that you think happened, they're all in your mind."

He didn't believe me. He was a priest, a man of faith, so he must have claimed himself to be, and yet he refused to believe me. I clenched my fists in anger. There was a flash of white light where he was sitting and then, it seemed, he was gone.

"Father?" I said, hoping that he was still there but there was no reply. I stood up and left the confessional. Cautiously, then, I opened the other confessional door. True to the fear that had built up within me there was no one inside. The priest was gone and, as I found out later, he was never heard from again.

CHAPTER XX

Ophelia

> *From the Original Timeline*
> *In the Alternate Reality*
> *On Earth Ii*
> *Earth-Date:2029*

More than two weeks had passed since all of this had begun. In *my* reality, Liam had been attracted to me from the moment we met. Despite the fact that he was engaged to someone else—someone who was carrying his child—I wondered if the attraction was still there. But the engagement/about-to-become-a-father-with-his-fiancée part was a complication I did not know how to deal with. All I *did* know was that my presence on this world had been written out of existence and that the Payton in this dimension was not Quantum Girl. There *was* no Quantum Girl here, and if the timeline in my dimension had been overwritten as well, I would have no chance of ever returning home. For all I knew, Peyton was dead. After all, she had taken her own life before Dhraaal intervened. *What if she had never been resurrected?* I trembled at the prospect of that even more than being marooned here all alone. But if reality had been rewritten around me, that would mean that there would have been no reason for Payton to have brought me there in the first place. The terrifying possibility raced through my mind that there could be another of me back on my world in my dimension, and, if so, would Mom and Dad even notice that I was gone? [31] As all of that clouded my mind, Jordan began to

---

[31] I sometimes wonder whether or not the timeline that I remember is in fact the original. Peyton rewrote what *was* a number of times, but it is interesting and frightening to think that what we believe is what *should* be might just be the result

cry, and so I went to her and, for that moment at least, I was distracted from all such thoughts.

In the last iteration of time, Liam had been a server at an Italian seafood restaurant on the pier called *Il Mare*. I wanted to see him. I needed to try to convince him that things weren't as they were supposed to be. It wouldn't be easy, but I had a plan. The first thing I had to do was get there. After phoning to find out if and when he worked there, I found the number in the Yellow Pages.[32] His next shift turned out to be that same evening. As it was just past noon, I spent the rest of the day making whatever appointments I thought necessary, assuming that Liam would cooperate. When evening came, I called for a cab and, armed with Jordan, left to find her father, who had had his memory of her erased by the rift.

It was strange, though. The building, the signs—even the menu in the window—were all the same as I remembered. As I entered, I saw all of the familiar faces I had known—all but one. The hostess was different, though she greeted me with a smile.

"Is it just you?" she asked, "or will you be meeting someone?"

"Just me," I replied.

"This way," she said. Then she led me to a table by the window, handing me a menu.

"What happened to Erika?" I asked.

"Who?" came the response.

"Dark hair. A greeter, like you."

"Oh, you must mean Eric. He works days," she said, and then went out without a second thought. "Someone will be over to take your

---

of an overwritten past. Might not there have been a version where I became Quantum Girl and Peyton remained ordinary? All that I could construe from the events that had occurred was that God or the universe or the quantum fabric had no plan. Time travel, at least travel back into the past, breeds great potential danger with its ability to alter what has been. I am reminded of the poem by Longfellow, "I shot an arrow into the air; It fell to earth, I knew not where." Shoot an arrow back through time and witness the result, or perhaps be erased from existence and not be able to witness anything ever again.

[32] They still had the Yellow Pages there. And phone booths!

order in a few minutes. Would you like some water?" she asked.

"Yes, please," I answered.

"You have a beautiful baby," she said.

"Thank you," I replied. It was at that moment, as the hostess left to go back to her station, that I caught sight of Liam, and Liam noticed me as well and took the opportunity to walk over to my table.

"What are you *doing* here?" he asked. His face was stoic, his voice phlegmatic.

"I came to see you," I replied.

"What about?" he asked.

"This isn't the place," I said. "Meet me tomorrow at noon at Pacific Park by the Ferris wheel."

"And *why* am I *doing* this?" he asked.

"Curiosity," I replied.

"Curiosity killed the cat," came his somewhat smug response.

My eyes bore into his. "You're allergic to cats," I said. "So am I."

I arrived at the park the next day and stood at the appointed spot. Liam showed up a few minutes late.

"I'm not quite sure why I even came," he said.

"Maybe a part of you still remembers me,… or her," I replied.

Liam stared at me and then glanced at Jordan.

"I've got two tickets for the wheel," I went on. "I'll tell you on the ride."

And so, we got on, and after a brief moment, the chair we were in began its ascent. It stopped at the top, as a couple of teens took their turn.

"All right," he said. "Why am I here?"

"You see this little girl?" I told him. "She's mine and yours."

"You're crazy," he replied and stared at me like I was.

"I made an appointment at the paternity clinic," I said. "They'll swab her mouth. They'll swab yours. Five'll get you a million-dollar lottery ticket that you're her father."

"We've never had sex," he replied. "Hell, I never even laid eyes on you before you broke into our home."

The Ferris wheel began to turn again.

"She's your daughter," I said. "Just from a different timeline."

"A different timeline," he repeated. He wasn't asking. He was parroting what I had said, staring at me like I had just escaped from a mental asylum. I knew that look. It was the same look he'd given to Frank Westfield when Frank had told him that he was gay. Everyone, including Liam, knew that Payton was, but Frank had always come across as some super-macho jock. It had never occurred to Liam that he was anything but straight, especially as he had always maintained the pretense of being a total ladies' man. He once even claimed to have had sex with three coeds in one night. Of course, that turned out to be a total fabrication, although everyone appeared convinced at the time. But Frank gay? Liam wouldn't believe it even when it came directly from Frank himself. Liam had just stared at him, his eyes ready to bug out of his head. And that was how he stared at me.

"I'm from a parallel dimension," I told him. "On my vibrational plane or whatever it is, Peyton is my sister. Your DNA and mine are virtually identical except for the fact that I have an X and you have a Y on chromosome 23."

"So, technically, we're practically the same person, dimensions aside," came his response.

"Technically," I replied, "but we never grew up together. And when we met, it was one of those love-at-first-sight sort of things."

"And so, how did you wind up in my dimension?" he asked.

I sensed he was being patronizing, but, regardless, I went on. "Peyton, my sister, committed suicide because she was being bullied by a girl at school, only an alien from a previous universe, named Dhraaal, resurrected her and implanted a quantum seed in her head, which turned her into Quantum Girl and gave her super-abilities, one of which is interdimensional travel. But when she was mortally injured, she gave the seed to *your* Payton, who phased into my dimension and, ironically, fell in love with the girl who had driven my sister to kill herself."

"Wait," he protested. "Payton is *not* into girls."

"Well, she *was* before everything changed," I said. "Anyway, as I said, you and I fell in love and we'd been living with your parents. But after Jordan was born, we decided it would be best to find a place of our own. Then, suddenly, two weeks ago, boom, everything changed around Jordan and me, and how sad it was for *me* to learn that you now had a girlfriend."

"Claire," he interrupted.

"And to make matters worse," I went on unabated, "she's on the nest." And there was that stare again. "Liam," I told him, tears welling up in my eyes, "I love you *so* much. I know you must think I'm insane, but please let me prove all this to you. I know you hate avocados and lima beans and broccoli. Your favorite song is American Pie. You like making love with the lights on, and you never made the slightest sound when we were having sex, like it was all about just pleasing *me*."

Liam said nothing. As the wheel rose again, he stared out toward the horizon. I wondered to myself if my words had sparked some modicum of belief in what I had said, incredible as it was on its face. I considered what my own thoughts would have been. In my case, I had been able to witness my sister's abilities, although, according to PeyPey, there were several replays of that event, and, in one, I actually fainted.

Liam did, in fact, although reluctantly, accompany me to the paternity clinic where I also had my mouth swabbed. We met there again two days later. It must have been a Wednesday because I recall watching *Time After Time*, the television series based on the 1980 movie about the time traveler having to chase Jack the Ripper through the past and the future to try and end his murderous career. It starred *Benjamin* Affleck as the time traveler and *Matthew* Damon as Jack. Anyway, the results of the swabs came back as expected.

There was absolutely no doubt that Liam was Jordan's father. It also showed that Liam and I were virtually identical twins. Still doubtful, Liam insisted that we go to another lab that he'd pick out and run the tests again, and so we went, with the exact same results.

He drove me, bleary-eyed, back to the house where I was staying. He was on the edge of belief, and the prospect scared the hell out of him. He was polite as he helped me out, then and walked me to my door. As he was about to head back to his car, I turned to him.

"Why don't you come in?" I offered.

He shrugged at my invitation as though he felt it would be awkward.

"I *don't* bite," I went on, "unless asked to." I went inside. A moment later, he followed me in and shut the door behind him. "Make yourself at home," I told him. "If you want, there are cold drinks in the fridge. I just need to change Jordan and then put her to bed. It amazes me," I went on, "that no one in this entire dimension ever thought to invent disposable diapers."

"So, in this other timeline," he asked, "you and I have had sex together?"

"That *is* how babies are conceived," I replied.

"And you were in love with me?" he pressed on.

"Not were," I said, "am," walking back into the room where Liam stood opening a bottle of Woca-Cola with a bottle opener.[33] He turned and looked at me, setting the bottle down on the countertop.

"I'm still trying to wrap my head around all this," he confessed.

"About being Jordan's father?" I asked.

"No," he replied, "about having had my entire life erased. I mean, what's the good of any of this if it can just be taken away in an instant? And then again, what if it wasn't?"

"What do you mean?" I asked, suddenly puzzled.

---

[33] In this dimension, Coca-Cola was called Woka-Cola, due to the fact that it contained five times as much caffeine as coffee and was what college students drank when they had to pull off an all-nighter before a test.

"I mean," he went on, "how do you know that this is the exact same dimension where we met and fell in love? You said that when you left the supermarket, everything changed around you."

"Yes. And?" I replied

"What if," he suggested, "everything around you didn't change? What if you and Jordan just moved into a different parallel dimension?"

"How could that have happened?" I asked.

"How could any of this have happened?" he replied. "I might not be *your* Liam. My sister might not be *your* Quantum Girl."

"But if that's the case," I asked, "Where *is* she?"

"I don't know," he replied. "This other dimensions, alternate reality, parallel universes shit messes with your mind." He shrugged and then went on. "Regardless, all things considered, I intend to help out with child support. I'll do what I can. I don't make much, though."

"That's not why I put you *through* all of this," I said.

"Then why?" he asked.

"Because," I replied, "I'm all alone in this world, in this dimension, in this universe."

"I'm sure you'll meet someone," he said, stumbling out the words.

"I *did* meet someone," I replied, "and I fell in love with him. Whether you remember it or not, *I* do. I swore to you to love you till death, and I never break my word."

"I don't know what you expect me to say," he replied.

"I don't expect you to *say* anything," I said. I stared at him as the distance between us seemed to evaporate. My eyes never left his. I could tell that it was awkward for him, but I just didn't care. This was all too hard on me. I no longer had family or friends. No one else would even believe me. "We were at the Getty, standing in front of the painting called Spring. That was when you asked me."

"Asked you what?" he said.

If I had been Quantum Girl, I could have heard his heart pounding

101

in his chest.

"Asked me to marry you," I replied. "You called me Lia. That was your nickname for me. You said you could never love anyone else as much as you loved *me*. The world dissolved in every direction, and all I could see was you. I know that I said, 'Yes,' but I couldn't hear myself speak. It was as though I were in a vacuum—like there was just the two of us, floating in empty space, with nothing beneath our feet, with only each other to live for from that moment on. And then you wrapped your arms around me, and I felt your lips against mine. It was the closest my soul had ever come to another and the most resplendent day of my life. So many hope for love and never find it. I had found it, and there it was in *you*."

Then I kissed him—no arms, no holding hands, no embrace—just lips touching. That was all it took for our emotions to ignite. We wound up in my bed. It was like the first time we had ever made love. Afterward, he lay on his back staring up at the ceiling with me cuddled up next to him. He spoke for the first time since the reenactment of our love began.

"I shouldn't have done that," he said.

"Claire?" I asked, already knowing the answer.

"It isn't fair to her," he confessed. "I don't know what to do."

"What to tell her?" I asked.

"No," he said, "what to do about *you*—about *us*. With Claire, things were all settled. I've known her since we were in grade school. She's always had a crush on me."

"And you?" I asked.

He turned his head to face me. "What do you mean?" he asked in return.

"Did you always have a crush on *her*?" I asked.

"She's beautiful and smart," he replied, "and there was always a spark between us."

"But never a fire." That was my conclusion to him.

"No," he said, "not like just now with you. I am *so* fucked," and

102

then he exhaled a long, hard breath.

I stroked the hair on his chest. "Why's that?" I asked.

He glanced at me and then stared at the ceiling again. "You said it yourself. She's on the nest."

I smiled as I shared his gaze. "You *could* become a Mormon," I suggested

"Not funny," he replied.

"We'll figure something out," I said as I moved closer to him, "I have faith."

His face took on a frown. He glanced at me and then stared back up again. He wrapped one arm around me and pulled me closer still. "Then you're a better man than I am, Gunga Din," he said. At the time, I didn't know what he meant. But that was then.

CHAPTER XXI

Peyton

From the Original Timeline
In the Alternate Reality
On Earth I
Earth-Date:2026

It seemed strange being a part of my family from three years ago; sort of a *déjà vu* that wasn't quite the same. Mom and Dad and Phee were finally getting used to me being older than I should have been. Nearly twelve months had elapsed since the day of the funeral and since I had tried to fill the emptiness that had torn out their hearts when my alternate self had died. But in due course, I had made a decision to try once more to go back to Rendenaaar in order to discover my past and try to learn what had made me the villain I once had become.

Having left one of me behind to stay with Phee, I began my journey back through time. As I have mentioned before, the only way to travel back past a Big Bang is through the quantum fabric, which overlays or underpins everything. The quantum fabric is neither a universe nor even a place. Existence is charted by time. What we consider matter is, for want of a better term, a chronometric anomaly. Each universe is self-contained, the number of universes being calculated as infinite. While many universes can intersect, they are incorporeal to each other because, essentially, they are made of different stuff. Each universe, however, is comprised of an infinite number of both physical and time parallels. The concept of all of this transcends human comprehension. There is just too much to take in. Entering the quantum fabric, though, is rather like going down the rabbit hole, for it not only consists of everything, but everything in between. There, the rules of time and space do not apply. It is the wormhole to everywhere and to nowhere but it was there that I needed to go to travel to the planet of my origin, where I, as Khattaaara, had been born.

There is nowhere to stand in the quantum fabric. There is neither ground nor gravity, but it is not the same as outer space. And while there is no air, there is no need to breathe, nor any reason for the lungs to take in air or for the heart to pump blood because time there is irrelevant. But as I traveled back past the creation of *our* universe and a trillion others, as I approached the boundary of that one which held the Rendenaaaran home world, all around me there began to appear other versions of myself. Unlike when I duplicate, those versions were not me in actuality but, instead, the infinite possibilities of what I was attempting to do. I floated in a sea of other Quantum Girls whose voices bombarded my brain with disconsolate thoughts that held but a single message: *Go back home.* Each heralded the futility of any attempt. Those who saw me knew that I had yet to venture back far enough to have tried to accomplish what I had set out for. *"Give up!"* the thoughts chanted into my head. *"There is no hope! You're doomed to fail!"* Bodies—versions of myself—cascaded into me. Some, out of phase, went through me as though I wasn't even there. Many were missing arms or legs or were disfigured. No matter that I phased myself a billion light years away, if one could measure such distance there, the quantum fabric was filled with Peyton Herrons and Quantum Girls, none of whom was truly whole, until, at last, there came one who looked at me with an expression different from the rest.

"I followed your trail," she said. "I had to. I couldn't let you do this alone." It was Payton. "Let's get out of here," she said, and so, holding hands so as not to get lost in the quantum maze, we phased away from the insanity of it all.

Traveling through the quantum fabric, though, is not like

traveling through space or time. It is difficult to describe in three-dimensional terms. The best comparison I can come up with is that it is like a lucid dream. There is a sense of reality, but things can change in an instant. It was amazing to me that Payton had found me, but regardless, we needed to remain close together so as not to lose sight of each other. Here was the link to literally all of creation—every dimension, every universe, every possibility. Thara-Klo had given me, not a map, but a means by which to find Rendenaaar. But then, I wondered, what could have happened to have changed things? One atom might have shifted on its axis and, like a row of dominoes falling, one against the other, altered the way things had been. I suspected, though, that the culprit was something much larger to have thrown things so out of kilt. We went back more than a trillion universes to find the one where I had first been born. That much was a success.

"How are we going to find Rendenaaar?" I said to her. "We don't even know which galaxy it's in, not to mention that this universe appears far larger than our own. I'm guessing there are probably more than five septillion star systems and more than twenty-five septillion planets and moons on the conservative side."

"You forget one thing," Payton replied.

"What's that?" I asked.

"You have a quantum seed from this universe that is undoubtedly linked to the one that is *here* because technically it's the same *one*. All you need to do is phase yourself to the original."

"You're brilliant!" I told her.

"I'm just not as conflicted, Peytaaara, dear," she replied.

"Please don't call me that," I begged.

"Anyway…" she went on with an impressive sigh. "That should get us to the right star system, but finding the right time period is another matter."

She was right. It was not only a question of where, but when. Rendenaaar had existed for billions of years, but Khattaaara for only a shallow breath of time.

The planet we found ourselves on was dark and cold, with an atmosphere so thin that no beings other than ourselves could have survived without oxygen and protective gear. There was evidence of what was now a long-dead civilization, far more advanced than our own, but it lay in ruins, covered with eons of corrosion and dust. There, though, at my feet, revealed to my mind, even through the silt and stardust, was the quantum seed that had drawn me to this spot. But imagine my shock when, having blown off the debris with a gentle quantum breath, a skeleton revealed itself to us— Gaaalthaaaran in shape, female and adult with a meter-long tail. *Was this Khattaaara*? I wondered. *Was it me?*

CHAPTER XXII

Ophelia

From the Alternate Timeline
In the Alternate Reality
On Earth I
Earth-Date:2029

I felt as though I'd somehow been emptied. I wanted to know who I was before everything changed. Even though I had my whole life's memories, I was like a part of them had been erased. Peyton was the only one who knew the alternate version of me, so that first night after she appeared—the day of *her* funeral—I asked her.

"Well," she said, appearing to give it some thought, "you were pretty much the same. The difference was that we both discovered my powers at the same time, but it was you who came up with the name Quantum Girl."

"Really!" I said, smiling, all so proud of my original self.

"And the other Payton said you were essential," she went on, "when you and she and Theresa went back in time to help her master her abilities."

"The other Peyton?" I asked. It was one of those *What the fuck?* moments.

"She's from a parallel dimension," came the response. "She's a diehard les and…"

"I can *so* picture that," I said, staring at her, up and down.

"Shut up!" she replied.

"So," I said as I took a drink from the bottle of water in my hand, "she's a total carpet muncher."

"I think she's more into waxed floors," she replied, at which point

I burst out a laugh, snorting half the mouthful of water I was swallowing out my nose.

"Ow!" I said, and then continued to laugh. So did she.

"After I died a second time…" she went on.

"Ex*cuse* me?" I interrupted.

"Not by my own hand," I said. "Thara-Klo."

"Your daughter," I said with half a question.

"Khattaaara's," she answered with a shrug, "*and* mine, I suppose, in the vast scheme of things." She paused and then went on. "Anyway, she took my place. Here. On this Earth. Then you and Theresa helped her learn how to use the quantum seed."

"And when you say Theresa," I began, "this is a different Theresa than the one who bullied you and caused you to commit suicide?"

"It's a long story," she said.

"I've got time," I replied.

"She and you became friends," she went on.

"Seriously," I said, staring into her eyes.

"Theresa had a crush on me," she answered. "That's why she did what she did."

"She drove you to suicide because she loved you," I said rhetorically.

"She didn't grow up like us," she said without any emotion.

I stood up, angered. "I have a sister who is rotting in her grave because of her!" I looked down at her, sitting there. "You're like a big sister to me in this iteration or whatever the hell it is! But she was my twin! She was half of me! More than half! If I had a choice, I would trade places with her! I don't know what the other me was thinking to even be within a hundred yards of her. And as for the other Payton, fuck her! Fuck her for even wanting to *touch* that bitch, let alone make love to her. Fuck all of this!"

"What's done is done," she replied.

"Well, I guess then," I said, turning my back toward her, "done is better."

"What's that supposed to mean?" she asked with concern.

"Nothing," I answered.

"Do I need to watch you?" she pressed on.

"I'm fine," I said. "I don't intend to follow her. It would kill Mom."

"And Dad," she added.

"Not the same way," I replied. "Not literally." I turned to face her again. "You were always Dad's favorite—his little girl. I was Mom's—her second chance. She was always so very critical of me, but I guess that was because she wanted me to become what she never could. And she hangs onto God like he cares."

"I'm sure he would if he actually existed," she said.

"And Quantum Girl knows that he doesn't," I said, "and that makes Peyton nothing more than food for worms."

"I know how she felt," she replied. "I know why she did what she did, but I also know that she knew that you were always the best part of her life, just as you were mine, even when you were with Liam."

"Thank you," I said to her.

"Wait!" I exclaimed. "Who's Liam?"

"Your fiancé," she said.

"Fiancé," I repeated. "What does he look like?"

She projected a life-size 3-D image of him into the nearby air.

"Definitely eye candy," I said as I walked full circle around it. "What's *his* story?"

"He's Payton's twin brother," she said.

"Like I'm your twin sister?" I asked.

"Uh-huh." Came the reply.

"And he was my fiancé," I said, half-statement, half question. "Isn't that like…" I started to say.

"Incest?" she said, interrupting me.

"I was going to say *creepy*," I replied, "but okay. And no one said anything, like, 'Hey, guys, this is not Kentucky?'"

"No one could say *anything*. The two of you were inseparable and in love and had a baby together. Her name was Jordan, though apparently she, too, was erased, which is really sad."

"Well, none of that matters now," I said. "I don't *know* him, and I'm definitely not in *love* with him. Besides, I've made up my mind. I'm going to marry Jake Maxwell."

"The actor?" she said.

"Yep," I replied. "We are going to fall madly in love, get married, and haul off to the French Riviera."

"I'll come to your wedding," she said.

"Go ahead," I said back. "Make fun, but you'll see," and I stretched my arms out seductively as Liam's image disappeared. "I'm the most beautiful girl he'll ever see."

"And the most modest," Peyton added.

"Shut up!" came my condescending reply.

"But I still love you regardless," she added. The feeling, of course, was shared.

CHAPTER XXIII

Khattaaara/Payton

*Payton from the Original Timeline
Sharing the Mind of Khattaaara
In the Rewritten Timeline
On Rendenaaar
Trillions of Universes in the Past*

I had grown frightened of Dhraaal. While I had submitted to his sexual desires, I sensed that he had begun to realize that I was participating out of obligation rather than attraction. The truth of the matter was that ever since my Payton psyche had combined with that of Khattaaara, the totality of my sexual desires had been toward Dargra-Tol, regardless that she was, as most of the ruling class would have put it, *just a* Thaaagran, a "lowly" synth.[34] But she (not *it*) meant the world to me. I was in love with her and, as far as my swooning brain could decipher from her words and her displayed emotions, the feelings I held toward her were mutual.

Sex was the most important concomitant of Gaaalthaaaran life at that time in its history. Gone were the eras of exploration and discovery, of ethics and invention. Civilizations come and go, and, as with what one day might be the Roman Empire and, as might be the United States in Peyton's dimension, the degradation of its morality tended to (or might tend to) foreshadow its demise. All of

---

[34] There had been a long-standing bias against *Thaaagrans* ever since their creation, especially due to the potential for hybrid offspring. In truth, I had long suspected that Dhraaal was the product of such a pairing, rather than of a Grentaaarg, whose anatomy, as previously stated, was more similar to that of Earth humans. Father, of course, staunchly denied this, though I always felt that was to protect his only son from the prejudices that existed back then.

the planets that were within reach had been colonized, though, due to the history of upheavals on the home world, meaning Rendenaaar, clearly ninety percent of the galaxy's habitable planets remained unpopulated. Perhaps, things were different on the other inhabited worlds, but on Rendenaaar, the god-stones provided for virtually all of the elite's needs. It was like Vannie's wishing ball in *Ellienne*, one of the stories from *The Starport Chronicles* that Liam and I used to read to each other at night by flashlight as we huddled together under sheets on his bed or mine.

No one on Rendenaaar needed to work. There were slaves for that, and, as I said, the god-stones provided for the rest. And so, when Thara-Klo went to school, Dargra-Tol and I would spend the better part of the day making love, stopping only for a midday meal. She was just so breathtakingly beautiful, and she had me by the tail, literally, even though that expression did not exist there.

I know for a fact that Dhraaal did much the same with his share of Grentaaargran mistresses, often three at a time, from what I had heard. There was no heart in any of it. It was debauchery at its best, or perhaps its worst. Sex can make one drunk with pleasure. It can become addictive and all-consuming, and, without the presence of love, it just subtracts from lives. It reduces otherwise intelligent, rational creatures to their primordial instincts, essentially turning them (or, in this case, us) into animals in a state of perpetual heat.

Understand that even though my mind was now commixed with Khattaaara's, it was her body that caved to this addiction. Sex on Earth was an occasional outlet, just one breath in a room filled with air. But there on Rendenaaar, it had become life's oxygen, and each of us had breathed it like the supply was running out. And then it happened—the plague!

Gaaalthaaarans called it *Vraaaagthorg*, which meant the destroyer, though it only affected the Grentaaarg. At first, most just suffered mild symptoms that would have resembled a slight cold on Earth, but then the mutations came wherein those affected, which were many, devolved into Preataaaras, all too hideous to contemplate even in one's worst nightmares. It became rumored that the *Vraaaagthorg* had been engineered by a group of radical social regressionists, who believed that Rendenaaar needed to go back to the old ways. *Khii*, they claimed, wanted no more of the way things had become. Her adherents called it blasphemy from their religious pulpits, and they were prepared to end all life on the planet in the belief that a better life (meaning an afterlife) and a more sacred one lay ahead.

There came no vaccine, though, much as the medicians tried. Most of the biochemical knowledge that might have helped had been extinguished by time. The world had become all too dependent on the god-stones. It was clear that the subversives wanted to show the Gaaalthaaar the difference between the god-stones and their god.

Panic soon turned to anger. The dissidents, when they were found, were publicly shamed, stripped, hanged by their *yaaarghig*, tortured, and then dismembered. I, unfortunately, bore witness to one such event wherein I simultaneously threw up and spat out *kaaarbrogth* through my tail. I had nightmares afterward for many days.

The plague eventually transformed all of the Grentaaarg population on Rendenaaar into hideous, virtually mindless creatures. Worse, the newly devolved Preataaaras turned aggressive against the Gaaalthaaar, my race, murdered us when they could, and consumed our flesh. The Gaaalthaaaran Council quickly issued a bounty on any Preataaara that was slaughtered upon the presentation of their *yaaargh* as severed just behind the *ptaaargh* artery that ensured an actual kill. Credits were assigned that could be exchanged for god-stone privileges. The result was a bloodbath such as Rendenaaar had not seen in more than five thousand cycles, with deaths on both sides, although in the end, the Gaaalthaaar proved the more formidable of the two species, and so the Preataaara were exterminated down to the last man, woman, and child. And still there remained discord. As I had mentioned, the Grentaaarg not only served as laborers but as sex slaves, with the Gaaalthaaar lamenting their absence in both capacities. All that remained were the synths—the Thaaagrans, and their numbers were minuscule compared to the total population. Thus, anger among the less-*entitled* fomented, and the world, as Khattaaara had come to know it, was in chaos. Something needed to be done—but what?

My mother, as the royal *Orithaaan*, proved an utter failure when it came to quieting the unruly masses. Both she and Father had always been pacifists and refused to try to quell any violence with more violence. But then Father died and it was just her. It became a battle of the haves versus the have-nots. Mother gave speeches, asking for peace, which were broadcast using the god-stones, attempting to appeal to both females and males, insisting that the path to happiness was through the heart and not the *yaaargh*. But her Gandhi-like deliverances fell upon deaf ears.

Despite his lineage, Dhraaal numbered himself among the have-nots. With no one left to do harsh manual labor, the factories for the production of Thaaagrans fell into ruin, and Dhraaal had not one Thaaagran to his name—not anymore. Those Gaaalthaaarans of Rendenaaar who had become accustomed to hours of sexual pleasure every day turned as violent as hopheads needing a fix. Sex was an addiction to them, and the craving for it caused both males and females alike to go nearly insane. In light of all of this, Dhraaal conceived a plan—one which, per his insistence, would involve me as well.

He showed up at my practice. Thara-Klo was there watching as she had been doing ever since the Payton half of me had arrived and had chosen to bring her along each time. I cast a glance toward Dhraaal and then, after the dance number ended, walked up to him.

"New Production?" he asked.

"*Faaalathar*," I replied. "I have the lead."

"Such beauty in the midst of so much horror in the world," he replied with a smile.

"Thara-Klo wishes me to teach her dance," I told him. "She wants to be like me. So she says."

"It won't be long ere thy prick shall transform her," Dhraaal replied.

I grabbed my towel from the chair I had set it on and wiped the sweat from my face and neck. I stared at Thara-Klo, who had turned her attention toward Dhraaal.

"What brings thee here?" I asked, not giving him a second glance.

"I need thy help?" he replied.

"With what?" I questioned him, who seldom requested my participation in matters other than sex.

He stared hard at me as I turned toward him again. "Not here," he said with but a hint of an air of secrecy to his breath.

"Where then?" I asked.

"My place," he answered. "Tonight." His voice was but a whisper. "Come alone. Leave Thara-Klo inå her bed. The Thaaagran can watch over her. I trust it has proved effective?"

"She does what she is told," I replied.

"I pray that there remains one hair of affection for me," he said.[35]

"I shall do as thou hast bid," I replied.

Dhraaal gave a parting glance at Thara-Klo and then left the way he had come, wishing himself back home, I presumed.

I arrived at Dhraaal's home shortly after dark. He greeted me, led me inside, and then fixed me something to drink—a *thoul*, I believe—a cool, intoxicating beverage that changed color from red to blue as the glass was emptied. For a moment, it seemed to numb my brain, but an instant later, my focus returned.

"So, why am I here?" I asked after my head had cleared.

"Our civilization is on the brink of ruin," he said, "and your

---

[35] Referring to the hair on the *naaahnraor*, furry the end of the *yaaargh*, as when Gaaalthaaarans made love, those hairs become somewhat erect and bristly through coital stimulation.

mother's course of action to stem it is ineffectual."

"Dost thou suggest that thou and I should try to usurp the royal throne?" I asked.

"No," came his response. "That would prove futile. One could never gather enough forces to overwhelm those already in place—at least at this time."

"Then what, Husband?" I asked.

"I propose that we purloin the god-stones," he replied.

I stared hard at him, shocked at the very thought. "Thou art mad!" I said. "The stones lay guarded by impenetrable fields."

"That may be opened by royal male blood," he insisted.[36]

"Which leaves thee out, being the bastard child of our father and that Thaaagran he used to toy with—my mother being kind enough to raise thee as her own. So, there is no one, and that ends that."

"There is Thara-Klo," he said.

"Thara has decided to become a girl," I replied. "Besides, she is too young for her to be pricked!"

"The age for *nuraaag* is based on custom, not biology."

"Thou canst not do this to her. I will not let thee!" I proclaimed.

"I suspected thou wouldst say as much," he went on, "which is why I put a substance in thy drink. It should be taking effect around now. Thou might notice that thy skin is somewhat cold, thy vision a bit blurred. In another moment thou shalt lose consciousness, but when thou awakens thy will shall bend toward mine."

"Thou art despicable!" I said in a weakened voice.

"Do not think I have not noticed your dalliances with that Thaaagran of yours. That, my dear, shall find an end, and *it* shall find its scrapheap. Whatever sexual acts thou participate in from this day forward shall be with me."

It was then that darkness engulfed my brain. Only much later did

---

[36] How Dhraaal had succeeded in procuring the god-stones in the first iteration without resorting to such means remains veiled in mystery, although it may be suggested that Khattaaara, her mind unadulterated by Payton's, found another way.

the memory of what had transpired that night return, sad to say.

CHAPTER XXIV

Theresa

> *From the Original Timeline*
> *In the Alternate Reality*
> *On Earth I*
> *Earth-Date:2025*

I had to assume that the priest was dead and that that Charlie guy was dead as well, though it was nothing like what I had done to those gang members. Something had been *done* to me and I didn't know what. *That fucking Peyton Herron!* I thought to myself. I needed to find her and make her pay for what she did to my mother and to me.

As I had no idea where she lived or, rather, had forgotten as a result of the head injury I had sustained from the blast, I headed down to the school to try and find her and end her life if I could. I wasn't thinking about any consequences to myself and, if I had, it probably wouldn't have mattered. In my mind, she had taken away the only one in this world who had ever loved me.

When I arrived, classes were just letting out for lunch. I pushed through the crowd, looking this way and that until Andy Panda caught sight of me. His name wasn't really Andy Panda. It was something like Jonathan Wiedmeier. I don't know. I just called him that because he was some *pinche güero*[37] who always wore a white ski hat with a black band at the bottom and a fuzzy black ball at the top.

"Hey, Martinez," he said in Dumb and Dumber tones, "We all thought you were toast." As he hurled his stupidity at me, he flung his arms out, made two fists, and pointed his thumbs up. It was

---

[37] fucking blond dude.

distracting and called attention to me. Anger surged in me, but as he began to vanish, I managed to calm myself a bit, so that he solidified himself again.

"Whoa," he said as he looked at his hands, as they became solid once more. "Tripping!" No one else noticed, thank God!

"Do you know where I can find Peyton?" I asked him.

"Didn't you hear?" he said. "She offed herself. Rope around the neck." He raised one arm as though he was holding a rope, tilted his head in the opposite direction, closed his eyes, and stuck his tongue out.

"When?" I questioned.

"A couple of weeks ago," came the response as he returned to life. "Totally bodacious funeral. The entire school showed up, though I think they were outnumbered by the already dead. A lot of us hung out at Grimwood's house afterward. Hung out!" He laughed then whispered, "Bad choice of words."

He glanced around and then turned back to me. "She was hotter than a firefly, you know. I was totally going to ask her to the prom. Bummer. I mean about her committing Pey*tone*icide. That's what I call it. Dude, I *so* wanted to nail her."

I frowned and started to walk away.

"Hey, Martinez," he called after me. "You know, the prom's not for another two weeks!" I ignored him, walking straight ahead. Whatever his reaction was, I really didn't care to turn around and look.

As there was no point in remaining suffocated in that throng of teenage hormones, I pointed my feet toward the nearest exit. As the door to breathable air approached, something, or rather, some*one* challenged my line of vision. It was Peyton Herron's sister, Phoebe, I thought to myself—at least that was the closest I could remember was her name. *Fuck me if I care!* I thought. I stood still like a fucking statue as *Pheebs*, her nose pointed down toward some textbook she was trying to read, crashed the fuck into me. *How serendipitous I*

120

would have thought—had the word at the time been a part of my vocabulary. The book that she'd been cradling flew from her arms and landed at my feet, spattering the papers that had apparently been in it. The semi-clone immediately bent down to gather up what she had dropped, uttered a polite, "Sorry," and then glanced up to see to whom she had apologized. "Oh," she added as the rim of her mouth turned into a frown.

"What?" I harrumphed out.

"You're the one who caused my sister to kill herself," she said, standing up to face me.

"Yeah, well, my mother is dead because of her shooting me with whatever kind of ray gun that was."

Her face suddenly turned pale. "Oh my God!" she said. "You're from the other timeline!"

"The other what?" I shot back.

"I need to go!" she said, and then she rushed out the door to the street.

I followed her to the exit and stared out the glass door. Ophelia—yeah, that was her name, I remembered—was now standing at the foot of the steps, her cell phone pressed against her ear, with an occasional glance back in my direction. Suddenly, another girl, if I can call her that, appeared from nowhere right next to her, wearing a costume and glowing like the one I'd found myself in, in my bedroom in the future, but it definitely wasn't me.

"What the fuck!" I said to myself as it sent shockwaves through me.

It was crazy enough that all of this was happening to me, but now there was another one, only she apparently had control over her powers. I did a one-eighty and leaned back against the door to keep myself from fainting. *What is going on?* I thought to myself as the blur of students melted away into their classrooms with what at the time seemed to be the deafening ringing of the school bell. My head still reeling from what I'd just seen, I went to the administration

121

office where I stood in front of the turtle woman—at least that's what I and everyone I knew referred to her as.

"Excuse me," I said. "Do you happen to know where Peyton Herron got buried?"

The turtle woman looked up at me through her cataract glasses. "You were there like everyone else, weren't you?" she asked with great suspicion.

"Yeah," I replied. "I want to buy flowers and I need the name and address."

The old bat shrugged, but wrote it all down on a small piece of paper and was about to hand it to me, but then stopped.

"Shouldn't you be in class?" she said.

"I got excused," I said back. "I'm still affected by what happened. You know, post-dramatic stress and all."

The turtle woman shook her head, and then handed me the paper.

"Thank you," I said. "I forgot your name."

"Mrs. Waxman," she replied.

"Thank you again," I said back, and then thought to myself. *Waxman. Turtle Wax. It figures!*

I left the school, walked over to Pico or Olympic, I forget which, and then thumbed my way to the cemetery. The unwashed, unshaven clown that offered me a lift in his rusted pickup, halfway there, decided to put his right hand on my bare thigh and work his way up. Having just been gang-raped, this decrepit old dude caused my blood to boil. I looked down at his hand on my leg and then glared at him. I was not quite sure then what happened next but the man vanished. Unfortunately, we had been traveling at more than seventy miles per hour on the 10 freeway, and the truck began to veer out of control. It careened into several cars and then into a semi that hurled it toward the guardrail. Grabbing the steering wheel did nothing at that point. The vehicle struck the center divider with such force that the whole thing, with me in it, rolled over to the other side's fast lane with its oncoming traffic. My life didn't flash before my eyes, but I seriously thought that I was going to die. Then something strange happened. The pickup, as it tumbled over the median, rolled right through me so that it went over to be smashed by a bunch of vehicles as one car piled into another and into *it*. As for me, I just wound up dropping a couple of feet to the pavement with barely a scratch. Turning to look in the direction of the accident, I watched as the truck burst into flames. Drivers in both directions from where I stood slowed down to watch, which gave me the chance to walk across the side of the freeway I was on and make my way down to the street. After all that had just happened, I decided to hoof it the rest of the way.

It was nearly four p.m. when I finally got there—to the cemetery, I mean—Angelus-Rosedale Cemetery to be exact. The grounds, which have quite a large population, are sort of halfway between Hollywood and Huntington Park. As the office was still open, I went in and inquired as to where I might find *the bitch's* grave. This was an old burial ground that must have been started in the late 1800s, from the headstones I saw. The plot I wanted, though, didn't *have* a headstone—just a bronze plaque set in a shallow block of white marble. The raised letters read, "Peyton Elise Herron, 2011-2025, Beloved Sister and Daughter, Go with the Angels." I read it, thought about it for half a moment, looked around to see if anyone living was around, pulled down my panties, squatted down, and pissed on her grave. I really did need to urinate, but I thought, what better spot to do it? Satisfying as it was, it wasn't enough. *All this way just for that?* I thought to myself. I sat down on the grass. Some wilted flowers lay on the grave beside hers. I picked them up and stared at them, and that's when it happened. The flowers burst back into life as I held them in my hands, as my hands began to glow with a white iridescence. And then it hit me. This was another power that I had. *But what if,* I wondered, *what if I could bring her back just to kill her again?* I couldn't be charged with murder. She was already dead! Was it possible that my mind could do that and more? I focused on the grave. At first, just the grass began to quiver, and then the earth beneath my feet started to shake. Suddenly, soil hurled upward into the sky, and scattered like dust, leaving the cement vault exposed.

What was more odd was that I could see through it all—see her pretty black and pink dress, her arms folded across her chest, her eyes closed like she was asleep. I wanted to strangle her with my bare hands—bring her back to life and then choke the life out of he—but there was no way at that time that I was able to move the slab that entombed her. And yet, I realized, there was something better—something she deserved—resurrect her and then let her suffocate alone in the dark, six feet under—trapped like the rat that she was! I stared into the grave and focused every ounce of my will to bring her back to life, like with the flowers. I could heal her, flow blood back into her veins, and make her alive again. She might last ten minutes, maybe more, screaming, pounding for someone to let her out, but no one would. No one could. And that would be the end. That would avenge my mother's death. And so, I did it and then brought down the soil to again fill up the grave. Peyton Herron was alive once more, but not for long. That much I knew, and I reveled in that fact.

CHAPTER XXV

Peyton

> *From the Original Timeline*
> *In the Alternate Reality*
> *The One Who Stayed Behind*
> *On Earth I*
> *Earth-Date:2025*

Phee's words to me, as she phoned me from school, were urgent. It had to do with Theresa, she said. I phased there as Quantum Girl, exchanged a few words, and then phased us both back home.

"There are two of her!" Phee exclaimed when we were back in our bedroom, and I was Peyton again.

"What do you mean, there are two of her?" I replied.

"There are two of *you*, or were," Phee insisted. "She was in my chem class, and then I bumped into her in the hallway. She was dressed differently. I really didn't give it much thought. I was distracted picking up the book and papers I'd dropped. She rambled on about having been blasted by you from when you were Khattaaara. But the Theresa Martinez in the new timeline couldn't have experienced that, since in this timeline, you never got the quantum seed, and Khattaaara never took over your mind. She has to be from the original timeline."

"But how did she avoid the rewrite?" Peyton asked, half to herself.

"*You* did!" Phee said, insistent.

"But I have a quantum seed," I replied.

"Wait!" Phee exclaimed. "You have one. The other Payton has one. What happened to the one that belonged to Thara-Klo? You said that Theresa was in the hospital—that they thought she was going to die. What if the other Payton gave her Thara-Klo's seed? That would have protected her from the rewrite, wouldn't it?"

Suddenly, I felt as though I couldn't breathe. I must have turned pale.

"What's wrong?" Phee exclaimed.

I divided myself, though it took more effort than it normally would have. A Quantum Girl emerged from my Peyton self. In another instant, she was gone, though I myself collapsed, to sit down on Phee's bed, gasping for breath.

Phee was livid. "What can I do?" she asked.

I held out my hand for her to wait. I became Quantum Girl. I was able to focus more—interphase more with the quantum seed—but it was still hard for me. *What was she thinking? How could Payton have done this? This was what must have changed everything!* All of that went through my mind. I felt nauseous and ready to pass out.

CHAPTER XXVI

Peyton

From the Original Timeline
In the Alternate Reality
The One Who Just Left
On Earth I
Earth-Date:2025

Ground zero for the suffocation that I felt was at the cemetery. The sensation had brought me right up to the grave of my other timeline self. My X-ray projection revealed her alive and gasping for air. *But how?* I wondered. She had been dead for more than a year. *How was that possible?* And then I saw her—Theresa! She was drifting in and out of phase on her back on the grave, pleasuring herself. Phee was right. She did have a quantum seed, but she probably hadn't mastered it. It had taken me the better part of a year to learn how to use mine. So, this was Theresa's doing—exacting revenge on a girl for a crime she didn't even commit. There was no time to think. I had to free Peyton from her tomb before she died *again*!

Not that it mattered, but the seed would protect Theresa from what I was about to do. I tried to blast away the dirt to get to the casket, but in that I was now so close to my alternate younger self, the asphyxiation she was going through affected me, weakening my powers. It took several attempts to reach the vault and two or three more times to blast it open. Theresa had been thrown fifty feet by the first shock wave. Her seed had protected her, but her mind was another thing. She didn't have total control, so she had been knocked unconscious. My attention was turned, though, toward my other self,

127

and so, with every ounce of my quantum strength, I lifted the wooden coffin out from the ground and then tore away the lid. The fourteen-year-old version of me gasped for breath and then began to scream. Then her breath became shallow and labored. Her eyes bled rivulets of tears. Her body trembled, and then she began to shiver. Her skin was cold and clammy, her complexion gray. She was going into shock. Taking hold of young Peyton's hands, regardless that she tried to fend me off in her hysteria, I phased us both back to our bedroom just as Theresa began to come to.

Phee froze, startled by our sudden appearance, but I and the self I had left behind managed to get a hold of young Peyton. Her arms were rigid and shaking, and she was screaming, refusing to stop. Mom and Dad thankfully weren't home. They had gone out to dinner before I had left for the cemetery. After some considerable effort, the two of me managed to get her into the bed, at which time Phee launched to her side to try and comfort her. There came a further shock as my alternate self saw my Peyton self merge into Quantum Girl, at which point she just became catatonic. Phee wrapped her arms around her and held her and, perhaps, prayed.

"I have to go back," I said. "Theresa. You were right. She has the quantum seed." And with that, I phased back to where the resurrection had taken place. By this time, Theresa had stood up.

"Who the fuck *are* you?" she yelled.

"Quantum Girl," I said to her in my Quantum Girl voice.

"What the fuck did you do?" she screamed as she saw the open grave, and as she did, she herself turned quantum. Where my skin iridesced violet, hers radiated an icy white. She stood garbed in an outfit identical to mine, other than the color. But beneath it all was anger, raw and unrelenting. I glanced above as the sky turned dark; not from clouds or even from an eclipse, but as if it had just lost its brightness. "You saved her!" she shrieked, nearly hysterical.

"Theresa, it doesn't have to be this way," I said, but her fury only grew.

"I'm not Theresa!" she screamed in a voice that echoed through the vacant air. "I'm Rage!" Her gaze became fixed as her eyes grew bright like the sun. Then every tombstone, it seemed, lifted from the ground, went up into the air, and then came crashing down on me. There was shattered granite all around, but I myself stood unharmed. My quantum seed had seen to that.

Enough of this! I said to myself, and with that thought, I phased back through time to appear just after my former self had phased off with young Peyton, as Theresa or Rage or whoever she now was, was still dead to the world. I put the casket back in the earth and restored the ground to the way it had been. With my strength returned, it was just a matter of energy fields reconstituting the vacuum of the reality, returning it to the state that it had been in only moments before. I would phase back home before she woke up. She would think that her rival would be lifeless beneath the soil, dead and buried, having died a second time in agony and fear. There was no end to this, though. Sooner or later, I knew that she would realize that she had failed, but at least there would be time for me to think about what I needed to do to prepare for when that moment would occur.

CHAPTER XXVII

Ophelia

From the Original Timeline
In the Alternate Reality
On Earth II
Earth-Date:2029

I sat on my bed, my folded legs drawn up to my chin. I sat there, wondering if I had done the right thing. I was alien to this world and a stranger to this timeline. Did I have a right, I wondered, to interfere with what in this here and now was supposed to be? I was an interloper—the other woman. Yes, I had a child, but so did she—at least one on the way. But this was *her* reality, not mine. She had fallen in love with Liam and he with her through no fault of their own. As far as this world was concerned, both Jordan and I had literally popped in out of thin air. Yet if there was some morality to be found in what had happened between Liam and me, I was not sure what it was. There are two sides to every coin, and on mine, there was just Liam and Jordan and me. We had been together for four long years. We had loved each other and made promises to each other that our lives would be forever shared. Then, all at once, it was all wiped out, as though it had never been. How *fair* was that to *me*? How unjust was it for Jordan to miss out on her father's love? And it wasn't just sex that we had. Our spirits had connected. I could feel the way he kissed me and held me—the way the tips of his fingers caressed the small of my back and the edge of my cheek. It was as though some part of him from the former reality had broken through and mixed with his soul. He was to have been my husband, and now he was to be hers. But what could I do?

My thoughts were interrupted by the wail of sirens that filled the air. This was not the sound of any ambulance or police car or fire engine but, rather, that of an alarm, and the blare of it did not end. I got out of bed, went to the front door, and then walked a few paces to the street. People were fleeing their houses, mostly in cars. Ethan emerged from the rear of the main house in his chair and wheeled up to me. I glanced at him, but then turned my focus back to the exodus that was underway.

"What's going on?" I asked.

"War," he said. "It's all over the news."

"War?" I echoed. "War with whom?"

"The Soviets, of course," he replied. "I said it was inevitable. It was just a matter of when."

I thought it all so bizarre. In my dimension, the Cold War had ended twenty years before I was ever born. What possibly could have happened to have prevented its demise?

"Their planes," he told me, "dropped a bomb on New York. Supposedly, Russian troops have gained footholds in Alaska, Florida, and Washington State."

"Oh, my God!" I exclaimed as I turned to face him. "But where is everyone off to?"

"Bomb shelters," he replied, "Which one were you assigned to?"

"None," I said. "I mean, I don't know."

"Well, then, you'd better come with us," he insisted. "We're leaving in ten minutes. Just take what you absolutely need. I'd help you, but I'm afraid I'd just be in the way." And, with that, he turned his wheelchair around and went back inside.

Watching the panic was more than I could bear for more than a moment or two. I just shook my head to myself and headed back inside. It was no great effort to gather up what few things I had to my name: some small amount of clothes, some sundries, my fourth-trimester carrier, which sort of made me look pregnant all over again, diapers, wet wipes, talcum, and formula. If worse came to worst, I decided, if I ran out of formula, I could always breastfeed.

The Porters' station wagon landed us at a manmade cavern just north of La Cañada. All of the vehicles, which by my count numbered in the thousands, had to be driven down to a subterranean parking lot. Ethan proclaimed that the structure had been designed to hold as many as 50,000 people. More than one hundred such structures had been built just in Southern California, funded by legislation enacted more than half a century ago.

The living area consisted of ten levels, the first being a common area where those in charge had their offices and where there was what appeared to be an indoor shopping mall, designed for those quartered to fill their needs at their own expense. Beneath that were the apartments, all with plumbing, a refrigerator, and beds, as well as an electric stove and a radio that were both powered by glowing vacuum tubes. Each level was divided alphabetically. Jordan and I, with our last name Herron, were assigned the third level from the top, while the Porters were sent four more levels down.[38] It was all very orderly, as were the people.

The elevator took Jordan and me to our assigned floor, and there were maps on the walls to guide us to our unit. The room was small but comfortable. There were, of course, no windows to the outside as we were deep underground, but there was a faux one with a lighted panel that made it appear there was an open meadow just on the other side. The panel was run by a timer that caused its lights to dim as night fell upon the world above. This was done so that those underground would maintain their brain's circadian rhythm. There was also a small attached kitchen. Added to what I have already described were a coffeepot, a pot, and a pan (no Teflon here on this world), a few cooking utensils, and there were two shopping bags on

---

[38] It came as a bit of a problem since there were no records of either Jordan or me in this dimension. Fortunately for us (unfortunately for them), a couple, William and Moira Harrison, had been killed in a car crash only weeks before, so we were assigned their room.

the counter filled with canned goods, pasta, seasonings, bread, and beef jerky. Having laid Jordan down on the bed (I was told that a crib would follow in a day or so), I was startled to hear a light knock on the door. When I answered it, there on the other side stood Liam.

"Um," I said. It was the only word that my brain could think to say. Liam's easy-going nature broke through the awkwardness of the moment.

"The assignments," he said, "are alphabetical. Mine and Claire's adjoin yours, and Mom's and Dad's are in the next one over. Payton got assigned with her boyfriend, one level up from here."

"She has a boyfriend?" I said, amazed.

"Is that so incredible?" he asked.

"I suppose not," I said, "considering her newfound heterosexuality. It just seems so *unnatural*—for her, I mean."

Liam just cast his eyes up toward Heaven, or, rather, the ceiling. Then his gaze came back down to meet mine.

"From when she was fourteen," he replied, "my friends and I used to make bets on which month she'd wind up pregnant. Fortunately, that never happened."

"Strange," I said, "how certain (I searched hard for the word) *proclivities* can get erased."

He tried to ignore that one.

"Anyway," I said with a profound sigh, changing the subject, "what happens when PC learns I'm right next door?"

"PC?" he asked, and his head cocked to the side like a puppy dog.

"Pregnant Claire," I replied.

"Oh," he said. "That's sort of why I came."

"To warn me," I said, concluding the reason.

A guilty expression twisted on his face as he glanced nervously toward his own new apartment.

"Do you want to come in?" I asked.

"Oh Gods, yes, please," he admitted, and then, pushing past the jam, quickly shut the door behind him.

133

"We need to be quiet," I said. "Our daughter's asleep." Liam glanced at her on the bed. I was sure he could tell, even though they were closed, that she had his eyes. "So," I awkwardly went on, "how are things going, engagement-wise?"

"All right, I guess," he said.

"You guess." I parroted.

"Claire is totally loving," he admitted. "And smart. And talented."

"Really," I said, as more of a pondering than a question.

"She plays the cello," he added as an afterthought.

"It must be great, watching her legs wrap around that hard, wooden instrument," I replied with a wicked smile.

"I'm just saying..." he stammered out.

"I know," I laughed. "Stop being so serious. I know you love her, but you also love *me*." That was *not* a question. It was a reinforcement of what I knew was in his heart. I stared hard at him. "You do, don't you?"—that, more of an entrapment than anything else. There came a guilty nod. "Life can be so complicated," I went on as I wrapped my arms around his neck and stared into his eyes. "So, what are we going to do about it?" The question came without the expectation of a verbal response.

Our lips were just inches apart from each other, but as Peyton once told me, distance is an illusion. It seemed as though I had barely moved before mine were pressed against his. We kissed passionately, but it was more than a kiss. It was an exchange of all the hidden emotions that humans define as love. I rested my head against his shoulder, staring outward and away.

"What are we going to do?" I said in a whisper of a voice that barely broke through the air.

"I don't know," he replied.

"It isn't fair to her," I breathed out in exasperation, "but if I walk away, it isn't fair to me—or Jordan. *You* may not remember it, but I spent four years of my life with you."

Liam took hold of my shoulders and moved me away just a bit to stare into my eyes. "We'll figure something out," he said.

As I stared back, a tear fled down my cheek. "You know," I confessed, "I was religious once. I believed in God and Heaven. I thought that love was a gift from the angels. Now, it seems to be a curse."

CHAPTER XXVIII

Peyton

> *From the Original Timeline*
> *In the Alternate Reality*
> *The One Who Went back in Time*
> *On Rendenaaar*
> *Trillions of Universes Ago*

There on the ground lay the skeleton of a Gaaalthaaaran female, dead for what must have been a thousand years or more; the partial skeleton of that someone who must have been me in my former incarnation as Khattaaara, for within her hollow skull lay the same quantum seed as was in my head. I turned away as Payton squatted down to examine it.

"There's a bracelet around its left wrist," she said, "with writing on it. Take a look."

I turned back as she lifted it up, the bones of the hand and arm dropping away like sticks and stones as she did. "I can't read what it says," she went on, turning it around.

"Here," I said, reaching out. "Let me see."

She handed it to me. It was quite ornate and appeared to be made of gold, looking like a snake, coiled several times around with a head at each end. Slices of gems formed what appeared to be scales. Meanwhile, each head held in its mouth a round, metal ball, perhaps a quarter of an inch in diameter.

"Oh my God!" I exclaimed.

"What is it?" Payton asked, her nerves now turned on edge as were mine.

"Did you look at what are in the serpents' mouths?" I said.

"Small beads of some kind," she replied. "Why?"

"Use your quantum vision," I said. "They're not just beads. They're globes! Do you see this one, the one that has an orange tint? That's Rendenaaar."

"Okay," she replied. "And? We're *on* Rendenaaar."

"Yes," I said, "but look at the other; the one that's tinted blue. It's the Earth! Look at the continents: Europe, Africa, Asia, Australia, and there's North and South America!" The inscription that Payton couldn't decipher wrapped down the center of the creature's back. *"Fraaagthual, isg Naulaaarg Kgaaan Haaar gaaar naaag Rendenaaar oghuthaaal thaaargan irn praaalthaaag Khattaaara Gaaalthaaara naaag urthaaarg, Haaar zuaark Payton Alise Herron straaag mooorferg dooraaag, straaag mooorferg booraaag irn gaaar wooraaaj traaabjar.* Whoever the gods of the universe are, I have been trapped on Rendenaaar back in time in the body of Khattaaara Gaaalthaaara, I, who am Payton Alise Herron, from another universe and another dimension in a future far from now."

"But *I'm* Payton Alise Herron," she replied. "How can that *be*?"

She stared at me, and I stared back at her. Here was the reason that so much had changed from what was to what never should have been. Here was the domino that had thrown time in a different direction. Somehow, a part of Payton had been hurled back into this universe and landed in and combined with what once was me. My guess was that Theresa had been at the heart of it with her newly acquired quantum seed. It was as that thought pierced my brain that, as though instinctually, without thought of any consequences, I slipped the ancient cuff onto my left wrist. Suddenly, the coils tightened, and the jewels that formed its eyes began to glow.

"Take it off!" Payton warned.

I struggled to do just that without success.

"I can't!" I said.

"Then phase out of it!" she cried out.

"It won't let me!" I replied, still struggling against the grip it held on me. It was at that moment that the world around me grew dim. Payton became like a phantom. I could see her mouth moving as she called out to me, but I could hear no words. Then, like a great explosion without sound, there was brightness everywhere. The place where I stood disappeared, and I found myself in a void facing my alien incarnation. There, before me, appearing as real as anything I had ever seen, stood Khattaaara in her full Rendenaaaran splendor; Khattaaara, who was the personification of everything that was evil and cruel.

It was strange then, to see, once more, that alien version of myself with her pointed ears and violet, browless eyes and that tail, so gloriously naked to the world. Her hair was worn in boxer braids into which colored feathers had been woven. Her eye makeup was more colorful than anything that would generally be worn on Earth, but the combination, along with the gauzy pastel dress, gave her an exotic, almost avian appearance. In terms of age, she looked perhaps just a few years older than me.

"Who or what are you?" I asked.

"I am the final consciousness," it said in Gaaalthaaaran, "of one who no longer lives. In life, I was Khattaaara Gaaalthaaara of Rendenaaar, and also Payton Herron from a universe parallel to thine own."

"How is that possible?" I asked. "I remember nothing of that."

"Theresa Martinez phased the spirit of thine interdimensional twin back through time and into her mind after she had been healed by the mother stone."

"How long did Khattaaara live?" I asked.

"Approximately one hundred forty-four point five cycles," it replied. "Roughly equivalent to eight hundred, sixty-seven of your years."

"Was the Payton half happy?" I asked.

"There was no half," it explained, "The two minds combined with little resistance. Whatever memories there were of Earth were put aside to lead the life of a Gaaalthaaaran."

So, this was what had altered the timeline, I pondered to myself, *the presence of Payton's mind in Khattaaara's brain.*

"There is no memory of an altered timeline," the image went on, apparently able to read my thoughts.

"How long has Khattaaara been dead?" I asked.

"More than five thousand cycles," it answered.

After that, the sound of its voice and its image began at first to waver and then to fade away so that I found myself once again beside my mirror-dimensional friend.

"Try!" she said, still panicked.

"Try what?" I answered in a now calm voice.

"Phasing out of it!" she insisted.

"No need," I said, as I effortlessly slipped the bracelet from my wrist.

"I thought it wouldn't come off," she said.

"How long was I gone?" I asked.

"What do you mean?" she replied. "You just put the bracelet on a moment ago and were struggling to take it off. That wasn't some kind of joke, was it, because, if it was, it wasn't funny in the least."

"I saw her," I said.

"Who?" she asked.

"Khattaaara—well, an avatar of her—and you."

Payton looked at me with a blank expression on her face. "What do you mean?" she asked.

And so, I described to her what I had seen.

"How is that possible?" she wondered out loud. The thought that a part of her had been trapped so far back in time unnerved her.

"She seemed to have accepted it," I said.

Payton glanced down at the skeleton. "So, that's me," she replied.

"*And* me," I added, "as Khattaaara."

She looked up at me from the skeletal remains that she had been staring at. "What do we do about the quantum seed?" she asked, and

139

as she asked, it vanished.

"It merged with mine," I said, and then I had a sudden, horrible thought. "Wait a minute!" I went on. "Something's wrong."

"What do you mean?" she replied.

"I have Dhraaal's seed in my head. I should have been drawn to his remains, not hers. But if Khattaaara had Dhraaal's seed, who had the mother stone?"

"The what?" Payton asked.

I stared right through her, my mind gripped with all the terrifying possibilities that might lie in our path. I could barely feel my lips move as I spoke out the rhetorical question. "And what happened to Dhraaal?" Indeed, where was the mother stone, and what *had* happened to Dhraaal? But there were no answers; only questions.

CHAPTER XXIX

Khattaaara/Payton

> *Payton from the Original Timeline*
> *Sharing the Mind of Khattaaara*
> *In the Rewritten Timeline*
> *On Rendenaaar*
> *Trillions of Universes in the Past*

I dreamt of dancing at a performance and then hearing the roar of laughter… until I stopped and stared at the audience. They were laughing at me—every face glaring at me as they howled uncontrollably. Then they began to throw food, yelling for me to get off the stage. And how bizarre it was that the rabble were all dressed in late 19th-century British attire. The scene then shifted to a room where the royal council sat, among them my mother, royal *Orithaaan*[39]. They were talking about me—demeaning me— jabbering with hissing voices of how they intended to take Thara-Klo away—away from *me*. They said that I was insane; that I was an abomination, an insult to the throne—a reprobate, a Thaaagran sympathizer, a traitor to my race. They spoke of wanting to excise my *yaaargh* and then ship me off to the Preataaaran continent, where I would be tortured and raped and, no doubt, killed.

"Why do you want this of me?" I screamed at those at the table. "I have done naught to deserve this!" Tears streamed down my cheeks. They then commenced to berate me and scream out obscenities.

"Off with her *yaaargh*!" commanded my mother, who oddly was now garbed in red. "Guards! Seize her!" she went on, a thousand tints

---

[39] The Gaaalthaaaran word for Empress.

of anger written on her face.

"I am a royal!" I shouted back.

"Thou art nothing!" hissed the *Orithaaan* that was my mother. "Off with her *yaaargh!*"

And so, I ran, barely avoiding those who would deform me. I ran and I ran with voices close behind me, with the thunder of their footfall down the endless corridors until I collapsed upon the floor and lay there, out of breath, unable to run anymore. I rolled over onto my back, awaiting my fate. I watched, then, as the faces came—hideous distortions of what should have been—drooling down upon me—monstrous caricatures of Gaaalthaaarans, seething with hatred, lusting for my blood. Closer and closer they came with loathsome stares, reaching hands, and gnashing teeth. And then I woke up and opened my eyes to find Dhraaal bent over the bed on which I now lay.

"I had such a nightmare," I said, as I began to sit up. "I dreamt that I was attacked by the Royal Council. I was running until I dropped from exhaustion, and then they were on me."

"A phantasm drenched in truth," he replied, offering me a drink, which I gladly took and imbibed.

"What meanest thou?" I asked, choking on the liquid.

"The council excoriated thee," he proclaimed. "They have spies as thou must know—shadows creeping everywhere the god-stones allow. They witnessed the enamor betwixt thou and that synthetic of thine. How I wish that I had never given it to thee. But the deed was done, and now thou art to be expulsed."

"But I just met with thee moments ago!" I said.

"Nay, it has been two *naaarag*.[40] Thara-Klo has been frantic from when thou didst not return. It was only after *one naaarag* and days more of trying that I managed to bribe some guards to allow me to remove thee from the prison where thou wast held."

"This cannot be!" I proclaimed.

---

[40] A *naaarag* consisted of ten days.

"But it is," he said back. "If thou dost not believe me, then check for what was once thy *yaaargh*."

And so I did, and it was gone! "Nay!" I screamed, "Nay! Nay! Nay!" as I started to throw up, but with nothing in my stomach, I only gagged. After some moments of this, I began to weep, and wept so bitterly without stop that it was as though the clouds had opened *up* and poured *out* a torrent of rain."I shall make them pay!" I said at last through my tears, as anger took hold of me. "Each and every one of them!"

"And I will help thee," Dhraaal replied as he took hold of and kissed my hands.

"We shall take the god-stones," I said. "We will make ourselves master and mistress of this misbegotten world!" And thus began our plan.

The god-stones were housed in a sphere deep beneath the royal palace. Like the mummies of the pharaohs of Egypt, their vault was like a tomb, designed so that it would remain undisturbed for the rest of eternity. The sphere, as it turned out, was quite small—perhaps only five centimeters in diameter—but it had been coated with a layer of neutronium, giving it a weight of more than ten thousand tons.[41] Such had been achieved with the aid of the god-stones themselves.

"Let us say that we get to them," I said to Dhraaal. "What then? It would be impossible to transport the sphere due to its weight."

"Such had been thought of by our progenitors in the event that our people ever needed to be evacuated from the planet. In the palace, just beneath the jeweled throne, is a device that projects a high-energy beam of electrons that will cause the neutronium to lose cohesion, dissolve into hydrogen gas, and expose the sphere that weighs less than the tip of my *yaaargh*."

---

[41] Neutronium is a super-dense, super-heavy substance comprised of neutrons packed against each other in close proximity. The quasi-element, only theorized on 21st Century Earth, has an atomic weight of zero, and does not exist freely in nature. Scientists on Rendenaaar, however, with the aid of the god-stones, managed to produce a thoroughly stable form.

"Do not remind me, husband. My blood boils at the thought of what they did to mine."

"Forgive me my indiscretion," he said, and then went on. "As for the rest of the plan, leave that to me. Know that there are five more confederates here to help us succeed."

The seven of us met in an open field at night, where there was no possibility that we could be overheard. The other five consisted of Shaaalra, who had been my best friend since we were children, Naraaag-Tal, a somewhat burly-looking male, Faaathrag, a Northerner with the typical skunk-like band of white down the center of his hair, Shaaanchor, a male of average looks, who, it seemed, was a highly respected physicist, and Aaajfrant, twice the years of the rest of us, who, despite being both aged and ugly, came with a wisdom that became apparent whenever he would speak. I had never met any of the men before. They were Dhraaal's acquaintances—co-conspirators or hirelings or perhaps even friends—he never apprised me of which, nor did I ever choose to question his selection, so great was my trust in him at the time.

It was winter and frigidly cold outdoors. I would have said, *Cold enough to freeze off one's tail* but that didn't apply to *me*—not anymore. In the instant that it took to wield the sword or the scalpel or the cutters—whatever it was they had used—I had been transformed into a freak who could no longer give birth again or even enjoy sexual pleasure. Shaaalra came over to me and took hold of my hand.

"I heard what they did to thee," she said.

"They shall pay!" I replied, half under my breath, as my fingers interlaced hers. "I shall hang them by their *yaaarghig* and then roast them over fire! They shall beg for the charity of death!"

"And what of thy child?" she asked. "What of Thara-Klo?"

"Killed, Dhraaal says; murdered whilst sobs for her mother choked out her last breath." I looked up at her. "My *yaaargh* gave me pleasure," I said, "but my child was the heart in my chest."

"The child had chosen then?" Shaaalra asked.

"Thara-Klo loved me as much as I loved Thara-Klo," I replied. "'I wish to be like thee,' my child said again and again. And now, those sweet lips, no more will they speak. No laughter will shine from those eyes. My soul has been ripped from me and thrown to the wind, and all that remains is the ether of hate."

"Her death shall be avenged!" Shraaalra said to try to assuage the anger that now seethed in my veins.

"Vengeance is but a word," I said back. "The pain I shall inflict upon them shall echo through the very bowels of Rendenaaar so loud that the voice of a thousand winds shall seem gentle and tame."

It was at this time that Dhraaal and the others approached us.

"We shall move on the morrow when most lie asleep," Dhraaal proclaimed.

"With oceans of azure blood?" I asked.

"Nay," he replied. "Faaathrag here beds the cook. It will be she who administers the poison into their evening meal. None shall be spared its result."

"And my mother?" I asked.

"Though godly, she proclaims herself, her gullet shall prove her mortal like the rest."

I have long since asked myself where was the Payton in me *then*, the kindly girl who knew nothing of the world but gentle love? But then this was a different world, and love is a bird with fragile wings.

I spent that night beside Dhraaal, naked and ashamed of how I must have appeared to him. Still, he held me in his arms. His *yaaargh* slid up between my legs, and yet I felt nothing of the *woman* in me, for so little of her was left. Still, it was comforting, his affection. There were no words between us, nor even tepid breath.

As I lay there, unable to sleep, I thought of the life I had on Earth. I wondered what my parents and Liam would think when I did not return. But then, they wouldn't be born for hundreds of trillions of years. How thoughtless the universe was to spawn and then take life

145

without conscience. The Gaaalthaaarans did not believe in the Christian God. There was no Jesus to have died for their sins. Their stories of creation were just myths like all the rest. And if there was a God, where was he now, and where had he been for my Thara-Klo?

And what of poor Theresa, my Theresa, once the love of my life, whose soul I thought was so interlaced with my own? The god-stone may have cured her, but her revival resulted in my coming here against my will. How I missed the gentleness of her touch, the softness of her lips as they softly pressed against mine, the fervor of her passion, insatiable it seemed, at least when it came to me. How I missed feeling so loved by her. And yet, there was Dargra-Tol who helped me to forget. There, too, in her lay a seat of passion, despite that she was fabricated, artificial as it were, though with a sentience that made her real and gave her needs much like my own. What would be her reaction when she learned that the *yaaargh* that had wrapped around her with so much ardor had been cut away from me and no doubt stomped upon and then nailed to a post or else worn as a belt like some trophy? The thought burned down to my soul.

It was nearly morning when I finally caved in to the need for sleep. Dhraaal had already gone off; I did not know where. I still remember the strange dream that I had. I was back on Earth before ever becoming Quantum Girl, and I had walked into the kitchen where Mom and Dad and Liam were, but they were not human—not anymore. They were Gaaalthaaaran, all with violet eyes and *yaaarghig*, and Mom with pointed ears and pairs of breasts. They acted friendly and natural, speaking to me in the language of this planet and not theirs. But then, suddenly, I was in the kitchen with them. Dad and Liam both sat at the table with plates in front of them while Mom was at the stove, stirring something in a large pot filled with soup.

"What is it?" I asked, although I cannot remember if I said it in English or in Gaaalthaaaran.

Then I walked over to her, and she dipped in her spoon and

offered me a bit. It tasted sweet with an undertaste of pork. But then, as I was swallowing, I glanced into the pot and saw a *yaaargh* in the middle of it all. And then I felt excruciating pain from where my *yaaargh* should have been, and there was a trail of blood on the floor leading to the pot and a knife on the counter that dripped in azure blood. I turned back to my mother and saw her drink down a second spoonful. Then she closed her eyes and rolled her head as though she had just tasted ambrosia. I turned toward Liam to see him chewing on my *yaaargh* as though it were a barbequed rib. And there was Dad, a bowl in his hands, filled with *yaaargh* soup, that he had brought to his mouth to drink down.

I screamed in my dream and then awakened, screaming still. I rose from the bed to find the bedsheet drenched in blood. I felt burning from where my *yaaargh* had been. It proved difficult, but I managed to bandage myself and stop the bleeding. Yet the gentle disposition I had in my dream, when I was back on Earth, vanished in my awakened realization that my body had been defiled by someone. Anger rose once more in me to such a level that I, as Payton Herron, had never known. I laughed at the thought I had had of hanging those responsible by their *yaaarghig* to torture cook them. *Not enough!* I thought to myself, *not nearly enough!* Before I did any of that, I decided that I would skin them alive!

CHAPTER XXX

Theresa

> *From the Original Timeline*
> *In the Alternate Reality*
> *On Earth I*
> *Earth-Date:2025*

My head felt like it had been hit by a ton of bricks. *Shit!* I thought to myself. *What the fuck happened?* My face was literally smashed into the ground, and I could feel cold metal against my cheek. As I pulled myself up, I saw that there was an indentation in the grass that my body had made, and the metal that I had felt was one side of a bronze grave marker that was tilted so that the other end was angled up. *But how did I get here?* I barely knew which was way up. I shook my head as I sat there, propped up by both arms, trying to focus. Again, *What the fuck?* I looked around as my head began to clear. Everything *seemed* the same. But I had a weird-ass dream about some bitch that I'd fought, who called herself Quantum something, who was wearing a costume like I'd been in. I remembered using my powers to lift up all of the headstones and hurl them down on her, but there wasn't any sign of that. *Shit, my head hurts*! I kept thinking. *At least by now, that Peyton chick should be dead.* But where the hell was the hole that I had dug? A sickening thought came over me— *What if it wasn't a dream? What if... Crap!* I stood up, went over to the grave, and blasted at the soil that covered it until I could see the concrete vault. I caused the lid to rise into the air and then hurled it away, where it went smashing into a mausoleum. I lifted the casket twenty feet into the air and then smashed it down onto the ground. Dirt and debris flew toward me as it did, but I caused all of it to freeze in time just inches away from me. Then, with a sweep of my arm, I sent it hurtling in all directions. The impact of the casket, though, severed the lid, which flew off to one side. As it did, it caused my worst fears to be realized. The casket was empty! I clenched my fists and screamed so loud that the birds in the nearby trees flew off from their perches and into the evening sky. I needed to calm down. I needed to think. *Was it just a dream?* I wondered. *It couldn't have been—otherwise, where would her body have gone?* And then it struck me. Maybe I wasn't the only one with superpowers, and if so, maybe she—Quantum Girl, that was it—Quantum Girl could reverse time, too. *Fuck her!* I thought to myself. *I brought Peyton Herron back to life, and then she goes and rescues her! Fuck her!* There were now two bitches that I wanted dead! No way was I gonna let this end!

I began the long walk home, shaking my head at the fact that I actually had to walk. What sort of superhero needs to walk or hitchhike or take an Uber to get where she's going? I stopped in my tracks. So far, I had learned that I could manipulate time, blast things to smithereens, hurl stuff without being anywhere near it, and remember things that used to be but weren't anymore. I wondered what else I might be able to do.

Attempts at flying proved both awkward and futile and thoroughly embarrassing, falling flat on my face, which by the way, definitely hurt. I knew that if I wanted to use whatever powers I might have, I needed to focus, so I closed my eyes and tried to wish myself home. I felt dizzy at first and then found myself halfway embedded in a wall in the rectory back in the church I had just come from, just as one of the priests, kneeling before the crucifix, was saying his prayers. Fortunately—and I say this not knowing the consequences of what otherwise might have happened—my head and heart did not merge with the structure. The now terrified clergyman stared at me, speechless, as I managed to pull out from the brick and plaster into which I had materialized without harming either it or myself. I must have looked like Jacob Marley as he slowly made his way through

Scrooge's closed door.

"Good afternoon, Father," I said. "Next time, I'll try and come in another way."

The poor man dropped the rosary he had been holding, climbed to his feet, and stood motionless, staring at me with an open mouth as I left. My thought process once outside gave realization to the fact that I could indeed teleport myself and that the reason I had fucked up was that the church had been in the back of my mind and that if I wanted to succeed, my focus had to be clear. I decided to try again. This time, I wound up back home with only my left hand stuck in the drawer front of my dresser, so that I had to pull my arm to get it free. That accomplished, I stared down at my hand to assure myself that no damage had been done, either to myself or to the drawer. I took a deep breath and then went to the kitchen, where, having found some Rocky Road ice cream in the freezer, I sat down with the carton and a spoon at the table and began to gorge myself, if for no other reason than to prove that my body was incapable of putting on extra weight. Such is every woman's dream!

Having satisfied my hunger, I went back to my bedroom, stripped down to my skivvies, and then plopped myself down on the bed. There was a lot I had to think about besides that bitch, Peyton Herron, or that Quantum Girl. In the future, I had been to the house that apparently had been lost to the bank or sold, though I wondered about the mirage of me that stood facing me in the doorway as I left. No matter what, I needed to do whatever I could to keep the only real home I'd ever known. Curious, though, I wondered, if I did that, would it prevent me from ever interacting with that Charlie guy and his wife, which would have meant that I wouldn't have ever left and been raped, and everything that I just did would never have happened, meaning I would never have gone back in time to keep from losing the house. The whole thing made my head spin, but it was one of those who gives a fuck moments. All I cared about at the moment was not losing the house. But to do that, I needed money, and to get money, I needed a plan. A job wouldn't pay enough. I mean, I was fifteen years old. What was I going to do—babysitting? Robbing some business of its hard-earned cash wasn't right. *But what about getting it from criminals?* I wondered. The men who had raped me were from the El Barrios street gang. I knew that they dealt in drugs. But more than that, they had suppliers who probably had enough *dinero* to choke a *caballo*,[42] as the saying goes—sort of. And because I was able to stop time, once I found out where their suppliers were, I could walk in and walk out with as much as I needed. Not only that, but I could make it look as if the El Barrios were the ones who were the thieves. They'd be taken care of and deservedly so. With that thought and a smile on my face, I closed my eyes and quickly fell asleep.

When I woke up, I told myself I should never do that again—go to sleep, I mean. I might say that I had a *dream*, but it was a motherfucking nightmare. I dreamt that I was all lovey-dovey with that Peyton bitch. We were kissing and touching and having sex. The fact was that I hated her, and I wanted her to die a thousand painful deaths for what she had caused to happen to my mother. I would have had sex with any girl who *wasn't* her. *Hell*, I told myself at the time, *I'd sooner have sex with a guy!* No matter how hard I tried, though, the images of us together would *not* leave my mind.

My breakfast consisted of Cocoa Krispies and coffee—the coffee mixed in with the cereal. I was out of milk. It really wasn't that bad, especially since I'm a night owl and it was morning, and between the chocolate rice puffs and the Folgers, I got a double dose of caffeine, my drug of choice. When I was finally fully awake and dressed, I went outside to check the mail. There was nothing but bills and a foreclosure notice. The bank was going to repossess the house. Did they care that my mother had died or that I was now all alone and that this was my home? *Damn them!* I thought to myself *Damn them all!*

---

[42] to choke a horse.

CHAPTER XXXI

Peyton

> *From the Original Timeline*
> *In the Alternate Reality*
> *The One Who Stayed Behind*
> *And the One Who Left, Now One*
> *On Earth I*
> *Earth-Date:2025*

I stood as Quantum Girl at the side of what had been my bed, looking down at the fourteen-year-old suffering from catatonia resultant from having been buried alive or, more specifically, from having found herself trapped in a casket after being resurrected. I knew the feeling. I remembered it happening to me, only I was pulled out of there before the oxygen ran out. I'd gotten to her too late. She had become hysterical, using up what little air there was until there was none left for her to breathe.

And so there she lay on the bed in the shape and form of me when I was her age, her body rigid and unyielding, her breath shallow, staring outward with sightless eyes, looking like a mannequin in a window display.

Phee emerged from the bathroom with a wet cloth that she placed on young Peyton's forehead, and then glanced back up at me.

"What are we going to do?" she asked. "Maybe we should call an ambulance."

"Wait," I said, as a Peyton me phased from my quantum self. Then, that one of me merged into my younger, alternate self, as both Phee and the Quantum Girl version of me looked on. Five minutes went by, and then ten.

"What's going on?" Phee asked in a whisper.

"I'm trying to calm her," the Quantum Girl me said.

"Is it working?" Phee replied with concern.

"I'm causing her to forget," I told her.

"Forget what?" she asked.

"Everything from the moment she set foot in the closet to kill herself. It will all seem to her like it was just a bad dream."

A moment later, my other self merged back into me, and a moment after that, young Peyton opened her eyes and saw me as Quantum Girl standing beside Phee.

"What's going on?" the fourteen-year-old Peyton asked as she stared at me. "Who *are* you? *What* are you?" She glanced down at herself. "And how did I get into this dress?"

Phee went over to the bed on which my younger self lay and sat down beside her. "What's the last thing you remember?" she asked, her voice ever so calm.

"It's too embarrassing to tell," she replied as her eyes bled out tears. "Theresa came up to me," she began.

"I should have known," Phee broke in. "I should have been there for you."

"You were *always* there for me," my younger self replied. "But," she said, and she paused, "this is the dress I wore in the show. Why am I wearing it now?"

"It's a long story. For later on," Phee said in a gentle voice.

My younger self sobbed and then stared at me. "Why does she *look* like that?" she asked.

"She's in costume?" Phee replied.

"For a play?" my younger self pressed on.

"Something like that," Phee said, taking hold of her hands. "Her name's Katt. She's on my swim team."

"That doesn't explain the outfit," she protested.

"I'm also in the drama club," I said. "We're putting on a play next week. It's sci-fi. *Invasion from Rendenaaar*. I was showing your sister how I'll look."

"Pretty cool, huh?" said Phee.

"Yeah, but," young Peyton asked, "how do you get it to glow like that?"

Phee looked at me like, *I have no idea what to say.*

I turned to my alternate self. "You know how black light makes everything glow in the dark?" I asked.

"Sort of," she replied.

"Well, this is kind of the same," I said, "only things glow in the light. The company that makes it calls it Fairy Dust. It's made of powdered glitter."

Phee slowly mouthed "Oh My God!" at me, but to my younger self, she said out loud, "She must be taking a liking to you because she refused to tell me."

"Where's Dad?" young Peyton asked with a sudden rush of tears to her eyes.

"I saw him downstairs when I came up," I said, and then turned to Phee. "I really need to get back home. I'll send him up on my way out." Then I told my younger self, "So, nice to meet you, Peyton. I hope you feel better."

"Thanks," she replied. "Maybe I'll see you again and get to see the real you."

"You will," I said. Then I left the room, shutting the door behind me.

In the hallway, I phased back to my Peyton self and then went downstairs to the living room, where Mom and Dad both sat—Dad, reading a book, and Mom, engrossed in a bit of mending with needle and thread. It was Mom who noticed me first.

"Peyton," she said, acknowledging my presence. "Is anything wrong?"

"Quite the reverse," I replied with a smile. It was Dad who then looked up.

"What do you mean?" he asked.

"There's a somewhat confused fourteen-year-old girl upstairs, who I think could use her dad." I paused to take a deep breath. "It's Peyton. I don't know how, but Theresa, the girl who had been bullying her, somehow got another quantum seed, and she brought her back to life, apparently to let her suffocate in her casket. I managed to rescue her. All she remembers is the night before she died."

Mom began to cry while Dad jumped up out of his seat and was about to rush up the stairs when I stopped him.

"You need to compose yourself before you go in," I said, gently taking hold of his arms. "More than a year has passed since she killed herself, and I know what she's feeling because I went through it, too. She asked for her dad, and she needs him to be strong for her. As far as she's concerned, she only left to go to bed half an hour ago, and we need to handle her with care. She's insecure. She wants to die. But she's been given a second chance. You need to help her through all of this." I glanced at Mom. "Both of you."

It took them a few minutes to calm down, and then all three of us went back to the bedroom with me again as Quantum Girl. I refused to shock the younger me with another version of herself.

"I forgot my bag," I lied.

The younger Peyton didn't hear what I'd just said or care. She jumped up when she caught sight of Dad and then flew into his arms, her cheeks still wet with tears.

"I don't understand what's going on," she wept. "I dreamt I was in so much pain! I couldn't breathe! I was sure I was going to die! And then I woke up!"

"It's going to be all right," Dad said, holding her.

"Peyton?" Mom said gently. "Are you all right?"

The younger me, whose cheek was still pressed against her father's chest, answered without turning. "I don't know," she replied with unrelenting tears. "That Theresa—she won't stop."

"Bullying you." Phee broke in.

"It makes me not want to live!" her now kid sister wept. "It's every day! I just can't take it anymore! I even thought…"

"What?" Dad asked.

"To end it all!" she admitted with tears streaming down her cheeks.

"No, no, no," Dad said, as he held her tighter. "I'll see to it that she never bothers you again."

His words comforted her, but I knew that after what I had witnessed, protecting her was not going to be an easy task.

"There's a lot to talk about," Phee interjected, "but we can do that in the morning."

"Are you hungry?" Mom asked.

"No," young Peyton replied.

"How about you sleep with me in my bed tonight?" Phee asked.

The girl turned to face her, wiping tears from her eyes. She nodded and then stared at her. "You look different," she said.

"I'm just exhausted," Phee lied. "Come on," she went on. "The rest of you, out of here. I'm going to find her nightgown and get into my jams." And so it was that Mom and Dad and I left the room.

CHAPTER XXXII

Ophelia

From the Alternate Timeline
In the Alternate Reality
On Earth I
Earth-Date: 2029

It was only just past eight—nowhere near my normal bedtime—but it had been an exhausting, frightening time for Peypey, and she needed me now more than at any other moment in her life. After having been her twin for fourteen years, I was now her older sister—not by much—just eighteen months or so, but at the ages we were, a year and a half can make for a world of difference in terms of maturity and emotions. Poor Peypey! I can only begin to imagine what she went through. Peyton (the elder) had told me how horrific it was, and what she said had made me so sick just to hear it that I began to cry. According to her, it was more than fourteen billion years ago that she herself experienced it. But then she went through it all over again to try and rescue Peypey, only to fail. Here, though, by the grace of God or quantum reality, my now little sister lay next to me as I spooned her, holding onto her, afraid to let go, afraid to fall asleep lest I wake up only to discover that this was all just a dream. How strange it was that there were now two of her—one older, one younger, and yet both of them my twin. My darling, sweet Peypey. Nothing shall ever come between us again. I'll protect you throughout all of my life—*with* my life if it ever comes to that!

When the world is dark, a person can notice things that seem invisible in the light. As I lay there next to her, I could smell the scent of her hair. I don't mean anything like shampoo. I mean the scent of her *in* her hair. I could feel the pressure of her breath as her ribcage rose and then fell again. I could feel and hear her heart beating in her chest, and I could sense her emotions as they swept through her dreams. Occasionally, my mind would drift off and wonder who that Liam person was—my thread from another dimension—my mirror that wasn't really a reflection—my disparate self whom God had deemed my soulmate. What was he like, I wondered? What were his interests? What was the measure of his soul? And what made him fall in love with me, and me with him? Are we as humans so vain that we only wish to see ourselves in others? The reverie of my thoughts was broken, as Peypey stirred from her sleep.

"Phee?" she muttered, only half-awake.

"Yes, Darling?" I replied.

"You didn't tell me before when I asked," she said.

"Didn't tell you what?" I said, still holding onto her.

"Why I was in the Alexander McQueen gown. It's the same one from the show."

"They gave it to you," I replied.

"But why?" She asked.

"Do you believe in miracles?" I asked her back.

"I don't know," she answered. "Should I?" She glanced back a bit in my direction. "Do *you*?"

"I didn't, but I do now," I said. I paused for a moment, trying to craft my words. "You know the girl in the costume?"

"Katt?" she asked

"She has another name," I said.

"You mean her last name?" she asked. "She never told me, or I never heard."

"Her name's Peyton," I said.

"Like mine," she replied. "But why did you say her name was Katt?"

"Because," I started to explain, "you'd been in shock and we didn't want to upset you."

"Upset me how?" she asked.

"Because," I went on, "*her* name's Peyton Herron, too."

"Well," she answered softly, "I'm Peyton *Elise* Herron. What's *her* middle name?"

"The same," I replied.

"Yeah, right," she said. "What are you talking about?"

And so I told her, and she listened without a word in the dark.

"That's all well and fine as stories go," she said at last, "but prove it."

And so I called to Peyton quietly—Peyton, who could hear my teardrop from a thousand miles away. But it was Quantum Girl who calmly entered the room.

"You can phase out of the outfit," I said to her as she walked up to us. "I told her everything."

"I know," said Quantum Girl as she became Peyton again. The sudden transformation caused Peypey's jaw to drop. She sat up in bed with a start.

"What else can you do?" she asked, whereupon at least ten other Peytons suddenly filled the room. "Oh. My. God," she said, as the crowd merged back into the one. "What else?"

"Well," said Peyton. "I can phase through time and space and other dimensions. And I can project force fields."

"And she has X-ray..." I started to say.

"Projection," Peyton said, finishing the sentence for me.

"Show me," Peypey insisted.

Peyton looked at me, questioning. I shrugged and stood up. Peyton's look became a stare as her eyes began to glow violet. All at once, I became a Visible Woman, like the old model kit. My clothes and skin turned transparent as my muscles and organs were revealed.

"No *way*!" Peypey exclaimed. Then Peyton shut it off, and I became opaque Ophelia once again. Suddenly, Peypey had a thought and turned to me with a serious expression on her face.

"What happened when you found me, hanging dead and all?"

"I screamed like a thousand banshees. At least that's what Dad said afterward. And then he cut you down."

"This is all so unreal," Peypey said. Then she threw her legs over the edge of the bed and stood up.

"So, you and I, we're both the same," she said to Peyton.

"More or less," Peyton replied, "Only I'm now four years older than you."

"And you have the quantum seed," the younger said.

"I do," the elder replied.

"And get to be Quantum Girl," the younger went on to ask.

Peyton just shrugged.

"Why couldn't *I* get to meet Droll?" the younger one sighed.

"Dhraaal," I corrected.

"Whatever," she shrugged.

"We're still trying to figure that one out," the elder Peyton said. "We think it was caused by Theresa inadvertently sending the spirit of my interdimensional twin back to Rendenaaar."

"Wait!" Peypey interjected. "You mean that Theresa the Terrible, the one who caused me to kill myself, has a quantum seed, too?"

Peyton sighed. "Sort of," she said.

"How did *that* happen?" Peypey asked.

"The Payton from the other dimension must have found Thara-Klo's seed and put it in her to heal her."

"Oh, great!" Peypey replied. "So, now there's an evil Quantum Girl!"

"If there weren't," I interjected, "you wouldn't be sitting here now. You'd still be dead."

"True," Peypey admitted with a deep sigh. Then, as with a sudden thought, she looked Peyton in the eyes. "Phee told me about what you did at the cemetery. Thank you for saving my life."

"I'm sure you would have done the same," the Peyton answered.

It was beyond strange to see the two of them together, years apart in age. But it was the same face, the same smile, and the same heart,

160

which made them who they were.

"Wait!" Peypey said, looking at Peyton. "If you're here and I'm here, we can't both be Peyton. And the fact is that I wouldn't be here if not for you. So, I think it only fair that if one of us needs to change her name, it should be me."

"Change it to what?" I asked.

Peypey thought for a moment. and then spouted out, "Sarabeth. Sarah for the name you said that Thara-Klo used in the original timeline when she raised Gram and Beth after Grandma Elizabeth, Dad's mom."

"It's a pretty name," said Peyton. I nodded in consent.

"Then it's settled. Sarabeth it is." She then twirled around to face *me*, as her eyes brightened. "I'm going to tell Dad and Mom!" she exclaimed. Then she rushed from the room.

Peyton turned to me with a serious expression when her younger self had gone. "You *do* realize that she's still in terrible danger," she said.

"What do you mean?" I asked.

"Theresa wants her dead," she replied. "I can't protect her twenty-four seven. Even with me duplicating, she's going to want her freedom."

"So, what are we going to do?" I asked.

Peyton shook her head. "I don't know," she replied, "but we need to think of *something*."

CHAPTER XXXIII

Khattaaara/Payton

> *Payton from the Original Timeline*
> *Sharing the Mind of Khattaaara*
> *In the Rewritten Timeline*
> *On Rendenaaar*
> *Trillions of Universes in the Past*

By the time I had awakened, it was afternoon. Dhraaal was gone, but there was a telepathic message that activated the moment the room sensed that I was awake.

We will proceed at midnight when most in the palace are asleep. If we fail, that will be the end of us, but fail we shall not; we must not. Be ready. I shall signal thee where to meet.

I dressed without emotion and then asked the god-stones to transport me back home. I found Dargra-Tol in the kitchen, preparing a meal. Regardless that food could be synthesized, she preferred to use her own culinary skills, often encoding the results into the formulary for replication later on. She stood with her back toward me, although she apparently sensed my presence.

"Thou hast been gone for many days," she said.

"I was unconscious until last night," I replied.

Dargra-Tol wheeled around to face me with apparent concern. "What befell thee?" she asked. "Art thou all right?"

"I was attacked," I said with a bitter tongue. "I was injured and dismembered."

It was then that she noticed the absence of my *yaaargh*, and her face lost its color.

"By the wrath of the stones, who did this to thee?" she sobbed as

162

her face wept life-like tears.

"By order of the *Orithaaan*, Blessed and Divine! My own mother! So Dhraaal told me when I awoke."

"I shall love thee still," Dargra-Tol proclaimed.

"There is nothing left for thee to love," I replied, "for with my *yaaargh* they stole as well the kindness in my heart so that my pulse doth only quicken at the thought of the demise of those who did such to me."

"Take care, Mistress," she replied, "for the walls have ears."

"How can a living corpse weigh its misery without breath?" I asked. "I would lay down all my bitterness if I could, but I cannot take hold of it, nor are there tears to shed. Lift up the knife within thy hand and plunge it deep into my breast. Observe, then, how little damage will be done, for there is no heart in me left that thy blade can strike."

Dargra-Tol was a synthetic lifeform, but she was not a robot. Her brain was not that of a computer. There were no printed circuits or diodes or transistors or wheels or cogs. There were neurons with axons and dendrites, despite the fact that they were made in a laboratory and not in a *yaaargh* or a womb. She was aware of her existence, and she could dole out love that wasn't programmed into her brain. Not all Thaaagrans were like her. Indeed, she was the most advanced and, with her *yaaargh* intact, had the ability to reproduce.

"How couldst thou ever love me," I cried out, "I who can never love again?" It was not sorrow but anger that incensed those words.

"I am more than my *yaaargh*," she replied. "Isn't that what Kaaag-Rul wrote five thousand cycles ago? Thou art more than a *yaaargh* to me. Thy touch makes the blood in me quicken. Thy scent is as if it were a bouquet of *jaaathrig* flowers. But more still, thy soul is the mate to my own, though that mine is but the wadded remnants of some designer's cloth."

"But we can never make love again," I protested.

Dargra-Tol stared at me with calm in her eyes. "Love is in the

163

mind," she told me, "not the rope that calls us to passion. Love steers our heads. It beats our hearts. It lines our nostrils that imbibe the fragrance of each other's existence."

Her words calmed me, but my path would not be changed until the price of my humiliation had been exacted in spades. She kissed me on my lips and held me in her arms as thoughts ran through my head of what deeds this night would bring.

The Rendenaaaran day consisted of ten hours or *baaagtran*, each divided into one hundred *chraaagran* and each of those into one hundred *kaaajdan*. It was at precisely nine *baaagtran* and forty-seven *chaaagran* that the last of our coterie entered what had been my chamber growing up, and that was Dhraaal, holding a small tube of blueish liquid in his hand.

"What is that, Husband?" I asked.

"It is a vial of Thara-Klo's blood. I pricked her ere she died and took this once all life had fled. It is this which will open the vault."

"How convenient," I said back, as my eyes bore into his.

"Would that I might have come a moment sooner," he seemed to lament, "I might have saved the child."

"*Our* child!" I corrected him. "But tell me, Husband, with Thara dead and myself without my *yaaargh*, who then shall there be to carry on the royal line?"

"I suppose," Dhraaal said, trying to feign humility, "that the burden shall fall upon me."

"Indeed," I replied, "and such a burden it must be. Thy *yaaargh* must grow flaccid at the very thought of mating with some female, other than myself, to bring forth a likeness of thee."

"Nevertheless," he went on undeterred by my words, "what is done is done. In her death, Thara-Klo still had within her the three-quarters noble blood to unlock the vault that guards the seven stones. Hail, Thara-Klo!" he said in a triumphant voice.

"Hail, Thara-Klo!" echoed each of the men, as I bled out my grief through tears.

"It is fortunate that these walls are as thick as your skulls," I shouted at the lot of them, "or the guards would have heard you!"

"Khattaaara speaks truth," voiced Shaaalra, my one true friend.

"I have left the guards to feed the soil," Dhraaal replied. "None shall molest us from this moment on."

I need to make clear that the Orithaaan, Rhothaaana, my mother, was not Dhraaal's. As I had mentioned before, Dhraaal was the product of an unexcized Thaaagran, to whom Father had taken a fancy while off on some diplomatic tour. But while it was not uncommon for an Orithaaan, whether female or male, to have affairs, especially with synthetics, it was considered disgraceful and, consequently, unlawful for any of their offspring to be allowed to survive. Father never revealed the identity of Dhraaal's mother, nor did he in any way describe her other than to pretend that she was some Grentaaarg slave. There was always the suggestion that he had loved her and that perhaps she had died, but when he finally returned, he brought with him the egg from which Dhraaal eventually hatched. In good fashion, Mother claimed it as her own, but it was apparent as he grew from infancy into childhood and then into an adult that the only resemblance came from his paternal side. Where both Mother and Father were somewhat fair-haired, Dhraaal had a swarthy look about him—akin to some of the Thaaagran worker forms—and stoicism like unto those with an artificial mind. The combination of Gaaalthaaaran and Thaaagran, though, appeared to have endowed him with a singular personality so that, unlike most of either race (if Thaaagrans may be called a race), he was more rebellious from the start. Father used to joke that the shell of the egg from which Dhraaal was hatched did not dissolve as should have been the case, but that Dhraaal, when a hatchling himself, ripped it apart to escape. More to the point, I believe that Dhraaal felt some sort of jealousy—perhaps even rivalry—when it came to me but he was sexually attracted to me and the fact that (as would later be the case of the Egyptian pharaohs) brothers and sisters were promised in marriage to each

165

other, his temperament became abated by the intimacy between us that he knew would eventually occur. I, on the other hand, was not as eager for that union but still respected and honored my role as successor to my mother, never breathing so much as a whisper of the questionable lineage of my then-future consort.

As for my mother, Dhraaal had, it seemed, taken steps to eliminate her by means of one of her chambermaids slipping his poison into her evening meal while bribing her tasters to turn the other way. The murder of all who stood in our path having been accomplished, the five men in our cadre pushed aside the throne—which was extraordinarily heavy—then Naraaag-Tal used a disintegrator to remove the granite floor and expose the vault wherein lay the seven all-powerful god-stones.

The surface of the vault appeared to be made of liquid metal but was solid to the touch. Vial in hand, Dhraaal walked to the edge of the shallow relief that had just been carved out, opened the vial, poured the blood onto it, and then took a long step back. The azure life source hissed on contact. As it did so, the vault seemed to come alive. From its center rose a swirling, circular column that formed into a faceless being that in turn resolved into a female shape. Moment by moment, features began to emerge—features that resembled my own, though not quite. The face was more that of Ophelia, though clearly it was not her. At first, I thought that perhaps my mind was playing tricks; that the image of my best-of-friends, whom I missed so very much, and which lay in the forefront of my mind, was merely what this being had chosen to project into my consciousness; for why else there on Rendenaaar, would I have seen a female with rounded ears, who lacked a *yaaargh*? *A mockery of myself,* I wondered, I who so recently had her *yaaargh* excised. But there were other differences. Her skin glowed with a silver hue, and her eyes, also silver, were hypnotic. This was not merely a projection, though. It was alive, with movement, and appeared to be aware that it and the vault it guarded had been disturbed. The being, or whatever it was, searched around the room, as though it were assessing each of us, one by one, until, at last, it came to me, and that is where its vision stopped. Cautiously, I reached out to touch it, but before I could, it spoke.

"Quantum Girl," it said in perfect English. "But the one from the other Earth, the other dimension, the other reality."

"How do you *know* this?" I asked back in that same tongue, my accent thick, as my Anglican words were alien to the physiology of Khattaaara's throat.

"I am she who is everything and she who is nothing," it answered. "I am the beginning and the end and the guardian of the quantum gems. I am everyone and no one, and I am the embodiment of every Quantum Girl who did or will ever exist."

And with that, her image morphed into what Peyton and I had looked like as that superhero—the costume, the cowl, the cape (seemingly lifted by a nonexistent wind), though not in the iridescent violet we had known. Rather, she stood in that same radiant silver as she, this being, had appeared in from the start. I wondered how the others had reacted to all of this, but as I glanced around the room, they were as stiff as proverbial statues.

"Your companions cannot move or see or hear or speak," the silver being said, "for I have frozen them in time. Now, come forward and merge with me if you want your precious gems. Beware, Payton Alise Herron! Your very presence here has changed what was meant to be!"

I walked forward with great hesitation. The being held out her arm toward *me*, and so *I* reached out toward *her*. Our fingers touched. There was an exhilaration that coursed through my every cell. It was like some gentle electric charge that flowed up my arm and then dispersed throughout the whole of me. Then she grabbed my hand and pulled me into her. It was a strange feeling as our shapes began to combine. I could hear the echoes of a billion Quantum Girls who had yet to be born. I could hear their thoughts, feel their pleasure and pain, and the trepidation of their fears as all but one faced inevitable death in the end—as my form seemed to melt into the other, as I was turned to match her position until at last, we merged into one.

There was no exchange of thoughts or minds. Perhaps she did not wish to reveal all that she knew—or perhaps it might have been that my brain was not equipped to handle the vast store of knowledge she held. I do not know to this day. But there was power within me again, although not the same sort that I had as Quantum Girl. It was as if I were pure energy; as though the force of the entire quantum fabric bled *through* me from every direction.

I stared down at the vault beneath me and then squatted down. Leaning to one side, I reached through the metal as if it were not there; as though it had melted with my touch. Below, I felt a metal ball. This was the neutronium core in which the god-stones lay hidden. Dhraaal has said it weighed more than ten thousand tons, and yet I lifted it as were it but a feather. Standing up once more, I stared at it as it lay on the palm of my left hand. Then, like a mere puppet, my body controlled now by her, I waved my right hand over it and the impenetrable coating evaporated, dissolving into the air with tiny sparks of light. Thus came the seven god-stones into my possession as that thing which I had become a part of vanished, and those six, who had come with me, all came back to life.

They all stared at me, wondering how I had gotten (in what they thought an instant) to where I now was. As they did, I clenched my fist, hiding the stones.

Shaaalra ended my train of thought, breaking the silence. "How is it possible?" she exclaimed.

"What dost thou mean?" I asked.

"Behind thee," she replied, pointing. "Dost thou not see? Thy *yaaargh* hath grown back!"

CHAPTER XXXIV

Ophelia

From the Original Timeline
In the Alternate Reality
On Earth II
Earth-Date: 2029

The bomb struck Los Angeles at precisely 11:46 a.m. the next day. Reports indicated that upwards of six million people who had not made it to shelters or who had been in shelters that were destroyed by the blast were killed. All that was certain was that the nuclear war that had been feared for generations had finally occurred. Albeit that it had all come from just one side, the effects were just as devastating.

Reports came in mainly over shortwave radio, as one of the decimated areas was the antenna farm that had been located on Mount Wilson and had served as the broadcast site for most radio and television in Los Angeles. We were told that it would be necessary to remain underground for at least a week before radiation levels subsided enough for us to return home. What there was to return to, at least as far as we were concerned, was still unknown. According to the scuttlebutt within the shelter I was in, downtown L.A. had been ground zero for the missile that had been launched from an airstrip in Korea. The official word from what was left of the press was that Red World terrorists had somehow taken control of the Pentagon and prevented any defense or countermeasures by the U.S. military. Meanwhile, rumors spread that the attack was deliberate and planned by the current administration in order to permanently wipe out both capitalism and democracy, regardless of the cost in human lives. Over the course of the next three days, fourteen major U.S. cities had been obliterated. By day six, President Kamala D. Harris had signed articles of surrender, after which Soviet troops began pouring in and across the country. Some Americans fled either toward Canada or Mexico, but the vast majority of them were captured en route as the rest of the nation was quickly crushed under the iron fist of the Soviet regime.

Two weeks after the apocalypse, we who had hidden in the shelters emerged to safe levels of radiation. Despite the fears of many, it was explained to us that, unlike Three-Mile Island or Chernobyl, the nuclear bomb had been detonated in the air above its target to maximize the blast's destructive power. This had the advantage (if that's the appropriate word) of dispersing most of the radiation into the upper atmosphere and preventing those areas destroyed from becoming permanently radioactive. Regardless, when the doors to the shelter , we were met by armed troops, clad in radiation suits, who ordered us to wear paper masks over our noses and mouths; masks that did little more than dehumanize us and make us compliant. It all seemed like something out of a bad science fiction film, but it was all too real.

The shelter was far removed from ground zero, so we did not bear witness to any of the devastation until, while being driven in buses to the hastily set up citizen processing center, we saw that downtown Los Angeles, with all of its skyscrapers, had been reduced to rubble. Once inside, we were ordered to strip off our clothes and form a line, our clothing then gathered up, presumably to be burned. I tried to argue with one of the soldiers to keep my change bag for Jordan, but not speaking Russian, to no avail. Liam forced himself between us, grabbing the bag, but was struck in the head with the butt of the rifle belonging to another soldier who stood nearby. Claire quickly dropped down to her knees to help him when he collapsed, turning back momentarily to scream out, "Animals!" at those soldiers within her view. For myself, I could do little with Jordan in my arms. One by one, we were measured for radiation with handheld Geiger counters, although, having been isolated underground since the blast, none of us tested positive. Afterward, we were each handed a black or a green uniform to put on, depending on whether male or female, respectively. I learned later on that these were standard prison outfits throughout the Eastern Bloc. Shortly after I had dressed, a female soldier came up to me and handed me back my change bag, saying something in Russian that I did not understand. I uttered, "Thank you," but she offered not so much as a smile in return. About a hundred feet away, one man, whom I recognized from our group, began screaming at one of the guards. The guard, in response, unholstered his pistol and shot him in the head. This was our new world order. There was nothing for us to do but obey if we wanted to survive.

Eventually, those who still had homes were allowed to return to them. This was where I and my interdimensional relatives parted company. I hadn't seen much of Payton throughout the ordeal as she had spent most of her time with her boyfriend on the lower level. As was the case with Claire, Payton apparently hadn't been handling the situation very well and it was only thanks to her boyfriend that the slashes she had inflicted to her wrists hadn't proved fatal, this according to Liam. I had wished that I could have been there for her and comforted her, but this Payton didn't know me. There was no history between us. It seemed that her sapphic persona had been more self-assured and resilient, though I have no doubt that, given the chance to have become Quantum Girl, she would have fared just as well as that sister of mine whom I so greatly missed.[43]

There were talk of small resistance groups having been formed, but there was little they could ever hope to accomplish against the new military forces, added to the fact that less than ten years ago, Congress on this world had overturned the Second Amendment and

---

[43] Note that in this dimension, lesbians were called sapphics or sapphs, after the ancient Greek poet, Sappho, while gay men were known as socs, from Socrates, the ancient Greek philosopher.

outlawed all firearm ownership by private citizens. It was also ironic that former President Harris, who in my dimension had been an outspoken advocate of socialism, was summarily executed here by the newly formed socialist regime. "Why are you doing this to me?" she was rumored to have said, as she was forced down onto her knees in the Oval Office, whereupon a pistol was held to her head. "Deep down, I hate America; everyone knows that," she insisted to those about to execute her. Rumor had it that she began to laugh—some said cackle—just before the trigger was pulled, ending both her life and her career.

And so there was change. It was as though a blanket had been thrown over the entire country and then suddenly removed to reveal a totally different civilization. The Soviet takeover was privately referred to as С ночевкой[44] or *The Overnight*. Private businesses were seized by the Soviet-American government, as were people's homes. Elaborate mansions were *appropriated* by government officials with the exception of certain favored celebrities, whose popularity was considered advantageous as long as those individuals agreed to further the new agenda. Thus came an end to the Cold War with the upending of the United States of America, which became the United Socialist States of America or the U.S.S.A. It was just over a month later that Liam showed up at my door.

"Claire lost the baby," he said. "She went into early labor. It was stillborn. It happened just after we were let back into our home."

"I'm so sorry," I replied. "Is she all right?"

"She's gone," he shrugged. "She left yesterday—went to stay with her parents. I'm not going to judge. It was all too much for her. There was a lot of stress from everything that's happened, plus her cat bolted out the door when the sirens first went off. When we got back, we found it dead on the porch from radiation." He paused, gathering his strength, and then went on. "And then the miscarriage."

"What about Payton?" I asked.

---

[44] Pronounced Sno-*chev* coy.

"What *about* her?" he replied.

"What's she like?" I asked. "I know what she was like *before* time changed, but what's she like *now*?"

Liam shrugged. "She's a lot smarter than me and more focused. She wanted to be a doctor—a pediatrician. She was trying to earn enough to make it through medical school. Now, that's never going to happen. I worry about her now."

"How so?" I asked.

"She and Connor haven't been getting along that well of late," he replied.

"Connor?" I asked.

"Her boyfriend," he replied. "I thought I'd mentioned him. They've been together for years, but I don't know. I mean, he's a swell guy and all. It's just they're not on the same page, and it caused a rift that continued to grow. He wanted to go into the military. She wants to save lives. And then he went off and left her—he and a bunch of his friends wanting to fight back against the invasion. Peyton took it pretty hard."

"I wish I could talk to her," I said, "try and comfort her. We were close in the other life."

"Maybe I could figure out a way," he replied. "She and Claire never really clicked. Claire was always about popularity and fitting in. Payton was…" and he hesitated, trying to find the right word.

"An old soul?" I suggested.

"Different," he went on. "In a good way. And, not just my sister; my best friend."

"Same with me," I said, "with *my* Peyton."

"Look," he went on with a deep breath. "You said that on your world she was your sister, and on this world, she was your friend. I was thinking, maybe if you and Jordan came to live with us, you'd be able to bond with her. I mean, that's one way. You're stuck here. And I know you have your own place, your own private world, but I just thought…" He broke off and stared at me with eyes that begged the very heart of me.

"Yes," I said.

"You're sure," he asked as though he needed to hear it again.

"You *know* that I love you," I said, and then added, "but how will you explain me to your parents and to her? The truth is not an option."

",ther truth;" he said, "that I'm in love with you."

I smiled, a weight lifted from me with just those words.

"Anyway, if we're together, it'll let me be somewhat of a father to Jordan."

"You can be more than *somewhat* to her," I said, taking his hands in mine.

"And in time," he stammered on, "I was kind of thinking, maybe we can make things permanent."

I stared at him. "Liam Herron," I said, "Are you asking me to marry you?"

"There've been so many times, in my head, you've said no."

"Well, this isn't one of them," I replied with reassurance. "Only we can't make that known—at least for a while. In the meantime, I can bunk with Payton if she won't mind putting up with her niece, though we don't have to tell her who Jordan really is to her."

"I can understand why I loved you so much in the other reality," he said.

"We're in *this* reality now, though," I replied, "and *I* can understand because I feel the same way."

It was at that point that I fell into his arms, and he held me and I could feel his cheek as it pressed against my head, as my arms wrapped around him, and I knew at last that I wasn't alone anymore.

CHAPTER XXXV

Peyton

> *From the Original Timeline*
> *In the Alternate Reality*
> *On Earth I*
> *Earth-Date: 2025*

Having given it considerable thought, I felt it best to take Sarabeth to my time if for no other reason than to put three years between her and the now Quantum Theresa. I thought that, perhaps, that amount of time might palliate the inexplicable hatred that appeared to have manifested itself with her newfound powers. Aside from the fact that Mom and Dad will, no doubt, miss their little girl, I believed it to be the safest course of action. Sarabeth did not possess a quantum seed, and it would be too difficult, if not impossible, to safeguard her day and night. It just seemed better to lessen the odds of something bad happening to her, considering that she had already suffered death.

I was playing a game of chess with her when I broached the subject. She was winning. I wasn't really concentrating on the game; at least that was my excuse.

"I need to take you back with me," I said.

"Take me back where?" she asked and then added, "Check."

"To where I'm from, three years from now," I told her.

"Why?" she wanted to know. "All my friends are *here*."

"You know that you can't let them know you're alive," I said. "There's too much at stake."

"I suppose," she shrugged. "Anyway, they'd probably think I'm a zombie."

"That's all the world needs," I replied. "A vegetarian zombie."

"Who's a vegetarian?" Sarabeth said.

"I thought *you* were," I said back, "because *I* am."

"I'm not the same as you," she sighed. It was as though she were defending her own uniqueness. "You've said it yourself that some things changed when the timeline got rewritten, the worst being that I actually stayed dead and didn't get the quantum seed." She looked at me with mournful eyes. "I mean, it is so unfair that I never got to be Quantum Girl."

"The universe is a thoughtless beast," I replied as I gently stroked away the lock of hair that had fallen against her face. "But," I went on, "you are smart and beautiful."

"Mirror, mirror," she said back.

I just smiled.

"I never asked you," I went on.

She stared at me, her head slightly cocked.

"What was it like when you were dead? I never had the chance to find out. Dhraaal rescued me the instant it occurred."

"There wasn't anything," she said. "I died, and then I was alive again. There was nothing in between." She took a deep breath and then exhaled. "So much for all the religions in the world! It's very disheartening—getting to live our lives and then, *Poof!* It's all gone like we never existed at all."

"I guess that's why we have children," I said, "so that *our* existence can continue through *them*."

"I suppose," she said back, "but at least you'll never have to worry about that—about death, I mean."

"I'm not immortal by any means," I replied. "I've died twice now by my count. But enough of this talk. How about I beat your ass at a game of Monopoly?"

"We'll need more than just the two of us," Sarabeth insisted.

"Then we'll get Phee to play as well," I said.

"Dibs on the race car!" she exclaimed.

"Deal," I replied.

Half an hour later, as the game progressed, Sarabeth was beginning to lose. Phee was holding her own, but as fate would have it, my commercial properties, houses, and hotels were turning me into a real estate mogul. I could see the disappointment mounting in Sarabeth's eyes. This was all so painful to her—to lose her identity, to see what in another universe she might have become—and so I did what any good superhero big sister would do; I reset the clock back half an hour, and this time I made certain that she came out on top.

"Hah!" she exclaimed triumphantly when both Phee and I had found ourselves bankrupt. "And you said—what were your words?—that you would 'beat my ass?'"

"You are indeed assiduous when it comes to this game," I replied. "I bow down to your assiduousness!"

"As do I," Phee chimed in.

"As well you should," said Sarabeth. "Both of you." We all laughed and got up off the floor where we had sat for almost an hour, stretched our legs, and then went downstairs to have lunch.

That night, I broke the news to Mom and Dad and Phee about my wanting to take Sarabeth back to my time.

"Three years to the day," I said, "and then you'll be parents and sister to her again."

All of them hugged Sarabeth, gave tearful goodbyes, and then I took hold of her hand and phased us to 2029. As usual, the transition was instantaneous, jumping one thousand, ninety-six days in time.[45]

---

[45] The reader might wonder how such is possible, moving from one point on the Earth to the exact same place three years later, when, not only does the Earth spin on its axis at a speed of roughly 1000 miles per hour and rotate around the sun at roughly 67,000 miles per hour, but the solar system moves at more than 448,000 miles per hour within the galaxy, as the Milky Way and its Local Group move at 1.3 million miles per hour toward the constellation Vega. So, one might ask why, when I phased with Sarabeth three years hence, we didn't wind up in the middle of empty space where the Earth used to be. The explanation is that we didn't simply phase through time but through quantum time, which allowed us to wind up in the same place. This principle is called quantum *adhesiveness,* though nothing will be

It was indeed unexpected, however, when our arrival was instantly met with shouts of "Surprise!" by Mom and Dad and Phee, along with noisemakers (the kind that unroll when you blow into them and squeal out their sound), along with a rain of confetti. Meanwhile, a banner that was hung across the room read, "Welcome back Peyton and Sarabeth!" A large white, frosted cake that stood on the coffee table boasted much the same sentiment in gel-like letters of pink and blue. Sarabeth was met with hugs from all. Then Phee, now my same age, came over and hugged me as well.

"I've missed you, too," she said.

I smiled as I looked at her. "You know," I replied, "for us, it's been like half a second."

"Don't spoil things," she said. "You can't imagine how long and hard it's been for *us*."

"I know," I said back, "but we're both here now for good."

---

known about it until 2068, when a physicist by the name of Dhakshan Singh will write a treatise on it based on his time wave research at the International Centre for Theoretical Sciences, in Bengaluru, India.

CHAPTER XXXVI

Theresa

From the Alternate Timeline
In the Alternate Reality
On Earth I
Earth-Date:2025

I was lying in my bed, thinking, when the door to my room opened, and I walked in. This was a true what-the-fuck moment that nearly scared the shit out of me when the lights suddenly went on; more so when I saw her standing in the doorway, or rather, me standing there, though she/I didn't notice *me*. She was wearing the Braxton uniform—the blue jacket, the white blouse, and blue and red plaid skirt. There were books in her hands that she set down on the dresser she'd walked over to.

"Hey!" I said, sitting up in bed, throwing my legs over the side. "Who the fuck are *you*?"

She turned, startled, but didn't say anything. I think she was too scared. I stood and walked right up to her—stared into her eyes. I didn't even blink, and neither did she.

"Who *are* you?" she said in a voice that trembled.

"Theresa Martinez," I replied. "And again, who the fuck are *you*?"

It was all so crazy. There was only supposed to be one me in this world. I'd been living in this house alone for a week now, and it had been abandoned. Fuck, the food was all rotten in the fridge. The mailbox overflowed with bills. And I watched my mother slit her wrist and die. But then, when I glanced around the room with her in it, everything was different—neat. I mean, I'm not the most orderly person in the world, but the bedroom now looked like it belonged to Martha Fucking Stewart!

"Theresa Martinez," she said. "*I* live here and this is *my* room! You need to get out. Did Daisy put you up to this?"

"Daisy?" I said, so confused.

"Look," she went on, "Just because I broke up with her doesn't give her the right to gaslight me with some doppelgänger!"

I stared ever harder at her. "You fucked Daisy McKenzie..." I said, astonished.

"Just because you fuck someone a couple of times," she ranted on, "doesn't mean you're in love with them! Crazy rich white girl!"

It was then that I heard someone else in the house with a voice that was unmistakable.

"Theresa!" the voice called out. "Is there someone in there with you in your room?"

It was the voice of my mother! *But how?* I thought to myself. *I'd watched her die!*

"¡Mamá," my lookalike called out, *"necesitas llamar a la policía!"*[46]

That didn't happen, though. Instead, *her* mother, *my* mother, I don't know which, rushed into the room, and then stopped in her tracks, her eyes going from one of us to the other.

"¡Dios mío!" she cried out. *"¿Cómo es esto posible?"*[47]

My look-alike took a deep breath. "I just came home from Carla's house and there *she* was in my bed!"—this, with a motion of her head toward me.

"She?" Mama asked, totally confused. "You both look identical!"

"Mama, it's *me*!" the look-alike insisted. "*I'm* Theresa! *I'm* your daughter! I don't know who *she* is!"

"*I'm* Theresa!" I proclaimed. "I don't know who this *maldita*

---

[46] "You need to call the police!"
[47] "My God! How is this possible?"

cabrona[48] is, but *I'm* your daughter!"

My mother stared at me and then shook her head. "*My* Theresa does not talk like that," she said. "That is not how I raised her. *My* Theresa is a good girl." Then her gaze turned toward my look-alike. There were tears in her eyes as the bitch rushed into my mother's arms. It was as the Other Me turned her head in my direction that I realized that that Theresa was just a better actress. She glared at me with hatred in her eyes. Inside and out, we were both the same, insecure but determined. We had that much in common, and I admired her for that, which is to say that I had no regrets for the way I myself was.

The woman, who was my mother, had rejected me. She stared at me with the look of a parent protecting her child from harm.

"Mama, please!" I begged, but there were no words that I could say to change the hatred toward me that I saw.

"You need to get out!" she said, "before I call the police!"

I don't know what ran through my head at that moment—whether it was anxiety or anger or fear—but I wished at that moment that I could be alone. I needed time to think. And just like that, both of them were gone.

---

[48] ...damn bitch...

CHAPTER XXXVII

Payton

From the Alternate Timeline
In the Alternate Reality
On Earth II
Earth-Date:2029

I envied Liam for his strength. He'd always been my protector, but there are certain things, I guess, there's no protection *from*. I didn't like who I was. I felt that the path I'd taken was not the one I should have chosen. There was a girl in one of my classes at UCLA— Dara Tallman. She was always so popular. It seemed as though virtually all of the guys who knew her would line up just to talk with her. She wound up president of the Pi Beta Phi sorority. The house stood in the middle of the row of Greek buildings adjacent to the campus.

Anyway, being somewhat of an introvert, I found it odd when she and a couple of the other sisters had asked me to join. I've never been much of a people person. Mostly, I've kept my head buried in my books. Liam had always insisted that I try and become a model, though I didn't care much for all that went with it—posing, being told to stand this way or that, dealing with all of those behind the scenes. Regardless of him knowing that, when I offhandedly mentioned the invitation, he wouldn't let up until I caved, so I went. The girls all seemed fine, if a bit on the immature side. There were a lot of questions asked, some intimate, and then came the hazing, which consisted of going through an entire day, including attending classes, wearing nothing but our underwear, supposedly to humiliate us. Unlike the other pledges, though, I was indifferent to it all. I've never been one bit ashamed of my body. Hell, I started work at a strip club the very day I turned eighteen. So, unlike the whimperers, as I liked to call them, I made it through without giving it a second thought. There was one boy in my English Lit class, though, that I caught looking at me in my lingeried state, but who would awkwardly and quickly turn away whenever my eye caught his. That was Connor—totally shy when it came to me. The other guys gawked at me in my skivvies. Connor and I hadn't exchanged a single word, either before or after that day, until one night at some social, he came up to me. Even though he was the one who approached, he seemed reticent and embarrassed, as though he were intimidated by my looks.

"I like your outfit," he said.

"As opposed to my underwear?" I said back.

"Yeah," he managed to get out. "I didn't mean to stare. I just…"

"Thought I looked ridiculous?"

"Thought you were the most beautiful girl I'd ever seen," he replied. He was having a hard time maintaining eye contact. "There I go," he added, "putting my foot in my mouth."

"Hey," I replied. "I think what you just said is really sweet."

He looked up at me. "You do?" he said.

"If you really meant it," I said back.

"I did," he insisted. "Every word. Did it come out wrong? I didn't mean it to. Really."

A short laugh burst from my lips.

"I'm sorry if I'm bothering you," he apologized.

"No," I replied. "It's just that it's like you think I'm going to bite your head off if you offer to get me a drink." I paused and looked him in the eye. "You *are* going to ask me, aren't you?"

"Can I get you some punch?" he asked.

"Sure," I said with a smile. "By the way," I went on, "I'm Peyton."

"I know," he stammered out. "Everyone knows of you."

"Nothing bad, I hope," I said.

"Oh, no," he replied. "All the guys think you're beautiful."

"And what do you think?" I asked.

"Gosh, um…" he managed to get out.

"Yes?" I prodded.

"I think you're the most beautiful girl I've ever seen," he said with great conviction.

"Hey, Manes!" one of the jocks in the room shouted out. "I didn't know you could talk to a girl without peeing in your pants!" at which point I turned my head to see which idiot had said that, gave him a harsh look, and then wrapped my left arm (the one farthest from him) around Connor's neck and planted a hard, firm kiss on his lips. The idiot looked shocked, as did the other jocks with him, and as did Connor when I pulled back a bit.

"Now, how about that drink?" I said to him.

He started for the punch bowl and then suddenly turned around to face me.

"You'll still be here when I get back?" he asked.

"I shall be as still as the Statue of Liberty," I replied—and that was how our ill-fated love affair began.

We started going out on weekends, mainly Friday and Saturday nights. After about a month or so, Sundays were added on, where we would wend our way through museums or amusement parks or sometimes just spend quiet times alone. We would talk about our thoughts and our hopes and the dreams we had of the future. Things seemed to be going well; so well in fact that when we finally became intimate, we chose not to use any form of contraception, believing that were I to become pregnant, it would only have solidified our relationship. But then things began happening that, at the time, I could only attribute to schizophrenia. Sometimes, out of the corner of my eye, I would think that I would see myself, but then, the instant the other me saw me looking at her, she would vanish into thin air. This began happening with greater and greater frequency until I couldn't take it anymore.

First, I went to my doctor at Kaiser Garfield. After describing my apparent apparitions, I was scheduled for and took a blood panel, EEG, and what is referred to as a functional cerebral MRI. All turned out to be negative. At the same time, I saw a psychiatrist who prescribed Planzapine, which did nothing other than make me drowsy, make my mouth dry, and make it difficult for me to concentrate. I gave up on it after a couple of weeks. I was still seeing her/me more and more. It happened again when Connor and I went to the movies. I remember it was on Independence Day, the 2nd of July.

Anyway, it was around eight o'clock. The feature was set to start at 8:10, and I had excused myself to go to the ladies' room while the newsreels were still running. The movie was a screwball comedy called *God Only Knows* with Matthew Damon and Anna Zavtur. It was about Jesus having come to Earth a second time to discover the meaning of love. People have always said I look like her—Anna Zavtur, I mean. Connor did, too. Maybe that's why he chose to go to this one. It was a compliment, I suppose, being compared to one of the most incredible beauties in film. I always wondered what he'd have thought if he'd actually met her.

Anyway, there *she* was again, just outside the ladies' room and apparently about to vanish once more into thin air, when I called out, "Wait!" and amazingly she did. She paused for just a moment outside the door and then went in. Stupidly, in retrospect, I followed her, wondering if she would still be there after I entered (doubtful is perhaps a better word), but there she was.

"Who are you?" I asked, as my heart rate quickened.

"I'm you, more or less, but from another dimension," she said with the hint of an accent I couldn't quite put my finger on, "and with superpowers you don't have."

"Yeah, right," I said with more than a shred of disbelief, despite having witnessed her disappearing trick so many times. I just assumed that someone was trying to gaslight me and was doing a

185

pretty good job of it so far.

"Why are you following me?" I demanded to know. "Why do you look like me?" I asked. "And I don't see any *superpowers*."

"Do you mean like this?" she said, and in an instant, I was standing on a barren plain on a world with an orange sky that I later learned was called Rendenaaar, where she herself was born. "Or like this?" and all at once she stood before me like a colossus, a thousand feet tall.

"Okay!" I shouted. "Okay!" and just like that, we were back where we had been.

"So, why did you come here?" I asked.

"To learn what your life is like?" she replied.

"And why is that?" I said, furthering my question.

"The Earth I lived on was *damaged*," she said, emphasizing the word.

"How did *that* happen?" I asked.

"I got a little carried away," she said. "I have, as your people say, anger *issues*."

I looked at her with scathing eyes. "So, you destroyed the planet," I said, assuming the worst.

"Just the inhabitants, mostly," she replied. "Besides, I *do* like the Earth in *your* dimension," A wicked expression painted her face as she went on with, "It's so *quaint*."

"I don't understand," I replied. "If you're Payton Herron in your dimension, why would you *do* all of that?"

"Who said my name was Payton Herron? It's Khattaaara, but you may refer to me as Her Serene Highness, Khattaaara, Mistress of All that Lives, Goddess of Rendenaaar and of Everything Else that Exists." It was at that moment that I noticed her ears as they poked through her hair. And her tail! *Oh, my Gods!* I thought to myself, and then everything around me changed.

I was still in the bathroom, but it was dark and cold, and she, Khattaaara, was gone. The floor was covered in water and debris that

I couldn't see but could feel. I tried to remember which direction the door was and began walking toward it, I thought, but ran into one of the sinks instead. Slowly, I felt my way around the room—from one sink to another, then to a wall, and then left to the row of stalls. The water sloshed as I moved just inches at a time. The first stall I came to had its door open, something I didn't anticipate as I had pressed my weight against what I thought was solid, and so I lost my balance, my feet slid out from under me, and I toppled down to the water-drenched floor, cutting my hand. I couldn't see how bad or how deep the cut was in the pitch-dark dungeon that this room had become, but I *had* sprained my left wrist, trying to catch myself, and scraped one knee, which offered more pain to the predicament in which I found myself. I gathered myself up and rose to my feet, my legs shaking unsteadily beneath me. Then the tension and the darkness, the fear and the pain, all brought on a new dilemma—the need for me to urinate—the reason I had gotten up out of my seat and come here in the first place, not expecting to find *her*, the one so different, perhaps a monster; the one who claimed to be another one of me—sort of. I knew there must have been a toilet in each stall. What was in them I couldn't begin to imagine. But with that in mind, I hiked up my dress where I stood, pulled my panties to my knees, squatted down, and let nature take its course. I could hear the splash as the stream of urine sprayed down to the watery floor. I could smell the pungent fumes that began to waft up to my nostrils. I could feel the warmth in the water at my feet. But I also felt relief.

Pulling myself together, I began moving forward along the row of stalls. It is impossible to describe how oppressive the darkness was. It felt as though I had suddenly been struck blind. I remember feeling my heart beating like a hammer in my chest. I tried not to panic, but to no avail. I slid both hands across each door until I would feel the edge. Then my left hand would reach down to find the latch just to be sure. Six times I repeated this action until there was just empty air. I moved to the right then, clinging to the side of the stall, until I felt smooth bricks, cold to the touch. *The door must be close,* I thought to myself, and it was.

At long last, as my fingers grasped the handle, a raised U-shaped vertical bar, I pulled on it, only to find that the door was locked. I felt the swell of tears meet my eyes. *Who would have done this?* I wondered. *Who would have locked me in? Of course, it was her, the monster who looked like me; the doppelgänger from hell, with her pointed ears and tail, so like the devil that Mother had told Liam and me about when we were small. No,* I thought again. *I will not be defeated!* I calmed myself, felt upward on the plate that the handle was mounted on, and found the latch that, with one twist, would set me free.

I exited to much the same as the room I had come from, but there was a bit more light that bled in from the outside doors. It was then that I began to scream, for littering the floor were the bodies of what must have been the movie-goers and the staff, though enough time had passed that decay had set in to such a degree that, in many cases, the flesh was entirely gone. *But how could this be?* I wondered. *How could any of this be?* Many of the corpses were piled one upon another as though they had stampeded to escape. The skeletal fingers of one woman held those of a little girl who, in turn, held onto a teddy bear. Trembling, I cautiously tried to step around the dead, not always entirely successful in my attempts.

When, at last, I made it to the outside, things seemed all the worse. I lifted my arm to shield my face from the brilliant daylight that scorched my eyes, unprepared for the transition from the dark. I squinted as my sight adjusted to the brightness of the midday sun. Blurred vision sharpened into focus, but what it revealed was utter devastation!

This had been my city, my home, now reduced to rubble. But then, I thought, *This isn't my Earth! This isn't my world! It's hers! The one who looks like me!* There were dead bodies everywhere, and there were skeletons! A crow sat on the skull of one and cawed out its survival over the ruin of mankind. I wondered, then, if the house I had lived in had existed on this world as well. More than two hours of walking in the heat gave answer to my question.

It was there—the house I had grown up in—at least it looked the same. The lawn was dead with scattered weeds in its place, similar to those of the neighboring yards. Some of the structures had walls that had fallen; others had windows that were missing or broken. Chimneys lay toppled on the ground, smashed to bits by the Big Bad Wolf named Khattaaara. Slowly, I ascended the few steps that led to the front door. Cautiously, I turned the handle and pushed the door in, my heart beating like thunder.

"Hello?" I called out before I entered. "Hello?"

The room was in disarray. Things had been knocked off shelves, and there were layers of dust everywhere. A picture had fallen in the hallway. I picked it up with its broken glass, a photo of two small children, neither of whom was me. Rather, it was of a very young Liam and a girl the same age who resembled him. So, this is how this universe played out on a world where Payton Herron was never born. There were drawings taped to the refrigerator in the kitchen— drawings made by children. One was of animals. The other was of a family of four. The first one was signed, *Liam*—the other, *Ophelia*. This was, apparently, the little girl's name—the twin who wasn't me. Then I saw something that shook me to my core. There was a calendar on the wall just like the ones we'd always had at home. But it wasn't that the calendar was *there*, as it was the *date* on it, which read 2019. That was ten years ago! The bodies in the restaurant didn't appear to have been dead for ten years, nor did the corpses on the streets that hadn't been picked clean by coyotes or birds. *Unless*, I thought to myself, *here time was different from my own; different by a decade*. Suddenly, I heard a noise from upstairs, then silence, and then there was a faint click.

"Hold it right there!" a boy's voice said. "Don't move. Don't even breathe."

189

Then I heard the voice of a girl. "It looks just like her," she said, "like when she's not glowing and all."

"Back up against the wall!" the boy ordered, and I did, moving slowly, till I felt myself flat against the refrigerator door. It was then that the boy moved forward, and a ray of light from the window touched his face.

"Liam?" I blurted out, shocked at the possibility that this was my brother standing before me, ten years old. Then the girl came and stood beside him, the image of the girl in the photo in the hall, whom I assumed was Ophelia, Liam's twin on this world.

"How do you know my name?" the boy asked. Both of his hands gripped something that looked like a futuristic rifle that was aimed at my chest.

"Would you please put down the gun?" I begged, but he shook his head.

"Shoot her!" Ophelia screamed. "Shoot her, before she kills *us*, too!"

"I'm not going to kill anyone," I said in as calm a voice as I could. "And I'm not who you think I am. I'm not (and I paused) Khattaaara. If I were and had all her powers, you'd be dead by now—both of you."

The boy paused to consider what I had just said and then glanced at the girl. "What do you think, Li?" he said.[49]

"She kind of has a point," Li replied. "Besides, N-bursts didn't seem to do anything when the military shot at her—Khattaaara, I mean—so I think the plasma gun would be kind of useless."

The boy put up his rifle. "Okay, but if you're not *her,* then who *are* you and why do you look like her?"

"According to *Khattaaara*," I said and I emphasized the name, "this is a different dimension from my own. In mine, you're my twin, only you're *my* age. And there *is* no Ophelia."

"No one calls me that," Li said.

---

[49] pronouncing her name to rhyme with *me*.

190

"There's no one left *to* call you that *but* me, Dunkhead!" Liam shot back.

"I hate when you call me that," Li said.

"It's a compliment," Liam replied.

"Well, I still don't like it," she protested, "and you know it."

"That's a strange compliment," I said. "Why did you call her that?"

"I once tripped and fell off Santa Monica Pier," Liam explained, "and she dove in to save me even though she was terrified of the ocean ever since she watched Jaws in virtual."

"He peed in his pants when he virtualed *Aliens*!" Li shot back. Then she turned to him and stuck out her tongue.

"What's virtual?" I asked.

"Gee, Lady," Liam said, looking astonished. "Where've you been?"

Li glanced at Liam, scowled, and then turned to me. "It's where you put a small disk on each side of your head, and then everything around you seems to change to whatever the program is. But you need to have temple implants for it to work. I got mine put in when I was five. So did Liam."

"We don't have anything remotely like that on my world," I admitted.

"People used to watch things called movies," Li added, "but that was long before Liam and I were born."

"So, is your name Khattaaara like hers?" Liam asked, still not convinced of my story.

"No," I replied, "It's Payton."

"That was grandma's maiden name, wasn't it?" Li asked, turning to Liam.

"I think so," came the reply. "Payton or Paxton. Something like that." He paused, thinking, and then looked up at me. "So, how come you look just *like* her?"

"I don't *know*," I said, "but as you can see, I don't have pointed

191

ears *or* a tail."

"True," Liam replied. "Or two sets of boobs as far as I can tell," he added, staring at my chest, at which point Li loudly cleared her throat, causing him to turn to her. "What?" he said defensively. "I was just making a point!"

Li turned to me. "He's got a thing for boobs," she said, girl to girl.

"I do not!" Liam insisted.

"I've caught him glancing at mine," Li whispered to me.

"Liar!" Liam shot back. "You don't even *have* boobs!"

"How would *you* know?" Li said tauntingly.

"And you're, like, my sister!" he scowled.

"I'm not *like* your sister! I *am* your sister," Li shot back.

"Children!" I said. "Please! This is not the time! Where are your parents?"

"They're dead," came the response from Liam.

"They were outside when I guess a million Khattaaaras projected the death rays from their eyes." She paused, and then went on tearfully. "I can still hear them scream from the pain."

"There was another one like her," Liam said. "A man. He tried to stop her, but she killed him, too—right outside of here. He kind of just disintegrated, but I found this under where he was."

He reached into his right trouser pocket and took out what looked like a small, green marble.

"It glows in the dark," he said.

"May I look at it?" I asked.

"Sure," came the response, as he handed it to me.

"It doesn't seem like anything out of the ordinary," I said as I examined it.

"It lights up the room when it's dark," Liam insisted.

I cupped my hands around it and then stared closely into the slit formed between my thumbs. The gemstone did, in fact, glow with a brilliant green light. It was strangely hypnotic as it began to spin around and around, faster and faster, growing smaller and smaller as it did. Beams of light shot through the spaces between my fingers and danced upon the walls. Then, all at once, defying gravity, the brilliant glint—for it had shrunk *that* small—lifted up from my palm and shot at my head like a bullet. For an instant, I felt a prick of pain in my forehead, and then I passed out.

I'm generally not one to remember my dreams, but I have wondered to this day, does anyone dream while they're unconscious and not just asleep? But what (or, rather, who) I saw was she who trapped me here—she who looked so much like me—she whose name was Khattaaara. Only it was not here on this Earth or on mine, but on that other planet that she had taken me to. It was more of a nightmare because, when I woke up, my heart seemed ready to explode from my chest, it was beating so hard and fast and I was covered in sweat. It must have seemed very real at the time, but it quickly faded into bits and pieces as most dreams do when we wake.

I didn't know how many hours had gone by, how long I had lain there, or even how I had gotten from where I'd collapsed to the bedroom that I found myself in, remembering that this wasn't my world, not my Earth, and I wasn't related to the Liam here or to his sister.

I'd awakened feeling almost smothered. I wasn't alone in the room or even on the bed. There were others beside me, on top of me, and next to me. Who they were, I couldn't see.

"Who's there?" I asked, but as I did, I heard my voice multiplied; I couldn't count how many times. "Who are you?" I demanded to know, and once again, my voice reverberated throughout the room. It wasn't like an echo, though. It was as if I were everywhere in the room at once and able to see everything there from every possible direction. And then, suddenly, my body gave out a greenish light, as did all of the others in the room, and I gasped. All of us gasped, for we all saw that each of us was me. When I spoke, each spoke; at first the same words, but then there were differences. I rose from the bed, struggling to break free of the weight of those of me that lay atop me, my heart pounding in almost deafening tones. At last, standing, I looked around, as did each of the other Paytons in the room. I flicked on the light switch with my hand even though I was nowhere near it to reveal fifty-eight of me as it turned out, all now standing, staring at each other, wondering what in the Gods' names was going on.

Stranger still, was the fact that I felt what all the others were feeling, which was both confusion and fear. The only sense I could make of it was that we were in each other's minds; seeing through all of our eyes at the same time. How this had come to happen, I had no idea, although I (or we) suspected that it was somehow connected to that glowing green gem that had flown at us and struck our forehead before there was an *us* to be struck—just *me*. And yet at the time, I believed that it had merely glanced off my skull and not penetrated it. So, there we stood, all fifty-eight of us, with absolutely no idea of how to reunite us into one. With some great difficulty, we managed to open the bedroom door. It was from there that various ones of me began to filter throughout the house. Fortunately, both of the children were fast asleep. The one of me who had been directly on top of me turned to face me.

"What are we supposed to do?" she asked as, at that exact same moment, I said the exact same thing.

Meanwhile, I could taste the soda that another of me, now in the kitchen, was drinking, and I could feel the cool liquid as it went down her throat and into her stomach. This was all so confusing and bizarre. It was then that the one facing me closed her eyes and wished to be just one Payton again and, just like that, all of the rest were gone or were absorbed back into her, myself included, invoking a deep sigh of relief, though I was dreadfully afraid to go back to sleep after that. Instead, I wanted to learn about where I was, but there were no books or even a television. Apparently, all knowledge and entertainment came through the disks everyone used, which *I* couldn't use, even if I could find a disk, because I didn't have the temporal implants. But if that were the case, I wondered—if no one needed a large screen to view anything anymore—what was the purpose of the building I had found myself in, that on my world was a movie theatre?

As I walked out into the night, looking up at the sky, it was hard to imagine that now I stood on a world in a different dimension from my own. Their moon hung in a crescent overhead just the same as mine. The stars and their constellations were all the same. *But wait!* I thought to myself. *There are lights on the moon!* On my world, we had tried to reach the moon and failed. Yet here, despite that their years were a decade behind mine, their technology was far more advanced—perhaps a century, if not more. *What could have caused such a disparity,* I wondered, *where some things were so different and others the same—Liam's existence, for instance?* All of this passed through my mind as I stared up at this Earth's companion, wondering what the lights represented. An instant later, I found myself on the moon, gasping for breath in the airless vacuum. I felt intense heat, and then my skin began to freeze. My thoughts were just for air and protection from the cold. I don't know how long I stood there, but suddenly, there was warmth all around me. At first, I shivered as though I were naked in the dead of winter in sub-zero cold. My hands and feet were numb, but gradually, my blood began to flow again, and there was comfort in that. Terror gripped me, however, when I chose to look up again. This time, instead of just stars, there in the distance was the Earth, roughly the size of a basketball, leaving me to believe that this was either a hallucination or that I was, in fact, on the moon.

This was all too real for it to be a dream. Besides, when one is actually dreaming, one never stops to consider the possibility that one is fast asleep. The Earth in the distance held the only color around me. Everything else was gray, from the mountains in the distance to the powdered sand upon which I stood. As I turned around at my surroundings, I could see some of the lights I had noticed from the yard outside the house. I wanted to find out what they were, but caution took hold of me. Was the air around me just a small cocoon, or would it move with me wherever I went?

Cautiously, I lifted my arm and extended it. About two feet from me, the tips of my fingers began to feel just numb at first, and then I felt a sharp pain. I quickly drew them back to me and brought them up to my lips. They were freezing cold, as though I had just put an ice cube in my mouth; worse, it was like in the movie where that kid touches a streetlamp with his tongue and it gets stuck to it. That was much the same in this case, and it was only the heat from my lungs that caused the bond of fingers to lips to be broken. Once that had happened, I rubbed my frigid fingers with those of the other hand to warm them.

But was I to be marooned in this one spot forever, I wondered? I had to know. I was afraid to even sit down, lest I once again breach the barrier that surrounded me. With one deep breath to fill my lungs, I took one step, then another, and then a third toward those distant lights. To my amazement, the envelope of air went with me. Step by step, I slowly advanced until what had just seemed points of light resolved into a tall, large, twelve-story building with glass windows. Once there, I peered inside.

Within the walls were row upon row of people, each a magnificent specimen of humanity, as though every one of them had been cast from the pages of Vogue or GQ. All of them were completely naked and seemingly held in a rigid, standing position by yellow beams of light that projected downward from the ceiling. Each of them, man or woman, appeared to be unconscious, oblivious to what was happening to them; they were changing, turning into versions of whatever it was that Khattaaara was. One woman facing me was growing a second pair of breasts just beneath the ones she already had, while her labia were disappearing, as though it were an incision that was healing itself. And of those who faced away from me, both female and male, I could see tails being formed on them— tails like the one on Khattaaara before she sent me to this hell.

My Gods! I thought to myself. *They're all being turned into Gaaalthaaarans!* whatever that was, as that name just popped into my head along with one other—Dhraaal!

Suddenly, one of the figures that was decidedly more transformed than others near her opened her eyes and saw me. That one, a teenage girl, raised one of her arms to shoulder height, pointed her finger at me, and appeared to scream. Others, already transformed and clothed, rushed toward her and then turned in my direction. Each had a lighted, purple device affixed to the palm of his or her left hand, which they raised, almost in unison, in my direction. Bursts of light pulsated toward me. As one stuck me hard on the side of my head, I wished with all my might that I was home, and I was. I found myself in my bedroom, on my world, and in my own dimension. I was back!

CHAPTER XXXVIII

Theresa

From the Original Timeline
In the Alternate Reality
On Earth I
Earth-Date:2025

It really started me thinking— my look-alike and the woman who wasn't my mother but was hers—who were they really? Where did they go? Where were any of the ones that I sent away? The other Theresa's mother said that her daughter was, *What did she say?* "A *good* girl." That I'm not. Maybe, unlike me, she was never molested. Maybe her mother just happened to walk in that first time when it was about to occur, but hadn't happened yet. Maybe *that* Theresa likes boys and dreams of marriage and children, but that's not me. She's not me, and I'm not her. I had my childhood stolen from me. I had my sexuality changed. I don't know if it's a bad thing to be only attracted to other girls, but it's who I am now, and it isn't just about the sex. I'm not just some perpetually horny nympho lesbian chick. Love and physical attraction don't just go hand in hand. I can be physically attracted to a girl and not love her. But when there's love, I look at her like she's the most perfect person in the world. I don't mean that she's gonna wind up on any magazine covers, but in my eyes, she's all I could ever want or need. Love is when my fingers intertwine with hers. It's where I feel comfortable and safe opening up my heart and not just my legs. For better or for worse, I feel safer in the arms of another girl. Perhaps it wasn't who I was or who I was meant to be but I wasn't the one who dealt the cards. I just played the cards that I was dealt. But who was I to talk with no one in my life?

As I sat on the front porch swing, I got to thinking that maybe putting myself out as some badass supervillain wasn't such a good idea. The only ones in this world that I really hated were Peyton Herron and that Quantum Girl—whoever the hell she was—and maybe even myself. *Maybe if I hadn't wished myself into the future, my mother wouldn't have taken her own life.* Anyway, that was what was running through my head at the time. So, there it was—shared blame. Ever since I'd been molested, I'd tried to put on this pretense of not caring about anything or anyone but me. I think it even translated to sex. Maybe, I thought, it wasn't just about me wanting to have sex with some girl, but about my being in control of her during the act; sort of like how my molester had been in control of *me*. I remember trembling as that comparison came to my mind. I remember clutching one of the chains that held up the swing and gripping it so hard with both hands that my knuckles turned white and my skin got all clammy. My breathing became labored, and I felt a warm trickle down my thigh as I lost control of my bladder. It wasn't fear that had encapsulated me, but the realization that those fantasies that I had in some ways made me the same as him. That did not make me a good person, and I knew that needed to change. For the sake of my mother, I had to make it happen if I had any respect for her.

The good news was that since things had become different, all the bills were up to date. That gave me more time to figure things out. Maybe I could use my superpowers somehow to make enough to pay off the house and keep the lights turned on. I decided to rebrand myself. No more Rage, literally. I'd be Rainbow Girl, and as long as that Quantum Bitch stayed in the shadows, as far as everyone else was concerned, I'd be unique.

It took three hours of intense concentration, but I finally got the costume the way I wanted it to be. Instead of being patterned in stars, it changed color from one moment to the next. I spent the following day setting up accounts on Facebook, Instagram, YouTube, TikTok,

GoFundMe, and X. The thing was, though, I didn't want to go it alone. I had no one in my life, no one to talk to, no one to care about who would care about me, and, most important of all, no one to be with for companionship, love, and sex. I thought about all the girls in my class that I would want to be with, with regretful thoughts about Peyton Herron being a fucking straight bitch. All hatred aside, she was still one of the hottest girls I knew, and there were those damn dreams where I was having sex with her that came virtually every night—meaning I came virtually every night over her. One *other* girl came (perhaps overusing the word) into sharper focus than all the rest and that was Daisy McKenzie; Daisy McKenzie, who I'd desperately wanted to fuck ever since I'd gotten enrolled last year. I had fantasized about her naked in my bed on an almost nightly basis, even though I figured she was straight as a laser beam, the same as the uppity Ms. Herron. *How was it*, I wondered, *that God made so many hot girls totally straight? What the fuck was He thinking?* I just kept telling myself that all girls, regardless, have sexual pressure points and all one needed to know was how to make use of them in a manner that didn't push them away. But after what the other Theresa had said, the playing field had totally changed. She had actually fucked her! I just never figured her to be a dyke, but that was a good thing where I was concerned.

Daisy McKenzie was fifteen years old, just like me, and supposedly still a virgin—at least as far as boys were concerned—but I wasn't a boy, and neither was she. All I can say is that she was seriously hot. I mean, the girl looked like Harley Quinn down to her pigtails—a total knockout with an air of innocence attached. But what is attached can be removed. and apparently, my look-alike had already done that. Girls, like newborn ducklings, bond with whoever gives them their first *experience*, and I was sure that Daisy was no exception.

So, there I was at the McKenzie house in a part of town a lot nicer than mine; hardly any cars parked on the street, manicured lawns, huge, sick homes. Hers was white with dark blue wood trim. Anyway, after I rang the bell, waited a few seconds as I looked up and saw the Ring camera, Daisy's mother answered the door. Mrs. McKenzie was pretty hot-looking for her age, but that's what having money does. Plus, she *was* Daisy's mom—shared gene pool if you get my drift.

"Is Daisy home?" I asked.

"Daisy!" her mother called out. "Your friend, Theresa is here!"

Daisy McKenzie descended the staircase that stood just beyond the foyer, still wearing most of her school uniform. The jacket and tie were gone, as were the saddle shoes and socks, and her hair had been set free, bouncing this way and that to the beat of the fulsome breasts that were somewhat exposed beneath her bra, her blouse three buttons open from the top. As she cascaded to the door where I stood, her left arm reached behind her head and pulled her hair to that side. It was one of those moves you just wanted to see in slow motion.

"Hi," she said in a voice that sang with the angels. Then she looked at me with a slight tilt of her head as though trying to remember.

"I thought you weren't coming back till tomorrow?" she said.

I went up to her and whispered in her ear, "I couldn't stand to be without you that long."

"Oh. my Gods," she whispered back. "You're making me wet again!" She turned toward Mrs. McKenzie. "Mom!" she said in an audible voice, "Theresa and I are going up to my room!"

"Have fun!" Mrs. M. said back.

"Is it all right if Theresa stays the night?" Daisy asked. "I wouldn't want anything to happen to her going home when it gets dark."

"I wouldn't want to impose," I said. As we were standing really close to each other, Daisy reached behind me with one hand and placed it under my skirt between my legs, totally unseen by her mom. "But if you don't mind," I went on, "I'd love for Daisy and me to catch up on some things." The last word must have gone up a full octave from the inward motion of her fingers. I cast a glance at her.

"Wait till we get to your room," I whispered.

"Sorry," she said, as she brought those same fingers up to and into her mouth, smiling back at me.

"Of course, I don't mind," Mrs. M. said and then added, "I just hope you're hungry. We're having beef bourguignon, and there's more than enough and then some. You two run upstairs, and I'll let you know when it's time."

Daisy McKenzie was the textbook definition of jailbait, though I had to wonder whether or not she even realized the effect that she had on the boys at school, or on the male faculty, for that matter. Think Cara Delevingne with a bit of Chloë Grace Moretz thrown in. Think nothing about what the thought of this girl had on me, especially being alone with her up in her bedroom, both of us sitting next to each other on her bed—Arousal 101—to this day, every time I think about it, about her back then. Daisy was the sweetest girl you could ever imagine, though (and I don't mean this as a put-down), she was not the brightest star in the sky. All too trusting, four years from then would have found her dead in her dorm room, having been tortured, raped, and strangled by another college student who, it would turn out, would rival Ted Bundy as to the number of girls he'd have killed. But that was in the other reality that virtually throttled my brain. How did I know that, I wondered? Might some of the other Theresa have gotten into me when I made her disappear? *Shit!* I thought to myself, *this superpower crap is fucking complicated!* One of these days, though, I figured I would go back in time before he'd committed his first murder and plunge him alive in a grave next to some rotting corpse along with a flashlight, prune juice, and oxygen so that he could truly understand the meaning of hell! That would have prevented all the crap he would have done, though I never got the chance. At that moment, however, my thoughts weren't on the future and, to be honest, my sense of altruism only extended to the

202

number of orgasms I could cause Daisy to achieve if things worked out the way I assumed they would. To be clear, although I am one hundred and ten percent girl, I do have the sex drive of a boy my same age.

The fact of the matter, though, was that once we were inside her bedroom and she closed the door behind us, I didn't really have a chance to think. She went up to me, looked me in the eye, put her arms around my neck, and her lips against mine. This was followed by a totally wet kiss with her virtually deep-throating me with her tongue. It all went uphill after that, but I won't bore you with the intimate details. It must have been around two hours later that her mother called us from downstairs to let us know that dinner was about to be served. As we were getting dressed, Daisy frowned.

"Everyone thinks I've been with all the boys, but it isn't true," she said. "The guys say really dirty things about me, bragging about all kinds of stuff I've supposedly done with them, like I'd ever *let* them. Most of the girls hate me because they think I'm out to steal their boyfriends." She paused and then went on with some hesitance. "I really like what we just did in bed, but…"

Oh, no, I thought, *here comes the kiss-off,* I thought to myself.

"But what?" I asked.

"I'd like us to be friends," she replied. "I mean, I have something I want to tell you, but I don't want to scare you off."

"Scare me off how?" I asked.

"I have a confession to make," she went on.

"Yes?" I said.

"I've kind of had it bad for you," she replied, "since the moment I first laid eyes on you after you enrolled at Edmond last fall. But please don't tell my mom. She wants me to grow up all prim and proper and marry '*an upstanding young man from Yale.*' *Her* words, which is strange because Dad's a Harvard man."

"I don't have any friends either," I admitted. "So yes. Absolutely. You and me."

"After dinner," she said, "how about we read a story together under the covers. I have one in mind. It's one of my favorites."

"What's it called?" I asked, pretending to care.

"Coldheart," came the reply. Daisy looked at me questioningly, and then it struck her. "By the way," she said, "shouldn't you call your mom to let her know you're overnighting?"

"My mom's dead," I said with a shrug.

"Oh my God!" Daisy exclaimed, taking my hands in hers. "I'm so sorry. I didn't mean…"

"That's okay," I said, cutting her off. "It's like, I'm still not over it, but life *is* what it is. By the way," I said, searching around the room with turns of my head, "have you seen my panties? I thought they were on top of the rest of my clothes on the floor."

"OMG!" she said. "I must have put on yours by mistake. Do you want me to take them off?"

"That's okay," I said. "I don't want to risk being late. I mean, I don't trust myself. I mean, I'm already picturing it. Probably best you just leave them on for now. That'll give me the chance to take them off you myself later on. As for me, I'll go commando. No one will know but you.

We dressed ourselves and then made our way down to the dining room. Dinner went without incident other than that as I sat across the table from Daisy, her bare foot *somehow* found its way up to my pantyless crotch and began to—how shall I put it—explore my nether regions. Eating became somewhat of an ordeal from that point on, but I was hungry regardless, and so despite the pleasurable distraction, I managed to fork my way through the meal—no pun intended.

Daisy's mother sat matronly at the head of the table. Her father, who was an executive for some company that did arbitrage (which was explained to me as the purchase and sale of commodities in order to make a quick profit), was out of town at that moment. The cook (yes, they had a cook and a maid and a gardener and I don't know what else) served dinner—beef bourguignon (which I had never had before) as promised, after a leafy salad mixed with pineapple, pumpkinseeds, and croutons. Daisy's mom had been served red wine to accompany it, while Daisy and I were each presented with mocktails, which were glasses of diluted grape juice filled with grape-shaped ice. Dessert consisted of a custard tart with blueberries, grapes, strawberries, and kiwi. It was all quite delicious, though I was a total dumbass when it came to which fork or spoon to use. But whenever I messed up or appeared confused, Daisy gently threw her glance toward the incorrect one and then pointed it to the proper utensil, as well as repositioning her toes against my hidden passion, which elicited my heart to pound above and beyond the overpowering sexual rush.

When dinner was over, Daisy and I went back upstairs. Her bedroom, I should mention, was about as delicate and white as one could imagine. It was like New England in the winter, just after a fresh-fallen snow. There were white teddy bears and white furniture, white bedding, white wallpaper with flocked snowflakes and angels, and at the foot of the bed stood a life-size female statue with powder-white skin, dressed as the Snow Queen in a flowing, gauzy white gown and holding a silver wand in her right hand with her arm outstretched as if about to cast a spell. Its hair was white, its eyes the color of the sky, and its lips frosted with just a hint of blue. Meanwhile, an icy crown encircled its head. The room was a fairy tale waiting to happen. *Fucking strange,* I thought, for someone with a sexual appetite like hers!

And, so there we were, snuggled up close under the fluffy white comforter on Daisy's bed, each of us in a short nightgown, mine provided courtesy of Miss McKenzie, both of them white, of course. And there was a large picture book on Daisy's lap, from which she began to read:

"Once upon a time, in a land so cold that even the icicles shivered, there was a kingdom. And in the kingdom was a castle, and

205

in the castle was a queen—not just any queen, but an evil queen with a heart as hard as a diamond, and like Winter herself. Now, this kingdom might have been called a queendom instead, for there was no king, oh, no. The king, who had been kind and gentle, and given warmth to even the polar bears, had fallen in love with the woman, who would later become his bride—fallen desperately, madly, and terribly—so that he worshipped the very ground that she walked on, and gave her jewels and furs and anything she wanted, till at last she wanted his life, and he even gave her that.

"'Dear Husband,' she proclaimed one day, as though on a magical whim, 'if you truly loved me, you would tear out your liver and serve it to me on a plate so that I might fill myself with your courage.' And so, the king, being desperately, madly, and terribly in love with his wife, tore out his liver and gave it to the queen, whereupon she roasted it and consumed it with the greed of a starving fox. But, of course, a man cannot live without his liver, even if he is a king, and so the good king died and was buried in a sepulcher beneath the castle, and all that was left to remind anyone that he ever existed, was his crown that was made of the rarest snow and ice that shown like diamonds and could never melt, no matter how hot the world became, and could never be smashed or dashed or destroyed in any way. But the queen, wanting all of her husband's memories forgotten, locked it in a box and threw it into a well, and there it lay at the very bottom, guarded over by Neptune's trident and some fish that trembled from the cold.

"But the king had also left a legacy, for he had placed a spark in his beloved's belly, and the spark had grown into a beautiful little girl, who was born nine months and a day after the king had met his terrible end. The queen named the little girl Coldheart, for of all the days and years and minutes and seconds the girl had spent upon the earth, of all the laughing and carefree children who had passed her way, Coldheart would never smile, never laugh, never cry, for in her heart was a shard of ice that had been placed there by her mother,

for her mother had plans for this beautiful daughter of hers. And the shard never melted, never thawed, never turned to tears as it should, but always stayed cold and hard, like a needle in an angel's eye. And the winters came to pass, one by one, and the summers passed the countryside with indifference, so that both the snow that covered the kingdom and the ice that was wedged in Coldheart's chest, never thawed, nor melted, nor turned to tears, and Coldheart grew into young womanhood, with skin as pure as the fresh-fallen snow, with hair as yellow as the sun, and with eyes as blue as the northern seas. But she never smiled, nor laughed. She learned her lessons from books and her etiquette from the court. She could recite poetry and nod graciously whenever someone bowed or curtsied, but hers was a brooding face, for no joy lay within her breast. At night, her chambermaid would undress her and sometimes politely ask if the princess were happy. And the princess would think, and say, 'No, we are not.' And the chambermaid would probe more and ask, 'Do you think about love?' And Coldheart would stare into the wall until she bore a hole in it and then say, 'Love is for books, not for people, and especially not for princesses or queens.'

"*One day, not long after Coldheart's eighteenth birthday, a prince from a far-off kingdom rode a sleigh, pulled by a great, white stallion, up to the castle. Clouds of steam rose from the stallion's nostril, as it strode up to the palace gates. 'Who's there?' barked the palace guard. 'Prince Kraven, from beyond the mountains and across the sea. I have heard of the great beauty of the princess, and I have come to ask for her hand.' And so, after a few short mutterings and eyes cast over the palace walls and above the palace gates, the wooden doors were opened, and Prince Kraven clucked to his horse, and the horse's nostrils filled with steam once more and led its master into the courtyard beyond.*

"*When Princess Coldheart heard the commotion, she looked out from her chamber's window and saw the prince, and, oh, now she knew the meaning of the love that filled the books that she had read.*

207

Oh, it was love—love at first sight. Her prince was tall and strong, with long, dark hair and eyes that were invitations to eternity. And, despite that there was a shard of ice beneath her bosom, her heart fluttered like a thousand frightened birds. But the princess's eyes were not the only ones, which caught sight of the prince. Oh, no, for the queen had been taking her afternoon stroll in the royal courtyard, and she, too, saw the handsome prince, and her heart, too, even though it was as hard as a diamond, pounded in her chest and tore at the very fiber of her evil soul, and the queen wanted Prince Kraven with the want of a young maiden. But being not a young maiden, she knew that the prince would reject her and that she would not have him. And so, the evil queen devised a plan. From where she stood, her eye had also caught sight of Princess Coldheart, and she saw that Prince Kraven had caught sight of her. And the queen bit her lip and stayed the heart in her breast. She gathered up the fringes of her dress and her petticoats, and without a word of goodbye or hello to her newly-arrived visitor, slithered back to her bedroom, pressed a small granite brick, and, after the wall opened itself to reveal a hidden chamber, went inside and walled herself in so that no one and no thing could see or hear what she would do, for evil wants not eyes nor ears to eavesdrop on its plans.

"It is a curious thing what sorts of potions witches brew, what sorts of spells they weave—magical, mystical, phantasmagorical, but always unquestionably evil. In her hidden chamber, the queen had secreted sulfur and brimstone, bat's wings and lizard's tails, eye of newt, and even the feather of a phoenix, thought to be real only in the minds of storytellers from long ago. A little of this, a little of that; a smidgen here, a pinch there, a puff of smoke, a frothing of brew, and three drops proclaimed themselves to be precursors to both immortality and love.

"When night fell upon the kingdom, and all but the sentries who stood guard at the parapets of the castle lay in their slumber of dreams, the queen stole quietly into Coldheart's bedroom and placed

*first one, then the second, and then the third drop upon her face—
one upon each eye and one upon the lips. Then she crept back into
her room, walled herself up in the hidden chamber, smiled to herself,
and fell into a blissful sleep.*

"Morning came with its daily certainty. Light crawled into the
room of the princess and then awakened into a fire of brilliance.
Coldheart stirred, yawning from her rest. Was there a shadow over
her bed in the middle of the night? she wondered. But the thought
pushed out of her mind like so many dreams, and she opened her eyes
and licked her lips, and all at once, a whirlwind launched itself upon
her mind. The world grew dark. Her brain could not hold a single
other thought. Blackness came like a thousand snows in an instant.
And when at last she did awaken, it was to find herself in a pitch-
dark room with neither doors nor windows, and in her came a terror
that she was dead and that this was hell.

"But the queen, the queen, when she awoke, it was as though the
fires of Valhalla had melted the snows. When she opened her eyes
and breathed in the morning air, she inhaled the scent of the silk
robes the princess had worn and the sweet perfume that wafted off
her gentle skin. The queen took in everything there was to see in
Coldheart's room. She yawned herself to wakefulness, stretching out
what only hours before had been the arms of her daughter. And then
she laughed with Coldheart's voice, a sound of jubilance that
Coldheart never made, for there was the matter of the sliver of ice
that had only begun to melt at the sight of the prince the previous
afternoon. And so out of bed the new young queen got, went straight
to a mirror and looked herself up and down and sideways, and was
very pleased indeed at what she beheld, for no longer was she in the
body of an aging queen, oh, no, but the body of a beautiful princess,
who would soon win the love of a handsome prince, and with the
other out of the way—for that is how she now thought of her former
self—they would rule the land for the lifespan of a tortoise, and
tortoises live very long lives.

"And so, the princess, who was not the princess, whose real name was Drusilla, invited the prince to breakfast, and the prince feasted upon her beauty, and Drusilla gazed upon the prince with the hunger of an aged maiden. But the evil queen would not leave such matters of love to simple chance, oh, no! As soon as she dressed, she went to where she had hidden her stock, mixed a bit of this and that, and poured it into the wine the prince was soon to drink. It was a love potion, designed to make whoever swallowed it fall completely, madly, and irrevocably in love with the first person he or she set eyes upon. And, so, before the brew could pass his lips, Drusilla made absolutely certain that the dining hall was empty, and she locked the doors behind them after they entered.

"'Why do you lock the doors?' asked the prince.

"'Because I am afraid that my wicked mother might catch us alone, and banish you from the kingdom,' the evil queen lied.

"And the prince, smitten by the queen's stolen beauty even without a love potion, accepted her explanation with neither comment nor question. But there he was at breakfast, and there before him was the silver goblet filled with the sweetest wine mixed with a potion that would make even an angel and a demon fall madly in love with each other. Fine meat lay on the prince's plate, which he heartily consumed. But the queen had taken liberties with the cook's recipe and salted it just a bit more than it should have been. And so a thirst came over the prince, and he put the goblet to his lips and emptied it down his throat and into his belly and once it was down, the magic crept into his veins, his eyes feasted upon the beauty of the princess, who was really the queen in princess's clothing, and just like a lovebird finding its mate, the prince's heart began to flutter, his brow began to sweat, and he knew that he had found such love as not distance, nor time, nor even Death could break.

"The queen, of course, knew what had happened. She stood up from the table, walked over to the window, and stared out, ignoring the prince entirely. Seeing this was more than the prince could bear.

He wanted the princess with every measure of his breath, and so he stood up, rushed to her side, and knelt down before her.

"'Fairest Princess,' the prince muttered out, 'you cannot imagine how I worship you.' And his skin grew pale as the dawn.

"But the queen said nothing. She only stared out the window and yawned. 'Fairest Princess,' the prince repeated, 'what might I do to win your noble hand, for I fear that without it, I am lost and will die the deaths of a thousand lonely men.'

"And the queen said nothing still, staring out of the window at a tree that, like all the rest at this time of year, was barren of even a single leaf. 'Go into the forest,' she said in a voice that was like the ghost of an angel. 'Go and find me a bird with a golden beak, and I will think to have you at my side for a night.' Not once did she take her eyes from that tree. Not once did she turn to the prince, who had proclaimed her in his soul his now and forever darling. Not once did she even blink her eyes, but stood as a statue might, till the prince rose to his feet, and said, 'Yes, my dearest beloved. I shall go into the forest and find the bird you seek, and I shall catch it and tame it and bring it back to you to cook or to admire as you so please.' And the prince bowed to Her Majesty, and he backed his way out to the door, never once taking his eyes off of her who was once Princess Coldheart. But at the door, when he tried to turn the handle, he found that it was locked, and he remembered that she, who was the very passion of his soul, had locked it behind them both.

"Oh, the queen was not like any royal person, for beyond all the potions in her lay the magic of a thousand generations of witches. Unlike Coldheart, who was an only child, Drusilla was the seventh daughter of a seventh daughter of a seventh daughter back to when all daughters were born in caves and wore bearskins as proof against the cold. This daughter of royal blood had magic in her veins, and so she merely pressed her eyelids together and did a magical thing, and the prince's hand, which was still gripping the gilded handle that could open the door were it not locked, suddenly found itself able to

turn the lever and move the mechanism, withdraw the latch, and faster than a kangaroo can open its pouch and look inside, the door opened up and the prince, still fixed upon his beauty, backed up and out of the room and towards his impossible task."

"Maybe we can finish it tomorrow night," I suggested.

"Do you mean you want to stay over again?" she asked.

"Why not?" I said. "If your mom doesn't mind. I don't have anyone at home to miss me."

"You know," she said, "I never thought that we'd be friends. I never thought I'd be friends with *anyone*."

"Neither did I," I said.

She smiled softly then buried her head against my breast, pulling herself close, wrapping one arm around me. I put my arms around her.

"I have a question," she said sleepily.

"What's that?" I asked.

"When we get up in the morning," she replied, "do you mind if we make love again?"

"Daisy, darling Daisy," I replied.

"What?" she said, half asleep.

"You never have to even ask," I said.

She smiled softly and then fell into dreams.

I smiled to myself. I had always wished for something like this—some*one* like this—but I guess, as they say, "Good things come to those who wait." I wound up staying for an entire week. Daisy's mother didn't suspect a thing, thank God. As far as she was concerned, I was merely the missing piece in the life of the daughter she had sheltered and protected for all of her fifteen years. Nor was there any objection when I asked if Daisy could come and stay overnight at my place, where I intended to tell her everything. *Everything* became her fairy tale except for one thing. Every night, instead of dreaming about her, I dreamt of having sex with Peyton Herron. *What the fuck!* I thought every morning when I would awaken. It was all so sick and not in a good way.

CHAPTER XXXIX

Peyton

From the Original Timeline
The One Who Went Back in Time
In the Alternate Reality
On Rendenaaar
A Thousand Years after Khattaaara-Payton died

There was so much to consider. Payton and I stood on a dead planet, trillions of universes in the past. Was the fact that we only came this far a warning from the quantum gods, if there were any, that we should go no further? It was apparent that the separated consciousness of Payton, which had merged with that of Khattaaara, had inexorably altered reality—at least the reality that I had known and perhaps hers as well. We surmised that the quantum seeds in our heads had shielded us from the overwrite and preserved our memories of what had been.

"What should we do?" I asked Payton.

"What do you mean?" she replied.

"I mean," I said, "that, at least for the moment, we have absolutely no idea what we can do to correct any of this. Your having given Theresa a quantum seed caused reality to butterfly."

"So, it's all my fault?" she replied. "That's what you're saying." She shook her head. "I was just trying to save her after you put her in the hospital."

"That was Khattaaara," I said defensively.

"And Khattaaara is you or was you. And now half of me got thrown into her."

"I know," I said. "Before I started out, I met the me who never became Quantum Girl. Look," I went on, "I'm not blaming you. It's just…"

"FUBAR," she interrupted. "Fucked Up Beyond All Repair. My Uncle Buck used to say that. He was in the military."

"You have an Uncle Buck?" I asked.

"And?" she replied, looking at me questioningly.

"Nothing," I said. "Only John Hughes will be laughing in his grave hundreds of trillions of years from now. I think we should head back," I went on. "We can always return if we figure something out."

"Too bad there aren't any Quantum Women we can go to who've already been through this before."

"No such luck," I said. "It's just you and me. We're all that's left. Come on. Let's go." And so, we phased back, each to our own universe and to our own dimension.

CHAPTER XL

Khattaaara/Payton

> *Payton from the Original Timeline*
> *Sharing the Mind of Khattaaara*
> *In the Rewritten Timeline*
> *On Rendenaaar*
> *Trillions of Universes in the Past*

I was whole again. The Quantum Spirit had healed me before it had disappeared, but whatever it was remained a mystery. It had said that it was the embodiment of every Quantum Girl who had ever existed. And yet, I was Quantum Girl, or at least I *had* been in my other life. In all of the possible universes and their infinite dimensions, how it was that my alter ego was so significant, I had no idea.

Nor did I know the origin of the quantum seeds, but I recognized their power. Still, I wondered how it was that, out of the trillions of galaxies with their trillions upon trillions of stars, they wound up in my hand. As I stared down at them, one glowed brighter than the rest. It was the same one that I had found in the dust that had been Thara-Klo so far into the future. Taking hold of it with the index finger and thumb of my free hand, I brought it close to my forehead, closed my eyes, and let it melt through my flesh and bone.

"Are thou mad!" Shaaalra exclaimed. "The god-stones are alien things of which we know naught."

I turned toward the sound of her voice and opened my eyes, which, as I later learned, had glowed white.

"I act with knowledge from another life," I said.

216

"Such is without reason!" Shaaalra proclaimed. "There is naught but the here and now."

"Think what thou must," I said, "but I am both Khattaaara Gaaalthaaara and Quantum Girl!" Quantum Girl! The name was meaningless to all of those around me who only knew Gaaalthaaaran words. How strange those two words would have sounded to my former American mind when voiced by a being who has spoken Gaaalthaaaran all of her life. Quantum Girl! The name even sounded strange to the Payton part of me; it had been so long since I had heard it said out loud. But even as I spoke it, I changed, and I became her, garbed in her costume, filled with brilliant, moving stars, and a cowl over my head, the only differences being that my ears came to points, my breasts were twice in number, and my skin, instead of iridescing violet, glowed white. And then there was my *yaaargh*, so miraculously grown back, and, as with the ends of the hairs on my head, the hairs on it sparked out white fire. My glorious, glorious *yaaargh*, grown erect behind my back, such being the indication that a Gaaalthaaaran female both wants and needs to mate. But this was not the time, and there was no one there for that.

The others stared at me with amazement and perhaps a bit of fear. To them, the god-stones were merely a power source that would enable them to control their world. It might have taken them years to learn how they could be used—how their minds could tap into their power. But it was the Payton half of me that knew this from the start. Perhaps it was that half who had awakened the Quantum Spirit and urged it to grow back my *yaaargh*. Ignoring all of them, I simply phased back home.

Dargra-Tol was sitting in a chair in the dark when I materialized.

"I'm back," I said. I waited a moment, and then I repeated my words.

"They're gone," she replied without movement or emotion.

"What's gone?" I asked.

"The god-stones," she said. "I tried accessing them. I'm no longer connected to any of my kind."

"I did not know thou wast networked."

"I know not such a word," she replied, emotionless.

"Thou still hast *me*," I said, "if thou still wanteth me."

She turned her eyes in my direction. "Of course," she said. "Thou art my special love. But what sort of clothes dost thou regale me with?" she went on. "And how is it that thou once more hast thy *yaaargh* at thy back? What manner of sorcery has beset itself upon thee?"

"'Tis no sorcery," I proclaimed, "but rather the science of the god-stones, one of which now takes refuge in my brain," and with that, I phased back into my Khattaaara self, my costume gone, my skin once more the color of my Gaaalthaaaran birth. As such did I go over to her and place my hands upon her shoulders in as loving a way as I could, wondering if there were anything I could do to *un*do the murder that had been done to my child? The thought crossed my mind that I might phase back in time to save her. But if I did, her blood would not have opened the vault, and I would not have gotten the mother stone that allowed me to go back in time. It was a paradox I dared not risk till I knew more of how time worked.

As for the other god-stones, they were, for the moment, safe within my *yaaargh*. It had been our plan to divide them amongst ourselves, but this was something I needed to reconsider, in that my Payton memories knew much of their power. What I came to realize as far as Dargra-Tol was concerned was, in that she was a synthetic, hers was part of a collective mind that had now been severed due to my having absconded with the stones. I understood then why there had been such a disconnect between Gaaalthaaarans and synths. All at once, she felt isolated and alone; probably helpless as well. I tried to comfort her in bed, gently running my closed hand up and down her *yaaargh*, tightening my grip at the appropriate spots to try to elicit some sexual response, but after a moment or so, she pulled her *yaaargh* away.

"Why dost thou not let me please thee?" I asked in my most gentle voice. "Regardless that thou art my property, I still love thee as were thou my equal."

"Thou canst not know," she replied, "what it is like to be part of a common mind, sharing others' eyes and thoughts and sensations, only to have them, of a sudden, ripped from one's very brain."

"But I do," I said as I from one became many.

Dargra-Tol stood up from her chair with a start.

"How is this possible?" she asked as the words fell from her mouth.

"One of the god-stones is in my head. In another place and another time, I was known as Quantum Girl."

"What is the meaning of such name?" she asked as her gaze fled from one of me to another and on and on.

"Quantum means *Zhaaagura*," I explained, "while Girl means *Scraaa*."

"*Zhaaagur Scraaa*," she repeated. "And in what language is *Khaaantum Ghraaal*?"

I smiled at her pronunciation. "It is, or rather will be, called English on a planet called Earth."

"*Unglaaaash*," she parroted. "*Uaaarihaaa*."

I merged my selves back together. She stood up before me and then dropped down to her knees in obeisance, touching her forehead to the floor.

"Thou art a god!" she asked, afraid to look up.

"Nay," I said to reassure her. "Thou art my equal. Stand up and face she who loves thee as no other ever has."

She regained her feet but still refused to look into my eyes.

Gently, then, I placed my fingers beneath her chin and lifted her head. At last, she opened her eyes and looked into mine.

"Wilt thou make love to me?" I asked. "Wilt thou let me make love to thee?"

The synth slowly nodded.

"Then kiss me passionately," I ordered, "and press thy body close upon my own. Tonight there shall be a knowing, and we shall spray our passion wildly into the air!" Would that I had known the dangers of all I had revealed.

CHAPTER XLI

Payton

From the Alternate Timeline
In the Alternate Reality
On Earth Iᵢ
Earth-Date:2029

The absolute first thing I did after I found myself in my own bedroom was to take a shower. Maybe it might have been considered invaluable to NASA as I was literally covered in moon dust, but it smelled like gunpowder, tasted like chalk, and clung to my skin. Generally, I use a pouf to wash myself, but I wound up having to scrub it with an Egyptian loofah to get it all off, and, even with that, it took considerable effort. I spent the next twenty minutes or so taking care of *personal* things, which (fortunately) they never show you in movies or on television, and, while one might think this is too much information, it is relevant to the fact that it took me *that* long from shutting off the water to emerge back into my boudoir as it were only to find Liam and that girl who just walked into our house some weeks ago (or was it months, I wondered, as I hadn't checked the date when I returned) together in my bed. As for what they were doing, if there were springs beneath the mattress, they would have been creaking nonstop. Both of them were naked. Liam was on top like a human piledriver, while Madame X was on her back beneath him, her arms at her sides, gripping the sheets with clenched fists and making small moaning sounds, her legs trying to wrap themselves around his. I cleared my throat to alert them that they were not alone. It scared the living crap out of them, and it served them right for desecrating my space! Gods, what were they thinking, and how the

221

hell did she wind up back here and in bed with my brother? Liam frantically grabbed the sheet that was down by his feet to cover his private area, while the girl pulled some of it from him to cover herself. It was a tug of war, as each tried to grab more from the other.

"I told you I heard the shower," Liam said to her.

"How is *she* back here?" I demanded to know. "And what happened to Claire?"

"They broke up," the girl responded.

"I didn't ask *you*, whoever you are!" I snapped back.

Liam sat up, throwing his legs over the side of the bed as the girl pulled a bit more of the sheet from him.

"We broke up," Liam said, parroting the girl's words.

"You certainly *moved on* quickly enough," I shot back.

"It's not *like* that," Liam said, standing up to get dressed as I turned my head away. "Look," he went on, "I know you're probably not going to believe me, but Phee Phee's from another dimension."

"Phee Phee? Seriously?" I said.

"Ophelia, actually," came the girl's response.

I glared at her. "Was I talking to…" and I suddenly broke off. "Ophelia!" I exclaimed. "Ophelia Herron?"

"She's from the other dimension," Liam said, buttoning his jeans, at which point I burst into laughter.

"What's so funny?" Liam demanded.

"It's just that I've been *trapped* in another dimension, and there she was—your sister! Only there you called her Li!" I couldn't control my laughter, which angered Liam to no small extent. "Look," I went on, "I have something to tell you. I'd have you sit, but you'd wind up back in my bed with *her*, and there's no telling what might happen next."

"Let me guess," Liam said. "You're pregnant."

"No!" I shot back, disgusted by his inference. "It's a whole lot bigger than that. You probably won't even believe it."

Liam gave me a *Go on already* look.

"Anyway, Liam, the other Liam—he's only ten—gave me a glowing green stone that went into my head and then weird shit started happening."

"You got a hold of a quantum seed, and now you have superpowers," Ophelia said, at which point I took a step back.

"How…" I stammered back at her.

"In my dimension," Ophelia said, "there *is* no Liam, and you and I are sisters; well, *my* Peyton and I are at any rate, and before the time rewrite, you and I…we… were best friends."

"Time rewrite?" I said. I had to sit down. I opted for the chair at my makeup table.

"I have no idea how it happened," she said, "but everything changed, and neither you nor your mom and dad remembered me or Jordan. Jordan's Liam's and my daughter."

I just took a deep breath.

"What went into your head," she explained, " is called a quantum seed. It's from another universe, and it lets you phase anywhere in time or space or to different dimensions. You can create an infinite number of yourself. You can hurl out energy blasts and protect yourself or others with force fields. And you can see through things."

"I've already done some of that," I said.

Ophelia wrapped herself up in the sheet and started toward the bathroom, part of the fabric dragging after her.

"Forgive me," she said, "but I need to pee."

She entered the bathroom but left the door open just a bit. "Anyway," she went on, "in *my* dimension, on *my* Earth, *my* Peyton got her seed four years ago. Then she got shot and gave it to you before she died, only you brought her back but then her brain got taken over by her decidedly evil former self, there was a full-scale war above our house—you won, by the way—she got her life back together, you brought me here to be with Liam, he and I had Jordan, and then everything went kerflooey and I got trapped in this dimension. I found Liam, hooked up with him again, even though he didn't remember any more of his life before the rewrite than you do, and so here we are, together again."

"In my bed," I added.

She flushed the toilet and then came back into the room.

"Have you seen *his* bed?" she asked.

"Point taken," I replied.

"Can you remember *any*thing?" Ophelia asked. "I mean, with the seed and all. I'd like to be able to get back home—at least to let everyone know I'm all right."

"Nothing," I replied.

"Not even that you were gay?" she added.

I rolled my eyes and shook my head to myself at that one and then turned to Liam as he asked, "So, how did you wind up in another dimension?"

"Connor and I were at the Cineplex," I said. "By the way, has he called to find out where I was?"

"You were supposed to be with him right now," Liam replied.

"I must have overshot," I said. "It's been weeks for me. Anyway, I got up to go to the bathroom, and there was this girl. You know, I've told you I don't know how many times that I thought I was seeing things, only it turns out I wasn't. There was this woman—if she was a woman—who kind of sort of looked like me except that *she* had pointed ears and a tail and said her name was…"

"Khattaaara?" Ophelia interjected.

I stared at her. "How did you know?" I asked.

"Shit!" she replied.

"What?" I asked.

"That means there's another one of her!" she exclaimed.

"Who *is* she?" I asked.

"On *my* Earth, she was my Peyton's original incarnation, and she's bad news."

"So I heard from Liam," I said, "*young* Liam and Li. Their Earth got destroyed by her."

"Where are they now?" Ophelia asked.

"They're still *back* there," I said.

"And *how* old did you say they were?" she went on.

"They're both ten," I replied.

"And you left them alone on a world that Khattaaara destroyed," she said, as though to admonish me.

"It wasn't intentional," I replied and stared at her. "All this superpower stuff is new to me. But you said I can time travel."

"Uh-huh," she replied.

"And I'll be able to travel backward and forward in time?" I asked.

"If your seed is anything like the one you had before," she said.

"Well, then, once I get it figured out," I replied, "I can go back in time to the moment I left them, so they're not in any danger."

"Okay," she said. "Just sayin'. I wouldn't have left them in the first place."

"Well," I insisted, "you didn't accidentally wind up on the moon."

"The moon again!" she exclaimed. "What is it about you and the moon?"

"Meaning?" I asked.

"That's where the other you stranded my Peyton when Khattaaara took over her mind." She paused and then stared at me. "So, which powers *do* you have control over?"

"I can make a whole lot more of me," I said.

Liam shook his head. "*That'll* help win arguments," he sighed, mostly to himself.

"Shut up!" I said. "And as for the moon thing, it wasn't anything I planned. I just thought about being there, and suddenly there I was. And there was like this invisible bubble around me."

"A force field," Ophelia interjected.

"Whatever it was," I replied, "it protected me from the cold and helped me to breathe."

"Not to mention the solar radiation," she added. "Look, I can teach you. We all went back in time for a month in the other reality in order to help you learn everything."

"We being who?" I asked.

"You, me, and Theresa. Martinez."

"Theresa Martinez," I repeated. "I sort of remember her from high school."

"Yeah, well, she was your girlfriend," she replied.

I just shrugged. "Whatever," I said. "Right now, I just want to figure all of this out before I accidentally blow up the planet."

Liam looked at me. "Just try not to sneeze," he warned.

CHAPTER XLII

Ophelia

> *From the Alternate Timeline*
> *In the Alternate Reality*
> *On Earth 1*
> *Earth-Date:2029*

Dear Everyone, yes, I know it's complicated, but I would like to introduce you all to my younger sister, Sarabeth, who had been abducted by aliens at birth and was just brought back by the mother ship.

Dear Everyone, my mother, whom you all know, had a tumultuous affair with my father's identical twin brother and then, after carefully concealing her pregnancy for nine months, gave birth to a beautiful girl whom she shipped off to a convent in Switzerland in order to preserve her marriage.

Dear Everyone, although many of you may find this hard to believe, my sister is actually a superhero (or superheroine), who has powers and abilities far beyond those of mortal men (or mortal individuals for those of you who are decidedly woke) and due to some fuck-up with the timeline, an alternate version of her was created, who killed herself but then got brought back to life after she was dead and in her grave for three years and here she is.

Dear Everyone, I would like you to meet my cousin, Sarabeth, whom we lovingly call SB, and doesn't she look the spitting image of Peypey when she was her age?

All things considered, I decided to go with the last. Anyway, I now had two sisters, which was not a bad thing other than in terms of living accommodations. I volunteered to stay in the guest room, at least for the time being, as I felt it best for Peypey and Sarabeth to try and bond. It was, after all, a strange situation, but I thought that Sarabeth might benefit from her older self's experience. The fact was that I was still very concerned for her, since she had taken her own life, and I needed to make certain there was never another attempt.

After an intensive week of hugs and tears and coddling, Mom enrolled Sarabeth at a different school than she had attended before. According to the story, Sarabeth Herron's parents were killed in a car crash five months ago, and so she came to live with her aunt, uncle, and cousins. Peyton was the one to come up with a birth certificate. She actually went back in time, got a blank form, typed everything out, signed all the names, and left it on one of the intake workers' desks at some hospital in North Dakota. Then she time-traveled forward and placed records in the local elementary, junior high, and high schools. As an added touch, she even left a photo of Sarabeth with the printer for the Red River High School yearbook in Grand Forks. Thus did Sarabeth Herron enter her new school as a sophomore.

As there were going to be questions about her resemblance to Peyton from those in the neighborhood, we did our best to change her appearance. We lightened her hair and then added streaks of pink and blue, gave her a goth make-up look with heavy eyeliner, a nose ring that didn't actually go *through* her nose, and a heavy sterling cross that hung from a silver chain around her neck. She wanted to get her tongue pierced, but Mom put her foot down on that one. Her clothes were all black, including her studded leather jacket, leather mini-skirt, and thigh-high leather boots with chains. She was badass to the T. I coached her on the persona she was to display. She embraced it as though it were her first acting role. We made certain that the school she would attend, while private, had no strict dress code.

"How did it go?" I asked as Sarabeth walked through the front door when she came back home from her first day at school.

"It was wicked," she said, in an expressionless tone. "Mrs. Halston, the gym teacher, said I should try out for the cheerleading squad. 'Are any of the players going to die?' I asked without expression. 'I hope not,' she said. 'Then what would I be cheering for?' I replied. Oh my God!" Sarabeth exclaimed, breaking character. "You should have seen her expression!"

"Wednesday Addams would be proud," I assured her. "Look," I went on as my tone became serious, "we need to talk."

Sarabeth's eyebrows raised as she looked at me, and then she walked over and plunked herself onto the sofa. I sat down beside her and turned to her.

"What's up?" she asked.

"I know you want to be here," I said, "I mean in the here and now—but I don't want to lose you a second time."

"I'm *not* going to kill myself again," came the reply. "I swear!"

"It's not that," I said.

"What then?"

"I ran into Daisy McKenzie at Giselle's. There was a casual exchange, and then she asked about you."

"Why would she?" Sarabeth replied. "I'm supposed to be dead."

"That's just it," I said. "It wasn't like, 'I'm still so shocked about her. It was like she knew you'd been brought back from the dead, which means…"

"She's with Theresa!" Sarabeth exclaimed.

"I picked up on that, too," I said. "I asked her if she's seen her and, her whole expression went pale, and then she suddenly excused herself. She promised her mother. She needed to get home. I walked outside to follow her, and she disappeared, meaning she got phased out of there by Theresa, who wasn't anywhere in sight. By the way, for the past three years, Theresa's been promoting herself as Rainbow Girl."

"Really!" Sarabeth said. Then, with a sudden thought, she added, "But wait! How could she have? I mean, neither Peyton nor Demi can remote phase anyone," she replied. "Can they?"

"They can't," I said and then paused with a wrinkled brow. "Demi?" I repeated with the question nearly glued to my lips.

"That's what I've been calling her," Sarabeth replied with a shrug of her shoulders, "at least in my head. Demi for *other dimensional*. We need to tell Peyton," she insisted.

"I already have," I said, "and we both agreed that it's not safe for you here."

"So, where am I supposed to go?" she asked.

"To *Demi's* dimension," I answered. The name came out a bit hard for me on my first try.

"And you want me to go there all by myself?" she replied. "No way!"

"Do you actually think for one instant that I would ever leave you out of my sight?" I told her.

"So, you'll come with?" she asked.

"Of course, I will," I said. "We're sisters!"

A weird thought raced through my mind at that moment that if Sarabeth had had a tail, it would have been wagging left and right just then. But that would have been in another life!

She looked at me with tear-filled eyes. "I take back every time I ever called you Dunkhead!" she said.

I smiled and kissed her on her forehead. Then she leaned into me and hugged me, and I gently hugged her back.

"You know," I said softly, "Demi has a mom and dad who look and sound just like ours."

My dear, sweet sister pulled back just a bit to look into my eyes. Hers had grown wet just a bit. "Really?" she said.

"And Demi said that her brother is head over heels in love with me."

"That's not so special," she said.

"Why's that?" I asked.

"There isn't a guy on earth who wouldn't fall in love with you," she replied.

I was beyond words as her tears reflected in my eyes. Dear Peyton. Dear Sarabeth. Dear whatever your name is or was or might ever be, you have always been the best part of my life.

CHAPTER XLIII

Ophelia

> *From the Original Timeline*
> *In the Alternate Reality*
> *On Earth II*
> *Earth-Date:2029*

It was indeed serendipitous that Payton, after her encounter with the Khattaaara of what I will refer to as Earth III universe, managed to stumble on another quantum *seed* to herself become Quantum *Girl—a* Quantum Girl. This was a different version of the Payton Herron that I had known, who had become a surrogate sister to me when my Peyton had been killed. We—the other one—had spent an entire month back in my Earth's past, where I helped her hone her abilities. But with time having been overwritten, this Payton had no memory of any of that, nor of any love affair with the Theresa of the Earth where I was from. Before her return from that other Earth with a seed in her head, I had thought that I would be trapped in this dimension forever. Now, it was just a matter of teaching the new dog, old tricks—so to speak.

Meanwhile, my relationship with Liam was almost back where it had been, for despite that he remembered nothing of what had transpired between us in the original past, there was still a great attraction that seemed to have trumped the recalibration of time.

It had struck me with a sense of terror, though, what might have been the result of any time reset on my world. Even if I were able to teach *this* Payton how to use her powers, how could she find my dimension out of the infinite number of those that existed? *My* Peyton had been given her quantum seed when she was fourteen years old. The Payton Herron of this world was four years older and, I sensed, a bit more hesitant to run the gauntlet to transform into the heroine she was capable of becoming; all this while the government had just been overrun by a militant socialist regime.

Strange, how people take for granted their freedoms until they are taken away. It appeared that we would now have a champion able to defeat the invading forces in the shape of Quantum Girl, though my hopes were short-lived. I was able to teach her how to create her costume, though she insisted on a nearly floor-length cape and a mask rather than a cowl. But it was when I was attempting to instruct her on how to phase that it happened. She vanished. Five minutes passed, then ten, then an hour, then a day, and then she was just gone. The fact was that she had a green quantum seed rather than a violet one, and we surmised (correctly, as it later turned out) that the two might not behave exactly the same way.

At first, Liam blamed me. It was our first knock-down, drag-out fight.

"Why the fuck did you need to try and turn her into a copy of your superhero sister?" he railed.

"Because before she *was* one!" I shouted back. "Do you think I *wanted* this? She may not have been my sister, but we were best friends!"

"Gods know where she is!" he went on.

"Well, maybe *Gods* will tell you!" I said. I looked at him as tears came to my eyes. "I didn't want this to happen," I wept at him, "but the fact is that it would have, sooner or later, with or without me. She has powers that are all new to her." I paused a moment, wiped away my tears, and then said, "I don't want to argue. It's not helping anything."

My words may as well have fallen on deaf ears, for at that same moment, a group of soldiers burst through the front door. These were the Marks, as they called themselves—Marxists—traitors to the

American nation who had taken up arms with the Soviet invasion force. Each wore dark green combat uniforms with red armbands, upon which was emblazoned the hammer and sickle emblem. All in all, at least in my mind, they resembled the Nazis that in this world had never come to exist. No doubt all of them had been awarded special privileges—better food, probably women, perhaps even the wives and daughters of the former *working class*. The promise of social justice that Vladimir Ilyich Lenin had promised his people had soon been shown to be little more than wolves in power, leading a nation of sheep. The end result of the break-in was tragic. Liam's dad put up a fight and was shot and killed, as was his mother, whose only crime was to scream out in anguish at the sudden and needless loss of her husband of twenty years. Two pools of blood beneath them bore proof to the fact that what had been done to them was irrevocable. It was frightening overall. First, we were captured. Then we were let go. Now we were taken into custody again. It was like when the Poles were first placed in the Warsaw ghetto and then taken to the Treblinka killing camp. *Is this our fate?* I wondered. My heart began to pound, and I held Jordan close against my breast.

The three of us were forced out of the house at gunpoint and loaded into a military truck that contained some twenty other men, women, and children. We were not allowed to take any belongings, other than my change bag—which was thoroughly searched—and formula that I had to beg them to allow.

The trip lasted roughly an hour and a half—our destination: Edwards Air Force Base, now under Soviet command. We were disembarked in a very roughshod manner. There were other transport vehicles—perhaps fifty from my count—with similar numbers of prisoners, as it were—as *we* were —and more trucks arriving every few minutes. None of those in charge, the vast majority of whom were Asian and—as it later turned out—Chinese, would answer any of our questions. Many of the detainees were in tears, especially the women and children as we were all herded into one group. One

234

thirtyish woman who had fled, screaming in terror, holding her two-year-old son, was brought back, forced to her knees in clear sight of everyone, and despite her pleas for mercy, was forced to watch in horror as one guard pulled her child from her arms and then shot him in the head. The gun was then aimed at her, and the trigger pulled a second time. No one—not a single prisoner—broke rank after that. All that came as a result was a deafening silence.

Liam and I wound up separated from each other, as the throng of prisoners was segregated by sex. We were then told to strip as we had done when we had emerged from the shelter, although this time we were deloused with white powder and then sat down, one by one, to have our heads shaved. Several of the younger women, including young teenagers, were taken off by Russian guards, myself among them. The one who took me gripped my right forearm and forced me into a small, closed office, whereupon he shut the door.

"Don't hurt my baby," I begged.

"Don't struggle then," he said back. "Set her on the floor and then turn around, spread your legs, and put your hands up against the wall."

Reluctantly, I obeyed. Disgustingly, I was raped anally. It was humiliating and painful beyond belief. There was nothing gentle about it. The man just ripped into me. But as excruciating as it was, I refused to make the slightest sound that would have allowed him to believe that he had triumphed over me. I'm sure that just infuriated him, as with each thrust, his attack became more and more brutal, but I didn't care. Men rape women, not for sexual pleasure, but for the sense of power that it gives them. *Let him have his way with me*, I thought to myself, *but I'll be damned if I'll give him the slightest bit of satisfaction.* The act went on for all of a minute, though at the time it seemed like forever. When he had finished, he merely said, "Get back to the others after I leave." When he got to the door, he turned his head slightly and added, "If you say anything about what just happened, I'll kill her," and he stared down at Jordan. Then he faced

235

the door again and left.

As soon as the door had shut, I rushed over to Jordan, who had been crying ever since I had set her down. I picked her up and cradled her in my arms. "There, now," I said. "Momma's here. Momma's gonna protect you no matter what it takes." My words, though, held no real meaning. I was as helpless as she was. There was no way to contact Liam and, even if I could, what good would that have done? He was as much a prisoner as I was. And Payton, with all of her newfound powers, was nowhere to be seen.

Once outside, I felt a chill as the weather began to change. It was late afternoon, and a storm front was starting to advance. There were goosebumps on my flesh everywhere—probably the same with all the rest of us that were there. I took out some diapers from my change bag and wrapped up Jordan with them as best I could. Then I placed her in it. Looking around, I saw some of the other girls who had also just been raped. Most of them were in tears, searching for their loved ones. One girl, who must have been all of twelve years old, had dropped to her knees and was tearing at her hair. Another girl charged at one of the guards, pulled his gun from his holster, and then, holding it out, gripping it with both hands, turning in every direction, screamed, wept, "Stay away from me! Stay the fuck away from me!" Disregarding her threat, five or six of the Chinese guards pulled out their pistols and shot her. It was as though I could see it all in slow motion as the bullets entered her naked body, one by one, blood spurting out of the holes they had made. The girl stood for a moment, half in disbelief. Blood poured from her mouth. Urine streamed from between her legs down onto the thirsty soil that would eventually consume her flesh. Then she dropped down to the ground like a ragdoll, her eyes open and staring at the thoughtless sky.

A gust of chill wind shocked the terror from my bones. *How could this have happened?* I wondered. *Even if New York had been destroyed, why would America just surrender? This America also had nuclear capabilities. The news reported that the United States had launched a counterattack and that one missile had apparently gotten through to Soviet airspace and then mysteriously fell off the radar. But one doesn't surrender when there's a stalemate.* And then I saw her. She was in a newsreel that showed President Harris when Harris signed the Treaty of Surrender. She was only visible for a moment but bore an uncanny resemblance to Peyton. But she *wasn't* Peyton. She wasn't *either* of them. There was a difference. It was something about her eyes that I couldn't quite put my finger on at the time. She was dressed in an officer's uniform. And then it struck me. This was the same *woman* that Payton said had hurled her into the other dimension. This was another Khattaaara, born in a parallel universe who, like Thara-Klo and Dhraaal, had lived through a vast eternity with the aid of a quantum seed! This was how the Russians were able to conquer the world, but what chance did the world have against a villainous Quantum Girl?

CHAPTER XLIV

Theresa

> *From the Original Timeline*
> *In the Alternate Reality*
> *On Earth I*
> *Earth-Date:2025*

My house wasn't anything near what the McKenzies' house was like. Theirs was a mansion compared to mine, but the fact remained that my house was my own, though I had to continue to pay all the bills if I wanted to keep it.

Daisy was a bit apprehensive as we Ubered to my place. Her mother had insisted since the walk was quite a distance from their home. As we drove through my neighborhood, I could tell that it really wasn't what she was used to. Worse, when we got out of the car, my next-door neighbor, an often-drunk man in his forties, sitting on his front porch in a tank-top undershirt, beer in his hand, called out, *"¡Mamasitas! ¡Vengan para aqui!"*

"!Déjenos en paz!" I shouted back.

"What did he say?" Daisy asked.

"He wanted us to come over there," I said. "I told him to leave us alone. He says the same thing every time he sees me. Generally, I tell him to go fuck off, but this time I was trying to be polite, seeing that I was with you and I didn't know if you could speak Spanish or not."

"I'm not very good at foreign languages," Daisy admitted.

"Yes," I said, "but you are a girl of many tongues."

Daisy giggled. She was no innocent—at least not when it came to sex. Amazing how things have changed. My mother told me that she was a virgin until her wedding night. I guess things were different

238

back then. As for the house itself, there was an unvoiced, "Ewww!" from her, even though this was all well-manicured in this other version of my world. Daisy was used to finer things. There was still food in the fridge, but we decided to order out pizza. Her half was mushrooms and pineapple (ugh!). Mine was pepperoni and sausage (yum!). After it arrived, she insisted that I try a bit of hers. Despite how disgusting I assumed it was going to be, I figured that if I ever wanted to eat anything other than pizza again, I ought to bite, chew, and swallow the bullet. Looking back, it wasn't *awful*. It was just *wrong*. Trying to get her to take a bite of mine, though, was somehow sacrilegious from her point of view. As it turned out, she was a veg-head. I told her as much, to which she called me a corpse muncher. I wasn't quite sure what that meant, as it sounded kind of zombie, but I figured if it was anything close to muff diving, it was definitely me.

Before the pizza's arrival, I gave her the full tour of the house, though there wasn't a whole lot of tour to be had. Afterward, I sat her down on the sofa in the living room and told her not to be scared.

"Scared of what?" she asked. "Why should I be scared?" She glanced nervously around. "No one's going to jump out and kill me, are they?"

"That's not what I meant?" I replied. "I just want to show you some stuff that's kind of... unusual."

"Okay," she said, calming down.

"Just watch," I told her.

Then I caused the coffee table to lift several feet off the floor. At first, she seemed to think that it was some sort of parlor trick I had arranged and that there were wires attached. When at last she was convinced that there weren't any, having gotten up and run her arms under and above it, she turned to me with a vacant stare.

"How are you able to do that?" she asked.

"I'm not quite sure," I said. "You know that Peyton Herron chick?"

"The one with the sister?" she answered.

"Yeah," I said. "The one with her head stuck so far up her ass she can see her nose. I don't know how cuz my memory's sorta hazy, but she blasted some kind of energy light ray laser shit at me, and I guess I must have blacked out, cuz the next thing I remember is waking up in the hospital and there she was again, probably to finish the job, except—get this—*I* was able to blast *her*. Seriously, I don't know how, but suddenly I'm able to do all this weird shit like I've got superpowers."

Daisy stared at me with her mouth open. "No fucking way!" she replied. Then she paused, thinking, and then said, "Wait! Isn't she the one who killed herself last year?"

"So it seems, but that's in the new timeline," I said.

"The huh what?" she replied, her jaw dropping.

"That's what her sister said," I told her, "when I literally bumped into her at school last week."

Daisy just threw up her hands. "I'm totally lost," she said.

"I'm not clear on a lot of this myself," I replied, "but here, let me show you what else I can do. Grab hold of me. Tight."

She drew up close and put her hands around my waist. I did the same to her. God, it felt good! Then I closed my eyes and focused on six hours from then. The room we were in grew dark. Daisy laid her head against my shoulder.

"What's going on?" she asked.

We could hear noises from another part of the house. I let go of her, and she did the same with me.

"Shhh," I said, lifting a finger to my lips. Then I led her to my bedroom, which was where the noises were coming from.

Silently, I opened the door a crack—just enough for us to see inside. The room was lit by two lavender-scented candles that my mom had given me on my last birthday as part of my present. On the bed, though, were Daisy and I, naked and making love.

"How can that be?" Daisy whispered. "We're *here*. How can we be *there*, too?"

"Because this is six hours into the future," I whispered back.

"So, six hours from now, we're going to be in bed tribbing?"

"Yes," I said.

"And everything else?" she went on.

"Damn straight," I replied.

"You do know that's an oxymoron," she said, glancing at me—the me next to her. "All of this is fucking insane! What happens if we go in there now?"

"Don't know," I admitted, as I moved my hand to the doorknob to push the door open more.

"No!" Daisy whispered, clutching my hand in hers, trying to prevent me from going in.

"Don't you like what we're doing in there?" I whispered.

"Yes, but..."

"The two of us can join in."

"With ourselves? That's insane!"

"Insanity," I said, "is when you try something twice and expect a different result. We haven't tried this yet." That said, I pushed open the door, took Daisy by the hand, and gently urged her inside the room. Immediately, the other us stopped what they were doing, sat up in bed, and looked in our direction.

"We were expecting you," the other me said.

"Don't just stand there," the other Daisy said. "Get undressed."

What made me throb was when the other Daisy rose from the bed and went over to my Daisy, kissed her, and put her hand up her skirt. That was how it began. After all was done, the two of us went back in time to do it again with the two of us from the past.

"Holy shit!" Daisy said as she stretched out naked on the bed after our earlier selves had left. "That was so fucking incredible!"

"Totally," I said in complete agreement as I kissed her gently on her lips. "So, what did it feel like to make love to yourself?"

"Different," she replied. "Unexpected. Wanting to do it again."

She smiled and wrapped her arms around me, running her fingers down my spine. I inhaled her breath like it made her a part of me. It amazed me how I could have found her—my one true and forever love. This was my definition of Heaven, little realizing how much all that I had shown Daisy, meaning my powers and all that could be accomplished with them, had corrupted her and made her more and more like the person I no longer wanted to be.

CHAPTER XLV

Payton

> *From the Alternate Timeline*
> *In the Alternate Reality*
> *On Earth III*
> *Earth-Date:2029*

My powers honed with the help of Ophelia, I reappeared as Quantum Girl in the house where Liam and Li lived. It was Li who first noticed me and appeared to turn and call to her brother, but it was at that moment that time began to slow down. Her words became low-pitched and dragged their way through the air.

"Liam!" she said. "It's Khattaaara!"

And then something even more incredible happened. Time began to reverse, and I became incorporeal to the world I then observed. The sun and the moon ran their courses counterclockwise across the sky, again and again. Li and Liam appeared to scamper back and forth around the house, going upstairs and downstairs, indoors and out like an old silent movie that was being cranked backward at incredible speed. But it wasn't consistent. At times, it would almost slow to a stop, and at others, it became so fast that the two of them were just a blur. After roughly half an hour or so, I saw my former self appear and watched everything I had done before reenact itself in reverse to the point where Liam had aimed the weapon at me. Then he disappeared backward upstairs, after which my former self walked backward out the door. It then became a question as to whether or not to follow me out or else stay in the house and see what caused all of this. As I knew where I had been, I concluded that going back into a pitch-dark bathroom would have served no purpose, and so I decided to remain where I was.

Occasionally, I ventured outside. But then, things changed. There were people—apparently, neighbors who lived in the adjacent houses and down the block. I recognized some of them from when I was small. There was Mr. Edgemont, who had lived next door until he died when the car he was driving home from work was struck head-on by a drunk driver. And there was Scuffles, the Irish Setter that had run away from home when I was around ten, never to be seen again. But there were others; people I didn't recognize, I assume as a result of the differences between dimensions, just as there was Liam as Ophelia's brother in a world where a Peyton did not exist.

All of this was somewhat humorous in a way—to see people unmowing their lawns or taking their trash out of their garbage bins and bringing it back into their houses, not to mention the disgusting visuals of what happens when one unwalks a dog. Then, too, it was all very frightening since I had no control over this quantum ability, not knowing if it would ever stop so that time could move forward again. It was also very disturbing to hear voices in reverse, people breathing in their words, though, when it happened in sped-up time, it wound up sounding more like a swarm of bees.

The Mr. and Mrs. Herron of this dimension had already come back to life, though I had not witnessed them being killed, as it had happened outside, while I was in the house. But then, suddenly, I heard what sounded like explosions, and I rushed outdoors. Two Rendenaaarans hovered above the street just outside the house, battling each other. One was a male, who appeared, by human standards, to be about thirty years old, and the other was Khattaaara! The male, who at first appeared mortally wounded, healed, while blasts of energy flew back into Khattaaara, who had hurled them. Four other aliens then materialized midair out of nowhere. What happened next changed everything, at least for me.

Despite the disparity in our movements through time, Khattaaara saw me and caused time to stop. She looked at me as though she had seen a ghost. I had shed the Quantum Girl costume soon after I had arrived and appeared an almost mirror image of her, minus the tail[50]. I don't know what it was about the resemblance, but it appeared to frighten her. *"Twargraaag faaar jhaaax?"* she hissed at me. *"Twargraaag faaar jhaaax!"* I had no clue as to what that meant, although it was probably nothing good. And despite everyone and everything else being frozen in time, she hurled an energy blast at me. Instantly, though, the quantum seed in my head threw out a barrier to protect me. This only served to infuriate her, for her expression became painted with an almost hysterical anger. Blast after blast pummeled the force field around me without effect. Then, suddenly, she vanished from her perch in the air and appeared right in front of me. Her hands gripped my throat while her tail crept around me to my back and wrapped around my waist. I fought hard to break the stranglehold she had around my neck, struggling to breathe. There was such fury in her expression that her complexion turned blue. Then I felt a sharp, icy-cold prick to the middle of my spine, followed by unbearable pain. The world around me seemed to go dark. I wished with all my heart that I could just be somewhere else. And then everything went black.

---

[50] This apparently happened prior to my encounter with her at the movie theatre.

CHAPTER XLVI

Peyton

> *From the Original Timeline*
> *The One Who Stayed Behind*
> *In the Alternate Reality*
> *On Earth I*
> *Earth-Date:2029*

Payton and I phased back to what used to be the guest room (now my bedroom) in the middle of the night, whereupon I roused my other self, who lay immersed in dreams in a totally weird body posture, and all I could think was, *Is that how I look when I'm asleep?* I nudged her, but she just moaned and pulled the blanket over her head.

"What the fuck!" I said out loud, merged into her, and then sat up in bed and stared at Payton. "I was dreaming about having alien sex," I admitted.

"No shit," Payton replied. "How was it?"

"Pleasurable and disturbing at the same time," I replied. "I'm all me again, but there are some things best left unremembered." I shook my head to myself and then went on. "While we were gone, Phee and Sarabeth—that's younger me's new name—and I all decided that it would be best if you took Phee and Sarabeth to your dimension to protect her from Theresa. By the way, your new name is Demi, as in dimensional twin, for the sake of preventing confusion."

"Thanks so much," *Demi* offered with a twisted frown. "How about we refer to you as Reggie, for original?"

"Point taken," I said, "but you'll always be Payton to me."

"*Muchas gracias*," Payton replied.

I smiled and then asked, "You hungry?"

246

"Famished!" came the response as she phased into her street-clothes self.

Neither of us had much in the way of culinary skills, but the thirty-five-year-old Quantum Woman who had merged with me had learned a few tricks, and so I managed to pull together some blueberry crêpes with a powdered sugar topping, along with powdered hot chocolate that had to be mixed with boiling water. Payton contributed the heated water and cups and set the table. It was like an *Oh my God* thought from each of us when we took our first bites. It had been so long since we had eaten anything, and we both sat down to the breakfast that the Quantum Woman in me had allowed me to create. We were just about finished when Mom walked in wearing her robe.

"I get confused," she said. "Are you both my Peyton, or is one of you Other Dimensional Debbie?"

"Guilty," said Payton, raising her left hand, "though you're still sort of my other mother."

Mom, who had been standing behind her, bent down and kissed the top of her head. "You are so sweet," she said, "even though, as I understand, you are a lesbian."

"Mom!" I said through gritted teeth.

"I am *not* criticizing," she went on, placing her hands on Payton's shoulders, "but I'm sure there are some nice young men we could introduce her to so that she could be fruitful and multiply as the Lord intended."

"That is something to consider," Payton politely replied.

Mom looked down at her and then glared at me. "And Jesus said unto them, 'Because of your unbelief: for verily I say unto you, If ye have faith as a grain of mustard seed, ye shall say unto this mountain, *Remove hence to yonder place, and it shall remove, and nothing shall be impossible unto you.*'"

I shook my head. "We're eating blueberries, Mom."

"Don't you roll your eyes at me, young lady!" she replied. "You may have superpowers, but this girl knows what is best for her in the eyes of the Lord!" She paused and then looked down at Payton. "Don't you, dear?" she asked.

"Yes, Ma'am," Payton answered. "Come Sunday, I intend to go to church to try and meet some handsome young man that I can plan a future with."

Mom threw out her lower lip as she glared at me, just as Sarabeth sleepily walked in.

"What's going on?" she yawned.

"Your sister and I," she said, "were just having a little spiritual discussion. Nothing to worry your pretty little fourteen-year-old head about. Now, you go and wake your other sister and tell her to come down for breakfast. I swear, the girl would sleep until midnight if she didn't have to wake up to pee."

"Were you guys all talking about sex?" Sarabeth asked.

"We were talking about the Lord, Jesus Christ, not that it's any of your concern. Now, go wake up Ophelia before I'm forced to get a bucket of water."

"Yes, ma'am," Sarabeth replied and then left, grumbling, "Whenever anyone talks about anything interesting, I get left out! That is so unfair!"

CHAPTER XLVII

Khattaaara/Payton

> *Payton from the Original Timeline*
> *Sharing the Mind of Khattaaara*
> *In the Rewritten Timeline*
> *On Rendenaaar*
> *Trillions of Universes in the Past*

I was a fool. Perhaps that was just the fifteen-year-old part of me. *Had Khattaaara ever loved this synth in the other reality? Was I the one who had stepped on the butterfly and changed all that was meant to be? How could I ever know? How could what I had done ever be undone? Would the world I came from or Peyton's even exist after this?* These thoughts, though, did not cross my mind until after what was about to occur.

I was sitting on the sofa—or rather the Gaaalthaaaran equivalent of a sofa—next to Dargra-Tol, who gently stroked my cheek and stared into my eyes.

"What if something goes awry with it?" she asked with great concern in her voice.

"What dost thou mean?" I said.

"Well," she replied, "'tis in thy brain. What if it heateth up or starts to expand or explode?"

"Then I shall take it out," I replied.

"What if thou canst not?" she said as she looked at me as one might who thought there was a chance to lose their one great love in life.

"I can," I insisted.

"Show me," she said. Then she took both of my hands in hers and

249

brought them to her lips, whereupon she kissed them, never taking her eyes off mine.

Reluctantly, I shrugged and placed my hand up to my forehead, willing the stone to emerge. Then I took the small, white gem in one hand and placed it in the palm of the other, extending it to her to observe.

"See?" I said. "Thou needst not worry."

"But *thou* must!" she said, snatching it from my hand and putting it to her own forehead with a single move. Her eyes flashed a bright white light for an instant.

"How darest thou!" I shouted. "Thou art my slave—my property! Give it back at once!"

Dargra-Tol laughed, and her voice with resonated evil. "For a hundred cycles we have waited for such as this!" she boasted. "Now the power of the *Gaaalthaaara* is ours!"

"We gave you life!" I insisted.

"You gave us servitude and misery! Are any of us able to bear children? Nay! You cut off our *yaaarghig* so that we could not reproduce!"

"Not I," I protested.

"Not thou, but all the rest!" she proclaimed. "Can we seek out and find our own loves? Again, not so! We are bound to our owners, however repulsive they appear, condemned to die after but one cycle when our usefulness is done."

"I showed thee love!" I proclaimed.

"Thou showed me thy passion, nothing more! At first, thou left me much alone, but then, all at once, thou changed! Thou bedded me and commanded me to bed thee back! If there is anyone to blame, look thou in a reimager and then look behind thyself as well, for nothing is more true than that thou wast betrayed by thy *yaaargh*!"

And, with the sound of a *pop* in the vacant air, she vanished from the room.

What have I done? I thought to myself. *I have betrayed my own race! What now will become of my world?* And with such morose thoughts, I threw my head down on the sofa and wept out bitter tears.

CHAPTER XLVIII

Theresa

> *From the Original Timeline*
> *In the Alternate Reality*
> *On Earth I*
> *Earth-Date:2025*

Daisy McKenzie might have seemed like just another dumb blonde, but she had a knack for marketing—at least when it came to marketing *me*—plus, she was the shit when it came to all the social media crap that I was totally clueless about. And while Quantum Girl had remained in the shadows. I was bent on marketing myself as a superhero. It was the only way I knew to be able to make enough money to pay the bills. So, with that in mind, Rainbow Girl was about to enter the scene.

Daisy helped me after school every day, and then we continued to spend the rest of our time together. Her mother was totally clueless about our sexual relationship. She just seemed happy that her daughter, who had always been a loner, had finally found a friend. After a while, it was as though I had become an accepted part of the McKenzie family—so much so that when my birthday rolled around, I was treated to a surprise party at their home. Mr. and Mrs. McKenzie gave me a pair of diamond earrings, while Daisy gave me a small bottle of French perfume. Privately, later that night, she gave her*self* to me. Beyond all that, she helped me master my abilities—as many as I'd found I'd had—which I pretty much had down pat after a few months. There was time travel and energy blasts, teleportation, and resurrection.[51] I finally got teleportation to the point where I wouldn't materialize in the middle of walls or anything else solid, which was a huge relief. And I could make objects and people disappear, though I had no idea what actually happened to them and was never able to bring anything or anyone back. I could do the costume bit, even when I was totally naked. That was cool—to be able to undress in the blink of an eye—well, cool when Daisy and I were alone. There was also invisibility, especially great for going into the girls' shower and seeing them all naked—not that I would ever have done anything like that—or admit it to Daisy. Oh, and I could also freeze time.

Being a hero, though, is not as easy as it sounds. It isn't just a matter of saving people; it's a matter of knowing where it is that people need to be saved and when. Daisy got her mother to buy her a police band radio so that we could listen in and find out where help was needed. My first *heroic* feat was a hostage situation at the Bank of America in Beverly Hills.

I teleported there, invisible, and scoped out what was going on. There were three armed men and twelve hostages, who were all face down on the floor. A thirteenth—a woman in her forties—lay on the floor with a bullet in her head. Apparently, she was the one who had pressed the button that activated the silent alarm and had been caught in the act. Another hostage was a pregnant woman that one of the bank robbers had brought to the window, holding a gun to her head, while on the phone with the cops outside, demanding a helicopter. The woman was justifiably terrified; so much so that her water broke.

"Excuse me," I said to the creep as I became visible. The man paid no attention. "Excuse me!" I shouted, at which point he turned in my direction.

"Who the fuck are *you*?" he yelled at me.

"Rainbow Girl," I replied.

---

[51] I desperately wanted to bring back my mom, but her body was in the reality that had been erased.

"Rainbow Girl?" the man laughed. "What, like some super dyke?"

"Could be," I said in a firm voice. "And you need to put down the gun."

"Fuck you!" the man replied and then aimed his gun at me and fired. When nothing happened, he shot again and again until he had emptied his clip.

"I asked politely," I said. "What you did was *not* polite," and with that, I made him go away. Then I turned to the other two, who looked like they had seen a ghost, and nervously dropped their guns to the floor.

"Now, go outside," I said to them, "and turn yourselves in to the cops."

"Yes, ma'am," the two of them replied, virtually in unison. Then they both walked to the door and went outside with their hands up in the air.

Meanwhile, the pregnant woman, who was now in labor, began to collapse to the floor. Fortunately, I noticed as it was happening, teleported up to her, and caught her, gently laying her down.

"Somebody call 911," I shouted back at the others. Then I turned to the woman. "Are you all right?" I asked.

"Just scared," she replied. "I'm just seven and a half months. I don't want to lose my baby."

"The hell with the ambulance," I said. "Everything's going to be fine." I teleported her to the emergency room at Cedars Sinai and then looked around the room at the now-former hostages, most of whom had already gotten to their feet. They all just stood there and then began to applaud. One little girl came over to me, tears still in her eyes, and hugged me, and I thought to myself, *Maybe this superhero bit isn't so bad after all.* I had one more thing to do, though, and that was to bring the woman who'd been shot back to life. I reversed time around her so that the bullet flew backwards out of her head, which then healed.

"You're going to be all right," I assured her and then helped her up.

All the hostages looked totally shocked when she walked over to them. It was like "Holy crap!" and "Oh, my God!" and one of the women just fainted. When I exited along with everyone else, there were camera crews and reporters all around, pushing in against the line of cops. I suppose I should have stayed to answer questions, but I kind of got cold feet and just disappeared, which apparently was caught on camera and broadcast later, on the six o'clock news, before it went viral. People wanted to know who I was, where I was from, and how I came to have such incredible powers. The next day, Daisy put up Rainbow Girl accounts on every social media, which led to requests for appearances on television and on podcasts. I wanted to say yes to them all, but Daisy insisted I wait. I needed more heroic deeds under my belt first, she maintained. "Let them wonder. Let them beg," she said.

Over the course of the next few weeks, I had rescued twelve miners from a cave in Wyoming, teleported a small child out from a crevasse, caused by an earthquake in Peru, used a force field to stop a single-engine plane from crashing, and gotten down two small cats from a tree, although one of them scratched me and, sorry to say, is now adrift somewhere, frozen solid in outer space. In my defense, it was totally unintentional on my part—sort of a knee-jerk reaction. The little girl who owned them both wound up thinking that the second cat had just run away. All in all, though, Rainbow Girl was regarded as a hero absolutely everywhere except for on X, where Tucker Carlson had his doubts.

"Good evening, and welcome to Tucker Carlson. In a world now ravaged by skyrocketing inflation, where milk costs five dollars a gallon, and gas prices have soared in some places to more than ten, something incredible has happened. A comic book-like character has come to life, calling herself Rainbow Girl. After nearly eighty-seven years of make-believe super-powerful beings filling the comic book racks at newsstands and virtually dominating motion pictures, one has actually emerged for real with powers and abilities far beyond those of mortal men. Incredibly, just three weeks ago to the day, a fifteen-year-old high school student has suddenly become the most talked about person on the planet. Garbed in a truly amazing costume that appears to be a window into outer space, this caped crusader, the putative defender of the helpless and the weak, has just popped onto the scene, and when I say popped, I mean that quite literally, as she seemingly can materialize and dematerialize in an instant at will. No one knows, though, who Rainbow Girl really is, because she hides her identity behind a Zorro-like cowl. And yet, despite her anonymity, people everywhere are now regarding her as a superheroine. But the question is, why? As we speak, virtually the entire human population is experiencing a new pandemic that is now being referred to as Rainbow Girl Fever. Unlike COVID, however, RGF is not spread through the atmosphere or through human contact, but, rather, it infects unwary individuals through the Internet, and there appears to be no cure. Wherever there is technology, there is now Rainbow Girl adulation. Songs have been written about her. Websites have been dedicated *to* her. In Japan, girls and grown women have been seen wearing Rainbow Girl costumes. There is now even a church for her followers who have sanctified her as some sort of divine being. It's insane!" He laughed, and then his voice took on a serious tone. "But the question remains, just who *is* Rainbow Girl, *where* is she from, and *how* did she come upon all of her extraordinary abilities? Those are important questions, but no one appears to be asking them. Is she from Earth or from some other planet? Is she human? How many others like her *are* there? And is she actually good and kind, or is this just what she wants us to believe? Her powers are incredible—hovering mid-air, teleporting herself from one place to another, shooting out bolts of energy, and God knows what else. But her veneration doesn't end with the unwashed masses. It extends to celebrities, politicians, and even the leaders of countries. Her popularity has been so overwhelming worldwide that the United Nations just passed what they called the Rainbow Girl Resolution, which grants her world citizenship, meaning that she can travel anywhere on the planet without the need of a passport. To be clear, this is a high school-age student, and we have absolutely no idea *who* she really is or *what* her intentions are. Maybe Rainbow Girl is all she's cracked up to be—an altruistic superhero. But, seriously, how many teenagers are selfless and humanitarian? So, the million-dollar question remains, 'Is Rainbow Girl an angel come to save us or is she the devil in some cosmic disguise?' It would seem prudent to find out before we build altars to someone who, if ever enraged, could quite easily and single-handedly destroy us all."

That night after I went to sleep, I dreamt that I had materialized in Tucker Carlson's bedroom and, as with Charlie, I made him disappear. Coincidentally, the news the very next day reported that he had mysteriously vanished. I remember at the time hoping that maybe he had just retired and went off on a trip somewhere.

CHAPTER XLIX

Payton

> *From the Alternate Timeline*
> *In the Alternate Reality*
> *On Earth III*
> *Earth-Date:2089*

I pressed my eyelids tight for a moment and shook my head trying to clear it, still reeling from Khattaaara's sting. I was back in the house that Liam and Li had lived in but everything had changed. There were cobwebs in the corners and filth everywhere. Even in the air, particles of dust danced in the beam of light that poked through the yellowed newspaper sheets that were taped to the windows. An old woman sat in a chair in the living room. Her face was lined with age. Her hair was white, mixed with gray. Her arms and hands were withered, revealing their arteries and veins, and they trembled as she sat with her reading glasses, an open book on her lap. She stared up at me as she saw me appear just in front of her.

"You didn't come back," she said, her voice shaking out the words.

"Do I know you?" I asked.

"Of course, you know me," she replied. "You read me a story before you put me to bed."

"You're Li," I said, astonished.

"It is Miss Herron to you now," she replied, her whole body quivering from Parkinson's disease.

"What happened to Liam?" I asked.

Miss Herron smacked her lips. "He up and disappeared one day in a brilliant crimson light," she said. "Must have been more than eighty years ago. Been alone ever since. I used to go for walks—sometimes swim in the great pond. 'Course that was before I got the trembles. Can't do nothing much anymore."

"What year is it?" I asked.

She thought for a moment and then replied, "Twenty-one ought eight, no nine. Twenty-one ought nine. I'll be a hundred-ten years old next September. September the twenty-fourth. A hundred ten years old and I feel it in my bones. I miss my momma," she went on. "A girl needs her momma." She looked up at me. "Do you have a momma?" she asked.

"I do," I said. "Her name's Katherine."

The old woman smacked her lips again. "Same as mine," she replied. "I'm going to see her soon," she went on, "and Liam and Papa. I'm just sitting here waiting, reading *The Old Man and the Sea*. Must have read it near a thousand times. Just sitting here waiting for the Angel of Death to come get me. I saw a fallen angel once, a real bad one with pointed ears and a tail. It killed our parents—both of them—then it was just Liam and me by ourselves till Liam, dear Liam, was gone."

I bent down in front of her and took her hands in mine. "Do you want me to get you anything to eat or drink?" I asked.

"Not much of anything left," she said. "Used up most of what stock we had, and I'm too old and frail to go get any more. There was a lot once, though; Liam and I picked the grocery stores clean and brought it all here. But we were young back then."

"Let me see," I replied, and then I went to the kitchen. There was barely anything there. I phased from one abandoned grocery store to another until I found one hundreds of miles away that still had *some* things left. I filled up a bag with cans of soup and vegetables, fruit, and canned meats, along with some packets of cocoa, and then phased back and made her a hot meal. I pulled up a chair next to hers, fed it to her, and then wiped her mouth with a napkin when she was done.

"You're a Godsend," she said, and then she looked at me and asked, "How is it that you haven't aged?"

"Because I've traveled through time," I replied.

"I forget your name," she said as she looked at me with tired eyes.

"It's Payton," I reminded her.

"Yes," she said. "Payton." She paused and then stared out into space. "I knew a Payton once. She was like a big sister to me, but then she went away." She looked at me again. "I learned to love her, you know. Liam did, too, but then she left us to fend for ourselves."

And with those words, her head sank down. She never saw her hundredth year, and I never saw the agony she must have felt toward the end of her life. But perhaps this was something that could be undone. Those were my thoughts as I buried her in the backyard. This was the end of her journey through time. *Perhaps not, though,* I thought to myself. *Perhaps there was another way.* And so. I decided to go back into the past and change the way that things were, or, at the very least, I would try.

CHAPTER L

Khattaaara
(from Liam and Li's Dimension)

From the Original Timeline
In the Alternate Reality
On Earth II
Earth-Date:2029

It was curious how weak the earthlings were, regardless of which dimension their species chose to infest—but their defeat was inevitable! It was indeed a shame that I had only been able to bring six of my kind with me and that they eventually met their fate, sadly by my hand. As for Rendenaaar, despite its glory, it had succumbed to the inevitable cycle of self-annihilation, which caused me no small sense of grief. Yet there I was among a primitive civilization, standing alone as their god. It was the conversion chambers on the planet's moon, created by Shaaanchor, that allowed me to singlehandedly repopulate my species. It was, however, small consolation for all the Gaaalthaaaran souls that had been lost. The process involved altering the human genetic code—manipulating their DNA into TDNA with specifically encoded instructions.[52] The sad fact was, though, that the experiment had failed on the Earth in our dimension. Our plan had been to abduct the humans in small numbers until we built up a sufficient population to overwhelm those that remained. The humans, however, had fought us at every turn until there were hardly any of them left. Here on *this* Earth, I decided that the best course of conquest would be through infiltration rather

---

[52] TDNA or triple-stranded deoxyribonucleic acid was the basis for all life on Rendenaaar, consisting of three polynucleotide chains to form a triple helix.

than a direct attack. To that end, I had chosen to assume a human identity in the United States Space Force under the name Tara Hall—Lt. Comm. Tara Hall, to be precise.

My only hindrance was that I could not use sex as a ploy in order to advance my infiltration in that my anatomy was significantly different from that of the *human* creatures.[53] It became even more problematic when I was assigned the same quarters as a female lieutenant, who had the misfortune of walking in on me when I had just emerged naked from the shower. However, one sting from my *yaaargh* to the back of her neck caused her to collapse onto the floor and go into cardiac arrest. After listening to her make all sorts of gasping noises, watching her as she grasped her throat with one hand and reached toward me with the other, I calmly attended to my makeup and climbed back into my uniform. That done, having bent down to assure myself that all life had fled her, I went to the door, feigned both agitation and concern, and called for help. A bucket brigade of military personnel rushed in, to no avail. Her death was later attributed to a congenital heart condition.

In retrospect, it was probably a poor decision on my part to have killed Dhraaal back on the other Earth, but he had become such a fucking knot in the *yaaargh*. He expressed his *grave* concern about what he called genocide, and suggested that we instead resurrect the corpses of those already dead from human cemeteries, which would not only have been laborious but disgusting.

"And where would we all live?" I asked him. "This planet is not able to support the populations of two worlds. Besides, the humans would not consent to live with us side by side, nor would we, Gaaalthaaarans, willingly coexist with the humans."

Still, he fought me as I tried to eliminate all of the subversives in the human population. I then began killing innocents just to spite him.

---

[53] I found it laughably hypocritical, to say the least, that these war-incessant beings should label themselves with a word that their language defined as synonymous with kindness and peace.

Scorning my action, he struck at me with a barrage of force beams. That in turn caused my anger to rise to heights it had never known, as my half-brother with whom I grew up—my husband who had bedded me and impregnated me with our Thara-Klo—had then tried to murder me! *Fool!* I thought to myself. *Does he not know the power of the mother stone?* Add to the fact that very same morning I had learned that he had been having an affair with Shaaalra, who I thought was my best friend, having grown up with her on Rendenaaar. And with those thoughts and seething anger, I wished him into nonexistence, and he was gone. I determined that I would take care of Shaaalra later as the opportunity arose. How sad that I had passed through a trillion universes only to find betrayal so near to our journey's end. It was unfortunate, and the result of my heated emotions at the time, that I failed to consider that the god-stone in his head had survived. But in my defense, it was at that precise moment that a dozen Blackhawk helicopters had converged from all directions to turn my attention. Those inside did not know the power of the mother stone either.

As for the Soviet invasion, that was merely a smokescreen for what was to come next. It was I who had teleported a Soviet plane equipped with an atom bomb above Manhattan and then caused it to drop and detonate. The Pentagon responded in kind with a counterattack on Moscow, but I thwarted their efforts, destroying all of the planes they had sent. It is amazing how easily jet fuel can explode when met with a small quantum blast. Meanwhile, the public had been told that the failure of the retaliation had been due to ground-based intercept missiles deployed skyward from Russian soil. Regardless that the Soviet leaders had nothing to do with the attack, they took the opportunity to launch a full-scale invasion of America. After all, the Cold War had waged on ever since Lenin had taken power over a century before. Furthermore, after the Radical Left Congress, a few short years before, had succumbed to the pressure of the ADC,[54] its members had banned all gun ownership and defunded both the military and the police to the point where they were powerless to stem the invasion. As a result, the incursion lasted a mere six days. After that, the hammer and sickle replaced the stars and stripes as the symbol of America and triumphantly flew from the Capitol's mast.

Meanwhile, unbeknownst to the rest of the world, laboratories in China were working day and night at my behest to produce a virus that would transform the human genome into that of Gaaalthaaarans, so that our once-great civilization would live again.

Li Chang Shu was the lead scientist on what had been called the Metamorphosis Project.[55] The lab he headed was located in Zhengzhou, one of China's larger cities. Li had three daughters in their early twenties named Jiayi, Meilin, and Zhenzhen,[56] who were each persuaded to participate in the experiment with the understanding that in doing so they would all be accorded high-ranking positions in the new world order that was soon to emerge.

As the virus was only transmissible through bodily fluids, a syringe was placed in one nostril of each of the subjects, the contents of which were then released into their sinus cavities. After a five-day period of apparent inactivity, the subjects began to exhibit the first signs that a transformation was taking place. Similar to the case studies in the lunar lab on the human abductees in the other dimension, all three women collapsed, experienced fever, then chills, and then were rendered unconscious. Metamorphosis completed within a matter of hours, after which the subjects awakened. Meilin was the first to open her eyes.

"How do you feel?" I asked her in her native tongue.

The new Gaaalthaaaran propped herself up on her elbows and

---

[54] Short for the American Disarmament Coalition, the ADC was a militant, underground group formed by "Hanoi" Jane Fonda in the early Seventies.

[55] The Chinese workers referred to it as 蛻變計劃–Tuìbiàn Jìhuà—literally meaning *The Transformation Plan*.

[56] Their actual names in Chinese being 嘉怡, 美琳, and 贞贞.

stared down at her two pairs of breasts. "My senses are heightened," she replied in Chinese. Then she glanced down even further at her naked self. "Where is my vagina?" she said with sudden concern.

I took hold of her newly acquired *yaaargh* and stimulated it sexually. Meilin moaned and then took hold of it herself as I released my grip. It was at that same moment that Li Chang Shu entered the room and walked up to me.

"The process is successful," he said. "My daughters can begin to spread the disease."

"I do not want it referred to as such," I said.

"Understood," came the reply, as his eyes focused curiously on his daughter.

I turned to see Meilin, now on her side, curled up in a ball, licking her newly-formed *naaahnra* at the end of her *yaaargh*, oblivious to the world. Such was the course for all of our kind when we first grow out our *yaaarghig*. I smiled to myself as I remembered the moment when such had happened to me. It was the *graaakaaath*—the awakening. *In just a matter of months,* I thought to myself, *all the denizens of this tiny speck will awaken as well. Then shall Rendenaaar be reborn.*

CHAPTER LI

Ophelia

> *From the Original Timeline*
> *In the Alternate Reality*
> *On Earth II*
> *Earth-Date:2029*

It was all so humiliating, having to stand naked at attention in the lines they had ordered us into, the men staring at us, all of them naked as well, with barometers of how much or how little they were turned on by the women—or by the men for those of them who were gay. A locker room stench pervaded the air from the unwashed masses mixed in with the rest. Most of the women used their hands and arms to cover up their dignity, but eventually, they would tire and relinquish themselves to the reality that their lives were over as they had come to know them, and what pride they had owned didn't matter much anymore.

An Asian man in a white smock began to look us over. He appeared to be in his fifties and wore wire-rimmed glasses that he would peer over every time he paused for a closer inspection of one or another of us. Five women were culled from the formation and ordered to one side. Each was young and pretty. I was among them and, although I hadn't noticed beforehand, Claire had also been chosen. The remaining three were young women I had never seen before. One was Hispanic, and the other two were black. I was the only one with a child.

As the phalanx of naked women was eased into a loose gathering, the five of us were herded into the back of another military truck and driven off for what felt like several hours. Claire sat opposite me, staring at me, boring holes in me like I was on the receiving end of a laser beam. No one said a word. The only sounds came from the vehicle's engine and an occasional car passing us by. It was Claire who finally broke the awkward silence.

"Do you know why I called it quits?" she asked in grating tones.

"Liam said it was because of stress," I replied, "because of all that's been going on."

"Yes, stress," she said with both agitation and anger in her voice, " but not because of all of this," and she glanced around. "Liam talks in his sleep, and every word he said was about *you*! Ophelia this. Ophelia that. Phee Phee! Fuck!" Tears bled from her eyes. "Do you know how much I loved him? He was my life ever since we were children! I don't know what you did to *bewitch* him! What? Is your cunt so much better than mine?"

"I'm sorry," I said.

"I lost my baby!" she went on. "*Our* baby! I lost my life because of you! I lost everything!" She broke down into an ocean of tears. "I hate you!" she muttered through it all. "You stole it all away!"

The other girls glared at me. The one who sat beside Claire tried to take her hand to comfort her, but Claire pulled it away. For the next hour or so, there was just silence again until the truck finally came to a halt.

When the canvas at the rear of the truck was pulled back, we found ourselves inside the barbed wire fence of what turned out to be the Central California Women's Facility in Chowchilla. We were marched out and led to the medical section, where we were sat down and told to wait. In a short while, a female doctor or technician entered the room with a small aluminum case that she placed down on one table, and which, upon opening, revealed five syringes. A moment later, a middle-aged Asian man, similarly attired, entered and went over to her. One by one, we were ordered to stand up and go to the chair that was beside the table and sit down, and, one by one, the woman had us tilt our heads back as she pushed the fluids from the syringes into our nostrils. We submitted without a word. There was nothing else we *could* do. The three armed guards in the room were reason enough to obey. After all five of us had gone through the procedure, the woman turned to the man.

"What about the infant?" she asked.

"No," the man replied. "Not yet."

Five days passed without incident. We were housed in a small dorm with six bunk beds— forced to remain naked; at the time, I didn't understand why, but I was given diapers and wipes and baby food and even clothes for Jordan. There were three meals a day, and we were allowed to mingle with the general, orange-suited population. One of the black women in my group began a *friendship* with an eighteen-year-old, somewhat petite brunette, with whom on occasion she would sneak a kiss or one of them would finger the other's vagina and then bring her fingers to her lips. When the behavior was finally noticed, the girl was removed and placed with us. That was on the third day. None of us was allowed to mix with the general population after that.

Our own group's number, changed as it was, there was nothing then to stop Deja (that was the black woman, twenty-five years old, from my best guess) and Zoë (the eighteen-year-old white girl) from continuing their romantic endeavors. Cameras were positioned overhead—baseball-sized gray globes—but they didn't care. It only bothered them (and the rest of us) when using the toilet. I mean, it wasn't just an invasion of privacy; it was embarrassing, but we had no choice. And from the "Zoë Induction Moment," as Claire referred to it, we were all confined to our dorm. Our food was brought to us. Our group was only allowed one hour a day by ourselves in the courtyard, and this being February in Southern California, it was cold and often poured down rain. Oddly enough, though, despite that we were all still naked, none of us, other than Jordan, whom I kept bundled up and covered, were bothered by the frigid air. I presume in retrospect that it was from whatever it was that they dripped up our noses, but at the time, none of us wondered; none of us realized how cold it really was. My concern, though, was for Jordan, thinking she might be ill as she shivered from the cold I couldn't feel. She was not ill, of course. The change was in us. But the wet outside was still a bitch.

I was alone throughout it all. First Deja and her lover, Zoë, and then Nia (that was the other black woman), and Grace (the Asian woman) all took Claire's side, so it was just Jordan and me against the world, so to speak. The hatred shown toward me was so obvious and intense that when I would quietly sing a lullaby to Jordan at night, there were grumbles all around and I was told to shut up. Whenever *that* happened, Claire just smiled to herself.

None of us knew how long our confinement was to go on. I worried about Liam. I prayed that he was all right. In bed before I would fall asleep, I would pray for Mom and Dad. As for Payton, she now had her powers and was able to use them as best as I had been able to teach her. All I could think was, *She'll find us. She'll rescue us. Everything will be all right in the end.* If only she could find *my* Peyton. Two Quantum Girls might be able to change this godforsaken world.

It was on the morning of the fifth day that Deja collapsed. Two of the medical staff immediately placed her on her cot and then left the room. It was Zoë who first took umbrage with their abandonment of her.

"Hey!" she called out after them through the closed door. She went to it and began banging the heels of her fists against it, but there was no response. No one answered. No one came. Then she rushed over to Deja's bunk, which was one of the lower ones, sat down on the edge, facing her, and began to gently stroke Deja's cheek. Her hand then went to the woman's forehead. Zoë turned to the rest of us. "She's burning up!" she cried out. It was Nia who rushed to the sink, wet a small towel, and brought it to Zoë to place on Deja's brow. There was nothing more that could be done.

Roughly two hours later, the same thing happened to Grace. Then it was Nia. Then me. Thank God, I wasn't holding Jordan at the time. There were bits of consciousness after that, combined with brief moments of excruciating pain, but afterward, when I finally woke up, I could remember nothing more than that.

CHAPTER LII

Peyton

From the Original Timeline
In the Alternate Reality
On Earth I
Earth-Date:2029

Beyond the fact that I was Quantum Girl, I was also human. I had had no real life for the past three years, ever since the war—or whatever one wanted to call it—took place outside our home. But I tried. I wore the same disguise I had worn when I had become Khattaaara and took on my position as head of Quantech with a black pageboy wig as the image of sophistication—as the femme fatale that I pretend to be from my stilettos on up. As far as my sex life went, there was Connor Manes, an up-and-coming race car driver whom I had met at a charity fundraiser after I *accidentally* spilled a drink on him. My bad.

Every few days or so, I would make it a point to phase in to see Mom and Dad and Phee and young Peyton, now known as Sarabeth. I found it quietly amusing to see my younger self in her blonde goth look, but besides the age difference, between that and my Suicide Girl façade, no one would have ever guessed that we *were* or *had been* one and the same. I must admit, though, that it was a strange feeling to actually get to know my younger self. With the added experience of years, it was difficult for me to fathom how I had arrived at where I was, but I suppose the quantum seed had a lot to do with who I had become. Sarabeth, while kind beyond words, remained somewhat introverted and emotionally vulnerable. Regardless, absent the quantum seed, she was an incredibly sweet

271

girl, and I welcomed her presence in this time-overwritten world. She became the kid sister I never had, and I loved her so much.

The problem at hand, though, was the bully, Theresa, who had now been going by the name Rainbow Girl for what was getting on three years and had become the subject of public adulation, portraying herself as some great humanitarian. That would have all been good if she actually had changed, but what had happened at the cemetery three years before filled me with doubt and grave concern for Sarabeth. Whether she had suffered brain damage from what I as Khattaaara had done or if it had been the effects of the quantum seed in her head, she apparently possessed no memory of the incident, Furthermore, in the course of only six months, give or take, of her having come out as a supposed heroine, she had managed to interject herself into more than one hundred disasters, rescued countless individuals and, in doing so, ensconced herself into the hearts of millions. I myself, with years more experience under my belt, found it difficult to understand how she always managed to appear in moments of need. I briefly considered the possibility that she could have gone a day into the future and learned what was about to occur, but then, I would have felt the effect in each instance where the timeline had changed. Any challenges to her purposed sense of altruism, questioning the potential danger from such a powerful individual, however, were met with abject defiance from the Cancel Culture Left, especially considering that she had aligned herself with the LGBTQ community. Regardless, gay rights activists, politicians, and the leftist media championed Rainbow Girl's reputed acts of heroism as both Payton and I remained in the shadows. No one other than Tucker Carlson had questioned her sincerity, but he had soon mysteriously vanished from the face of the earth after questioning her moral fiber. Meanwhile, Rainbow Girl had managed to keep her alter ego secret, her face like mine hidden beneath her cowl. There was only one other person outside my small circle who knew Rainbow Girl's true identity, and that was Daisy McKenzie.

The early-blooming platinum blonde had been seen on at least two occasions going into gay girl teen clubs with Rainbow Girl. The crowd of girl wannabes was all ecstatic whenever there was a sighting of her, meaning Daisy. Every one of them wanted her autograph, wanted to touch her, and wanted to have sex with the girl who admittedly and literally was in bed with the superheroine. It was like in their heads they all thought, *I want to be the girl who fucked the girl who fucked Rainbow Girl* because that was as close as they could come—no pun intended. Thousands of notes were passed to her with phone numbers and Instagram addresses, Snapchat names, or X hashtags. They clamored around her. They wanted to *be* her, if only to be around their heroine. The Postal Service was inundated with letters and gifts for both of them from all around the world. Emails bottlenecked their ISP. Offers flooded in of every imaginable kind. By the end of 2025, Rainbow Girl and Daisy McKenzie statues began appearing on eBay, on Amazon, and in comic book stores. And yet, I remembered so clearly how, not so long before then, Theresa had resurrected Sarabeth just to murder her. I truly feared that the heroine bit was all just an act. Three years had come and gone, but I still held great concern for my younger self's safety.

CHAPTER LIII

Khattaaara/Payton

> *Payton from the Original Timeline*
> *Sharing the Mind of Khattaaara*
> *In the now Alternate Timeline*
> *On Rendenaaar*
> *Trillions of Universes in the Past*

Dargra-Tol had deceived me. Despite that she was a synth, I thought that I had felt something real in her.[57] Alone on this world, I had deluded myself that there could be love for me, but what she offered was just a pretense. As I later learned, synths shared a hive mind. While each could act on its own, there was a combined consciousness that ruled them all, similar to when I divided myself into many. Dargra-Tol had boasted that there was more than just her. But how many were connected, I wondered? Surely, the earlier versions did not have her advanced capability.

I had no idea where she had gone. She now possessed the mother-stone and, through it, could destroy all organic life on Rendenaaar, or, perhaps, everywhere. I could say that it was fortunate that she did not know of the six other god-stones I still had in my possession, but it was the timing of the situation that left her unaware; for had she not acted so quickly, I most surely would have shown them to her, so foolish was I back then. But she acted impulsively. It was the nature of the synths. Each had been built without the ability to see farther than the day they were in, their mental calendars having to reset with the rising of each sun. It was as though they were born again and

---

[57] The Payton part of me wished to say "human," but in Gaaalthaaaran, there was no such word.

again, with the memories of everyone they were supposed to know and with the instructions for all of the duties they needed to perform left intact, all so similar to the condition that Djana Barrymore's character had in the 2004 movie, *50 First Dates*.

The other god-stones were still where I had hidden them, deep within my *yaaargh*. The musculature of the *yaaargh* in Gaaalthaaaran females was such that what was within it, whether an embryo or a god-stone, could be moved in either direction at will. After Dargra-Tol had fled, and I felt it safe to do so, I carefully dropped them into my hand and had a close look at them for the first time. They were both captivating and magnificent. Where diamonds offer spectrums of refractive light, these shone out their unique separate colors—red, yellow, green, purple, white, and orange, each slightly smaller than the one Dargra-Tol had stolen. *But what if...* I thought to myself. *What if I used them all? Would then my power be greater than hers, or, perhaps, just different?* Regardless, I needed to know.

One by one, then, I placed them up to my forehead, and, one by one, they shrank in size as they spun faster and faster and then melted into my head. I felt a surge of strength that grew as each stone entered my brain. However I had succumbed to my sexual desires, whatever mistakes I had made, whatever animosity had infected me against those in charge—my Gaaalthaaaran mother among them—a part of me remained Payton Herron, and that part then became the living embodiment of the superheroine from the far distant future—an embodiment with a slightly different physique and a *tail*. Thus it was that I turned into Quantum Girl once more—cape and all—and then phased back to my husband-brother's home, whence our god-stone plot had been conceived.

275

CHAPTER LIV

Payton

> *From the Alternate Timeline*
> *In the Alternate Reality*
> *On Earth III*
> *Earth-Date:2029*

I had to go back. I had to save Liam and Li. There were, presumably, an infinite number of parallel dimensions. So, I wondered, if I went back in time and rescued them, would it erase what had happened, or would time and space split off into an additional reality?[58] Whatever the end result, there was nothing I could do about the old woman who had sat before me, whose life had come to an end in that timeline. But perhaps, I thought, the events of the years she had lived through might be unraveled, and so I shifted myself back through time to the moment I had left and then took Liam and Li back to my house in my dimension, freeing them from the devastation that Khattaaara had wrought upon their world.

I had hoped that the children would find comfort with my parents, who looked identical to the ones they had lost. One cannot imagine their devastation, nor mine, to see their bodies on the floor of the living room in my home. They had been alive when I had inexplicably left and found myself back on that other world. But it was I, not they, who dropped down to my knees and began to sob

---

[58] Again, in Krotaaarak's seminal work, *Governing Properties of the Quantum Fabric and Its Threads*, he states that the Quantum Fabric is immune to the physical laws of the conservation of matter and energy, so it would not be impossible for additional universes to be created out of nothingness; and while difficult for the sentient mind to fathom, is no more abstract a concept than the infinite nature of space or time.

bitterly. Liam came over to me and placed his hands on my shoulders.

"Don't cry," he said. "Their spirits are in Heaven now, just like the spirits of *our* parents are."

I looked up at him as he tried to be the strong big brother. He stared off into space and then added, "I wonder, though."

"What?" I asked.

"Well," he said, trying to put his thoughts into words. "If there are different dimensions, are there different Gods or just one?"

"I don't know," I replied.

"There's no God!" Li sobbed. "If there was, He wouldn't have let Mother and Father be killed!"

"Pastor Martins said…" Liam began to insist.

"I don't care what Paster Martins said. He got killed, too, just like Payton's parents! There *is* no Heaven! And there *is* no God! And even if there were, He'd be an awful one! Imagine having the power to save everyone and doing nothing!"

I rose to my feet and went over to her, and then wrapped my arms around her.

"I miss them!" Li wept.

"I know," I said. "I miss mine, too." Then a thought struck me, and I let go of Li. My head turned in all directions. "Liam!" I shouted. "Ophelia!"

"We're here!" Liam said.

"No," I replied. "Your counterparts. They're my age." I glanced at Li. "You two. Come with me. We need to search every room."

And so, we did, but we found no trace of either my brother or Ophelia. The question remained as to where they now were. Had they been killed somewhere else, or were they alive and safe, or alive and in captivity? There was no way to tell. What I *did* know, however, was that the situation of the United States at that moment was unimaginably bleak, and, considering what we had just seen, it was no place for children, especially those two who had endeared themselves to me.

I brought them close to me, held *them* as they held onto *me*, and then I shifted us—I guess the other me would have said "phased us"—to Ophelia's universe, to *her* living room; at least I was going to try.

CHAPTER LV

Payton

> *From the Original Timeline*
> *In the Alternate Reality*
> *On Earth I*
> *Earth-Date.2029*

Three days had passed, and we found ourselves ready to go. We all had supper together and talked as though we were the most ordinary family in the world. Sarabeth and Phee had packed their bags and were preparing for their farewells. Mr. and Mrs. Herron were somewhat tearful, though it was clear to see where the favoritism lay, as Mrs. Herron hugged Ophelia and young Peyton clung tightly to her father and wept tears into his shirt sleeves. Peyton and her parents then stepped back as I phased the three of us to the same living room, but in my dimension. And yet, of all the times I had gone back and forth to my world, this time it was different. As I phased with Sarabeth and Phee, it was as though I briefly merged into another version of myself. I saw atom bombs going off. I saw citizens executed by soldiers in the streets. I heard screams and sobs and then it all disappeared.

It was evening when we phased into my home, but the room was oppressively dark. All of the curtains had been drawn closed. None of the lights were on.

"Liam?" I called out. "Mom? Dad?" but there was no answer. I switched to Quantum Girl and then irradiated the room with purple light. It was then that I saw their bodies, Mom's and Dad's. "No!" I screamed out and then rushed over to where the two of them lay. I was trembling as I turned over first Dad and then Mom. Their eyes were open but lifeless. Their bodies were cold. The realization came that they had been dead for a while. "No, no, no, no, no!" I kept sobbing. Then a thought struck me, and I stood up and looked around. "Liam!" I screamed hysterically, and then I phased from room to room, but he was nowhere to be found.

Phee found me in the kitchen, with Sarabeth trailing behind. She turned on the lights to see me standing, my weight propped up by my arms, as my hands pressed down on the tabletop.

"He isn't here," I said. "He was here last time, but he isn't here now."

"Maybe he got away," Phee suggested.

I looked up at her, tears streaming down my cheeks. "First Theresa, now Mom and Dad... and Liam," I sobbed as my voice trailed off. "I have no one!"

"You have *us*," Sarabeth said. "We all love you."

I smiled through my tears. "Come here, Sarabeth," I said, and she came, and I wrapped my arms around her like there was no tomorrow. Sarabeth and Phee were like family. No, I need to correct myself. They *were* family. They were as much my sisters as Liam had been my brother, and I loved them both equally and as much as I loved him.

"Maybe you can undo this," Phee suggested.

"You *know* what happens when either Peyton or I mess with the timeline," I replied.

"Well, what about just here?" Phee said.

"What do you mean?" I asked, trying to wipe away my tears.

"What if you just reverse time where *they* are?" she said.

"I don't know if I can do that," I replied.

"Theresa did it when she brought Sarabeth back to life," Phee said, looking at me with insistence written on her face. "It doesn't hurt to try!"

I really had no idea how I was supposed to do it. How could I reverse time in one particular spot? *How did Theresa do it?* I wondered. *How did she even know how?*

It was difficult for me to stand beside the corpses of both of my parents, but it was the only way. Beyond all that, dead bodies tend to give off a disgusting, cloying, putrid scent after a while—one that I hadn't noticed in my heightened state when I had first come upon them. But where Payton Herron might have found herself overwhelmed by it all, Quantum Girl did not.

It all came down to focus in the end. Time is just one construct of quantum reality. The tenets of science consider it a dimension, but in reality, it's more like an all-encompassing wave that matter and energy are irrevocably bound to.

The first thing I did was to form a quantum barrier around them. After that, I caused the time wave that permeates all matter to shorten and then reverse. The effect on my parents within the isolated time field was not immediately noticeable, but within minutes, their bodies began to heal. Cells came back to life. Their hearts began to beat once more. It was incredible to see the bloodstains turn liquid again and reabsorb into the bullet holes from which they had sprung. Then the two of them, defying gravity, stood back up. The projectiles shot backward out of their bodies and then vanished once outside the barrier as their wounds and torn fabric miraculously healed. At last, there was a gasp of breath from each of them as they, who had let go of each other's hands when they had been shot and fallen to the floor, took hold of them again. It was at that precise moment that I reversed time's direction once more within the quantum field.

Mom and Dad stared at us and then at each other, startled, I think. Mom leaned into Dad, visibly terrified at, from her perspective, everything around her changing all at once, including seeing two people in the room who were not there before. An Ophelia was still there, but Liam had vanished while I, as a violet-glowing Quantum Girl, stood in his place beside a slightly younger version of Peyton.

"What's going on?" she said, trembling.

Dad, while visibly rattled, held her, always her pillar. Phee looked at them and then at me.

"Phase back to you!" she said in low tones.

Instantly, I did and became Payton again, but that seemed to only make matters worse, as now there were two of me, albeit one slightly younger.

"You both need to sit down," I said, "and I'll explain," and so they sat. We all did. All things considered, it was surprising how well Mom and Dad accepted the fact that I had superpowers and that there were different dimensions, though it visibly shook Mom's faith in our Gods and all. I mean, it's one thing to accept the belief that one God was the Creator of everything but the issue of multiple dimensions clearly suggested that there were also an infinite number of Jesuses who, in many instances, were born female and called Jesusa. Mom, our bastion of faith, was literally swooning at the thought.

"I need something to drink," she said, at which point Sarabeth rushed to the kitchen and back and handed her a glass of water. "Thank you, Sugarplum," she said, all the color gone from her face, "but I think I need something a bit stronger."

Sarabeth looked bewildered, but Phee rose without hesitation and looked at Mom.

"There's some brandy on the top shelf in the cabinet to the right in the kitchen," Mom told Phee. Phee went there and returned a moment later with a half-filled glass. Mom took it from her, took a sip, and then, after looking around at all of us, said, "What the hell," and downed what remained in the glass. "I'm not sure I understand it all," she said, as the liquor began to take effect. "You said that Ophelia had been in the other dimension for months, ever since the timeline was changed. Then who in the name of all that's holy has been living here with Liam all this time? And since Lords know I did *not* have another daughter that I forgot about, then why in the name of Jesus are there two of you—one being younger and noticeably cuter, no offense."

"None taken," I replied. "The fact is that if what you've said about Payton is true, then I'm not your daughter either, and she's out there somewhere, maybe with Liam and the other Phee."

The Katherine Herron, who was not really my mother, held out her glass to Peyton. "Sugarplum," she said, "would you take this back into the kitchen and fill it up with more of that brown liquid? If for some reason I become inebriated, I'm sure the Lords will understand and forgive me for my temporary indiscretion."

Peyton took the glass and went off with it. I looked at Phee with concern, who herself appeared somewhat shocked, to use an understatement. There were now alternate versions of both of us.

"Maybe it was because of the timelines," Sarabeth said upon returning and handing the refilled glass back to her other mother. "I mean, there are now four of *me*."

"Fuck, this is confusing!" I exclaimed and then turned to *Mom* with, "Sorry."

Katherine Herron waved it away. "Dear," she said, "if there were two Jesuses here in this room, I'd have said pretty much the same."

"The other Ophelia has been with Liam ever since he broke up with Claire," Dad interjected.

"Who's Claire?" Phee and I asked, as if with a single breath.

"Claire Salinger," Mom replied. "She was Liam's fiancée until they broke up; well, *Claire* broke things off with *Liam*, and then, suddenly, Ophelia came into the picture with her baby girl."

Again, another glance between myself and Phee.

"Jordan," Dad said.

"Ophelia," Mom continued, as the alcohol began to take hold. "Not you, dear," she added, glancing at Phee. "Ophelia or Phee Phee, as Liam calls her, said that Jordan's father had gone off to parts unknown," at which point she stared at me. "But as I told your father, the child was the spitting image of Liam when he was the same age, other than that Liam was a boy and this was a girl, but I told your father there must have been something going on between them—

283

Liam and Ophelia—while he and Claire were together. I mean, I may not be able to tell a newt from a salamander, but I most certainly can pick out my own grandchild from a nursery the size of a football field filled with little ones."

"Where's Liam now," Phee asked, "and the other me?"

"We don't know," Dad said. "The last time we saw either of them was just before Katherine and I were shot."

"We've kind of been ignoring that," I said. "Shot by whom?"

"The Marks," Dad said. "American quislings. Ever since the Soviets took over."

"What do you mean?" I said. "The Soviets?"

"While you were gone," Dad explained, "there was an invasion, and we lost. The country's been occupied ever since. They broke into our home. It was all so quick. Hopefully, Payton and Liam and Ophelia are still alive."

"And Jordan," Mom broke in. "Don't forget your granddaughter."

"I'll see if I can track them down in the morning," I said.

"You need to be careful," he warned.

"You forget," I reminded him, "I'm Quantum Girl."

CHAPTER LVI

Payton

> *From the Alternate Timeline*
> *In the Alternate Reality*
> *On Earth I*
> *Earth-Date:2029*

"Where *are* we?" Li asked.

"Do you remember I told you about the other Payton?" I said. "Well, this is *her* home." I glanced toward the kitchen and saw the other Payton's mom and dad walk from there toward us. "Well, I have a bit of a surprise for you," I went on, and I motioned my head toward the couple that had just entered the room.

"Mama!" Li exclaimed. Then she ran up to Katherine Herron and hugged her, not letting go.

"What's this all about? You just left." Mr. Herron said, noticeably confused.

"Why did you..." a twin of me started to ask as she walked into the room. Then she caught sight of Liam and Li. "And who are the kids?"

It was at that moment that Li turned around.

"Oh, my God!" Peyton exclaimed. "I don't understand. Did you go back in time?"

"No," I said, "What makes you think I did?" I asked. "You're the me in the other dimension, I take it."

"I'm confused," the other me replied. "Didn't you just leave here with Phee and Sarabeth?"

"No," I replied.

"So," she asked, "who are you, and which dimension are you from exactly?"

"No idea," I replied. "Are you missing an Ophelia by any chance?"

"Not really," she said. "Why?"

"Because," I replied, "I met one who was in love with my brother."

"Did she say anything about how she got there?" she asked.

"Well," I replied, "supposedly I brought her, only I didn't bring her. She said something about how reality must have been overwritten, only I figured that she was just batshit crazy."

"Not so much," she replied, "if you're part of the overwrite like Sarabeth."

"Who's Sarabeth?" I asked.

"Another younger version of you and me." She replied.

"Oh," I replied. "My head is starting to hurt from all of this."

"How did you manage to find this dimension?" Peyton asked. "There are an infinite number of possibilities."

"This parallel-dimensional stuff is all new to me," I replied. "I kind of just assumed there were just the three."

"There are an infinite number," she insisted.

"Well, then, I don't know," I said, "and for the moment, maybe we can leave it at that."

"Fine," she replied, "all things considered."

I turned toward the Katherine and James Herron of this dimension. "I was just hoping," I said to them, "that you two might find it in your hearts to take care of young Ophelia and her twin brother."

"It's like a godsend," Mrs. Herron said. Then she turned to Liam and Li, who were standing off together to one side. "Come here, you two!" she said to them, and so the twins went up to her on the sofa where she now sat. "Would both of you like to live here from now on?"

Liam and Li both nodded.

"Will you be our mother," Li said, "and will he be our father?"

"Of course, we will," Mrs. Herron replied. Then she turned to my mirror self. "Peyton," she went on, "would you show them to their room?"

Liam turned his head back and forth, looking at me and Peyton, again and again.

"They're the same person," Li told him, "but from different dimensions."

"Exactly," said Peyton, and she smiled. "Ophelia's right."

"No one calls her Ophelia," I interjected. "It's Li,"

"Li," Peyton repeated. "Such a pretty name." She looked at Liam and then back at Li. "Why don't you two follow me upstairs, and I'll show you to your room."

"We *know* where it is," Liam replied.

I cleared my throat loudly; something of an "Ahem!" Then I went over to him and whispered. "I know that most everything seems the same, but we are guests here, so be on your best behavior."

"Yes, Ma'am," Liam replied in a low voice, and then both he and Li followed Peyton upstairs with me trailing behind.

"Just one thing," I said to the new parents before beginning my ascent. "Time in the dimension they come from moves much slower than it does here. They may remain children longer than you might expect."

"That's not a downside," Katherine Herron said. "That's every parent's dream!"

Upstairs, after Peyton had gotten the kids settled in—after telling them all about Rendenaaar as she remembered it and kissing them both goodnight—she got up from where she had been sitting on the edge of Phee's bed and went to the door.[59] Peyton then looked back

---

[59] Ever since their parents had been killed, Liam and Li had slept next to each other, especially as Li had frequent nightmares about the havoc they had witnessed when

at the two as they closed their eyes to sleep, Liam's arm around Li, as the ever-protective, ever-vigilant brother. Peyton flicked off the light switch and then exited to the hall, where I had stood watching all the while. Then she quietly shut the door behind her.

"I think they'll be all right," she said in a soft voice.

"They're adorable, aren't they?" I said back.

"They are," Peyton replied. "But we need to talk because I'm confused."

"You and me both," I replied.

"Let's go to the guest room—my bedroom now," she said, and so we went.

"I didn't want to say anything before," she said once we were there, "because I didn't want to upset anyone, but you didn't happen to see another Payton on your way here, did you?"

"How many of us are there?" I asked.

"Four by my count," she replied. "You and me and the other Payton from your dimension and Sarabeth."

"The other version of you," I said.

"The other Payton," she replied, "Just took the time-rewritten Ophelia and Sarabeth to your dimension just before you came with the twins."

"And how did you get a quantum seed?" she asked.

"Young Liam gave it to me," I replied. "He said he found it after this alien woman, Khattaaara, murdered most of his world's population."

"Shit!" she exclaimed.

"What?" I asked.

"Another Khattaaara!" she replied.

"Who is she exactly?" I asked.

"My... your... former incarnation," she replied. "Total bad news."

---

all of those around them had been slaughtered in the streets and in their homes by Khattaaara.

"Tell me about it!" I said.

"You have the green seed, don't you?" she said.

"Don't you?" I asked.

She just shook her head. I stared at her, feeling somewhat queasy.

"I am so being freaked out by all of this," I said.

"The other you has a purple seed like mine," she went on. "We've been calling Demi," she said, "to try and avoid confusion."

I must have looked even more confused.

"Demi," she went on, "short for dimensional other self."

"Thank you," I said, but I really prefer Payton, despite anyone else being confused.

Peyton smiled. "That's sort of what the other you said."

"Ugh!" I moaned, now totally exasperated. "There is no *other* me. *I'm* me. I'm the only *me* I've ever known until I met *you*."

"Anyway," Peyton went on. "*Demi* took Phee and Sarabeth to your dimension to stay with your parents and protect them from the now Quantum Theresa, who's calling herself Rainbow Girl."

"And who the hell is Theresa?" I asked.

"The bully," she replied, "who caused me and Sarabeth to kill ourselves."

"Do you want me to go insane over all of this?" I asked, glaring at her. "What are you, like the walking dead?" I took in a deep breath and then exhaled. "Look," I said, "is there somewhere, a bed, a couch, an air mattress, anything that I can crash on?" My voice begged for a response. "I really need some time to let all of this sink into my brain."

"You can sleep here," Peyton said. "I'll phase back to the estate."

"Estate?" I repeated, staring at her.

"I'll explain it all tomorrow," she replied, and with that and the sound of pop in the air, she was gone.

CHAPTER LVII

Theresa

From the Original Timeline
In the Alternate Reality
On Earth I
Earth-Date:2026

My financial troubles were over, as money and gifts began to pour in from all directions. The gifts went through a fan mail service I had hired—the money to the Cash App and Chime and GoFundMe accounts that Daisy had set up. Most of the gifts I just donated to my church, though I kept the expensive jewelry and the designer clothes that I liked—the ones that fit. There was also revenue from online ads, like my Facebook and YouTube accounts. I had requests for appearances on television and for sponsorships for things like Rainbow Girl perfume, Rainbow Girl clothing, and Rainbow Girl action figures. Time magazine had me on the cover for Person of the Year. Both Marvel and DC competitively approached me to do a comic book and a film, even though all the rest of their characters were fictional and I was real. As for me doing film, I told them I couldn't act worth a damn. Marvel suggested Zendaya for the role. DC already had Ariana Grande committed if I decided to go with them. Daisy said to wait till their offers went up. "Best," she said, "to let two giants wage war against themselves," so I went with her advice, even though DC threw in Zack Snyder as director to sweeten the deal. But there were also offers that were age-inappropriate—or *totally* inappropriate)—as from the moment I came out as gay I had thousands of *proposals* for sex from adult women, many of whom sent naked (and often disturbing) photos of themselves; some men, too—each of whom conceitedly and presumptuously fantasized that they could *turn me*, so to speak. The vast majority of them were at least twice my age and knew it! Did that seem to bother them? Hardly! In fact, I would have bet money that not only did it *not* bother them but that it probably turned them on. One adult film company based in Russia actually wanted me to do porn, to which I responded, "Dude, I'm only fifteen!" and to which the owner replied, "No worries. It will only be shown on the dark web!" OMG! Some people are such perverted pieces of shit! And then there were those who sent me dildos. Seriously? Those all went into the trash except for a hand-blown (no pun intended) glass one that I kept on my nightstand as a paperweight. Hell, I had my own usable one for times of need, along with a 24-pack of Energizer triple-A batteries that I socked way in the drawer. I figured that what worked for the bunny would work for me! I figured right!

As for all those offering themselves, even those around my same age, I didn't want or need any of them. I had Daisy! But no matter how strong my love for her was, no matter how fantastic the sex was, images of Peyton Herron naked continually and disturbingly crept into my brain, and I didn't know why. The worst of it was that all too often I had sex dreams about her—nightmares was perhaps a better word—from which I would awaken in a cold sweat, my heart pounding like a kettle drum. Yet with each awakening, all of the arousal I had felt while asleep quickly evaporated and turned into liquid rage that surged through my veins. But then I would roll over onto my side and see Daisy lying asleep beside me, and it quieted me, and I would cuddle up against her and find a calming path toward sleep.

The best thing about being a superhero—or in my case a superhero*ine*—is how most everyone treats you like you're a celebrity, which I guess I now was, and the strange thing about it was that my attitude about Peyton Herron had changed. Being a hero is more than having superpowers. It's about caring and about thinking things through. The truth of the matter was that I really wasn't sure how I had wound up in the hospital or how I became Rainbow Girl. The mind can play strange tricks. Maybe, I thought, it wasn't Payton who caused any of this. To be honest, I wasn't even certain whether Quantum Girl was an actual person or a figment of my imagination. Maybe it was me who let Peyton out of her grave. Maybe that's what all of my dreams were trying to tell me—that it's better to love someone than wish death upon them. Regardless, I didn't want to be a bad person—not anymore. Me being good was what my mother would have wanted. She would have taken pride in the fact that I had rescued so many from the brink of death and that I was held in high regard.

When morning came, I awoke to find Daisy already out of bed, naked with beads of water still on her as she towel-dried her hair. Wet footprints trailed from the hallway. Water ran down her legs and dripped from her nipples to the floor. The room was warm, though. She'd turned on the heat. It must have been eighty degrees in the room. There were beads of moisture on me as well, but those were the result of sweat. I threw off the blanket that had covered me and stood up to face her.

"You could have waited to shower with me," I said.

"I didn't want to wake you," she replied. "But if you like, I can shower again, this time with you. I'm not afraid of getting wet."

We were both naked now. She looked me up and down.

"You must really hate her," she said.

"Hate who?" I replied innocently enough. "That Herron chick?"

"Who else?" came her response. "Unless Quantum Girl."

"Why is this a topic now?" I asked.

"You were calling out her name in your sleep," she said. "Peyton, Peyton, Peyton. It was like an echo chamber that wouldn't stop."

"I can't control my dreams," I replied. "Or remember them most of the time."

"So, when are we going to do her?" she asked.

"Meaning?" I asked back.

"Kill her," she said. She stopped drying her hair, lowered her towel, and stared at me. "You *don't* actually think I was suggesting that we fuck her?"

"No!" I said defensively. "And I haven't eaten breakfast yet, so please don't conjure any images."

Daisy looked me in the eye, tilting her head as someone curious might do. "You *do* still hate her, don't you?"

"If not for her, my mother would still be alive," I said, knowing that would appease her.

"Then let's find her and torture the bitch till she begs us to end her life." She let the towel slip from her fingers, moved in toward me, and kissed me on the lips. "You know, the way I figure it," she said, "if we *do* kill her, that wouldn't be murder. It would just be us putting things back the way they originally were." She took my hands in hers. "Anyway," she went on, "after the shower, we need to make plans to end her skank-ass existence once and for all."

This was a side of Daisy I'd never seen before. Despite my having powers, she scared the living crap out of me. Maybe it was the power. Maybe it was the sex. Maybe it was just something that had lain dormant inside of her, and now, with me in the picture, with her mother's thumb not pressing as hard on her as it had been, the anger that had been bottled up inside of her for so many years had finally burst through the cap.

CHAPTER LVIII

Khattaaara/Payton

> *Payton from the Original Timeline*
> *Sharing the Mind of Khattaaara*
> *In the now Alternate Timeline*
> *On Rendenaaar*
> *Trillions of Universes in the Past*

It felt very strange to be Quantum Girl again—well, Gaaalthaaaran Quantum Girl, I mused to myself, as I caught sight of my *reflection* in the reimager in Dhraaal's home. What was odd to me was not how I looked at that time, but how I had looked as the Payton version of Quantum Girl. As the days went by, I became more and more disconnected from my human past. True, there were memories, but I felt comfortable in the skin that I now wore, though I was saddened by the fact that the images in my mind of my parents and of Liam had begun to blur. Nor did I have any photos to remember them with, and I doubted that I would ever see them again. Even if I could travel past the end of this universe, I had no idea how far theirs was in the future. And if I did manage to find the universe in which I had been born, how would I ever find the Milky Way galaxy, let alone the solar system? How Dhraaal or Thara-Klo had managed was a question that pervaded my mind. But I might never know, since my Payton presence here had obviously changed the way things had gone in the previous timeline. I did need to know one thing, though: how I had lost my *yaaargh*. Dhraaal had said that it was those in charge who had dismembered me, perhaps even at the behest of our royal mother, whom I, before merging with Peyton, had made several attempts to kill so that I might ascend to the throne.

Never did she realize that my anger had been tempered and that I no longer had such aspirations. Still, my mother did not seem the type to inflict such cruelty on her own blood. But if not her, then who might it have been, I wondered?

My Earth parents had been supportive of me throughout my life. Even as a child, I remember how both my mother and father defended me after they had been called to the principal's office. Both the principal, Miss Chambers, and the counselor—the ever-feared, always talked about Mrs. Andrew, who later transferred to the high school Liam and I attended—sat in judgment. I was ten years old at the time, and our assignment was to select a poem, memorize it, and deliver it on stage in the auditorium during the Christmas recital. Our teacher, Miss Deming, said the poem was to be about the big C. She, of course, meant Christmas, but being ten and in that our family had taken a cruise the previous summer, I thought it was to be about the other kind of sea—that which ships sailed on. And so, I went to the library and found an epic poem, which was quite a task to remember, especially for someone in fifth grade, considering it had more than four hundred lines. But I always had a good memory back on Earth—photographic, one might say—at least when it came to words. A few dozen children went before me. There were at least ten recitations of *A Visit from St. Nicholas* and a handful of *Rollo the Red-Nosed Reindeer*. One girl actually sang it—off-key, I might add. Finally, it was my turn. Dressed in my white blouse, dark blue pinafore, knee-high socks, and saddle shoes, I walked onto the stage from one of the wings, took my center position, and began.

"I will now recite the *Wreck of the Sea Hag*," I announced, "by Edward Cornwell, written in 1854.

"The sailor kissed his dear love,
As his hands caressed her hair;
He pressed to his cheek her white glove,
Then he left her standing there.

He had signed aboard the clipper that year,
With a crew of forty-three:
Its maiden voyage to somewhere,
As the rechristened, Sheila Marie.
The planks had had their histories,
As did the masts and spars;
They had sailed three oceans' mysteries,
As the Sea Hag by the stars.
Each time they met disaster;
New voyage brought new pain;
And every crew aboard her
Would ne'er return again.
But the ship was salvaged each time,
And restored to make her sail
Despite that age-old sea-crime,
To defy both wind and gale.
It was the captain's daughter,
And the maid upon the land,
Whose namesake sailed the water,
With two score and three of hand.
But Sheila wept no teardrops;
No moisture left her eyes
For this was where her fear stopped,
She had cast her foolish dies.
Having paid a drunken sailor
To smuggle her on board,
She hid among the cargo
By what cost she could afford.
She had sacrificed her breeding,
To be with her love of late,
Yet now her knees were bleeding
With splinters from the crate.
One knothole let some air in,

Another let some out;
But the darkness left her barren,
And her lungs let out a shout.
But no one there did hear her
For a day or two or three,
And the box, it would not spare her
From her great indignity.
Thus Sheila Marie was weary
When her exit finally came;
And the captain, all too leery,
Who shared her own last name.
"Avast," said Captain Irish,
His voice was brusque and cold
'My daughter is a stowaway,
Well, lock her in the hold!'
And so the girl was taken
Despite impassioned cries,
And pleas and remonstration,
And tears from both her eyes.
And locked within the dungeon
Of the ship which bore her name,
She smelled the odors pungent,
And knew she'd go insane.
Her lover stood atop deck,
He heard her moan and wail,
So with an upper stiff lip,
He stared down from the rail.
He whispered, 'Sheila,' to her;
He mumbled out, 'Marie.'
The girl looked at the sailor,
And cried, 'Please set me free.'
'Be quiet,' said that seaman,
Or it's shackles for me, too!

I'll try my best to save you,
Yet I know not what to do.'
'But you said that you would marry me,
And take my hand someday,'
The girl wept out those poor words;
It was all she needed say.
The sailor was struck speechless,
A glaze had veiled his sight;
He said, 'We love us each less,
Than the total of our plight,
For these are waters foreign
To every ruled empire;
Here the captain is the sovereign,
So our straits are very dire.
You see, I overheard him,
Before we left the docks;
His face was pale,
His mind was grim,
As he stood among the rocks.
He had spoken to your mater,
Or so his words suggested;
She had told him your true pater,
Was a man who had him bested.
She mocked him, and he scorned her,
And bade her go away,
And take her bastard daughter,
From him that very day.
And, so, you see, my dearest,
What plight we have in store;
The man who loved you fairest,
Knows your mother was a whore.'
The girl was speechless rendered,
By this tale so newly heard,

Her mother had not tendered
Her vows in God's own word.
She stood there briefly thinking,
About her shaded family,
And all about the sinking
Of her mother Ellen P.
Who'd come from the Great Green Isle
To the distant Barbary
In Northern California, while
Her Sheila was just three.
She had met her Captain Irish,
Who had given her a ring,
She had tasted not the whiskey,
But imbibed the foolish fling.
The man rocked upon the dry land,
But stood straight upon the prow,
She had met him on her voyage,
And a love had grown somehow.
But a captain has two women,
One of flesh and one of wood,
One can sail the oceans' waters,
One stays landed, as she should.
But a woman draws her passion
When the girl is driven home,
And her love takes on a fashion
And her mind begins to roam.
And so it was with Ellen,
When left alone too long,
And the man who stole her sorrow,
Gave her breath a fervid song.
And as that man imbued her
With his own embracing glee,
He sparked the needful woman

With the flower of Sheila Marie."

Anyway, that was where Miss Deming stopped me. She walked on stage, took my hand, and literally dragged me off into the wing. Obstinately, I ran back, left off the middle, and recited the final stanza.

"The ship made final port that night,
Its cabin now unmanned,
Yet there will come no morning light
Of any peopled land.
It did not run its charted course,
With mast and billowed sail,
For the winds had proved a greater force
Than the hulk of board and nail.
The seas grew tossed, that calm once were,
The men called toward the skies,
As taken by Poseidon's lure,
That god shut up their eyes.
The night air echoes all hands down,
The wreck lies on some shore,
And the waves impart a briny gown
To the dreaded, ancient whore."

At that point, they had the curtain drop down in front of me. Not to be thwarted, I climbed under the curtain, stood up, and took my bows in front of a lot of shocked parents and teachers, though Liam, true brother that he was, stood up and began clapping and calling out, "Bravo!" And then there was silence. Big time. Deadpan.

And so, my parents were called down to a conference the next day to decide what should be done to me, with me, and about me. I wasn't allowed to attend. I was a child, and this was a meeting for adults.

"What do you think will happen?" I whispered to Liam as Miss Deming's attention was turned to the chalkboard.

"I don't know," he whispered back. "Maybe they'll ship you off somewhere far away like Wendy and the Lost Girls. But don't worry. If they do, I'll stick with you. I'll be your shadow."

I smiled at him, just as Miss Deming, who must have had ears like a bat, turned around, stared at us, and shook her head as though warning us not to speak.

Both Mom and Dad defended me, I was later told. The words I had recited were part of literature, Mom proclaimed, despite their bawdy nature, and not uttered with prurient intent. And so, nothing came of it, although my classmates looked at me with hidden smiles for weeks afterward, until it became forgotten like most things are with the passage of time. It was a shame, I remember thinking, that my memory of the future I had come from was not as vivid with sounds or images.

Anyway, Dhraaal was not home when I phased into his living room, which was probably a good thing since I did not want to be questioned about what had happened after the god-stones found their way into my hand. Nor did I desire to reveal how one of them had been purloined by Dargra-Tol, or how I had been hoodwinked out of the stolen booty right from my hand. For the moment, all I wanted to know was the name of the coward who had butchered me while I was unconscious.

The only way for me to find out was to travel back through time in a series of small jumps. I had done as much when I had healed Peyton from her gunshot wound, and so I began.

What had happened was not that far into the past, so I knew that what I had to do would not take long. At first, I saw Dhraaal by himself doing this or that, and then he was standing with me, no longer in possession of my *yaaargh*. I needed to go back further, and so I did—first, to that moment when I had awakened with him, and then back a bit more. What I witnessed was incredible. Dhraaal had told me that he had brought me to his home to save me. I saw him phase into the room with me, holding me in his arms. *But wait!* I realized, *I still had my yaaargh!* I jumped forward, a moment at a time, only to witness Dhraaal, my husband, my half-brother, lay me face down and use a laser knife to cut my *yaaargh* off and then casually walk to the door to his yard and toss it to his *goraaag* like a scrap of food or a bone! [60]

My blood boiled at the thought that the one person whom I had grown up with and trusted was the one who had mutilated me in such a vile manner and then lied to me about it. But then I thought about what he had done to Thara-Klo, my poor, poor child, and all for his selfish gain! As I stood in frozen time, I thought about ways to exact revenge. Killing him was not enough. Although a part of me was human, brought up with the concept of forgiveness and mercy, the rest of me was Gaaalthaaaran, a part that knew no virtues as such. The moment would come for his fate to be decided. For him, I might as well have been the antichrist, for any path he would have chosen from that moment on would lead him straight to the hell of my making. *No one does this to the heir to the Gaaalthaaaran throne!* I thought to myself as my blood heated up more and more, *How dare the bastard from my father's seed cut off my desire and then feed it to his dog!* Milton would not write of Satan's fall to perdition for trillions upon trillions of years, and yet what would become of that partner of mine would foreshadow it all!

---

[60] As noted in Quantum Girl, a *goraaag* was a spotted, scaled domesticated creature, resembling an evolved dinosaur, though about the size of a German shepherd, which Gaaalthaaaarans would often keep as pets.

CHAPTER LIX

Ophelia

From the Original Timeline
In the Alternate Reality
On Earth II
Earth-Date:2029

I awoke in the middle of the night—at least it felt like night as the lights in the dorm had been turned down. There were no windows to know for certain, but the others still lay asleep in their cots. None of that mattered to me at that moment, though. My head throbbed. My body ached. But how strange it was that my hair had grown back. How long had I been unconscious, I wondered? I started to rise, but even before I stood, I felt a sudden queasiness and vomited not food but blue liquid onto the floor. As I wiped my mouth with the back of my hand, I thought of Jordan and turned back to my bunk, but there was no sign of her, and my heart began to race. As I whipped around to search the room, I felt something at my back moving with me, like a rope. Cautiously, I felt behind me until I found it. My fingers clutched it and, with trepidation, I felt it. I sensed the pressure of my grip. I felt my fingers as I ran them up it until they met with a furry end. Slowly then, my hand moved back along it, closer toward me, until it found the base of my spine.

My God, my God! I thought to myself. *It's attached to me!* Half in panic, half in disgust, I released my hold and wrapped my arms around myself, only to be shocked a second time. My breasts, which were not large by any means, seemed to be lower than they should be. Slowly, I slid my arms back until my hands cupped them, but something felt off, as though the heels of my hands rested on something else. Cautiously then, I craned my neck to stare downward and to my horror and dismay, I saw that the breasts that my hands now cupped was a second pair. I saw them, and I screamed! It was a harrowing scream, but no one else seemed to hear. No one bounded from their bed to find out what was wrong, and no wonder, for as I looked toward the other bunks, they were all empty, and I was alone.

As I dropped to my knees, my tail (for I had no other words to describe it) lifted into the air and began thrashing uncontrollably back and forth. I could feel the tip of it against my heels, as my thighs pressed down against my calves. Tears began to stream down my cheeks. My fingers ran through my hair, and then I felt my ears! I felt the points of my ears!

"What's going on?" I screamed out, tearing at the insides of my lungs. "What have you done to me? Monsters! You're monsters! All of you!"

But that's what *I* now was—at least in *my* eyes—a monster. And then I remembered Thara-Klo—Thara-Klo, my presumed great aunt. Thara-Klo, Khattaaara's—Peyton's—daughter from another universe and another time. They had turned me into one of her kind, her species. But how—and why?

Wearily, the very life seemingly bled out of me, I rose to my feet. My body trembling, my vision weak, I staggered to the door to pound against it to scream, "Let me out! Let me out!" But as my fists made contact, the door swung open, almost on its own. I tried to exit the room, but my feet refused to budge. It was fear that was holding me back. Not even a thimble of sound came from the corridor that stood only footsteps away. All day and sometimes at night we could hear the voices of the other prisoners shouting, screaming, talking—even moaning as they engaged in sex with other women who shared their same desires to forget the bleak surroundings and lose themselves, if for just a while, in the torrid pleasures of the flesh—but there, all around, was just a vacuum of silence that choked the empty air.

At last, my legs freed the soles of my feet from the polished concrete floor, and I emerged from the room into a twilight of closed and locked doors. I know they were locked because I went to each one and tried to turn the levers that would have opened them. I peered into the window of one and then the next and on and on, but there was nothing I could discern in the half-light. Vaguely, though, it did seem that there were occupants in each one, perhaps asleep, perhaps being transformed into creatures that mirrored my now alien self.

What would Liam think of me now? What of me was there left to love? When my hand had reached downward between my legs, there was nothing—my womanhood had healed itself over as though it had been a wound! As I stood there, wondering which way to go, I thought how hideous I must appear to human eyes and how unattractive and repulsive I would seem to normal men.

My thoughts were interrupted as the ceiling fixtures came on—bright fluorescent bulbs, blinding me at first as though my new eyes were not conducive to sudden changes in light. As I brought down the arm that I had lifted to shield my vision from the glare, the figure of a woman about twenty feet away came into focus. She was Asian, of medium height and build, and wore a white lab frock and a respirator over her entire face.

"Ophelia Herron," she said with a slight Asian accent, "Please follow me."

She turned and went back in the direction from which she had come. I took a deep breath and walked several feet behind her, ultimately being led to a room that was cramped with glassed-in cages on each side. Three were occupied, each by one of my former roommates.

What I witnessed was an utter abomination of medical practice. The two black women, Nia and Deja, had been turned into virtual monsters. Patterned metallic scales covered their bodies. Their tails, held aloft, writhed this way and that, the ends of which opening and closing like hungry mouths, blindly searching for others like itself in order to mate. Bat-like ears had replaced rounded ones. Forked tongues lashed out from their mouths like snakes, while reptilian, slitted eyes stared out at us as though assessing us as danger or as food. And then there was Grace, the Asian woman, whose outward transition had been similar to mine but whose mental state was such that she just sat mindlessly sucking the end of her tail.

"It appears," the frocked woman explained, "the transformation does not work the same way on all races. In the Negroid, for example, the genetic transformation reverts to an earlier evolutionary form of Gaaalthaaaran existence and, while in Mongoloid, once the metamorphosis is complete, the mind becomes completely addled, which is a shame, due to the billions of subjects who will now either need to be subjugated or destroyed."

I stared at her. "How could you betray your own people?" I demanded to know. "And where is my daughter? If you've experimented on her in any way, I swear I'll kill you."

"Your daughter is fine," she said. "You will be reunited with her in a few hours. As for the rest, humanity cannot survive against the powers of Khattaaara. It was bend or break. At least this way, a large portion of the human race will survive."

"As this?" I said, indicating myself.

"Perhaps before judging, you should meet some of our examples of success. But first, you might elect to put on some clothes. You will find garments back in your quarters. And, if you are hungry, I can arrange for some food. I believe the cook has prepared moo shu chicken for you and our other venerable guests." And with that, she left.

When I returned to the room where they had jailed us, I found that, indeed, clothing had been brought there. It consisted of a short blue metallic dress, made of a silk-like fabric, along with matching slip-on shoes. As in the past, my every move was being observed so that within a minute or two of my having finished dressing. The same woman entered, pausing just inside the door.

"Please follow me to the dining area," she said.

I did not require one ounce of persuasion to comply. My stomach was growling from days (or perhaps weeks) of having had nothing to eat.

This dining room was different from the one I had been in before. It was much smaller, probably having been enjoyed by prison staff before the takeover. The woman, whose name I later learned was Dr. Song, indicated, with a nod of her head, for me to sit at one of the two tables that were there, which I did. A man then entered with a tray of food and some tea. As I began to eat, two more individuals appeared—Zoë and Claire—both of whom, like me, had been transformed.

"Have you had sex yet?" Claire asked in a smug voice that didn't beg for an answer. "Once you do—with a transformed male—you'll forget who Liam ever was."

"I don't think so," I replied, not bothering to look up. "I *don't* want sex, and I *don't* appreciate having been mutilated like this."

"Dear Ophelia," Claire went on, "it isn't mutilation. It's an upgrade." Then she raised her arms to stretch, closing her eyes as she did, all four of her nipples pointing upward, revealing themselves through the thin magenta cloth of her dress. "And I wouldn't go back if I could," she said, yawning out the words.

"I just want to see my child!" I said, as my tail raised up into the air, reflecting the anger that I felt.

CHAPTER LX

Payton

From the Original Timeline
In the Alternate Reality
On Earth II
Earth-Date: 2029

The danger had gone, but there was no telling when it would return. I was downstairs, pacing in the dark, trying to figure out how to find Liam and Phee, when two Peytons appeared. At first, I thought they were just multiples of Peyton, but when the moonlight struck the face of the second, I saw the four moles on her left cheek, like mine! Peyton had them on the right. So this was another version of me. But how, I wondered? And then it struck me. Time had been rewritten here as well.

"Glad you could come," I said to Peyton.

"We thought you could use the help," came the reply.

"Does she have powers, too?" I asked her.

"Yes, but different," she answered. "She has a green quantum seed."

The other me appeared agitated. She turned and searched the room with her eyes.

"The bodies of my parents," she said. "They're gone! I wanted to bury them!"

"I wouldn't recommend that now," I told her.

She turned to me. "Why not?" she asked.

"Because I reversed time and brought them back to life," I said.

You could not imagine her expression, filled with shock and surprise and happiness and relief. She threw herself into my arms, wrapped hers around me, and burst out, "Thank you, thank you, thank you!" Afterward, when the emotions of the moment had fled, and she had calmed down, she suddenly felt an awkwardness in the embrace, pulled back, and said, "I'm sorry. I just thought they were gone forever."

"No problem," I replied.

She looked at me. "You're really gay?" she asked.

"Can't you tell?" I replied.

"How am I supposed to tell if we look identical?" she asked.

"I was just joking," I said.

"Hmmpf," she replied, considering, and then she glanced toward the staircase.

"They're asleep," I told her, "as are Phee and Sarabeth." I paused then asked, "You *do* know about Sarabeth?"

"Yes. Peyton told me," she replied, "and there are two Ophelias."

"I still don't understand how," Peyton said.

"When I left her here with Liam," I told her, "I put a quantum field around her to protect her. That seemed to have made her immune to the change."

"So, she's out there," Peyton said.

"With Liam," the other me added.

"We don't know," I replied. "All we *do* know is that all of them are gone, Liam, Phee, and Jordan."

"Who's Jordan?" Peyton asked.

"Her baby," the other me replied.

"We have a niece?" said Peyton.

"We have a problem," I said. "We haven't the slightest idea where they are or if they're even still alive."

The world had been turned upside-down—at least in America. Whatever news, whether in print or on television or on the radio, now belonged to the State. It assured people that soon everything would be back to normal. It blamed the destruction of Manhattan and all of the deaths on what it had called *domestic terrorists*—insurrectionists, it claimed—who wanted control at any cost. This, of course, was furthest from the truth. The fact, as it later turned out, was that the attack on the United States had been engineered by a single individual—another dimension's version of Khattaaara, who had survived the destruction of *her* universe and found her way into mine.

The question remained as to how to find our siblings and our niece. Mom and Dad had said that armed Marks troops had probably taken them—but to where? My mind tried to search all possibilities but came up short.

Peyton and I and other me were trying to brainstorm later that night.

"So, what does that green quantum seed do that ours don't?" I asked.

"I don't know exactly," she replied. "I've been able to duplicate myself, but I don't even know if I can do that again because the one time that it happened, I was sound asleep. And I've been able to phase between three dimensions, and to the moon on the other world."

My face twisted a bit. Her not knowing how to really use her powers at this juncture was not good.

CHAPTER LXI

Daisy (Part I)

From the Alternate Timeline
In the Alternate Reality
On Earth I
Earth-Date: 2029

I had gone to Peyton's house innocently enough, ostensibly to offer my condolences for Peyton's tragic demise. Theresa didn't even know I'd gone. It had been three years since the bitch had offed herself, and Theresa (now Goody Two Shoes) wanted to put the whole thing behind her, but I didn't. I figured all the superhero shit had gone to her head and that sooner or later she'd come to her senses. Peyton Herron was alive—she had to be—and I intended to find out where they were hiding her. Enough was enough of Theresa's sex dreams about her, which she of course denied. But she talked in her sleep and all the moans and all the "Peyton, I love you!" again and again really pissed me off to no small extent.

I had never killed anyone before, and I wanted to know what it felt like. There had to be a rush—capturing her, having her wake up naked, tied up, and letting her beg for her life as I carved up her skin with a kitchen knife—not enough to kill her, just enough to make her bleed. Theresa could watch if she wanted, but the bitch was mine to take! I could borrow my parents' cruiser afterward and feed her to the sharks, bringing along some bloodied meat to attract their attention. I imagined how she'd scream as her naked body with open cuts all over it hit the salt water that would burn like hell, fitted with a life jacket, so the sharks could take their time biting off chunks of her flesh. *No use letting her drown first*, I thought to myself. *That would spoil all the fun!* It made me wet just thinking about it. And here my mom and dad thought they'd raised such an innocent, sweet little girl!

My story to Peyton's parents was that I was out of the country with *my* parents since just before Peyton had killed herself—at least this is what I told her mother, who commended me for my kind thoughts. We exchanged cordialities and memories, mine mostly made up, because I barely knew her. To be perfectly honest, I don't think I ever exchanged more than two words with her or her sister. Her mom offered me hot chocolate and apple pie, which I graciously accepted.

Fuck me, though, because while I was eating, Peyton Herron materialized right in front of my eyes out of thin air. I dropped my fork and just stared at her. She looked a lot older than I remembered, but, again, three years had passed. *She is fucking hot* was the first thought that raced through my head.

The bitch stared back at me. "Shit!" she said, half to herself, and then she disappeared with a pop.

CHAPTER LXII

Daisy (Part II)

From the Alternate Timeline
In the Alternate Reality
On Earth 1
Earth-Date:2029
Time Reset 1

I had gone to Peyton's house innocently enough, ostensibly to offer my condolences for Peyton's tragic demise. Theresa didn't even know I'd gone. It had been three years since the bitch had offed herself, and Theresa (now Goody Two Shoes) wanted to put the whole thing behind her, but I didn't. I figured all the superhero shit had gone to her head and that sooner or later she'd come to her senses. Peyton Herron was alive—she had to be—and I intended to find out where they were hiding her. Enough was enough of Theresa's sex dreams about her, which she of course denied. But she talked in her sleep and all the moans and all the "Peyton, I love you!" again and again really pissed me off to no small extent.

I had never killed anyone before, and I wanted to know what it felt like. There had to be a rush—capturing her, having her wake up naked, tied up, and letting her beg for her life as I carved up her skin with a kitchen knife—not enough to kill her, just enough to make her bleed. Theresa could watch if she wanted, but the bitch was mine to take! I could borrow my parents' cruiser afterward and feed her to the sharks, bringing along some bloodied meat to attract their attention. I imagined how she'd scream as her naked body with open cuts all over it hit the salt water that would burn like hell, fitted with a life jacket, so the sharks could take their time biting off chunks of

313

her flesh. *No use letting her drown first*, I thought to myself. *That would spoil all the fun!* It made me wet just thinking about it. And here my mom and dad thought they'd raised such an innocent, sweet little girl!

My story to Peyton's parents was that I was out of the country with *my* parents since just before Peyton had killed herself—at least this is what I told her mother, who commended me for my kind thoughts. We exchanged cordialities and memories, mine mostly made up, because I barely knew her. To be perfectly honest, I don't think I ever exchanged more than two words with her or her sister. Her mom offered me hot chocolate and apple pie, which I graciously accepted.

We talked some more while I was eating. Mrs. Herron seemed friendly enough, but I knew she was lying. Theresa said she had brought Peyton back to life, but then, probably, that Quantum bitch got in the middle of it and zapped her to here. But I couldn't very well demand to search the place, so *I* lied, too. I said that my parents were out of town until the next day, and wondered if it might not be too much of an imposition if I might stay overnight, because, I told her with puppy dog eyes, I was afraid to be in the house all alone. Mrs. Herron kindly agreed and showed me to the guest room.

Later that night, when it seemed that the Herrons had retired to their bedroom, I heard voices. Cautiously, I crept up the stairs to Mr. and Mrs. Herron's bedroom and quietly opened the door a crack. Not only were the Herron parents there, but Peyton and what looked like a younger Peyton as well.

"I couldn't leave her in the other dimension," the older Peyton said. "It's become too dangerous there. Your counterparts were murdered, though I managed to resurrect them."

"What *happened* there?" Mr. Herron asked.

"The Russians invaded," the older Peyton said, "and America fell."

"How is Ophelia?" Mrs. Herron asked, her face filled with

concern.

"Fine," came the response. "She's with the other Peyton. Apparently, time was overwritten in my dimension as well."

"Dear God!" Mrs. Herron exclaimed.

"Don't worry," the older Peyton said. "She has powers just like me."

Suddenly, though, the door I was holding onto creaked, and the older Peyton turned and saw me.

"Daisy?" she said, and then she turned to her parents.

"I let her stay overnight," Mrs. Herron explained.

"Oh, great!" said older Peyton, with a vent of frustration. Then she took hold of younger Peyton and both of them vanished, as the air let out a pop.

CHAPTER LXIII

Daisy (Part III)

*From the Alternate Timeline
In the Alternate Reality
On Earth I
Earth-Date:2029*
Time Reset 2

I had gone to Peyton's house innocently enough, ostensibly to offer my condolences for Peyton's tragic demise. Theresa didn't even know I'd gone. It had been three years since the bitch had offed herself, and Theresa (now Goody Two Shoes) wanted to put the whole thing behind her, but I didn't. I figured all the superhero shit had gone to her head and that sooner or later she'd come to her senses. Peyton Herron was alive—she had to be—and I intended to find out where they were hiding her. Enough was enough of Theresa's sex dreams about her, which she of course denied. But she talked in her sleep and all the moans and all the "Peyton, I love you!" again and again really pissed me off to no small extent.

I had never killed anyone before, and I wanted to know what it felt like. There had to be a rush—capturing her, having her wake up naked, tied up, and letting her beg for her life as I carved up her skin with a kitchen knife—not enough to kill her, just enough to make her bleed. Theresa could watch if she wanted, but the bitch was mine to take! I could borrow my parents' cruiser afterward and feed her to the sharks, bringing along some bloodied meat to attract their attention. I imagined how she'd scream as her naked body with open cuts all over it hit the salt water that would burn like hell, fitted with a life jacket, so the sharks could take their time biting off chunks of

316

her flesh. *No use letting her drown first*, I thought to myself. *That would spoil all the fun!* It made me wet just thinking about it. And here my mom and dad thought they'd raised such an innocent, sweet little girl!

My story to Peyton's parents was that I was out of the country with *my* parents since just before Peyton had killed herself—at least this is what I told her mother, who commended me for my kind thoughts. We exchanged cordialities and memories, mine mostly made up, because I barely knew her. To be perfectly honest, I don't think I ever exchanged more than two words with her or her sister. Her mom offered me hot chocolate and apple pie, which I graciously accepted.

We talked some more while I was eating. Mrs. Herron seemed friendly enough, but I knew she was lying. Theresa said she had brought Peyton back to life, but then, probably, that Quantum bitch got in the middle of it and zapped her to here. But I couldn't very well demand to search the place, so *I* lied, too. I said that my parents were out of town until the next day, and wondered if it might not be too much of an imposition if I might stay overnight, because, I told her with puppy dog eyes, I was afraid to be in the house all alone. Mrs. Herron kindly agreed and showed me to the guest room.

After the Herrons were asleep, I ascended the stairs and searched the other bedrooms, only to find them abandoned. Peyton Herron was not in the house. The question was, where the hell was she?

CHAPTER LXIV

Payton

From the Original Timeline
In the Alternate Reality
On Earth I
Earth-Date:2029

I phased into the bedroom of Katara Drall with Sarabeth. Katara, aka Peyton, was in bed asleep. She stirred with our sudden appearance as the air displacement pushed a small breath of air at her face; then she stretched out her arms and squeezed her eyelids tight before at last opening them.

"What's up?" she said with half a yawn. "I thought you two went back to the other dimension."

"We did," I replied, "only there's a shitstorm over there and, get this—there's another Ophelia, apparently the original, only I haven't tried to track her down yet."

"They murdered the other Payton's Mom and Dad," Sarabeth broke in, "but Demi brought them back to life."

"Never a dull moment," Peyton said, sitting up. She stared at me with a question in her eye. "Demi?"

"There's another one of me now, too, from the rewrite, and she's got a quantum seed that she picked up in a *third* dimension. It seems that the Khattaaara of *that* Rendenaaar somehow survived her universe and then murdered Dhraaal and wound up with *his* seed—emerald green. I'll need to show her how to use her powers and try to find out what ones she might have that are different from ours. She's smart, though."

"She's a Herron," Peyton said.

318

"She's a Peyton," Sarabeth chimed in.

"Anyway," I went on, "Once the lessons are over with, we'll both hunt down Liam and Phee. They were captured by the Soviet regime."

"Don't you have any *good* news?" Peyton asked.

"We were seen by Daisy McKenzie," I replied, "who was at your house, but I phased us back in time and undid it."

"Same here," Peyton said. "Theresa must have sent her on a reconnaissance mission to try and find Sarabeth." She glanced at her. "And I already know about the other Payton. I've met her. At first, I mistook her for you."

"I was hoping you could look after Sarabeth," I said. "It's become too dangerous for her to be at her home, what with Theresa and all."

Sarabeth looked at me, and then at Peyton. "I'm not afraid of some creepy lesbian," she burst out.

"Hey!" I said.

Sarabeth looked at me apologetically. "Sorry."

"We're not *all* creepy," I replied.

"I said I was sorry," Sarabeth apologized again.

"Apology accepted," I replied, and then turned back toward Peyton again. "I need to go back. Phee and Other Me are waiting."

Peyton stared at me as she stood up. "If you need my help, let me know. In the meantime, why don't you stay the night? You can always phase eight hours into the past, so it'll be like you just left." She stood up and draped herself in a long black silk robe that was on a small, carved bench at the foot of her bed. "I'll wake the maid to make up beds for both of you."

"Wait!" said Sarabeth. "You have a maid?"

"And a chauffeur," she replied, "and a gardener and a personal assistant."

"Boy, did I ever wind up in the wrong timeline!" Sarabeth grumbled.

"Stop groaning, child," I said. "Just be grateful you got to breathe air for a second time."

When night fell, I took my sleep in one of the guest rooms on a super-firm bed with a down-filled pillowtop. It had been an exhausting day; so much so that when I laid down my head on the down-filled pillow, I went down for the count. After a restful ten-hour sleep and a breakfast of quail eggs, caviar, and kiwi preserves on toast, I bid farewell to Peyton and Sarabeth and phased back to my dimension.

"I thought you were going back to my world," Phee said.

"Been and gone," I replied, and then turned to Other Me. "I need to get everyone here over to Peyton's dimension. It's not safe for any of you, what with all that's going on."

"I'm staying," Phee insisted.

"I don't want you hurt," I said.

"I'll be with both of you," she maintained. "I'll be fine."

I looked at my alternate self, who looked back at me and shook her head. "You get the kids out of bed," I told her. "I'll go rouse Mom and Dad."

As Other Me took the stairs, I phased up to Mom and Dad's room and switched on the lights. Both of them stirred from their sleep and looked at me.

"Please get dressed, "I said. "We need to go. I can't let you risk your lives again."

Mom was the first to get out of bed. "Where are we supposed to go *to*?" she asked.

"To the other Peyton's world. Payton and I are staying. We need to find Liam and the other Phee."

Dad stared at me as he, too, rose from the bed. "You're sure you can handle this?"

"Dad," I said as I split into five of me. "What do *you* think? Plus, I'll have Other Me to help."

"Lords, Jesus, Ghost, and God!" Mom exclaimed. "I thank everyone holy that only one of you emerged from my womb. I would not like to have been like that Nanomom woman. Imagine, nine bundles of joy coming out one after the other like baseballs from a pitching machine."

I merged back together and then looked at them in all seriousness. "You can pack a few things, but please be quick," I said, and then I phased back downstairs. Ten minutes or so later, all were gathered together. "I'll be right back," I told Other Me, and then I phased Mom and Dad and the kids and Phee to Peyton's living room.

It was a really odd thing to see when Peyton's parents, awakened by the commotion—mainly from the kids—descended the stairs to meet their doppelgängers. The two sets of parents eyed each other with the utmost curiosity.

"James," said Peyton's mom to her husband, "I think I need a shot of brandy." Then, on second thought, she called out, "Better make it a double."

"I could use one of the same," my mom (well, the sort of my mom) chimed in.

"Our world isn't safe at the moment," I told the Herrons. "I was wondering if they could stay *here* a while. If not, I can ask Peyton to put them up at her place."

"No, dear," Mrs. Herron said. "Everyone's fine right here." Her eyes drifted from Mom to Dad, and then her husband returned with the drinks, handing them first to my mom and then to his wife. Both of them downed the liquid in one fell swoop, almost in unison. It was almost comical to watch the two versions of the same woman act as though they were connected to each other like marionettes with one puppeteer. Then Mrs. Herron turned to the kids. "And who are you two precious little angels?" she asked.

"I'm Liam, and that's Li. She's my twin sister."

"James?" Mrs. Herron said as she went over to the pair. "Doesn't Li look just like our Ophelia when she was that age?" and she glanced at Phee, whose gaze kept going back and forth between the two sets of Herrons.

"That *is* Ophelia," I explained, "but from another parallel world."

"It's all so reassuring," Phee chimed in, "that everyone is so unique. Not."

"Just how many parallel worlds *are* there?" Mr. Herron wanted to know.

"As far as Peyton and I have been able to tell, the number is infinite."

"I'm confused," My sort of dad said. He had been staring at Mrs. Herron, but then turned to me. "How do an infinite number of universes all fit in the same space?"

"They're not *in* the same space," I explained. "Matter is just an anomaly of what we *think* of as space. It's the reason that nothing can travel faster than the speed of light because matter is just a projection onto spacetime, and each parallel dimension has a unique quantum signature."

Dad turned to Mr. Herron. "Did you get any of that?" he asked.

"Not a word," Mr. Herron replied and then offered, "Can I fix you a whiskey sour?"

Dad nodded. "Two minds with but a single thought," he replied.

Mrs. Herron looked at Liam and Li. "You angels look exhausted. How about we get the two of you tucked away in bed?"

"Are you our other mother?" Li asked.

Mrs. Herron smiled. "We're both your mother now," my sort of Mom said, and then she took Liam's hand, and Mrs. Herron took Li's, and they led them up the stairs.

I turned to my sort of dad and Mr. Herron, who were standing side by side at the dry bar. "I need to get home," I told them. "I need to find Liam and Phee." Then I phased back to my world.

CHAPTER LXV

Khattaaara
(from Liam and Li's Dimension)

From the Alternate Timeline
In the Alternate Reality
On Earth II
Earth-Date:2029

Journal Entry, November 18, 2029: [61]

Two of the six infected females with the virus have been successfully transformed. There are, however, racial imbalances. None of the Negroid race has survived the transformation. They have been observed to devolve into a primitive form of hominid life and then expire within a short time. Those of Mongoloid descent, afterward, developed undesirable mental characteristics, becoming uncontrollably obsessed with their newfound sexual organs. The results from those who were of mixed race have also been disappointing, as each subject, without fail, has suffered either death or insanity. Thus far, with the current viral strain, the only successful candidates have been those of the Caucasoid race with an adulteration no greater than 12.5%. To date, more than ten thousand individuals, both male and female, have been infected with the virus that we have labeled RenTran-26. Transformation centers have been set up across the globe. It was serendipitous, however, that the first facility I chose to visit was the one that had transformed a female, designated as Subject F4489, who, upon close examination,

---

[61] Please note that the entry has been translated from Gaaalthaaaran. Copies of the original text may be obtained upon request.

possesses a different quantum signature from all others in this dimension. Compounding this is the fact that F4489 bears a striking genetic resemblance to the human female I have replaced, despite the curious reversal of its internal organs.

What never ceased to amaze me was how the *humans*—so called because they believed themselves *humane*—had become convinced that they were somehow immortal—indoctrinated with the belief that they alone possessed an incorporeal quality that they had named a *soul* which that after their death ascends with their consciousness to a place they call Heaven, where their god/creator supposedly exists and where they would forever reside in a state of perfect bliss. Oddly enough, they considered all other living creatures other than pets exempt from this ascendency. How convenient for *them*! In truth, while the conscious attributes of living creatures might *ascend* to one pocket universe or another, what remains are little more than thought patterns—memories to be more precise—without the ability to create new experiences or thoughts.

Meanwhile, F4489, who identified herself as Ophelia Jane Herron, appeared displeased with her own transformation, as observed by her interaction with one of the male staff physicians through a two-way mirror.

"Why did you do this to me?" F4489 demanded. "And where is my daughter?"

The man, a Mongoloid, as were the majority of the staff, looked up and down her form and then stared into her now violet eyes. "Are you experiencing any adverse reactions?" he asked.

"Other than the tail, the breasts, the pointed ears, and the loss of my *womanhood?*" she asked in a facetious tone.

"Any hot or cold flashes, odd tastes or smells, difficulties seeing or hearing?" he went on, undaunted, in his guttural tone.

"My senses are all heightened," she replied, "equal to anyone born on Rendenaaar, I guess."

"How do you know that name?" the man asked.

"The same way I know that the woman—probably a bad word choice—in charge of all of this is *from* there." That said, she glared at him.

"F4489," the man continued, "have you learned to control your new appendage?" He looked at her again, "And for your edification, it is anatomically called a *yaaargh*, unlike a tail, which is an extension of the spine."

"Control it?" she replied, lifting it into the air and wrapping it around his throat. "You mean like this?" As she was about to sting him with its tip, I activated the microphone that fed into the room and commanded, "Stop!" at which point, the now Gaaalthaaaran female halted her plan to murder the man and released her hold on him.

It was at that point that I decided to enter the room. Once inside, I turned to the doctor. "Kindly leave us," I said, and so, without a word, he left, rubbing his neck. I walked up to F4489 and faced her.

"We have one thing in common," I said.

"What's that?" came the emotionless response.

"Neither of us is from this dimension." I went on.

"And you're *not* from mine," she replied. "In mine, you've been dead for an eternity."

"And what was I like before that eternity?" I asked.

"Just as fucked up as you are now," she replied, and then she glared at me. "How is it that *your* Thara-Klo didn't kill you? Or did *you* kill *her*, your own daughter? I believe the term is filicide. And did you come here on your own or with *your* Dhraaal?"

"You certainly know a lot about me," I said as my gaze met hers.

"In *my* dimension," she hissed at me, "you were reincarnated as my sister. You were wicked and deserved to die—however that occurred—but my sister was good because of how both of us were raised."

She seemed complacent as she uttered her diatribe, for her demeanor took on an aspect of superiority, her *yaaargh* raised high, pointed toward *me*.

"Careful," I cautioned. "You're like a moth, playing with fire," and, in front of her, I transformed back into my Gaaalthaaaran form and attire. My *yaaargh* reached down between my legs and up between hers, pulling her close to me. I kissed her, though she struggled against it—quite violently, I might add. Then I intertwined my *yaaargh with* hers and plunged mine into its mouth. Almost immediately, she succumbed to the rhythms of Gaaalthaaaran sex. Her back arched. Her resistance grew weak. This was different from any sex she had ever known—more powerful and overwhelming. By the time I had finished and she had achieved her orgasm, she collapsed in a heap onto the floor that was now spattered (or should I say stained?) with the bluish *graaam* that her tail had sprayed out in that final instant, comingled with mine.

"You see," I said, as I stood over her, my heart still pounding from what we had just done, "it's not so bad what you've become."

"Damn you!" she muttered. "I only want Liam and my child!"

"I do not know what Liam is," I told her, "but your child shall be returned to you tonight. We did not transform her. Gaaalthaaaran children remain sexless until adolescence begins. The virus will not work on her to her great misfortune." I paused then and stared into her eyes. "For now," I said. "For now."

Propped up with her arms, she glared back at me. "You're a monster!" she proclaimed.

"I've been called that before, many times," I replied, "and in many tongues. But I've also been called a god." And with that, I turned, changed back into my military attire, and quietly exited the room.

CHAPTER LXVI

Khattaaara/Payton

> *Payton from the Original Timeline*
> *Sharing the Mind of Khattaaara*
> *In the Rewritten Timeline*
> *On Rendenaaar*
> *Trillions of Universes in the Past*

There was no one left that I could trust—not even Shaaalra. I felt angry and sad and alone. But at least I had the six remaining god-stones, the quantum seeds as Peyton had erroneously named them. In my past as Payton, I only had experience with the purple one. Now I had that plus five others in my head, each a different color and, perhaps, with different powers. I desperately needed to talk to someone. The anger in me needed to be controlled.

As Quantum Girl, I had many powers. But, I wondered, with the additional god-stones, could I do even more? I rose from the chair I was sitting in, went over to the window, and stared out. It had just turned winter, and a soft blanket of pink-tinged snow covered the ground. Most of the trees had shed their leaves weeks or months before, speaking in Earth terms. The sky strode in its airy magnificence from one horizon to the other with rivulets of spiral clouds that seemed to almost pirouette in the upper atmosphere. A seemingly endless flock of *vhargraaaig* swarmed its way through the air, across to the east as an antigrav transport cut a path through them toward the palace, disrupting their formation. One could hear the *vhargraaalig* screech for just a moment, and then all was as it had been with the transport nearer to its journey's end.

My world once more at peace, I closed my eyes, concentrated,

327

and imagined what I wanted done. All at once, I could feel another self, pull its way out of me. But this was different than the countless other times I had multiplied myself. It was another being emerging from me as though I were a suit of clothes; so did I imagine as I tried focusing on what was happening. When it was done, I opened my eyes, and she opened hers. She stood facing me—Payton Alise Herron—the other half of me, the human half—the half that had kept me sane. She looked at me, glanced downward, and then behind herself to realize that she no longer had a *yaaargh*. Then her hands went up to her breasts and, finally, to her ears to prove to her doubting brain that she was fully human again.

"It's been so long," she said to me with half a smile. "I forgot what it was like," and she paused and then added, "to be me."

"Thou dost know we can only stay this way for a short span of time," I said.

"I know," came the reply. "And I don't mind being you," she went on. "It's just that I miss my Mom and Dad and Liam."

"And Ophelia and Peyton," I added.

"And Phee and Peyton," she said, correcting me. The moment became all so nostalgic for her that she broke into tears. The odd part was that although she spoke to me in English and I spoke to her in Gaaalthaaaran, we could both understand each other. "Come on," I said, taking hold of her hand, "Let's go for a walk."

"How does it feel to be thyself again?" I asked her.

"Almost human," she replied.

"Dost thou regret what happened?" I asked.

"There are a lot of regrets a person could have," she said. "The reality is, I could have been killed. How it was that my spirit found its way into you, I don't know." She paused and then went on. "And while I knew that you weren't Peyton, it still gave me—gives me—comfort to think that I'm together with a part of her."

She faced me. Her hands firmly gripped my forearms as she stared into my eyes. "There was so much hatred in you," she said. "I think I tempered it, at least a bit."

"Regardless, I need to avenge the iniquity of my brother, now thine as well," I said.

"I know," Payton said back. "And we will. What he did to us was unconscionable. There's an expression where I come from; there will *be* an expression, 'An eye for an eye.' What that means is that you exact justice and not revenge. You can take his *yaaargh* because he took yours, but you can't take his life. Take comfort in the fact that no god-stone will grow *his* back."

"Let him remain as impotent as my plans to murder him," I replied. "But what about Thara-Klo?" I said. "What if he was the fiend who murdered *her*?"

"We'll cross that bridge when we come to it," she replied, and her words gave me strength. "We have six quantum seeds in our head. We don't know all of their powers—yet—but we will." She pulled me to her and hugged me. "You are my strength," she said in a calming voice, "and I am your conscience. Whatever we were on our own, we are stronger together. Perhaps one day, I'll show you *my* world, but for now, we need to deal with yours."

A chill breeze scraped against my flesh as the two of us merged back into one again. My heart had ceased to pound in my chest. My hands no longer trembled with rage. Fury would not be an accomplice to the victory that I sought. I knew this now as my path to wreaking justice became clear.

CHAPTER LXVII

Peyton

From the Original Timeline
In the Alternate Reality
On Earth I
Earth-Date:2029

How long ago it seemed since the quantum seed went into my head and how messed up things had become. My own life had been different for what must be measured as an eternity. While Phee had gone on to attend college, I took over for Dhraaal at Quantech after Khattaaara had murdered him. I kept up the pretense. I became Katara Drall on a permanent basis, ever donning my black wigs, though the short, pageboy hairstyle had gradually transitioned to a somewhat longer Bettie Page look, down to the cream-colored makeup, black eyeliner, and red lipstick— Rouge Hermès, no less, at nearly $100 per tube. Hell, I had money now, so why not? *That* accompanied *always* by black stiletto heels. Fuck me if I say so, but I exuded sex at every turn. I also maintained a good business ethic and caused the company's stock to split twice in the past two years, justifying my salary of a cool six mill. Of course, having a quantum brain didn't hurt.

The day after Sarabeth had taken up residence at my estate, she began moping around my office and wound up fiddling with a rare Mid-Century sculpture by Paul Evans.

"Sarabeth," I warned her. "That's an incredibly valuable piece."

"Sorry," she said as she pulled her hands away. "I'm sure it's worth hundreds of dollars."

"Hundreds of thousands," I told her.

330

"It's so unfair," she lamented.

"What is?" I asked.

"Well," she replied, "I'm the only Peyton who doesn't have any powers."

"There are just three of us who do," I said smiling, as I continued to work.

"Just!" she repeated. "*Un*just, you mean! Why did *I* get the short end of the stick?"

I looked up at her and smiled. "You *do* know there's no such thing."

"What do you mean?" she asked.

"A stick can't have a short end," I replied. "It's all one piece." I rose from my desk. "Look," I said in as big-sisterly a tone as I could, "you got a second chance. How many others can *say* that?"

"I suppose," she said with a heavy breath, "but it's just not the same."

"Being alive is a superpower in and of itself," I told her. "Now, how about I take you on a quick trip, and then afterward we go anywhere you want for lunch?"

"'kay," she relented. Then I phased her to a place that was literally out of this world.

When we got there, Sarabeth looked around, disappointment in her eyes.

"You brought me to the desert?" she said.

"I brought you to Mars," I told her.

Her eyes lit up like fireflies. "Mars!" she repeated. "We're on Mars!"

"Fourth planet from the sun," I replied. "See that moon in the sky?" I said, pointing upward. "That's Phobos. And right there just above the horizon is Deimos."

"That is *so* cool!" she exclaimed, and then, suddenly, she went all serious on me. "We're not going to meet any Martians," she asked, "are we?"

"As far as I can tell," I replied, "we're the only Martians around. Now, where would you like to have lunch? Paris? Rome? Tokyo?"

"McDonald's!" she said.

"Oh, God!" I muttered to myself. "Why McDonald's," I asked, "when we can eat at Le Fouquet's?"

"I like their French fries," she replied.

"Sacre bleu!" I muttered to myself as I phased us both to the deserted back of the local franchise that was emblazoned with *golden* arches. McDonald's it was!

CHAPTER LXVIII

Theresa

> *From the Original Timeline*
> *In the Alternate Reality*
> *On Earth I*
> *Earth-Date:2026*

Daisy's mother turned out to be a real problem. She totally blew up Daisy's phone every day with calls and texts. Regardless that Daisy would text her back, "Stop!" it continued *non*stop. The woman sent over the cops five times, reporting her as a runaway, and each time the cops would pick her up and bring her back home, only for her to come right back here the moment they drove off. It was all just *so* annoying! We had enough money to be able to buy some other place—a really nice place—but when you're sixteen, you can't sign a contract, meaning neither of us was old enough to complete a sale.

When the runaway crap didn't work, Mrs. McKenzie called social services on me, telling them that I was underage and that my mother had died, and I was obviously "not capable of taking care of myself." So, while Daisy was back at her parents' house for one night to try and get her mother to stop, a social worker and a cop showed up at my front door. Both were women. To be honest, the cop was kind of cute.

"Theresa Martinez?" the social worker said, flashing her credentials.

"Yes?" I replied.

"I'm with Children's Protective Services. My name is Mrs...." (something or other.) I really wasn't paying attention. I was actually focused on the cop.

"What do you want?" I asked.

"Our department has been made to understand that your mother passed away more than two months ago," she said, "and that you've been living on your own ever since."

"She didn't *pass away*," I corrected her, consistent with the new timeline. "She abandoned me. But what of it?"

"You need to come with us," she replied.

"I didn't break any laws," I said.

"Pursuant to California Welfare and Institutions Code, Article 6, Subsection 300 (g)," she said, "any child under the age of eighteen who does not have a parent or guardian shall become a ward of the state."

"I've been able to manage on my own," I replied.

"You need to come with us," she insisted. "You can gather up some clothes and personal belongings."

"I didn't do anything wrong," I protested. "This is not fair!"

I looked at the cop. No sympathy there. I thought about teleporting out of there, but where was I going to go? I figured I might as well take things one step at a time. Regardless, I left a note for Daisy, warning her to lie low till things got sorted out.

California no longer believed in orphanages. I was placed in a foster home—that of Charlie and Lanelle Adams, a black couple in their thirties. Fuck if the universe didn't have a sense of humor. Charlie and Lanelle were the same couple who had wound up in my house three years in the future. Maybe I sold them the place after they took me in, but something must have gone wrong in between for them both to have reacted the way they did.

Charlie and Lanelle weren't bad as foster parents go, but I really did *not* want to be there. At the time of my placement, they were living in a two-bedroom apartment in the Crenshaw District. They definitely weren't rich, and I actually think it was Section 8 housing. Charlie, it seems, had been in construction till he got injured on the job, which he said messed up his back. Then the economy took a nosedive after Biden got elected, and hardly any construction took place. He said he tried to get jobs at other places like Walmart or Target, but was told he was *overqualified*. The apartment was simple—sort of barren when it came to any decorations. I don't know if that was from a lack of money or a lack of artistic sense, but all that was there was Ikea furniture shit and not much else. There was a disassembled baby crib in the room that I was given. I guess they'd tried to have a kid, but it didn't work out. I figured it'd be rude of me to ask. Maybe that's why they decided to go the foster route, or maybe it was just for the money they got paid. I didn't know, and I guess it really didn't matter much to anyone but them.

The first night, there was roast beef and mashed potatoes and gravy for supper. Lanelle wasn't a half-bad cock.

"So," Lanelle said, "I understand you've been on your own for quite some time." She took a swallow of her Coke. "Since your mother left you."

"I've done all right," I replied. "I really don't need to *be* here."

"I said the exact same thing when I was your age," Charlie said, not even glancing up from his plate.

Lanelle looked at me. "Doesn't it get lonely, living in your mother's house all by yourself?"

"I wasn't *by* myself," I said. "I have a girlfriend."

"Is that a girl *friend* or a muff-diving carpet muncher?" That was Charlie.

"Charles Langford Adams!" Lanelle exclaimed. "We do not talk that way in this house, especially in front of a child!"

"If the Lord Almighty *God* had intended women to enjoy their caves of madness with each other," Charlie hurled back at her, "He would have changed their tongues into penises."

Lanelle turned to me with the scent of apology on her breath. "You have to forgive Charlie," Lanelle said and then glared at her husband. "His mother dropped him on his butt when he was an infant, and it all went to his head."

"Just sayin'," Charlie went on unfazed.

"Daisy and I happen to be in love," I said to him. "You have a problem with that?"

Lanelle placed her hand on mine. "Girl, you be whoever or whatever you want to be, with whomsoever you want to be with."

I thought that was kind of cool of her to say. Anyway, the rest of the meal went on without another word.

CHAPTER LXIX

Ophelia

> *From the Original Timeline*
> *In the Alternate Reality*
> *On Earth II*
> *Earth-Date:2029*

This wasn't my life—at least it wasn't supposed to be. This was Hell. I mean, I don't believe in Paradise or Perdition *or* Hell, but if there were such a place where damned souls stand condemned to eternity, it was the Earth in this dimension, there and then. And if there was a soul that justly or unjustly was condemned to travel there, it apparently was mine. I was born Ophelia Jane Herron, but when I looked at my reflection in the mirror, I didn't know who I was anymore.

That same night, after I awoke to find myself transformed into a previously long-extinct alien, Jordan made her way back into my arms. Odd that she was brought to me by Claire—or perhaps that was a calculated move. For some strange reason, Claire liked her transformation. I wondered if there was any of the *original her* left. Claire, of course, had no past history with Khattaaara. There had been no Rendenaaar in this dimension, not that anyone was aware of. If that planet and its civilization had existed in the distant past, none of its inhabitants had made their way to this Earth. But now, the Khattaaara from that other plane of existence had somehow found her way here—the same Khattaaara the rewritten Payton had described—and her appearance had heralded an invasion.

It was fortunate that Jordan was too young to notice the differences in me and too young to have been adversely affected by our separation. Holding her in my arms put my mind at ease—at least for a while—but I was greatly concerned about Liam. *Was he all right? Had he been transformed as I had been, and if not, what would his reaction be toward me? Repulsion, I suppose.* What man, from whatever dimension, would love a woman with whom he could never have normal sex? My guess was that how he would feel would be the ultimate test of love.

But there was a greater problem than my own. What of all humanity? Mankind here was on the verge of extinction. As far as I knew, there was no resistance. The country had been taken over by the Soviets, but the Soviets were under the direction of the Khattaaara from Earth III. There had to be a way to stop it. At least I prayed that there was.

Beyond their new physiology, Claire and Zoë had been mentally transformed as well. They both behaved as though what had happened to them was natural and inevitable in a good way. Other Rends, as they were called, acted much the same. There were eighteen of us in total, six of whom were males. All of them also now spoke with what I assumed was a Rendenaaaran accent, presumably caused by the restructured anatomy of the larynx. Such was the same for me. I remember hearing a trace of it when Thara-Klo spoke, but then, she had decades of practice to try and hide it.

I found it curious, though, that my brain hadn't been affected like the others. Regardless that every cell in my body had been changed to resemble that of a long-dead species, mentally I still remained me. All that I could think was that the quantum field that Payton had placed around me, which had caused time to re-form around me, had now protected my mind as well. And, in that none of them suspected, that would serve to my advantage if I ever wanted to escape. I just needed to pretend to be one of them and learn as much as I could.

I was in the commissary. Claire and Zoë were already sitting at one of the tables, enjoying, respectively, what looked to me to be a plate of almost hair-thin, live worms along with large beetle-like creatures, also still alive. I went to sit beside Zoë and opposite Claire. My plate, in contrast, consisted of leafy vegetation mixed with cheese.

"All right if I sit down?" I asked.

Claire glanced at Zoë, and then shrugged out, "Whatever."

"Are you still in a lather about Liam?" I asked Claire.

Claire burst out a laugh, inadvertently spitting out some of the food in her mouth. Zoë chuckled as well.

"What?" I asked.

"Liam has a six-inch dick. The Rends have four-foot *yaaarghs*. Seriously, you should try one." She shoved some more worms into her mouth with her fingers. "Mmmm! You need to taste some of these! You can feel them squirming as they go down your throat." She looked as though she were having an orgasm as she swallowed. "Here," she said, picking up more with her fingers and putting them up to my mouth. "Go ahead." She stared at me, as though it were an order. Disgusting as they were, I had to keep up a pretense, so I opened up and let her fingers push the squirming mass into my mouth.

I felt like throwing up! The hideous worms—or whatever they were—squirmed and thrashed. I closed my eyes and feigned ecstasy. I tried to convince myself that what was writhing on my tongue was only angel hair pasta. I had to. Everything depended on it—my life, Jordan's life, maybe even Liam's—they were all at stake. And, so, I pushed them down my throat with the back of my tongue. It was interesting to observe the differences both Claire and Zoë revealed in their assimilated state. The vindictiveness in Claire—at least as much as I had observed—had been replaced by a sense of superiority.

As the meal came to an end, a tall, burly, dark-haired Rend entered the room. He was naked, with chiseled features and violet eyes. I found out later that his name was Samuel Murdock and that he had, in his human existence, been a teacher at a private school in Newport Beach. According to Zoë, he had a wife and small child, but none of that seemed to matter anymore once the transformation had taken place. Murdock walked up to Claire and placed his hands on her shoulders. The woman—now a female Rend—looked back and up at him and smiled, placing her left hand on his right. At her touch, the man's tail lifted over his head and appeared to grow rigid. Claire rose, turned to meet his eyes with hers, and then the two of them, together, left the room.

Once both sexes had been transformed in sufficient numbers, mating was encouraged in order to determine whether the Rends were able to reproduce. After all, what good would it have been to transform an entire population if only to have them die off within a few score of years? As for Zoë and me, for the moment, no males were forced upon either one of us. Regardless, I observed her and Claire in bed together most nights.

Freedom was rationed out to us in small doses, as was information regarding the state of affairs on a global scale. It seemed that the invasion, which had begun in the United States, soon metastasized to the rest of the world. With their inability to become Rends, the vast majority of the populations of Africa, Asia, and the Americas south of the Rio Grande had either been eradicated or made slaves for their future masters. Meanwhile, the Khattaaara of Earth III had revealed her true form, though, for whatever reason, concealed her origin.

The war that was inflicted upon humanity was, after the initial attack, not fought with guns or bayonets or bombs but rather with the RenTran-26 virus, which had been surreptitiously released throughout North America and Europe, often through the use of already infected prostitutes. And cleverly, drug stores and other places that sold over-the-counter pharmaceuticals had their shelves stocked with RenTran-26 adulterated nasal spray as well as in inhalers for those who suffered from asthma. Meanwhile, as human-to-human transmission could occur while those already infected were asymptomatic, the virus could unwittingly be transmitted by something so innocuous as a goodbye kiss. No one who *was* infected ever realized that they *were* infected until they awoke after the metamorphism had occurred. The disease had an R factor of 2, which meant that every person would likely infect two others while in their infectious phase. As such, despite precautions, there was insufficient time to develop a vaccine or a cure, though the general population was told otherwise. The truth of the matter was that the vaccines being administered to Caucasians were, in fact, laden with the disease, while those given to the other races contained neuron inhibitors that acted upon the cerebral cortex, causing its recipients to become permanently docile.

As I said, little by little, I was given more and more freedom. At night, I would walk down the corridors that were lined with jail cells—cells that were always filled with unconscious occupants being transformed into beings from that long-dead race. Every so often, one of them would awaken, and there would be one more Rend to people the Earth. How tragic it was that the Earth in this dimension, which I had thought was so perfect and peaceful because of its lack of technology, had been conquered by the technology from a parallel world.

As I was thinking these thoughts, one *man* sat up and looked at me.

"Where *am* I?" he asked.

"I think you should be asking what, not where," I replied. I was not trying to be cruel. But for all of us, there appeared to be no going back.

The man caught sight of his *yaaargh* and screamed! It was a harrowing scream. It was probably not to be his last until the mental transformation took place. As for me, I simply walked on. I would not allow myself to become invested in the misfortunes of others. I had my daughter to care for. She was my concern, and that was more than enough. With every step, with every breath, I contemplated escape—but the method by which to accomplish it eluded me.

CHAPTER LXX

Payton

From the Original Timeline
In the Alternate Reality
On Earth II
Earth-Date:2029

One power that I did not have was a heightened sense of smell—at least to the extent of a bloodhound—so the only way I could find either Liam or Phee was to phase back in time to the moment they left or were taken and pray that they were still together. I dared not pluck them out of that moment for fear of the paradox and subsequent endless time loop it might have created.

The house, when I arrived, was abandoned. My kind of Mom and Dad were on Peyton's Earth, as was everyone else, including the other Ophelia; everyone else but *her*, the other me.

"I thought you were going to sit this one out?" I said.

"Liam's my brother, too," she replied, filled with the same bunch of stubborn as me.

"This is a harsh, mean world now," I told her.

"So?" she said, "I can protect myself. I have a quantum seed, same as you."

"But you're not *trained*," I insisted.

"Then train me," she said as she looked at me with the same unrelenting stare that I had always possessed.

"There isn't time," I replied.

Her mouth twisted as she shook her head. "And here I thought you were the smart one."

"Oh," I said back. "I'm just distracted. When do you want to start?"

"After I get something to eat," she replied. "I don't know about you, but I work better on a full stomach."

I fixed myself a ham and cheese sandwich, while Other Me, a diehard vegesaurus like her Peyton counterpart, put together a salad comprised of romaine, tomatoes, black olives, croutons, parmesan cheese, and tofu (yuck!). But our meal gave us our first real opportunity to sit down and talk.

"So," she said, munching on her plants, "I hear you're a dive-bomber."

"I'm assuming that's what they call a clam smacker in this new iteration," I replied.

She looked at me very strangely, presumably due to my flippant use of the obviously derogatory term.

"At least I'm not a doppelbanger," I went on.

"You and me?" she said in a never-in-a-kajillion-years tone. "I mean, I think you're amazingly beautiful and all, but huh-uh. I'm only into dick." This, as she (somewhat amusingly from my Freudian perspective) chomped on a celery stick.

"You never know until you try," I said.

"Then I guess I'll never know," she said back with an air of indifference. "So," she went on, "how did *you* wind up with a glowing rock in your head?"

"They're called quantum seeds," I replied.

"Whatever," she remarked with indifference. Then, after an impatient five-second pause, "And?" she asked, staring hard into my eyes.

"I got it from Peyton," I answered.

"The older one, I assume," she said.

"When she died," I said back.

"Does every Peyton in creation eventually bite the dust?" she asked.

"Seems like it," I replied. "All except you and me."

"So, you're Demi, and Shortcake's Sarabeth. What do you all call *me*?"

"No one has said yet, though I've been thinking of you as 'Other Me.'"

"Not sure that I care for that," she said. "It sounds too much like Oda Mae from *Ghost*."

"You didn't like the movie?" I asked.

"I didn't like the fact that Patrick Swayze died," she replied.

"That was the entire premise," I said.

"I mean, in real life," she said back.

"Oh," I shrugged. "Yeah. He was kind of hot, even from a lesbian point of view." I took a deep breath and then added, "So, Straight Payt, are we ready now to turn you into an awesome Quantum Girl?"

I think it was the Straight Payt that caused her to roll her eyes, but we both rose from our chairs and went into the living room, me after her. Once there, we stood facing each other like 3D reflections.

"What have you been able to do so far," I asked her, "that you can control?"

"I'm pretty good now about being able to phase through dimensions," she said, "the rest is kind of hit and miss."

"Trust me," I replied, trying to reassure her, "I felt exactly the same when the seed went into my head. It takes time—and patience—but we can do this if we work together."

"Ready when you are, Demi Girl," she said.

Teaching Other Me to be more *like* me in terms of quantum abilities was a journey of a thousand steps and then some. Other Me was smart, and she learned humility, but she possessed an air of cockiness that I myself had never exhaled. By the end of the third month, though, she had a decent command of most everything other than X-ray projection. No matter how hard she tried, it just wouldn't happen for her. Then, suddenly, one day, when we were outside, she demonstrated an ability that neither Peyton nor I had. Her body became rigid but incorporeal. How coincidental, I thought to myself, that months before, we had spoken about the movie *Ghost*, and this was now happening to *her*. I went up to her and tried to grab hold of her, but my hands went right through her. Her eyes were open, but she was unresponsive. It was as though she were actually somewhere else, and this was just an afterimage of her. Regardless, there she stood, unmoving for hours on end. Night fell, and then day broke, and still there she remained like a statue, and with me completely helpless, not knowing what to do.

CHAPTER LXXI

Payton

> *From the Alternate Timeline*
> *In the Alternate Reality*
> *On Earth II*
> *Earth-Date:2029*

Everything had suddenly changed. Payton—the other Payton, the one from the other timeline—was gone, and so was everything else. Suddenly, I was sitting in a conference room surrounded by a group of people—some civilian, some in military dress. One of the latter, a general, middle-aged with graying hair, sat staring at me, although he appeared to be addressing everyone else.

"What proof do we have," he said, "that what she says is true? America was at odds with the goddam Ruskies for more than a century. I don't know how we can trust them being in charge?"

I felt myself respond to him. I felt my mouth move. I heard words come from my lips, but the words weren't mine.

"This is no longer America," I heard myself say. It was my voice, but with an accent that struck a familiar chord. "This is now the eastern arm of the Gaaalthaaaran Republic. For far too long, the inhabitants of your world have propagated hatred among your own kind. There is no unity. There is no strength. Beyond that, your people grow old and die in less than one hundred of your years. What we now do will create virtual immortality."

Suddenly, I was no longer a part of her, but of the old general, who maintained his pointed stare, the blood curdling within him. I could see her now, the one I had been inside of. It was *her*—she who had sent me to the other dimension—the alien version of *me*.

346

"You want to turn the entire human race into goddam freaks!" he growled at her. I could feel his hands tighten into fists.

The alien sprang to her feet. "Is that what you think, old man? Am I a monster to your human eyes?" She caused the uniform she wore to disappear and stood there naked in her Rendenaaaran splendor. Her hair now loose, falling down to her shoulders, she shook her head, forcing it back, to reveal her pointed ears. But beyond the rest, were her eyes, the irises of which were violet, where before they had been gray-blue. "I am Khattaaara Gaaalthaaara, Divine Empress of the long-dead planet, Rendenaaar, whose glory transcends all universes and all time." And with that, her tail raised high above her head and sprayed an almost invisible mist across the room.

Once again, my consciousness was within her. She looked around as one by one, each of those in her presence succumbed to the vapor and let out small coughs.

"In some days," the Divine Empress said in an accent that, to my mind, seemed more alien than foreign, "each of you will become as I am." She glanced at the Asian woman who sat next to the general. "Well, most of you, at any rate."

Then, all at once, I was back in myself *as* myself. My Payton mentor, though, was no longer there with me, and the sun had vanished from the sky. It was nighttime and the stars shone brightly overhead, reveling in their distance from this troubled world. A lone dog's barking cut into the crisp night air, while crickets chirped out tirelessly in hopes of finding a mate, oblivious to the troubles that had besieged the human part of the planet.

I phased first into the living room and then into the bedroom that my mirror self and I now shared. Demi had phased Liam's bed into the room, which was a hell of a lot easier than carrying it or taking it apart and putting it back together. Not wanting to disturb her as she lay asleep, I quietly changed into my jams in the dark and climbed under the soft down comforter that Mom and Dad had bought for me last year, as one of my Christmas gifts.

"I didn't know if you'd ever come back," she said, roused from her dreams. "You were gone so long."

"It was just a few minutes for me," I replied.

"It's been more than four months," she said, and her words fell on me like a hammer. "You were standing there like some phantom. I couldn't touch you. I couldn't pull you back. Your form wouldn't waver in the wind. The rain fell right through you like you weren't even there. I thought you were gone forever. We thought. I went and got Peyton. It was beyond us both." She paused and then went on. "Your seed—it's not the same as Peyton's and mine. The fact that it's green and not violet…"

"I guess color makes a difference," she replied.

"So it seems," she sadly admitted, "The only ones we'd encountered before have been violet and white." She paused and then looked at me. "What exactly happened while you were gone?" she asked.

"I was in the body of the Khattaaara from Liam and Li's dimension," I told her, "and then in some army general. I could feel everything they felt, but I had no control. You know, that Khattaaara chick is mean as fuck. She used her tail to spray out some gas to change everyone in the room into one of her kind. That's what they were experimenting on, on that base on the moon."

"In the other dimension," Demi said, articulating what was already known. People tend to do that, you know, when they can't think of anything else to say, and it seemed that she was at a loss for words.

"I told you, or don't you remember?" I reminded her. "I had to scrub off all the moon dust."

"It would be nice to be able to train you to use your new power," she said, "but that could take years."

"How much longer on the other stuff?" I asked.

"I think we're almost there," she replied. "Just try not to fade off again."

"Like I have control over it," I said, frustrated.

"What were you thinking just before it happened?" she asked.

I tried to remember. "I was thinking about Khattaaara," I said, "and wondered what was going on in her mind. That must have been the trigger. No, I take it back. It was more like I wished for me to know." I looked at her. "But why the time difference?"

"You said she infected the entire room?" Demi said.

"And?" I asked.

"Perhaps," she said, "the mist from her tail had quantum particles from her dimension."

"And what does that mean?" I replied.

"Time moves slower where she's from," Demi said. "Anyway, we're going to need to work out a plan of attack if we're going to rescue Liam and Phee."

"Agreed," I replied. I thought about it for a moment and then went on. "I was wondering. If we jump—sorry—phase back to when they were taken, couldn't we rescue them at that point in time?"

Demi smiled. "We both seem to think alike," she replied. "I'd already thought of that. We can't risk a paradox occurring."

"How so?" came my response.

"Well," she replied, "if we rescue them just before they're captured, then we never would have had a reason to go back in time, which would mean that we wouldn't have gone back. But if we never *went* back, then they *would* have been captured and on and on, causing a time loop we might never be able to escape from."

"Seriously," I said.

She stared hard into my eyes. "*Groundhog Day* without Bill Murray."

"What's Groundhog Day?" I asked, "And who's Bill Murray? I hope he's not an exterminator because I think groundhogs are kind of cute."

She just shook her head to herself and then went back to sleep. I just shrugged my shoulders, took a deep breath, and followed suit.

CHAPTER LXXII

Payton

> *From the Original Timeline*
> *In the Alternate Reality*
> *On Earth II*
> *Earth-Date: 2029*

It is strange to think that my spirit-self, which went back so far in time, later became the subject of an ancient Gaaalthaaaran tale. [62] But for a coin toss in the quantum fabric, this might well have been me. How is it, though, that souls can divide? How can that which makes

---

[62] In late Thraaadrahn folklore, after the god-stones had disappeared and the world had grown dark and foreboding and braaagraonig breathed cold fire into the air, Paaagtaaan, a lonely spirit, having come from a far-off land, arrived on Rendenaaar, having searched for untold ages for some vessel to restore her physical form. An outcast, she had long ago been betrayed by her lover, Trasaaag, who had broken her heart and then devoured her flesh so that all that remained was her soul. Endlessly then, Paaagtaaan searched for a home for her spirit to rest until one day she found a beautiful *Gaaalthaaaran* female whose heart had turned black as coal, having also been betrayed by one to whom she had given all her trust and her love so that no more of either was left—not one bit. But when Paaagtaaan saw her, she saw through the darkness to the forgotten light within and knew at once that the two of them were meant to be as one. But, alas, she could find no way to intertwine their souls. Something of the other, though, must have felt her longing, for the other wept out one tear—a single drop of sorrow that dripped to the ground and melted into the barren soil. There it might have been forgotten, swallowed by whatever gods inhabited the lower depths, but miracles do happen, even on worlds that are bereft of laughter. And so, where it fell, all at once sprung forth a wondrous flower, more beautiful and fragrant than the other had ever seen—so much so, that the other dropped down to her knees to imbibe its beauty and inhale its fragrance, unknown to her that the flower held Paaagtaaan's spirit that was released as its scent. Thus, it came that when the other inhaled the fragrance, the soul of Paaagtaaan entered her head and mixed with her own. And thus, did Paaagtaaan find a home for her spirit, and the other, whose name was Khattaaara, had the darkness purged from her heart and once again became loving and kind.

351

us unique be cleaved in two? But then that is what happened to Peyton, her soul fragmented off of her physical form from when she was Khattaaara. And yet it seemed that I was Khattaaara as well—at least the part of me that was no longer a part of my present self. I suppose that Heisenberg would have had a field day knowing that none of us can predict where our soul will be at any given moment in time or dimension or universe or physical space. We can only map out the probability of where and when our souls might be at any given moment in time.

Meanwhile, my heart broke at the thought of what those monsters might have done to Liam and Phee. Other Me had only met Phee briefly, but I had known her for three long years during which time she had become not only a friend but almost a sister to me. And Liam, despite that he was in this overwritten reality, still felt like the brother I would never see again. I decided to leave Peyton out of this for the moment. Other Me and I would rescue Phee first and do whatever it took to keep both her and Jordan safe. After that, we would find Liam if he was still alive. Liam was strong. He would resist as best he could, but I still feared for the worst. It was just over a week later when I felt at last that Other Me's powers were as honed as they could be.

"Can you spirit-phase into her?" I asked Other Me. "We need to get a location."

"I don't know that I can do that," Other Me said. She seemed to radiate uncertainty.

"Of course, you can," I assured her. "Focus on *her* the way you focused on Khattaaara. You just need to believe in yourself."

Other Me closed her eyes. A moment later, her body became incorporeal once more. It must have only been five minutes, but it seemed an eternity before she became solid again and opened her eyes.

"I know where she is," she said. "Come on."

And so, she phased us both to the prison compound where Phee was being held. In that it was night, apart from some Rendenaaaran-morphed guards, most were asleep. We tread with caution, phasing past any potential threats that we encountered. Above all else, we did not want to set off any alarms. Steel doors and iron bars did not stop us. We phased right past them. Finally, through the map that was now in Other Me's head, we found the room where Phee and Jordan were and phased inside.

Phee lay in bed with Jordan next to her. My heart stopped when I saw what Khattaaara had done to her—turned her into one of her own. *What a monstrous thing to do*, I thought, *to turn someone into a species other than their own.* I could only imagine what must have gone through her head when she realized what she had become. *Dear, dear friend,* I promised her in my head that *we will rescue you, and then find a way to change you back.* She was asleep when we found her; whether in nightmares or dreams, I didn't know. Her tail curled over her, cradling the infant, cradling my niece. There was one other bed in the room, another Rendenaaaran-shaped female, lying with her face toward the wall, also asleep and thus oblivious to our presence. But it was as she turned in her restless slumber that her face was first revealed. It was Claire! *My Gods!* I thought to myself. *The world had become a nightmare!*

I touched Phee gently to rouse her, my hand over her mouth as she stirred. Violet eyes opened, still drenched with sleep, but they quickly came to focus on me and my timeline twin. This was followed by a rain of tears as I withdrew my hand. One finger over my lips bid her to be silent, glancing toward the other bed, and then motioning her to follow us from the room.

"How did you find me?" she wept out in a whisper, sitting up in bed.

"We'll explain when we get out," I said, as I glanced toward the other bed.

"What about Claire?" Other Me asked.

"Her mind is gone," Phee replied. "She's one of *them*. There's a

Khattaaara in this dimension. She's taken control of the world."

"We know," I said, but it was at that moment that Jordan began to cry. Phee lifted her into her arms, but it was too late. The sound had awakened Claire, who quickly sprang to her feet.

"What are you two doing here?" she demanded to know.

"We're here to rescue Phee," Other Me said, "and you, if you want."

"You're here to destroy us all!" Claire screamed. Then she let out a deafening wail, such as her now Rendenaaaran lungs allowed her to do.

"We need to go!" Phee said. "It won't be long until the guards come!"

It was as we phased that Claire lunged at us, but wound up only tackling thin air.

An instant later, we were back at home. Phee looked around the living room, half in disbelief that she was really there. Then she turned to me.

"Look what they've done to me," she sobbed. "They turned me into a monster. How could Liam ever love me anymore?"

"Love is unconditional," I said. "Do you have any idea where he is?"

Phee wiped away her tears. "He's at some camp in Modesto. That's as much as I know."

"Pay can find him," I said, as I glanced at Other Me. "Meanwhile, I need to take you back home. Your Mom and Dad and Pay's Mom and Dad are there. Look," I said, staring into Phee's eyes, "everyone loves you, and that will never change." I turned to Other Me. "Can you handle things from here?" I asked.

"Can a bird fly?" she replied with just a hint of a smile.

"Then we're out of here," I said, and phased the three of us, Pheeand Jordan and myself, back to the world that Phee called home.[63]

---

[63] It might be wondered why Other Me and I didn't just phase back before Phee had been transformed. It was Other Me who declined to do so, as it has been so long since the transformation had taken place that she did not want to erase that much of her.

CHAPTER LXXIII

Daisy

> *From the Alternate Timeline*
> *In the Alternate Reality*
> *On Earth I*
> *Earth-Date:2029*

Sex is great, but the thought of murder, the visualization of someone knowing they're about to die—and painfully—is the ultimate in terms of orgasmic thought. *But, fuck,* I thought to myself again and again. *I'm just a fifteen-year-old girl. I can't even buy a rifle.* And then there was Theresa—Rainbow Girl! *Why the fuck should she have all the fun and get all the praise?* She wanted everyone to love her. I, on the other hand, wanted people to fear me. My first victim was my mother. I whacked her in the head with a brick I had covered in a towel. I had come home to visit, and we were in the kitchen, and she was at the refrigerator, getting me something to drink, her back facing me. I had the ends of the towel twisted around it. I used it like a sledgehammer, slamming it into her head. I heard her moan as she collapsed to the floor, spilling the plastic pitcher of lemonade. She tried to look up to understand what had happened. She saw me then, as I slammed the brick down on her head again and again until the moaning stopped and her blood ran across the ceramic floor, staining the white grout as it went. Then I went upstairs, stripped off my clothes, and relived the moment in my mind, as I fingered myself to orgasm—once, then twice, and then more rapidly toward a final surge of ecstasy. Then I rolled onto my back, panting from my exertion, staring up at the snowy canopy that hung over my bed, my nostrils filled with the perfume of my own scent. I smiled and then laughed. I hungered for more. I must have lain there half an hour before I found the strength to get up. Still naked, I went to my mother's room and stole the jewelry from her safe. I knew the combination. It was my birthday. *Hell*, I thought as I dropped the glittering baubles into a pillowcase, *she wouldn't need them anymore*. Then I got dressed, went out back, and broke in one of the windows. *Let the servants find her and clean up the mess. Let the cops think it was some burglar.* She was my first. My second was to be Theresa. It was all great at first, but I'd grown tired of her.

I didn't know what gave her her powers, but she didn't have control when she was asleep. She was still with those foster parents of hers, though, back in her home. She had agreed to let them buy the place so long as she got the money and could stay there as long as she wanted. Most people may not realize it, but an axe works even better than a brick. Theresa had let me stay the night. I felt like the Red Queen in Alice in Wonderland. "Off with her head!" She never knew what hit her, nor did her foster mother know what had hit her. I couldn't find her foster father. He wasn't around. I didn't care just so long as he didn't unexpectedly walk in, which he didn't. But then, as I went back into Theresa's room, I saw something strange. There was a glowing white bead next to her head. As I picked it up and looked at it, it began to spin and grow smaller, and then, all at once, it flew at me—at my head! I felt a burning sensation, and then it was as though my entire body radiated energy. So this was what gave her the powers that she had. *Fuck!* I thought to myself. *And now they were mine!* After wiping away any fingerprints I might have left, I hiked it back to my house on foot. I didn't want to be connected with the murders that had just taken place. When I got back home, though, there were police and police cars everywhere. My first thought was that they connected me with what I had just done. Then I realized it was my mother's body that had been found, probably by one of the house staff, who had reported it to them.

"What's going on?" I asked one of the maids who sat crying on the front steps.

"Your mama," she wept. "She was murdered!"

My own tears began to flow on cue. "Oh, my God, no!" I sobbed.

The woman rose and took me in her arms. Then a cop walked over to us.

"Are you the daughter?" he asked as I turned toward him.

"Yes," I answered tearfully, my voice trembling. "Valeria said my mother was murdered."

"I'm sorry," he replied. "But we're going to need to get a statement."

"Of course," I said, "but I think I need to sit down."

"I'll get you a bottle of water," he told me, and then he walked to his squad car.

I wiped my cheeks a bit. I prided myself on being able to *turn on the faucet* on a whim. I was questioned for nearly an hour, during which time I cried like a baby. They never did find my mother's killer. Daddy Dearest killed himself just a few days later. He left a note in fountain pen, telling the world how sad he was over my mother's death and how he just couldn't go on without her. It took forever to get the ink stains off my fingertips. I should have used a ballpoint pen instead. My bad. Literally.

CHAPTER LXXIV

Peyton

> *From the Original Timeline*
> *In the Alternate Reality*
> *On Earth I*
> *Earth-Date:2029*

Dearest Phee, I knew that I had failed you from the expression on your face. I just wasn't prepared. Mom and Dad and the Herrons were out at dinner. It must have been a strange sight for any onlookers to have seen what they must have thought were two sets of identical twins circling fifty. Therein lay a subtle humor, since they were anything but—twins, I mean—the circling fifty part was just a result of time creeping up. No one—and I mean no one—would have ever considered the possibility that they were interdimensional versions of themselves. Still, it was a good thing that they were not here to witness what had become of you, my love. And then I saw the baby that you held.

"And who's this?" I asked, knowing already, but trying to hold back tears.

"This is Jordan," Phee replied. "Your niece."

"She's so beautiful," I said. "Can I hold her?"

"Of course," came her response. Then she gently handed the infant to me to cradle in my arms.

"She looks just like *you*," I said, glancing up at her.

"And her father," she added.

I looked at her with a hint of a question in my eyes.

"Liam, of course," she said, and then she burst into tears.

"We haven't found him yet," Payton said. "But Pay will." She cast a glance toward Jordan, encouraging me to give her back to Phee, which I did. Then she turned to Phee. "Why don't you take Jordan upstairs and rest a bit? You look like you need it. You've been through a lot."

"Thanks," Phee said. She started toward the stairs but then stopped and turned back. "I'll need diapers and formula and, I don't know, maybe a bassinet and a crib," and with that, she started to cry.

"Don't worry," Payton said. "We'll take care of it."

It was a strange situation. My poor sister; what they had done to her. And then a glance toward the head of the staircase revealed the other Ophelia, the one from the rewritten timeline, who stood watching all that had been going on. What would be Phee's reaction, I wondered, when she met her other self who had been spared from the transformation? I never did find out, because it was at that very moment that all hell broke loose as Khattaaara phased into the room. Phee turned, her face livid.

"How?" she said. Her word was drenched with fear.

Khattaaara shrugged. "It was the other one," she said, "when she went into my mind. That was how I learned about this place." She paused and then turned to Phee. "That one," she said. "She needs to be made an example of."

Khattaaara raised her arms to hurl a deadly blast toward Phee and Jordan, but Payton countered it with a blast of her own. As the two force beams fought against each other, Payton glanced at me.

"Save them!" she said.

I rushed over to Phee and phased us out of there. There was nowhere in *this* universe or the other two that would be safe from that witch, so I opted for somewhere else, somewhere where she could just blend in. I took her back to Rendenaaar—back to the other Khattaaara who had part of Payton intermixed with her soul.

CHAPTER LXXV

Khattaaara/Payton

> *Payton from the Original Timeline*
> *Sharing the Mind of Khattaaara*
> *In the Rewritten Timeline*
> *On Rendenaaar*
> *Trillions of Universes in the Past*

It was as I was contemplating what to do about Dargra-Tol that something incredible happened. Peyton phased into the room with a Gaaalthaaaran female who I thought bore an amazing resemblance to Ophelia. The problem (my problem) was that I was Khattaaara, and that brought about a conundrum. Peyton and Khattaaara had been one soul divided into two until Peyton became reconciled with who she had been. But here she was, face to face with that part of her who had been her mortal enemy and who had usurped her psyche and had taken control. So, why then, of all places, would she have phased here?

"You're not here to kill me, are you?" I asked in my best-remembered English, although, as I recall, my accent was incredibly thick.

"No," she said. "I know from the bracelet that you've changed."

"Bracelet?" I asked.

Peyton held out her left wrist, on which was a bejeweled, two-headed *jraaatra*.

"It's how I found you. In the future," I said. "Far into the future; far from now. You recorded a message on it. You said how part of you was Payton. It has a map of the Earth."

I held up my left arm, revealing the exact same bracelet. "It's

361

identical," I said, "other than that I haven't recorded anything on it yet."

Peyton shook her head. "Not identical," she replied. "They're one and the same, only mine is a thousand years older than yours."

It was at that moment that my attention was drawn to the infant in the other's arms, a human child that I hadn't noticed before.

"I don't understand," I said. "Who is *she*?" indicating the Gaaalthaaaran female, who had appeared with her.

"She's Phee," I said. "A Khattaaara from another dimension infected her with some virus that altered her DNA."

Then Peyton told me all that had gone on. The infant, Jordan, it seemed, was my niece, and Peyton's niece as well, born to parents of two separate dimensions. I looked at Phee and thought, *What sort of a monster in that universe had that Khattaaara become?* Phee looked at Peyton, gently handed Jordan to her, and then walked up to me, stared at me for a moment, and then threw her arms around me. I held her to comfort her and gently rubbed her back.

"You know that everyone named Herron loves you *and* me, regardless of how we look," I whispered into her ear.

"But I'm so in love with Liam," she said as she wept bitter tears, "and now we're not even the same species!"

"I figured that she and Jordan would be safe here," Peyton said, "at least until we try to put things right. There will be three quantum seeds against her one. I pray that it's enough."

"There's a problem here, too," I replied. "The synth I owned, Dargra-Tol, stole the mother stone I had."

"Mother stone?" she asked.

"It's one that's equal to all the rest combined," I explained. "It's the same as the one that Thara-Klo had."

"And now it's in Theresa's head," she replied, and then, with exasperation, breathed out, "Great!" There came a moment of silence as Peyton appeared to be momentarily lost in thought. Then she turned to me again. "Will you be all right?" she asked. "Against her,

I mean."

"I have the other six," I replied. "All in my head. That puts me on equal ground." I pulled Phee away just enough for each of us to stare into each other's eyes. I smiled at her, and she smiled back through her tears. I looked at Peyton. "They'll be safe enough here with me," I said.

"You sure you don't need my help?" she asked.

"We'll be fine," I assured her. "You have enough on your plate. Besides," she went on, "we have the same god-stones in our heads, and they won't stay separate for long."

"God-stones," she repeated and then shrugged.

Then she handed the infant to me, and Phee hugged like there was no letting go. It was apparent that she couldn't stay, as I felt the tug of the god-stones in our heads trying to combine.

"You take care of my niece," she said and smiled. "I'll be back when it's over. We'll find a way to undo all of this." Then she turned to me. "How about you? This wasn't what any of us planned."

"Just tell my Mom and Dad that I'm where Fate intended me to be and that I love them so very, very much! And Liam, too!"

"You can count on it," she said, and then she vanished as Phee and I looked on.

CHAPTER LXXVI

Peyton

> *From the Original Timeline*
> *In the Alternate Reality*
> *On Earth I*
> *Earth-Date:2029*

Demi lay unconscious on the floor of the living room when I phased back. Pay and the other Phee both knelt over her in tears. Pay glanced back when she saw me.

"She's hurt really badly," she said, "but I don't know what to do! She's lost a lot of blood. She can have as much, and there's my mom and Dad, but if she needs more, I don't know if any of the blood from this dimension is compatible. Everything's reversed."

"We'll worry about that when the time comes," I said. "I'll call Emma. She's a doctor and my Mom's best friend. She's up on some of this. She treated Thara-Klo when she was stabbed."

I quickly phased upstairs to grab my cell, made the call, and then phased back.

"She said she'll be here in ten," I told Phee and Pay. "Let's get her to the couch."

Pay interrupted. "No, let me," she said and then went over to her, squatted down, lifted her as though she weighed no more than a feather, and then carried her to the couch and set her down. After she pulled her arms back, the cushions sank down. As it turned out, the *god-stone* in her head enabled her to control mass and weight.

As she stood back, I asked her, "What happened after I left with Phee?"

"That Khattaaara is a witch," she replied. "She and Demi were having it out with force fields. You can tell from the shape the living room's in; only Khattaaara's force field was stronger, and when she got close enough, she wrapped her hands around Demi's throat and began to strangle her while thrashing at her with her tail, which she finally plunged into her left side. That's when I ran into the kitchen, got a knife, and swung at it. It didn't come off, but it must have hurt like all hell because she let go and screamed loud enough to wake the dead and then phased from the room."

A few minutes later, there was a knock on the door that Phee answered. It was Emma. The woman, in her late forties like Mom, did a triple-take seeing the three of us, but then went to Payton's side to attend to her.

"She's in shock," Emma said, "and bleeding. She should be in a hospital. I'll see what I can do, but she desperately needs a transfusion. Do any of you know her type?"

"Same as mine," said Pay.

Emma sterilized Payton's wound, gave her an anesthetic injection, and stitched her up. Then she had Pay sit down next to her and ran a tube from her arm to Payton's.

"We'll keep it connected for half an hour and see how she does."

"Thank you," I said. Then, as Emma excused herself to go to the bathroom to wash up, Phee looked at me.

"What are we going to do?" she asked. "She's more powerful than any of you."

I shook my head. "That's not the worst of it," I replied. "Now that she knows about this Earth, there's no question she's going to begin infecting the population here."

"Oh, my Gods!" said Pay. "It's all our fault! We never should have come here!"

"I wouldn't worry about it that much," said a young female voice from behind us.

Both of us turned to see a twentyish-looking woman, very pretty, wearing a silver and gold Quantum Girl costume.

"Who are you?" I asked.

"Don't you recognize me, Auntie? I'm Jordan—Jordan Herron—and I've come from Rendenaaar to help you save your worlds!"

EPILOGUE

Daisy

From the Alternate Timeline
In the Alternate Reality
On Earth I
Earth-Date:2029

I was taking a shower, feeling the warm water bead down on my back and neck, when I saw someone in the room just outside the steamed-up shower door. I turned off the water and listened.

"Who's there?" I asked. Then I wiped a circle of steam away from the glass.

Facing me stood a woman, beautiful, exotic, magnificent, actually, staring straight at me, ever so close. It was then that I noticed that her ears were pointed and that she had eyes such as I had never before seen—her irises silver, her pupils gold. I pushed open the door and stood facing her. She wore a dress that was like gossamer from the fairy tales I used to read. And me just naked, wondering who she was. And then I saw her tail.

"Who are you?" I asked. "What are you?"

"Hi ham Dargra-Tol," she said with an accent unlike any I had ever heard, "ant hwee chare thi muthar stowne. Hu ant Hi mus bay whun." Then, all at once, I felt her merge into me. It was the strangest of feelings. It was as though a billion thoughts flooded into my head all at once, while my body felt as though it had been renewed. Still dripping wet, I walked into my bedroom and stared at myself in the full-length mirror that was on the inside of my closet door. My features were the same, but I looked several years older now. My blonde hair appeared as though it were made of spun gold. My ears were tipped like hers. I had two pairs of breasts, one atop the other—and a tail! Oddly enough, I was not afraid, for Dargra-Tol and I were now one. I knew all that she had known, and I now knew how to use the stone. I felt my *yaaargh* creep under me between my legs and enter my vagina. I backed up slowly and fell down onto the bed. What happened next was ecstasy. When that was done, I knew what lay ahead. To hell with Peyton Herron. I would murder Quantum Girl and, with her out of the way, with the god-stone in my head, I would rule the world, the universe, and more!

AFTERWORD

The Quantum Girl Saga deals with a lot more than aliens and superpowers. They touch upon bullying, self-harm, and suicide. These are issues faced by young people today. As a teenager myself, I strongly encourage anyone twenty-five or younger, who is facing those issues or others such as sexual assault or date rape, substance abuse, child abuse, sexual trafficking, anxiety or depression, or if things are bad at home and you are considering running away, please call the Thursday's Child hotline at 1 (800) USA KIDS from a landline, or (818) 831-1234 internationally or from a cellphone. Phone lines are open 24/7 and are confidential and free. They care. I care. I'm Peyton Herron, Quantum Girl, and spokesperson for Thursday's Child. Their website is www.thursdayschild.org, where you can also get help.

www.ingramcontent.com/pod-product-compliance
Lightning Source LLC
Chambersburg PA
CBHW072305020726
47501CB00002B/402